Fated in Darkness

The Sanctuary Series
Volume 5.5

Robert J. Crane

Fated in Darkness
The Sanctuary Series, Volume 5.5

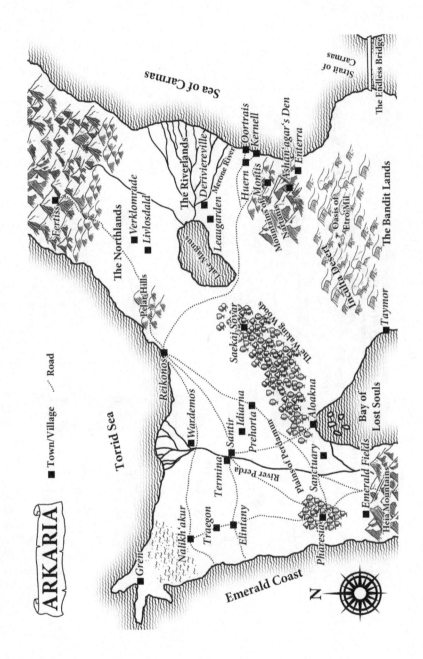

ARKARIA

Town/Village ■ ····· Road

Torrid Sea

Sea of Carmas

Strait of Carmas

The Endless Bridge

Fertiss

The Northlands

Verklomrade
Livlosdald

Pelar Hills

The Riverlands

Deriviereville

Merone River

Leaugarden

Lake Magun

Reikonos

Wardemos

Santir

Idiarna

Prehorta

Termina

River Perda

Plains of Perda

Tragon

Elintany

Nalikh'akur

Grenc

Emerald Coast

N

Sanctuary

Pharesia

Emerald Fields

Heia Mountains

Bay of
Lost Souls

Aloakna

The Waking Woods

Saekaj Sovar

Taymor

The Bandit Lands

Inculta Desert

Oasis of
EtroMil

Mountains of Nartanis

Ashan'agar's Den

Enterra

Kernell

Oortrais

Huern

Montis

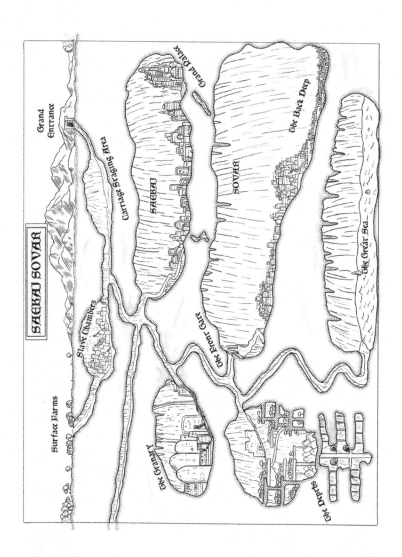

Prologue

Aisling

She waited in the quiet place, in the darkness, with not so much as a candle to shed light. The smell of the linens, the scent of blood all reminded the woman who called herself Aisling Nightwind of nothing so much as approaching death. The bitter taste of it was upon her tongue as she drew a ragged breath and closed her eyes.

Here in the caves of Saekaj and Sovar, the chill lingered upon her skin. *This is the way of things here,* she thought as pain surged through her. Her fingers came up warm and wet from the site of the pain, and she was reminded of battles and woundings past.

Have I ever hurt worse than this? she thought. It was hard to recall, with the burning agony rolling hard within her. She couldn't move, could barely breathe, and the darkness did not help.

How did I get into this mess …? she wondered into the quiet. She held back a scream for fear of what attention it might draw. She suppressed it, held it tight inside and clenched a hand. She ran fingers over the ridged blade of her dagger and the pain subsided, giving her space to think for a moment.

Ah, yes … that's how it began, she thought, tasting the bitterness within once more. *Hard to forget unless you're addled by absolute anguish … which I am.* She drew another shallow breath and opened her eyes to the darkness. *Darkness is familiar to me. I have lived in darkness most of my life … as have we all … and it is into the darkness that we are fated to go when our time is up …*

1.

Terian

One Year Earlier

The descent into Saekaj reminded Terian of human myths of an old underworld, a place where souls lived in torment and pain for all eternity, locked into a prison of fire and darkness to suffer endlessly. *Just like home,* he thought, looking out the window of the rattling carriage as it bounced along the rutted road that stretched from the gate to the open, sky-framed world above down to the depths of the dark elven capital, surrounded on all sides by rough and rocky cave hewn out of rock.

"You stare out as though you could call the light to shine down into the tunnels," his traveling companion said in that slow, nearly hissing way that he had.

Terian took a whiff of the stale, still, chill air, of the earthy aroma and fetid scent of spider dung and pulled his head back into the carriage. *Was I looking longingly behind me?* "No light comes down here from above," he said, turning to look at Malpravus, the Guildmaster of Goliath, "I recall that well enough. It would be anathema, even if it could reach."

"Oh, don't be dour, dear boy," Malpravus said, his cowl over his eyes, his lips stretched into their usual grin, "I offered you a path. On an auspicious day such as today, one would think to find you overjoyed. After all, should things go well, you will finally be able to return home."

Terian's muscles tensed involuntarily, a fevered shot of hope ran through his stomach and departed just as quickly. "Home," he said, almost under his breath. "Yes. It would be nice to go … home."

"You might just be there, soon enough," Malpravus said, tilting his scrawny neck to look out his own window.

I doubt it. "Indeed," Terian said, without much in the way of feeling. The cold of the tunnels crept in on him, through the spiked, hardened armor that he wore like a second skin. He blinked as a thought bubbled up to his mind. "How did you find me?"

Malpravus simply grinned, his smile widening. "You mean, how did I know to look for you on the far distant shores of Arkaria, far from any portal or civilization?"

Terian did not look at the necromancer, instead gazing out the window at the passing of cavern rock. *All of it looks the same. All of it. I suppose it's like a blue sky in that regard.* "Yes. That is what I meant."

"I heard the call of death, my lad," Malpravus said, and now his cowl swept over his eyes, shrouding them in darkness. "An inescapable, rushing wave of death so significant that it was as unto the trumpeting of an entire army outside one's window."

"The scourge," Terian whispered, and a vision of grey-fleshed creatures, low like dogs, with skin like rotted elephants, eyes devoid of life, went flashing through his mind. He watched in his mind's eye as a long bridge collapsed into rubble, carrying thousands of the rotting wraiths into the watery embrace of the Sea of Carmas. Thousands of them, perhaps tens of thousands—

And one other. The vision of old armor played in front of Terian's eyes, made him feel he could almost reach out and touch the man within, take his hand—

Alaric is dead. "You heard them coming," Terian whispered, "and came to see?"

"I came to see," Malpravus said, though he seemed to be holding something back. "One does not merely stand aside when something of that nature comes whispering into one's thoughts. Though it was hardly a whisper. More like a rising scream in the still night." His grin returned to manageable proportions. "Still, I was glad to see you, to catch you after your … altercation."

The thought of Cyrus Davidon staring him down flitted into Terian's thoughts once more. *Now, Terian?* he had asked, weary and earnest, as though it were some simple matter, easily disposed of.

This isn't over between us, Terian had said. He had meant in every sense, though his mind flailed at his reason in order to find a way that this could be so. *Not yet.*

"It was opportune timing." Terian looked back out the window as a clatter sounded ahead of their coach. He saw movement as the coach turned, the spiders at the fore responding to the driver's command.

Shouts echoed through the tunnel, harsh sounds in the dark. A guard wearing the distinctive bracer of the Saekaj militia clanked in light armor as he walked up the window and butted his head through the window. "A thousand pardons, General Malpravus," the guard said with a hard bow of his head, "but I must account for your guest. Sovereign's orders; no entry to the upper city without registration."

"But of course," Malpravus said with a simple bow of his head. "A very sensible precaution in these troubled times." He glanced at Terian. "Identify yourself."

Terian felt frozen in the moment, mind warring with him for what he should say. "I am Terian," he said after a brief pause, "of House Lepos. I am a citizen of Saekaj."

The guard listened intently but showed no sign of recognition. "Very good, sir. I'll record you in the logbook as a guest of General Malpravus, here on his pledge of good conduct." The guard backed his helmeted head out of the window and his boots made a soft clanking sound as they left the carriage's step and found the ground below. "Open the gate for the General!" he called, voice echoing through the tunnels.

"What the hell was that about?" Terian asked, almost to himself.

"These are dangerous times, my boy," Malpravus said, long fingers steepled in front of his face. "The war has been raging for two years now. The seeds of discontent are well and truly sown in the lower city, for the brunt of the privation has landed much harder on them than Saekaj."

Terian felt himself nod slowly. "There's rebellion afoot in Sovar."

"They are never more than a step away, those dregs," Malpravus said, sniffing, "but this time the Dragon's Breath seems well and truly lit, primed to explode with but the slightest spark. The moment is ill for that, though; one would hope that it could be put off until this war is concluded."

"With the victory of the dark elves over the humans and elves, yes?" Terian asked. He worked to keep the cynicism from ripping through his words like a knife cutting silken cloth.

"With the victory of the Sovereign over his foes, yes," Malpravus said, eyes hidden but mouth in a thin line. "Be wary of how you speak in these tunnels, Terian Lepos. The tongue is still considered a most dangerous weapon in this place, as well it should be."

"I was merely asking about the war," Terian said, "in a most subtle way."

"Hmm," Malpravus said, almost indifferently. "Then I will tell you about the war's progress, in perhaps blunter terms than you might expect outside of this carriage."

"Is speaking the truth of its progress a crime now as well?" Terian asked.

"No," Malpravus said, "merely a harbinger of disloyalty, which is perhaps worse in these times." He paused, cocking his head. "Our armies remain on this side of the River Perda, choked off from the Elven Kingdom by that cursed river. The Sovereign does not wish an advance in any case; he wants to fight the humans and finish his business here before moving forward with an invasion of elvendom."

"Probably shouldn't have picked that fight in Termina, then," Terian muttered.

"Oh, yes," Malpravus said quietly. "That was where your father died, wasn't it? Killed by Cyrus Davidon?" The necromancer grinned again. "I would imagine you should very much like to have a reckoning for that one."

This isn't over between us. Not yet. "Perhaps," Terian allowed as a stinging barb of regret sprung into his stomach. *Termina. That was where it all began to go wrong.* "So that front is stalled. What about against the humans?"

"We move closer to Reikonos," Malpravus said, "but are preparing to take the war into the east, to the Riverlands and to the Northlands. Into the places where humanity finds its last remaining supply of food. A solid conquest of either, and Reikonos will starve, what with the Plains of Perdamun already devastated and the elves bottled up from shipping to the human capital."

Terian blinked. "The plains are …?"

"Like a skeleton picked clean," Malpravus said with a leer. "The

Sovereign's forces have culled the farmers' crops and encircled your former guild in preparation to crush them." He sighed. "Such a shame. A hundred thousand of our soldiers are laying siege to Sanctuary even now. I had heard that they were poised to move in and end the thing; perhaps once it is done the Sovereign will grant me what is left of that ailing fortress to establish his presence in the plains."

Sanctuary … under siege? About to be destroyed? At last the emotions warring within Terian broke, casting him firmly in one direction. He wanted to scream, to cry out in the carriage, to draw the glowing red blade of his father and put it to fine use spilling Malpravus's blood all over the wooden interior, to rip through the door and charge back up the slope of the tunnel and run hard across Arkaria to the Plains of Perdamun, to throw himself against a hundred thousand dark elves—

But instead he sat, frozen, in the seat next to the necromancer and controlled his breath lest Malpravus notice anything amiss. "Interesting," Terian managed to get out without sounding strained.

"Indeed, these are interesting times," Malpravus agreed. The carriage was rattling over the stone streets of Saekaj, passing through the quiet markets. Ahead, Terian could see one of the waterfalls that bracketed the Sovereign's palace, pouring forth out of the cave walls like a bath being drawn by a servant. "This is the place to be at this moment, I will tell you, dark knight."

"It would seem that the dark elves are on a bit of a roll," Terian said with muted enthusiasm.

"The entirety of Arkaria is destined to be controlled from within these caverns. I stand close to the Sovereign now, high in his estimation."

"What does it take to get there?" Terian asked, strangely curious. *Sanctuary …*

"You should know," Malpravus said, "I have heard from the Sovereign himself that you were in his inner circle once, and that he would not have parted with you but for your strong argument."

"I was in his inner circle?" Terian mused. "I didn't know that."

"The Sovereign keeps his ways mysterious," Malpravus said. "He keeps his council in darkness—"

"Like everything else."

"—but he speaks highly of you, even in spite of that little incident two years ago," Malpravus finished.

"The one where he sentenced J'anda and I to death for personal betrayals?" Terian felt the full weight of his armor upon him, the armor and something else, perhaps. "He's not the forgiving sort."

Malpravus smiled thinly. "I admit, I am interested to see how this meeting goes."

Terian blinked. "You're taking me to him? Right now?"

"Oh, yes," Malpravus cooed, "of course. I could scarcely bring an exiled person into the upper city without immediately presenting him for judgment to the Sovereign." He grinned. "I am intrigued to see his reaction to you."

Terian's lips stiffened before he could betray his sudden, rising fury. *Strange to whip around with these emotions, like a horse gone mad, bucking in all these different directions.* "He might well kill me without another word."

Malpravus regarded him almost indifferently then shrugged. "You are my gift to him, and this is the trial through which you must pass if you wish to come home." He turned, and his cowl rose just a few inches so that Terian could see his dark eyes. "Do you wish to go home?"

Terian met his gaze, channeling all the deceit he'd practiced in the last year into his eyes to make them match Malpravus's cool indifference. "I want to go home," he said and meant it.

"Then speak that loyalty to the Sovereign, and he may grant you your wish," Malpravus said, turning back to the window. They had begun to pass the stately, sculpted manors that lined the road to the Sovereign's palace, hewn out of the rock and decorated impressively.

"Or he may grant me death," Terian said.

"I won't leave you dead, dear boy," Malpravus said with a fearsome grin, "you're much too valuable to discard in such a manner."

Terian's blood froze in his veins as they passed an estate on his right. He could not tell which was the greater chill; the veiled promise of Malpravus exercising his dominion over Terian's corpse or the sight of his old home out the window. *Could be either,* Terian decided. *Either is almost a fate worse than death; coming back here or being Malpravus's puppet.*

The carriage rattled on, passing through the gates ahead with nothing more than a wave from Malpravus. "We are expected," the necromancer said, sounding pleased with himself. "The guards must have sent a runner."

"Or perhaps the Sovereign is merely thrilled to see you," Terian said. "How long were you gone?"

"It was two days' ride to the bridge," Malpravus said with a shrug, "so not terribly long as far as these things go."

Terian considered Malpravus shrewdly. After Terian had accepted the necromancer's offer, Malpravus had wrapped his bony arms around Terian in the jungle and cast his return spell, taking them both to a building in a place that Terian did not recognize. There were black curtains over all the windows, and the furniture was so nondescript as to defy placement with any culture. A half dozen members of Goliath were there, waiting, and a wizard had teleported them to the portal outside Saekaj Sovar's entrance, from where they'd begun their steady descent to this moment.

"I'm sure that everything is quite all right," Malpravus said with that same indifference. "Otherwise, we would have been greeted with a much different reaction."

The Sovereign does not suffer failure lightly, Terian thought, agreeing silently with the Goliath Guildmaster. "What is your task in all this?"

"I help command my armies against the humans at present," Malpravus said. "Did you not hear them call me General?"

"How big is Goliath now?" Terian asked, trying to decide how to approach the subject. "Did you lose many in your exile?"

Malpravus let loose a light chuckle that was disturbing as the carriage came to a stop. "We are now almost twenty thousand strong, so no. The exile from Reikonos was actually a boon to our recruitment. We were able to gather unto ourselves some of the, shall we say, less savory elements of Arkaria."

Terian looked at him through slitted eyes. "Did you go to the bandit lands? Did you pull from the ranks of the lawless?"

Malpravus's grin stretched wide once more. "They are quite bitter toward the great northern powers down there, did you know?"

Terian bottled his feelings inside. *No wonder he didn't mind traversing to where he found me all by himself; he'd have used that last portal in the southeast before if he's been recruiting the bandits and savages to his guild.*

The door to Terian's side of the carriage was pulled open with a squeak of hinges, and a guard held it open expectantly.

"Well, dear boy," Malpravus said, gathering his blue robes about him, "this is it."

Terian regarded the open exit from the carriage with a surprising lack of nerves and nodded once. "This is it," he agreed. He had not been here in nearly three years, and the thought of how he'd left this place lingered on him like a swarm of flies buzzing about him, harrying him as he stepped forth from the carriage to meet his judgment.

2.

Aisling

Aisling Nightwind lingered about out of doors, on the grounds of Sanctuary, the breeze of the dark evening all around her. Corpses lay strewn about the trampled and muddied grass, bodies that had not yet begun to putrefy, fresh as the flowers that might have been popping out of the ground were it still the pristine, untouched landscape it had been when she'd left Sanctuary over a year ago.

"Things change," she breathed, so low that she didn't think anyone could hear her.

"Oh, they do indeed," came a near-whispered reply that caused her to turn her head. Some thirty feet away stood a woman in a grey robe as dull as a cloudy sky. She clutched an ebony staff in her fingers, and had the vestment marking her as a wizard. Her face was unwrinkled but showed slight wear; Aisling could not have placed her age to the nearest millennium if she'd been suspended over a pit and forced to make a guess with her life in the balance. "But," the woman went on, "as they change, I find they also stay remarkably close to the same."

"If you say so," Aisling said with a polite incline of her head. Smoke rose from beyond the massive curtain wall of Sanctuary, and grains of dust still floated through the air after the mighty battle that had led to dark elves swarming over their grounds and breaking down the doors of the massive building at the center of the compound. *Almost kissed death on that one. I saw the white-bleached skull, and his teeth were poised to swallow me whole.*

"I say so," the woman said, inching closer, her staff thumping against the broken earth, slapping against the bodies beneath her as she walked. "Don't you think it's so? That no matter how much we think things have changed, they stay remarkably close to what they always were?"

Aisling blinked, giving it consideration before replying. "When I left this place to go to Luukessia, it was whole. When I returned a few days ago, it was under siege. Now, the walls are cracked, and it is both filled with and surrounded by corpses too numerous to count." She glanced down at a dark elven officer and rolled him enough to get at his coin purse. It was fairly light, as though he'd had liberty recently or not been paid for a while.

"But it still stands," the woman said. "Still houses the same guild, with the same loyalties."

"Alaric is gone," Aisling said, parroting what she'd heard, oddly indifferent. "That is change."

"Yet things roll along," the woman said, gathering up the hem of her robe as she stepped over the large body of a troll. "The wagon wheels still turn inexorably."

Aisling rolled her eyes. *Elves.* "Are you annoying me for any particular reason, or do you simply have nowhere else to be? Surely, there is room for a wizard's work to be done around here, especially at present."

"Yes, a wizard's work is never done," she agreed, "always ferrying people to and fro; pushing off one's own appointments to help others keep theirs. You have an appointment of your own, did you know?"

Aisling stooped low, hand on another dead dark elf's purse when the words reached her ears, and they froze her in place as surely as an ice spell to the back. "Do I?" she asked, as coldly as if such a spell had crawled all the way up to her face and forced its way down her throat, chilling her words as they spilled forth.

"You do," the woman said, now close enough to strike out with her staff if she chose. Aisling watched her cannily, out of the corner of her eyes, afraid to focus all her attention on her new acquaintance. "You have been gone a very long while, after all."

"I was not aware that anyone in Sanctuary had marked my absence," Aisling said. "And I have been back for a few days, though rather busy with the business of the siege."

The woman stepped closer. She was not terribly tall, but she was a couple of inches in height greater than Aisling and looked down on her. The wizard's pointed ears were nearly hidden beneath her grey hat's wide brim. "You have obligations to those beyond Sanctuary. Obligations that your *benefactors* wish to insure you have not forgotten."

"I have a keen memory," Aisling said, standing upright again. "I forget little."

"A valuable attribute in a servant." The elven woman cocked an eyebrow at her. "My name is Verity—"

"A fitting name for a spy," Aisling said, so low that she was certain even the warriors passing fifty feet away could not hear her.

"Indeed," Verity said with a nod and a smile that hinted at a certain pleasure derived from the irony. "It was almost as though my parents named me with my eventual flexibility in loyalties in mind. When yours named you, did they have your ..." Verity looked Aisling up and down, "... rather birdlike qualities in mind, do you suppose?"

Aisling met her stare with a long-practiced ease, smiling lightly. "One would presume I was too small at the time to have displayed any of my current waifishness." *And my parents did not name me Aisling, in any case, but you don't need to know that.*

Nobody does.

"I am to take you with me," Verity said, stepping closer, voice dropping to a raspy hush. "Dagonath Shrawn wishes a report on your progress."

Aisling let her eyes dart about the grounds, looking for something, anything, to excuse her from this task she didn't want to fulfill. "We've just finished a siege. The grounds are in chaos; hunting parties still rage across the plains killing the last of the dark elves. The guild's council is still meeting, and refugees from the land of Luukessia are pouring into this place by the thousands." She felt the night close in on her, black and still and hard from above, not held at bay by the great torches and braziers that burned across the grounds and cast light across it all. She felt as an island in the middle of it all, unnoticed, as the darkness prepared to take her in its embrace.

"A perfect time to slip away unnoticed," Verity said with a slight smile. "We shan't be gone long, and there is far too much occurring here for them to notice a slippery thief's absence for just a small while." Verity leaned in, whispering in her ear. "You are indebted.

And you are here for a purpose. Or do you need a reminder?"

"I recall all too well," Aisling said with a nod of surrender. "Do as you must."

"Let us away," Verity said, smiling, as she whipped the ebony staff into the air. "Hold tight to me; I will return us to the Shrawn estate directly."

Aisling hesitated before closing on the wizard, looking around her once more. Mail-clad warriors milled about in a formation of ten roughly a hundred yards away. A few rangers with bows stood atop the nearest segment of wall, their backs to Aisling and their green cloaks whipping in the gentle wind. The darkness was complete beyond the curtain wall, a night closed off to all outside. Their attention was focused beyond the gates, beyond the broken stone barrier that surrounded them. They were worried about great armies like the one that had sieged and surrounded them, fearful of dangers outside their gates.

They should have more care for the ones that are inside them, Aisling thought as she closed her arms around the wizard in an unfeeling embrace. Verity smelled of herbs, of mint perhaps, and something lingering and artificial, one of the perfumes that the elves employed to cover their own aromas. She clutched to the grey robes as the energy of a spell consumed her, taking her along with the wizard back to a point of binding half a land away, and back to a destiny she could not seem to leave behind no matter how she tried.

3.

J'anda

J'anda Aimant found the letter waiting under his door when he returned from Council, and he wondered how long it had been there. He had been gone for a very long time, over a year, far across the sea in a distant land, watching it burn and die in a way he had not seen since the days of his youth, and the thought that all that while something so simple as an envelope with a missive might be awaiting him here had never once occurred to him. *And why should it?* he wondered. *I thought anyone who cared enough to write me a letter was either with me or here the entire time, aware of my prolonged absence.*

The lettering was a simple scrawl, the hand of someone educated but not proficient in matters of calligraphy, and written in the language of the dark elves. His curiosity grew, but he tempered it like a sword dipped in water before hammering; he laid it upon his desk and savored the moment of curiosity, not quite ready to put an end to the sensation just yet.

He stared at the faded parchment of the letter, sealed by simple wax without so much as a mark to suggest where it had originated. No, it was a simple spot of red, pressed closed by a circle without any identity of its own. It reminded him of himself when he left Saekaj; almost formless in its way, and keeping its secrets, giving away nothing to those who might look for them.

He had almost resolved to open it and put to death the mystery when the knock sounded at his door. It was heavy and thudding, the sound of strength matched against wood, like a battering ram to a gate. It echoed in his chamber, resonated off the walls and in his ears.

He smoothed his robes with tired, wrinkled hands and gathered them about him for the walk to the door. Before he had left, it would have been a simple jaunt, easy. Now his bones protested every step, and his muscles ached. He could not run as he used to, not that he often had before. He was an enchanter, and enchanters were meant to disguise themselves, to hide in plain sight if need be. He did not run, no, not unless he had to, but now, with his aged bones, it felt impossible.

The weariness was the worst of it. Now he was tired in a way he had not been before he had left, before he had bled out his life's blood, life's energy, on those far distant shores, trading his magic to conjure food for a starving people, and trading his life for more magic when that power ran out. He glimpsed himself in the clouded mirror as he passed the full-length glass that stood in the middle of his quarters, and he stopped in shock.

The vibrancy was leeched from his hair, which was straw-like and withered, and deep wrinkles were stitched in his skin like canyons cut through hard earth. The once vibrant, navy blue flesh of his face was now a shade paler, the furrows and folds those of an old man. J'anda stood, staring, blinking at the unfamiliar face in the mirror, his mouth falling open slightly as he raised a wrinkled hand to his cheek to inspect it by feel. Even his hand was not his own, but at least he recognized it. He looked at it every day, after all.

The knock at his door sounded again, full of feeling and heavy with urgency. J'anda licked his cracked and dry lips and tried to remember the simplest of glamours. He ran a hand over his face as he struggled with his fatigue. He had been awake for days, and his mind could not concentrate as it once might have. The words did not spring to mind; he came to the second line of the language of his magic and it was utterly gone, as if it were a handful of dust thrown into the wind or a bottle of good wine set before a sumptuous dinner feast.

The knock came once more, jarring him out of his attempt to remember the spell. "Coming," he said, pulling himself away from the cruel reflection. There was so much going on; surely it did not matter if he had an illusion on his face. People were in need, after all, in need of help and food and everything else. His face and how it looked was the last of a long line of concerns.

But for a man whose whole life had been the business of illusions, pulling himself away from that mirror with the job undone was almost an admission of surrender. Surrender to the perils of age that had overtaken him, to the fact that he had given up so much of his life in a land that he had never even heard of before he had gone there.

And surrender to the idea that keeping up the illusion was perhaps a game for the young, and he no longer had the time to waste on such a trivial thing.

J'anda opened his door slowly. It weighed more than he remembered, as though his stringy arms had somehow grown weaker in the time since he had left. *They probably have*, he reflected. *I am not what I once was, and I am certainly not aging as gracefully as Curatio.*

As the door swung wide, J'anda found he had to look up—and up—to see the face of his visitor. Black robes wrapped his guest's mighty frame, and he carried with him a staff with a glowing white crystal at the top.

"I thought maybe you were trapped in your privy," Vaste said as he barged past J'anda, giving the enchanter only a moment to step back before entering the quarters. "Or maybe luxuriating in a bath. Can't have been an easy thing, traveling for a year without any opportunity to bathe yourself."

"There were forest streams, and the occasional castle," J'anda said, surprised by the sudden entry of the troll, unbidden, into his quarters. "There was a waterfall, once, in the mountains, with the most crystalline water coming down from the snowcapped peaks far above. It was … picturesque."

"I'm certain it will make a fascinating anecdote in your inevitable travelogue," Vaste said, stepping over by the bed and clicking his staff against the stones of the floor, head swiveling slowly to look over the room. "Though, I might suggest you hurry and get to writing that if you're going to."

J'anda felt his eyebrow creep upward and did not fight it. "I beg your pardon?"

Vaste's dark eyes flickered in the light of the torches hanging in sconces on the walls. "Oh, come off it. Are we truly going to dance around this?"

"I'm afraid I don't feel much like dancing at the moment," J'anda said, drawing the door closed with a gentle click of the mechanism. His eyes drifted back to the mystery of the sealed letter and he found himself suddenly aching with impatience to read it, to break open the seal with a satisfying tear, to hear the crinkle of the yellowed paper and feel its smoothness between his fingers.

"As well you should not," Vaste said, immovable, a pillar in the middle of his quarters. "Fine. I'll just say it, then, since no one else has: J'anda, it doesn't take the sharpest pair of eyes to see you've aged like one of those hole-riddled elven cheeses in your travel."

J'anda felt a stillness settle on his bones, a strange quiescence at this truth simply spilled forth like a knocked-over cup, its liquid contents running over stones in a race to find their level. "I can only hope that I am as delicious as one of those cheeses."

"I'm sure that many a young man would love to find out," Vaste said, prompting a slight tremor deep within J'anda. To have it stated so boldly, even in passing, still curdled the blood in his veins even after all these years and far removed from the dangers of his particular brand of deviancy in Saekaj. "But," the troll continued, "I'm more concerned about the possible effects of this change on your health."

J'anda ignored the momentary tremor that the troll's first comment had prompted within him. *More than a hundred years, and I still fear for it to be said aloud.* "I feel fine," he lied.

"What did you do?" Vaste asked, the troll's great green head shaking slowly left to right, but not enough to sway his gaze.

J'anda found himself caught in a great sigh, one that drove home the weariness within him. "Something I do not regret," he said, and found it to be perhaps the most honest thing he'd said since this peculiar conversation had begun.

"You've killed yourself," Vaste said quietly. "You've drained your days away with magics."

"To good purpose," J'anda said, "but yes." He looked at the hearth, softly crackling as it appeared to consume a log that no one had thrown upon it. None of the fine ash one would expect from such a thing was within the room, and its gentle orange light radiated out upon them, turning the troll's skin a lighter shade of yellowish green.

"Oh, J'anda," Vaste said, shaking his head slowly. Was there a hint of mournfulness in there, somewhere?

"Why, Vaste," J'anda said in surprise, "are you concerned?"

"Yes, I'm concerned," Vaste said, "I'm concerned that if you die, I'll be left on the Council with Ryin Ayend, without the required helping of intelligence to counterbalance his all-consuming idiocy." The troll's voice was higher than usual by an octave, as though he himself were trying to deny something he could not quite muster the force to make sound sincere. His voice lowered. "All right, fine. I am simply concerned, regardless of any Council idiocy."

"I have missed you, my friend," J'anda said. "But you cannot mourn for me yet."

"I wasn't supposed to mourn you at all," Vaste said, and for the first time, the troll's gaze was now downward, to his feet, to the stones on the floor. "You are young—"

"I am over a century old," J'anda said, wryly.

"You are younger than me in the years of your people," Vaste said, his yellow eyes coming up to regard the enchanter. "You could have lived some nine centuries more, perhaps."

J'anda let the words hang in the air for a moment before he replied. "There are many things we could have done in our lives, my friend. Many paths we could take; but only one I have chosen to take. And as I said, I have no regret for it."

Vaste's massive shoulders bore the hint of a slump, a half-moon's angle between one to the other, broken only by the rise of his mammoth neck out of the middle. It was an unusual look for the troll, whose buoyancy and absurdity were practically hallmarks of his liveliness. The despair hung heavy on him, weight his frame did not need added to it. "First Niamh. Then Terian went round the bend. Alaric ... well ... and you—" He shook his head. "It's too much. Just ... too much." He sank back, onto the bed, his robes folding with him as he went. The bed's frame shifted and strained under the weight, and J'anda fought back the urge to say something in concern for his furniture. "I just don't know if I can wrap my mind around it all."

J'anda struggled to find something to say that would reassure the troll. What was there to say, though, truly? "We never know what the future holds," he said, but it sounded flimsy to him, like the wing of a lame bird, flapping almost noiselessly, trying to hold him aloft and failing.

"I think you know what your future holds," Vaste said, "now, anyway."

"That was always in my future," J'anda said, easing toward the troll. "It is the one thing that binds all of us together; the inevitability of an uncertain end."

"Yes," Vaste agreed, "all of us except Curatio. That bastard."

J'anda felt a chuckle rise, unexpectedly, within. "I do not know if, after what I have seen this last year, I could properly tell you whether what Curatio has is a great blessing, or the worst form of curse." Something about that tugged at a thread of memory within him, and his eyes went back to the waiting letter once more, remembering another time when he'd received a letter sealed by markless wax, and his blood held pause within him, his breath refusing to come for a long moment.

"I call it a fortunate thing," Vaste said, prattling on, unaware of the catch in J'anda's chest, the sudden fear clutching at his innards, "because who wouldn't want to go on living, in perfect form, ageless, for thousands of years? I mean, having children at the ripe old age of twenty thousand? Who wouldn't—?"

"You needn't concern yourself with me, friend," J'anda said abruptly, like the clangor of a bell of alarum at midnight. "I am quite fine." He found himself suddenly glad that he had not bothered to put on the illusion. "Though very tired. I hate to cut short our reunion, but … could I trouble you to let me rest? I would be very glad to take up our conversation in the morn, if you'd like to continue then."

Vaste's expression rippled with subtle doubt. "Would you? Would you, truly?"

"I would, truly," J'anda said, as sincerely as he could. "But I have been awake for the space of days, have cast more magic than I thought I had in me, and find myself depleted … much like …" he waved a hand, as though he could pull the desired words out of the air itself.

"… like the larders of Sanctuary, I would imagine," Vaste said, nodding. "Very well, I'll leave you to collapse into your bed without further ado." The troll started to stand, and a great cracking came from beneath him. The yellow eyes widened in panic, but the troll's reflexes were insufficient to the task before him.

The bed crumbled beneath Vaste's large frame, the mattress crushed beneath his weight. The troll's legs flew up in the air as his back fell. There was an explosion of feathers as the entire mass came to the stone floor with a thunderous sound that faded into stark silence.

"Ow," Vaste said.

J'anda stood there, feathers drifting around him like a gentle, falling snow. "Are you all right?" he asked, finally. Rushing forward to help the troll, who outweighed him immensely, seemed an exercise in futility, so he simply stood his ground, a hand on his chin, watching with a curious mixture of resignation and dismay.

"I believe I've just ensured a terrible night of sleep for you," Vaste said, legs in the air and his robe fallen down to expose his boots and thighs as large as the trunks of small trees. J'anda averted his eyes politely as the feathers and dust settled from the destruction. The troll was flat on his back in the wreckage of the bed. The white staff rattled as it dropped out of Vaste's grasp, rolling in front of the hearth. "For that, I apologize."

"You, ah," J'anda said, focusing all his attention on the fireplace, "you should probably get up."

"I am trying," Vaste said, and J'anda could hear the strain in the troll's voice. "Could you help me?"

"I doubt it very much," J'anda said, watching the crackling of the fire.

"Oh, right," Vaste said. "Well, I suppose I could—" He strained again, making a sound not dissimilar to a mule grunting under a heavy load. "Okay. All right. I'm good now."

J'anda turned to find the troll on all fours, robe up above the crest of his back. "I do not think I would define that as 'good,'" J'anda said, looking swiftly back to the fire again.

"I believe you've just insulted the quality of my ass," Vaste said, getting to his feet. The troll stepped on a piece of the bed's frame and it cracked loudly. "Errr ... which is, admittedly, perhaps a little outsized." He adjusted his robes back into place and the hem fell all the way to the floor.

J'anda watched the whole proceeding out of the corner of his eye, still detached from the destruction of his furniture and considering the letter once again. *If that is from ...*

"Well, I should probably leave you now," Vaste said awkwardly, stooping to retrieve his staff. "Let me know if you want me to destroy any of your other furnishings."

J'anda struggled to find the polite thing to say, with his mind so occupied by other matters. "It is of no consequence," he said with only a moment's pause.

"You say that now," Vaste said, "but you'll change your tune in about two hours, when your old bones are rattling across the cold stone floor. I think it actually might be more comfortable out in the yard, if you can believe it—"

"I will make do," J'anda said, the desire for haste finally setting in. He forced a half-smile, something wry, and opened his door, as quickly as he could without appearing rude or hurried. "I do thank you for your concern, my friend."

"Well," Vaste said, taking the hint and moving out of the door with less haste than J'anda would have preferred, "it's not out of the way for me, you know. I'm always concerning myself with everything."

"I have often said that about you," J'anda said, drawing a curious look from Vaste. "That you are a concerning individual," he added.

"Oh, very funny," Vaste said, pausing outside the door. "You know—"

"Tomorrow," J'anda said and closed the door without allowing for a reply.

"Right," Vaste said through the closed door. "Tomorrow it is, then. Good night."

J'anda leaned against the door, his eyes traveling slowly over the broken bed and back to the desk in the corner, where the yellowed paper rested, waiting. He let the inviting, smoky aroma of the hearth drift over him, the warmth of the room drift over his skin, and he eased his way to the desk and picked up the sealed letter. He ripped it open, but found the tearing of the paper not at all satisfactory.

And then he read the words within and wondered if anything would be satisfactory ever again.

4.

Terian

Returning to the shrouded dark of the Sovereign's throne room would have been a strange experience, even absent the extenuating circumstances that hung heavy on his mind like an extra set of armor. Terian passed through the intricately carved double wooden doors in the antechamber, the scent of some lingering aroma, incense perhaps, drifting deep into his nose.

A wooden floor stretched into the distance of the throne room, far ahead of him. Dim lanterns hung on the wooden walls to either side, but their light was diminished, less than a normal candle, as though they were shrouded in dark glass.

Terian walked alongside Malpravus toward the throne in the distance. He'd seen the creature upon it before; spindly grey legs that were disproportionate to the size of the body, a face with tusk-like protrusions jutting from either side of his mouth and a third tusk that extruded from the top of his head and curved between his red eyes. The Sovereign's body was nothing like a dark elf's; his torso was strangely thin, almost insect-like in its appearance, but with grey flesh that reminded Terian of the scourge. He saw the Sovereign's eyes turn toward him as he entered, the three-fingered hands of the leader of Saekaj and Sovar grasping the arms of his ornate wooden throne as he shifted to consider his impending visitors.

This is bound to be interesting.

"Do mine eyes deceive me, or does Terian Lepos approach my throne?" the Sovereign asked. His voice was the same cold hiss as always, his face inscrutable. The tall creature rose to greet his guests.

26

"Your eyes don't deceive you, my Lord Yartraak," Terian said, curiously uncaring about the outcome of this meeting. *Either I'll live or I won't. Or I'll live and be tortured horrendously. Or maybe he'll make me his loyal servant again—which might be worse, honestly.* "I present myself for your judgment."

"And at an auspicious moment, no less," the Sovereign said, eyes locked on his. "Do you know of what I speak?"

Terian halted as Malpravus did, the click of his boots against the wood floor dying away. "Are you speaking of the incursion of Mortus' dead that Sanctuary just turned back in the east?"

"I speak, of course, of—" The God of Darkness halted in the middle of his thought, his jaw pausing in a jutted position, giving the god a strange underbite. "Explain what you mean by that."

"Mortus' collected souls," Terian said, catching a glimpse of naked curiosity from Malpravus at his side. There was a slight shroud of darkness around the throne, but Terian could make out a figure stooping next to one of the arms of the seat, a man in the garments of a servant. "They poured out of a portal into the land of Luukessia, beyond the Endless Bridge, taking physical form and putting to ruin the entirety of the land."

The Sovereign made a deep, hissing noise, a sound born out of the back of his throat. "But your guild halted this … incidence?"

"Alaric Garaunt destroyed the bridge and sent the—we called them a scourge—" Terian began.

"A fitting name for those malformed wraiths," the Sovereign agreed, though his eyes flashed curiously at the mention of Alaric's name, crimson glowing in the artificial night.

"—to the bottom of the sea of Carmas," Terian said and controlled his instinct to swallow heavily with the pronouncement that followed, crushing it down into his insides. "Alaric was also lost in the commission of this action."

The Sovereign made a broad wave of his hand, as though sweeping the thought of that away. "I find it disquieting that Mortus's failure to seal that portal led to such a grand error. Those … things could easily have spilled over the bridge and created a great difficulty in these lands."

Terian paused, trying to decide how best to address his question, then remembered he might die at any moment. *Best to just get it out there, then.* "You've seen this sort of thing before."

The Sovereign stroked his nearly nonexistent chin, and for a moment Terian struggled to remember that he was in fact a living god; he looked so very normal in his mannerisms, though his form was truly bizarre. "Of course. It is well known to us that transitioning a disembodied essence through a portal creates a monstrous physical form. Mortus, being a collector of … well, he should have known better." Yartraak's gaze swiveled back to Terian. "Should I thank you for bringing me these tidings? Or should I kill you for the other news I have received on this night?"

Terian wondered whether he should ask if the 'us' the Sovereign referred to was a royal one or an actual one, but he decided not to press his luck once the threat was leveled. "I have no idea what other news you've received, having just returned to these shores."

The Sovereign's crimson eyes narrowed. "Perhaps you do not. Cyrus Davidon returned with you, then?"

Terian's calm wavered, just for a moment. "In spite of my best efforts … yes."

Yartraak's voice rumbled. "You tried to kill him?"

"Tried," Terian agreed. "Some."

"And failed?" Yartraak asked.

"I cursed him and cut his horse's throat while he was fleeing the scourge," Terian said, pursing his lips, "in payment for what he did on the bridge in Termina."

The Sovereign sat heavily on the throne. "Interesting. But he survived, as he always seems to."

The God of Darkness does seem to take an inordinate amount of interest in Sanctuary and its players. "It's becoming something of an annoying habit of his," Terian said. "Defying the best efforts of all to kill him." Terian searched for any trace of feeling in the matter, and found it curiously lacking.

Shouldn't I still want him dead? Didn't I just swear it wasn't over between us?

So why can't I seem to feel regret for my failure to kill Cyrus? He fixed his gaze back on Yartraak. *Maybe it's the company I'm keeping. Cyrus Davidon somehow seems quite the minor concern at the moment, for some reason.*

"He led an army against mine this very eve," the Sovereign rumbled. "The one I had perched in siege 'round the neck of

Sanctuary. They were to be my vise, my strong hand, to squeeze that pustule until the infection was purged out of the Plains of Perdamun." He raised a three-fingered hand, his claws catching the light and glistening. "Cyrus Davidon broke them."

"I beg your greatest pardon," Malpravus said, bowing as he took a step forward to stand next to Terian, "but how many of the Sovereignty's soldiers survived?"

"Nearly none," the Sovereign said in a low hiss, "Davidon's forces came in on mounted cavalry and ran our army to ground. We lost spell casters, our own horsemen, and infantry beyond the counting. Our officers were taken, caught out in the charge. General Vardeir has failed to report in; I can only hope that it means he has died with the rest of the fools."

Terian blinked. A small giggle escaped him, then another. He broke into an unquenchable laughter, bending double at the waist, unable to control himself, and looked up to find himself laughing at the Sovereign directly. "I'm sorry," he said, not remotely meaning it.

"You find this amusing?" the Sovereign asked. Terian could see Malpravus creeping away from him in slow steps.

"As you know," Terian said, composing himself, "my candor with you has always been ... stunningly frank. And I see no reason, perched as I am with my very heart on the tip of your blade, to change that at present. So, yes, I find it funny that Ardin Vardeir and his army were broken in their siege of Sanctuary. I find it hilarious, actually, a heady moment of levity in the midst of what has been a most depressing year, honestly. And probably not for the reason you think."

"I think you are so loyal to your Sanctuary friends," the Sovereign said, unmistakably dangerous, "that to let you leave this throne room alive would be to allow a traitorous worm to writhe his way out of my grasp."

"Well, then, I might as well hit you with the full weight of my honesty before I get killed," Terian said, "and we can make it an execution for the ages. Spilled entrails and whatever else." *Why, oh why, do I always find it necessary to be a bracing ass in the presence of the most powerful being I've ever met? He must bring it out in me.* "Why would you waste your time and effort attacking Sanctuary when it would be better spent crushing Reikonos?"

"You question my efforts?" the Sovereign asked, fury creeping into his voice.

"Yes," Terian said flatly. "I question your strategy. I question it most vociferously. I wonder if your advisors are completely incompetent, or if they're merely traitors who hate you with everything they have, because thus far, they've squandered the single largest army in Arkaria by throwing it wildly against everything that moves." He ticked points off on his fingers one by one. "Why would anyone even think of broadening the war to the elven kingdom by invading Termina when the Sovereignty was already at war with the humans? That's a staggeringly stupid maneuver, as was driven home in obvious terms over the last year, I assume—"

"You assume much," the Sovereign said, but his red eyes flared. "I gave the orders to take Termina, to cut off their aid to the humans up the Perda."

"Then your advisors should be gutted for not opposing you tooth and nail," Terian said. "Did even one of them raise the possibility that you were extending your army too far?"

"My advisors are loyal subjects," Yartraak hissed, "unlike you."

"Yet they marched your armies into a catastrophic battle on the bridges," Terian said, "without even advising you as to the potential consequences? That's not loyalty; that's fear for their own hides holding them back from informing their Sovereign of the downsides inherent in a military campaign. That's Dagonath Shrawn trying to keep from letting a breath of bad news pass from his lips to your ear."

The Sovereign settled in his throne. "After all this time, your grudge against Shrawn still governs your thoughts, Terian of House Lepos."

"He's a traitor, but let's leave that aside," Terian said, letting his opinions roll off his tongue unheeded. "I understand the desire for revenge, believe me," Terian felt a cool prickling inside at the admission, "but there's a time and a place, and the time to take on a third army is not when you're already fighting two others to a stalemate."

"I'm sure you find it easy to criticize those actions, now," the Sovereign said, "with the benefit of hindsight and time as your allies, aiding you in seeing to the truth that is brought only through the course of events being carried to their natural conclusion."

"The natural conclusion," Terian said, "of this war was that you would win it by crushing humanity's largest city and then mopping up their lesser territories in the east and north with little effort. That you would own them, break them, put them under the heel, and once your gains were consolidated you could extend your boot to the throat of the gnomes, the dwarves, the goblins and the men of the desert, if you so desired, before stretching across the Perda and breaking the dying kingdom of the elves. A strategist with half a brain would have opposed the idea of pledging as much of your force to Sanctuary as you did, because you couldn't afford to lose them and keep the fight going."

The Sovereign's clawed fingers clutched at his throne's wooden arms, and the sound of scratching wood filled the chamber. "Then what would you counsel now, Terian? Now that these setbacks have been dealt, now that your former guild has hobbled our efforts."

"I don't know," Terian said casually. "I'd need to know what you have, where you have it, and what you truly want before I could offer a decent assessment of what should come next."

"I have armies around Reikonos," the Sovereign said, "and in lesser numbers along the Perda."

"How many?" Terian asked.

The Sovereign stared at him with harsh, glowing eyes. "I do not trust you to know."

"So you're not going to kill me?" Terian asked, resisting the urge to smirk.

"I called for your return to me once before," Yartraak said, "before the outset of this war. You and the other traitor, J'anda ... I called you before me to answer, to prove your loyalty to me, and you did not hasten to my call, did not respond to my offer to betray your fellows—"

"As compelling as it was," Terian said, "I was in exile—"

"At my behest," the Sovereign rumbled.

"—and I despise Dagonath Shrawn," Terian said. "I assume he's still your chief advisor?"

"He is one of a few," Yartraak said roughly. "But you cannot hang your betrayal, your steadfast refusal to come back to me at the rise of the tide, upon Dagonath Shrawn."

"I could hang a lot on Dagonath Shrawn if I tried," Terian said.

31

"Have you met him? I mean, I've met some treacherous sons of bitches in my time, but that guy—he can tell you what you want to hear like no one else. Honeyed words couldn't come any sweeter if you dipped them in the comb and let them soak for five thousand years. Has he ever delivered ill news to you that didn't come with personal benefit to his house attached?"

"You cannot explain your failures so easily," the Sovereign said.

"If I may," Malpravus said, easing forward once more, "I do not believe that Terian Lepos has attempted to explain away any of his past failures. I believe he is presenting a compelling case for a slightly wider circle of advisement."

The Sovereign's throaty voice whispered over them. "Have I not already broadened my circle by including you and yours, Malpravus? And in spite of your attacks on our shipping with the accursed goblins, no less."

"I gave you the excuse for war that you sought," Malpravus said with a bow, "and my guild continues to make restitution for that indiscretion through our loyal service to your cause."

"Yes," Yartraak said, and his claws returned to his mouth. "I have received the better bargain from you in this dealing, Malpravus, this is truth. Your eternal service in exchange for some convoys dealing goods to foreign powers and the ability to make this war on justified terms … yes. It was well bargained, your parole." *That's a steep price*, Terian thought. "But this does not excuse the disloyalty of young Lepos."

"I serve who I pledge my loyalty to," Terian said, shrugging. "If I just flipped about like a carp in a boat, going from loyalty to loyalty, I think that would make me a mercenary. You turned me loose of my leash, my Sovereign, after your loyal servant Shrawn betrayed my house and crushed us underfoot with no more concern than you might give to a single slave being flogged to death by an overseer. You wanted me gone to pain my father, and I went. But the world is not kind to exiles without money, without lord or land, and I did what I had to in order to seek power. I swore my loyalty, and I didn't merely renounce it as soon as the moment was convenient and you asked me to come answer to you. If I had, you could be assured that were I to give it to you again in the future, it would be worth less than any of your current advisors' strategic plans."

"And what makes me think I should attach any weight to your strategic plans?" the Sovereign asked.

Well, Terian thought, *now's as good a time as any to see if I'm right … because this is either going to throw him into a rage, or save my life.* "Because I learned much in the way of these things in my absence, Lord of Night," Terian said, drawing a subtle flinch from the Sovereign, "from Cyrus Davidon … and Alaric Garaunt."

The Sovereign's expression was a strange one, his inhuman features difficult to read. Oh, the obvious emotions were there, and more plainly stated in his voice than anywhere else, least of all his face. But this time, Terian could have sworn he saw a flicker of rage behind those eyes, one that was swiftly replaced by … desire.

"I will give you rope, Terian Lepos," the Sovereign said at last.

"The better to hang me with, no doubt," Terian said.

"I will let you walk a path for a time," the Sovereign said. "To prove yourself my tamed servant." His eyes snapped to Malpravus. "You brought him to me. Does this mean you wish him to join your army?"

"I would have him as my adjutant, yes," Malpravus said, stooping in a low bow that Terian was surprised the old skeleton pulled off without collapsing into a pile of bones. "Unless you require him elsewhere."

The Sovereign gave it a moment's consideration. "I can think of many uses for Terian Lepos. He has proven himself versatile and candid in a way that few are in my presence but that all are outside my company. Very well, Lepos, you will live to serve another day. Do not test my resolve or betray me, or you will find the rope that I give you wrapped tightly around your throat, and—"

"Yes, I know, you'll torture me slowly to death," Terian said. "I'm very familiar with how the Sovereignty works, having done my share of this for you in the past."

Yartraak's eyes followed him. "Go on, then. Find your place in my graces once more, and prove yourself more than a facile user of fragrant words. Go to your home, tend to your house—" The Sovereign smiled unnaturally. "Take up with your wife once more."

Terian felt his jaw tighten. *Kahlee? Good gods, I would have thought they'd have granted her an annulment by now.* "As you would have it, my Sovereign."

33

"I think you will find House Lepos in a most curious position," the Sovereign said, and his gaze swiveled to the servant still kneeling by the arm of his throne. "It is, at least, not where you left it."

Terian looked sidelong at Malpravus, who seemed to incline his head in acknowledgment. *They moved in the Shuffle?* "I'm sure I'll find them where they deserve to be," Terian said simply.

"Undoubtedly," the Sovereign said. "Perhaps you could raise their fortunes ... help return them to the path. Otherwise, I suspect this will be the end of House Lepos."

Exactly how far have they fallen? Terian merely managed a perfunctory salute. "I'll do what I can."

"See that you do," the Sovereign said, dismissing them with a wave of the hand. "Oh, and Terian?"

Terian, already beginning to back out of the throne room alongside Malpravus, turned his attention back to Yartraak. "Yes, my Lord?"

Yartraak's hand moved subtly; so subtly that Terian almost missed it. The claws on his left hand only seemed to twitch for a second from their place on the arm of his throne, but the servant kneeling next to him balked at the motion, and Terian realized that the Sovereign had lashed out in some small way.

It was not until he saw the bloody line across the servant's neck that he realized exactly what form that lashing had taken.

"Do not speak to anyone else of what you saw over the sea," Yartraak said, "nor of the threat you faced in that place or from Mortus. Do we understand one another? It is a secret I wish kept."

Terian watched the servant fall to the floor, a puddle of navy blue blood seeping out onto the hardwood. "As you command," he said.

"Good," the Sovereign rattled, then turned his head to look at the servant's fallen body. "Get my steward in here as you leave. I do not wish my floor to stain."

Terian froze in his retreat, the inhumanity of the Sovereign driven home to him once again. *You are a cold and worthless sort of bastard ... and I guess I'll be serving you. Again.* "As you wish, your Grace," Terian said, and bowed as he joined Malpravus once more, and they left together.

5.

Aisling

"So this is the house of the man who would be the Sovereign's own right hand," Aisling said, loud enough that she knew Verity could hear her. She said it with that in mind, in fact, knowing full well that anything she repeated in the presence of one of Shrawn's servants would doubtless make it to his ears eventually. She had seen it happen enough times with others to realize that Dagonath Shrawn's greatest strength was his ability to overhear things that no one else seemed to. She pictured him as a spider in the center of a web of lies and flies, listening to the twang of his threads as others moved around him, always aware of where his prey was located.

"Indeed," Verity said as they stood in the rich wood parlor. The smell of varnish hung in the air, as though the surfaces had recently endured a refinishing. Other than hints of amusement at her own self-importance, Aisling had little read on the elf. The light in Shrawn's manor must have been dim indeed for someone such as Verity, used to life in the outside world, but the elf seemed to have little trouble seeing.

"I expected grander things, I suppose," Aisling said, again calculating the time it would take for her simple proclamations to reach Shrawn's ears. She'd learned to play the role, to curb her thoughts around others. *Cyrus Davidon proves that well enough*, she figured. *He has no idea. And if Shrawn had any inkling of what he himself has failed to realize about me ...*

She suppressed a shudder. It was second nature to her by now, burying those feelings within and reviving them later for some occasion when she needed them for purposes of acting in the manner expected. All the world was her stage, and a simple thespian's job seemed so easy to her now, acting only during a performance. *My performance is always, and the stakes are my life—and the life of Norenn.*

"I suppose we'll need to wait until Shrawn can accommodate me in his schedule," Aisling said without judgment.

"He is a busy man," Verity said with a little snap.

"Of course, of course," Aisling said, playing the role of one who did not wish to give offense. "I only mean to say that my use to him is going to be much reduced if I'm found to be a spy in Sanctuary. And the longer my absence—"

"You overcalculate your own importance to them," Verity scoffed. "No one will know you've left. And even if you were asked, you need merely say that you wished to visit family that you have missed whilst away." She shook her head and made a *pfft!* noise out of the corner of her mouth. "Foolish girl."

Aisling stood standing in the middle of the room. Her stomach rumbled, her tongue tasted of the bile born of that hunger. *How long has it been since I've eaten? What day is it, actually?* Her head swam slightly, fatigue rippling through her muscles. *I may need some sleep as well …*

Verity snapped to attention in the moment before the double doors at the parlor's entry clicked to open. Aisling listened to the lock mechanism move. She'd assessed it when she came in and found it wanting. *Not many people want to rob the second most powerful person in Saekaj, I suppose. Dangerous business, that.* A trace of sadness rippled through her, soul-deep. *Only the most careless would do something so foolhardy.*

People like me, then. Or at least how I used to be.

The double doors swung open, guided by a dark elven woman in heavy armor. She clanked slightly as she moved, but she did so with much more grace than most of the armor wearers that Aisling had seen. *I didn't even hear her in the hallway,* she realized. *A dark knight? A female dark knight? In Saekaj?* The woman's faceplate was up, her armor curved in harsh ways, a hole in the back where her ponytail spilled out of the top of her armor. The white hair snaked down her back and her red eyes surveyed the room, Aisling, and Verity in swift order, apparently trying to determine seriousness of threat posed.

She settled her gaze on Aisling. "I'll need your daggers," the woman said coolly.

Aisling thought, just for a moment, of resisting. *If they want me dead, I'm dead anyway.* She plucked both blades from their sheaths on her belt and handed them over without question, blade-first.

The woman eyes flashed in annoyance, but she kept emotion off her face as she took the daggers by their blades, burying the steel in her own armored palms with only a subtle noise to mark her grasp upon them. She withdrew them and held one in each hand, prompting Aisling to raise an eyebrow at the tactic; it left the woman's hands filled, unable to draw her own sword, which hung at her belt. Aisling's eyes swept over the curve of the scabbard, which was broad and long, considerably larger than Cyrus Davidon's sword, which was the gold standard by which she judged all blades. *The weight on that thing must be terrible. It almost looks like a meat cleaver rests on her belt, and one with a curve like a hunchback's spine.*

"Nice sword," was all that Aisling said with the woman caught her looking.

The woman gathered both the daggers in her left hand, the sound of blade on gauntlet clanking in the quiet room. She watched Aisling impassively, withdrawing to stand a few feet away. "His Grace will be along momentarily."

"Then I will wait, I suppose," Aisling said, bleeding any sarcasm out of her reply through careful practice. Sanctuary had been a place where she'd often let her thoughts bubble forth, because so many of them did not require her to keep her own counsel. *A curious place, in that regard. I was a freer prisoner there than here, where I am required to keep even more of my self hidden. More even than the place where I am a spy. How strange is that!*

She did not have long to wait. Dagonath Shrawn appeared in the open doors within a minute, his belly sagging over his belt, even larger than when last she'd seen him. His jowls seemed to have grown larger as well, like flaps of flesh hanging upon his cheekbones, sagging under his withdrawn eye sockets. His white hair was longer as well, skin wrinkled as though he had pruned in the time since last she'd seen him. His walking stick did not tap the wood floor as he went, however, and she knew that he only used it in public, to make himself seem weaker. Though she couldn't be certain, the affectation had just enough resemblance to a spell-caster's stave that she wouldn't have wanted to challenge him in a battle, despite his advancing years and infirm appearance. *He's a spider,* she thought, *of the worst kind. The kind that makes play that they're a fly, as helpless in the web as anyone else.*

Until he grows hungry.

"So there you are," Shrawn said, in a husky voice. "Returned after your little sojourn across the seas."

"Just the one sea, really," Aisling said, unable to keep from politely barbing him. "I would have gone farther for my mission if needed."

"And what do you have to report?" Shrawn said, slipping into the room and eyeing the woman in armor to his right. "Sareea … you may go."

"She's dangerous," Sareea said. Aisling mentally filed her name away.

"She is as a kitten," Shrawn said, not taking his eyes off Aisling. "Her claws hold no fear for me. Verity, you as well."

Verity stiffened, but nodded in a bow. "As you wish, your Grace," and she promptly withdrew from the room.

"It's all right, Sareea," Shrawn said, shifting his walking stick from one hand to the other in a subtle motion designed to remind the other woman of who he was, Aisling figured.

"I will be right outside," Sareea said with a bow, her red eyes flashing hard warning to Aisling. "In case you need me for anything." She, too, withdrew to the hallway and shut both doors behind her, her eyes the last thing to recede behind them.

"Sareea Scyros," Shrawn said, pointing the walking stick toward the door, "the first female dark knight in the kingdom."

"Oh my," Aisling said, strangely indifferent. *So I was right about her. Things are changing in Saekaj Sovar. A lady knight? How peculiar for this place.*

"Soon enough women will be on the front lines, the way the elves do," Shrawn said, bringing his walking stick back to the fore. "Personally, I find the thought distasteful, but we are in a war and fresh blood is needed, from whatever vein it need be drawn."

"Indeed," Aisling said, holding back a choice comment about what kind of blood she thought needed to be let.

"What do you have to report?" Shrawn said, tapping the end of his stick against the ground.

"I was able to enter the affections of the subject," Aisling said, matter-of-factly. "I was in his confidence for a time."

A line stitched itself down Shrawn's brow, like a scar dividing his forehead. "'For a time'?"

"Cyrus Davidon does not trust with greatest ease," she said simply. "He has been … distracted."

"Distract him further," Shrawn said, the crease deepening. "Get into his undergarments and do not relinquish your hold. Do I truly need to instruct you on how to go about this?"

"I think I have a sense of what's required by now," Aisling said, tossing a blistering dose of resentment down the pit inside where she threw all her excess and deadly emotions. "The man's mind is clouded, though. He has much upon it."

"Make yourself the most pressing thing," Shrawn said, dropping the staff to his side once more, utterly caught up in what he was saying. "By pressing, I mean—"

"Yes," Aisling said. "I understand."

"I don't think you do," Shrawn said. "A man in his position has weight upon him like few in the world. You are to be his soothing balm, the thing that cures his ache at the end of the day. From that place, you could hear everything of import to us, from the great to the trivial."

"I have tried," she said. "He resists."

"Try harder," Shrawn said, countenance darkening. "Go to him, this very night."

"I suspect he's tired—"

"You have just won a dual campaign," Shrawn said coldly. Aisling let slip a small measure of surprise, calculated to stoke his ego. "Yes," Shrawn said with great satisfaction, "I have heard where you have been already. About the bridge, about the siege. He mourns your guildmaster's loss, but he has just saved your hall and destroyed one of our great armies. He is alight with feeling at this moment, I guarantee. If ever there was a root ripe for the harvest, this is it. Go to him, tonight, immediately, as soon as you return, and seduce him. Worm your way into his graces and," Shrawn reached out and grabbed hold of her leather gherkin and tugged her off balance. She let him, reluctantly, even though she saw the motion coming from a league off. "Never let him go again." He released her from his grasp. "Do you require a reminder of what is at stake here?"

Aisling hesitated, speeding along the path of her thoughts, playing the probabilities to their inevitable ends. Better to be coy and give him a glimpse of her playful, insolent wit—which he expected at some point, no doubt—or play loyal and risk him thinking her false? That was a simple enough answer. "The entirety of the future of the Sovereignty hangs upon Cyrus Davidon's armored cod, no doubt," she said, putting just enough of long-suffering resentment into the statement to make it ring true.

"Girl!" Shrawn said sharply and rapped her across the cheek with his staff, just hard enough to ring her skull but not enough to leave a mark. "Your impudence does you no favor."

"No one does me favors," Aisling said, holding her stinging face, "I have to do all the favors, it would seem."

"And you will continue to," Shrawn said and turned his staff toward the door, hitting it twice with a knock that echoed through the air.

"I—" Aisling began, but the doors snapped open and stopped her mid-thought.

A small parade of people made their way into the parlor, a spectacle she had half-expected. *He has to re-assert his authority, to kick me back into line. There is no way to do that but to hang the threat over me, once more, for the first time in over a year.*

Two guards brought forth a dark elven man in tattered rags, manacles binding his hands and feet. Their chain mail rattled with motion, their swords were sheathed with no threat in sight. With practiced hands they shoved their prisoner into the room, and then to his knees, with an air of theatricality, a showcase for the cruelty of the house in which she stood.

Aisling let her carefully concealed expression break through with genuine horror. It was not hard to summon. "Norenn," she whispered, as though the whole theatrical exercise was a very great surprise to her, unexpected in every way and deeply disquieting in the ones that mattered to her host. She kept her eyes off Shrawn, focusing them on Norenn, even though she did not want to look upon him. Not like this.

She dropped to her knees, not having to work hard to summon up the desire to do what a lover would do for the man she cared for. His face bore fresh bruises, and she suspected that Shrawn had long planned for this moment, for her insolence. Freshly clotted blood hung in dark blue patches under his eyes and nose, and as she brushed his face with delicate fingers he flinched, squinting at her through a badly swollen eye. "… Ais?"

"It's me," she said, letting fright and joy shoot through her words as she knelt and touched him for the first time in over year.

"Oh gods, Ais," he said, breathing hard, as though the simple act of movement were a labor, "I thought you were dead. You were gone so long …"

"Not dead," she said. "Just away for a while. I wouldn't … wouldn't leave you here …"

Norenn's swollen eye darkened. "You should. You should le—"

A hard whack to the back of the neck with Shrawn's staff crumpled Norenn, and Aisling let an automatic "No-o!" escape her with little effort. She felt it inside, truly, but on a deeper, more complicated level. She let only the horror and fear shine through, now, keeping the relief that he was still alive hidden within—along with her satisfaction that she'd judged Shrawn correctly and that other trifling emotion.

"This is the carrot and the stick," Shrawn said, brandishing his staff. "Faithful service and success will be rewarded, insolence and failure punished." He jutted the end of the stave in her face. "Cyrus Davidon. You will write me a full report and give it to Verity, a full disclosure of your entire year away and all that happened, with as much excruciating detail as you can recall. Make it a diary, plausibly denied in case it is discovered, something frilly and heartfelt, but lacking not a whit of even trivial detail."

"Yes," Aisling said, letting herself sound suitably cowed. "I'll do what you want. Exactly what you want. Just … please …"

"I see you remember your place," Shrawn said, nodding. "See that you do not forget it again, lest I am forced to remind you in a harsher and more permanent way." He snapped his fingers. "Sareea: Have him healed."

Bastard, Aisling thought, letting the tears fall freely as she let the hard wood floor bite into her knees with its unyielding hardness. *You beat him before you came in. You were going to showboat him in front of me even if I'd been perfectly submissive and well behaved.*

The dark knight Sareea stepped into the room and over to Aisling, sliding both her daggers back into her scabbards, unasked. That done, she grasped Norenn by the upper arm, half-dragging him out of the parlor, the guards following behind as the dark knight did her cruel job. Norenn, for his part, struggled to keep up with the woman in armor. The only sound was the shuffling of Norenn's shoeless feet as his manacles clanked and he tried to keep his balance. There was a soft thump as he ricocheted slowly off the wall. "Stupid shite," Sareea Scyros said, loud enough to be heard as she dragged hard on Norenn's arm and produced a yelp.

"Are you clear on what needs to happen next?" Shrawn asked, clasping his staff in front of him like a ward.

"I will go to Cyrus Davidon this very night," Aisling said, bleeding all life out of her tone. *He wants absolute submission, and I can give him at least the appearance of that.* "I will seduce him and enter his trust, and never let go of him until ordered otherwise by you." She gave her voice the inflection of a broken thing. It was something she had perfected in Luukessia, listening to the voice of the Baroness Cattrine in moments of absolute desperation. A new tool that Shrawn hadn't heard from her before.

"Very good," Shrawn said, sounding only mildly satisfied. "Verity … take her forth."

"No," Aisling whispered, already reconciled to much worse than this. "I … just a moment with Norenn, please …" She threw out the plea knowing that it would almost certainly go unheeded. *He'll be fine,* she knew.

"His death will not be swift if you do not obey," Shrawn said, expression darkening. *And so he asserts his authority once more.*

"I know," she said, switching to pleading. "He is … broken of mind. He knows not what he says, what he faces … but I do. I do." She nodded swiftly, for emphasis. "You have been … truthful in all your dealings with me, and I know you will honor our pact." To this she added hope, though from where she drew it within, she did not know.

"I will honor our pact when your task is done," Shrawn agreed, with just a moment more hesitation than he should have had.

"I will go," Aisling said, her head hanging, as Verity stepped to stand next to her. "I will do as you have asked immediately." She made herself sound hopeless, will-less, and the wizard wrapped an arm through Aisling's own, as though they were going to skip merrily together through a field.

"Do not leave me room for doubt in this matter," Shrawn said, "for it would be costly to your friend, whose life and well-being I know you value."

She nodded, calculating that saying nothing was better than any feeble words added to the fire at this point. Verity, for her part, raised her staff and muttered something under her breath as the swirls of magical energy began to roil around them.

This was the hardest part, Aisling knew, watching the magic rise, knowing she was set to disappear but keeping her head firmly down, her last emotion tight within her while Shrawn was watching, while Verity could see her. She did this thing, though, stiffening the muscles in her neck so that she could not look up without pain. The storm raged within her as the magic passed before her eyes, striking the vision of Shrawn out of her sight and replacing it with the fields of Perdamun, with a vision of Sanctuary, glistening, a tower of light in the distance.

Aisling stood there next to the wizard—the spy—with her head still bowed for a long moment after their arrival, not trusting herself to give a performance worthy of what she needed to accomplish. *No, not yet. Not until it passes, until I contain it. I haven't had to hide it, not like this … not in a long time.*

"You have a job to do," Verity said stiffly, but still, Aisling kept her head down, and did not say anything.

Let her think I'm mourning my lost freedom. Let her think I'm cowed into inaction. Let her think anything, anything … until I can …

She pictured the pit in her mind, saw herself at the edge, in a fight. There she stood, on the very lip of an abyss, warring with her quarry, a wild, furious one, hissing, angry, spitting and thrashing. She pictured herself putting a dagger in her foe's belly, stabbing it over and over until the fight bled out of it and she could move the arms out of the way. Then she drove her blade into its heart, over and over, until the eyes glassed over, and the rage died, along with the rest of her enemy.

She saw the furious purple eyes fade, and knew them to be her own. *Shrawn is not my enemy*, she thought.

I am my enemy. Control yourself. Control your fury.

She lifted her head, the hot anger turned to cold and dropped unceremoniously in the pit with all the other feelings she could not allow. She knew it lived, though, growing more frigid by the day, hiding in her belly, waiting to strike.

"You should be going," Verity said, tapping her foot in the dirt with impatience.

"Yes," Aisling said quietly, under control at last. She took a step toward the guildhall and made it look like it was the hardest thing she had ever done. The heat had subsided from her face, and her breaths came slow and resigned now as she let the weariness of days of battle wash over her, take her over.

"You won't seduce anyone looking like that," Verity said at her back.

"I'll be ready when I get there," Aisling said, trudging back toward the towers in the distance, toward the curtain wall with its dark gaps in the places where it had been broken open. "I'll have to be. I'll make myself."

"Glad I'm not in your boots," Verity scoffed, walking a dozen paces behind her.

"They'd be tight on you," Aisling said, devoid of almost any feeling. She heard a slight grunt behind her and allowed the hint of a smile. If she were seen, it would be expected after such a snippy comment.

And I can only allow what is expected, for now. Because ... Shrawn is not my enemy.

Fury is my enemy.

And I will beat my fury, mask it, bury it, let it grow cold with the rest of my anger.

Because Shrawn is not enemy.

Shrawn is a dead man.

And only my raging, indignant fury can defeat me in this endeavor.

The smile she allowed herself was sincere. She thought carefully about the death of her hot, raging fury, and the colder, calmer form of it settled in instead, awaiting the moment where she could release it to do its work, satisfying that desire for vengeance that had been growing, unfettered, in that pit in her mind for years.

6.

Terian

The carriage rattled away from the portico covering the Grand Palace of Saekaj's main entry, Terian's mind racing far faster than the giant spiders that pulled his coach. *I just landed myself another chance with the Sovereign—should I be thrilled or disgusted about that?* He wavered, thinking it over, and ultimately landed somewhere between the two, a practiced cynicism washing back over him.

"You did well," Malpravus said, a surprisingly soothing quality in his voice. He leaned against the hard wood seat. "I was not certain you would be able to pull yourself out of the jaws of death, and yet you managed. I suppose I should not have underestimated your facility with making yourself sound different than the courtiers and suck-ups that the Sovereign is accustomed to."

"Yes, it's surprising how little anyone tells the God of Darkness the honest truth of things," Terian said. "It's as though they want him to grow like a mushroom in the dark."

"I wouldn't go too far in airing these opinions of yours," Malpravus said, putting his fingers together. "There is certainly a limit to how far total honesty will get you in Yartraak's estimation, to say nothing of the others in power in Saekaj."

"Well, as I'm apparently the only one exercising it in his presence," Terian said, "I think it's my best interest to remain as close to the truth with him as possible, lest I lose all value."

"I would be cautious if I were you; better to lose value than your head."

"I suspect that my loss of value would be followed by the loss of my head."

"A precarious position," Malpravus said, "but at least you realize it."

"Yes," Terian agreed, "I'm dancing on the edge of a blade, and if I fall, I'll split asunder. What fun. Serving a Sovereign whose generals have led him into a series of defeats that are ..." he paused, looking at Malpravus. "How bad are they? With tonight's loss in the plains considered?"

Malpravus looked at him shrewdly before answering. "Untenable."

"Define 'untenable,'" Terian said, a ripple of anxiety running through his chest, leaving his breath feeling as though it stuck in him. "Do we have enough soldiers under arms to maintain our current conquests, or will we have to surrender territory?"

Malpravus focused his dark eyes ahead, toward the wooden wall of the carriage. He considered his answer for a space before saying, "If our current manpower levels remain the same, we will not be able to hold the line to the River Perda or continue our advance on Reikonos."

"What about Goliath?" Terian asked. "Can't you—"

"We have our hands full at the moment," Malpravus said with uncharacteristic sharpness. "We are the bulk of the magical army that keeps the 'Big Three' in check on the Reikonos front. I remain uncertain how long we can maintain our strategic edge in that location given our losses." His lips stretched into a smile. "Though I do have an idea of how to, shall we say, allay some of those concerns." The smile faded. "There are, however, elements I have yet to work out in the execution of this plan."

"It appears you were in error; I've returned to a land where hope is near lost." Terian shook his head. "Sovar is on the brink of uprising, yes?" He waited for Malpravus's nod. "More battles than we can fight, more territory than we can hold, and an army that I'm guessing has dragooned more people into service than Saekaj and Sovar can safely afford to give."

"To say nothing of the lack of provisions," Malpravus added lightly. "Expect a starvation diet to begin soon, with the winter at its end but no significant level of outside crops to reach us this year." He paused and looked to Terian. "Last year we liberally raided the Plains of Perdamun for their goods to answer our need. This year, no such source exists."

"Sonofabitch," Terian said, the weight settling on his shoulders like he'd put on eight pairs of pauldrons. "If Sovar starves while we're feeding our army, that spark you're looking to extinguish is going to light up pretty damned fast."

"I am all too aware, my boy," Malpravus said. "I am in constant consideration of the problem, I assure you. This defeat at Sanctuary is perhaps the tinder upon which the fire will begin that will consume us all."

"Not enough spell-casters to conjure bread?" Terian said, and Malpravus shook his head. "The Great Sea—"

"The Sea is dying," Malpravus said. "Surface farms are producing more, but the bulk goes to Saekaj and little falls through the cracks to Sovar; even the bones of animals are being handed off to the servants in Saekaj for their families. With no new conquests since our gains last year, the flood of treasure and supply has slowed to a bare trickle."

"Well," Terian said as the carriage rattled to a halt, "'untenable' was the right word, then."

"Cheer up, dear boy," Malpravus said without expression, "more is still ahead of you."

"Why is that cause for cheer?" Terian asked.

"Look out your window," Malpravus said, and Terian did, catching sight of a squat building, only just inside the gates, carved out of the rock with little ornamentation.

"We're in the front of the city," Terian said, shrugging, "where the least favored perch. Why—" He froze, the cold reality crashing in on him. "Here?"

"Here," Malpravus agreed. "This is your family home now."

"Lucky me," Terian muttered. "Then my mother—"

"Lives here, yes," Malpravus said coolly.

"By herself?" Terian asked. "Because this sort of residence wouldn't suggest much in the way of help—"

"There is another," Malpravus said, waving at the building, which housed probably four apartments in its walls, "but you should see this for yourself."

Another? Terian wondered, his eyebrow inadvertently rising. *Is it ... Kahlee? Why would she leave her family?*

"Go on," Malpravus said, using a nearly limp, bony hand to wave him away. "We will talk more tomorrow, after you've had a chance to ... settle in." He looked straight ahead, but that smile pursed his thin lips once more.

"All right," Terian said, a cloud of suspicion resting on him like a smoky fog on Sovar during the days of chimney clogs. "I suppose I'll see you on the morrow, then."

"Yes," Malpravus agreed as Terian closed the door behind him. "Good evening." With a tap against the wood, he stirred the driver into motion, lashing the big spiders that pulled the carriage. Terian watched them go, disappearing under the phosphorescent cave ceiling's dim light. The carriage turned a corner out of sight, and Terian surveyed the building before him with disgust.

How far we have fallen, he thought, eyeing the common door that gave access to the building. It was built up on a stoop, hinting that there might even be a basement, which would be the least favorable housing within. *Whoever lives there is scant days from losing all grip on Saekaj and their citizenry therein; they could be in Sovar tomorrow even without committing any error at all.*

He walked up the hardened steps, carved out of the rocky floor of the cavern, letting his gauntlet clank along the bannister that rose out of the ground. It, too, was stone, and carved with some effort and craftsmanship, probably done over the course of a hundred years as the sculptor responsible could tear himself away from more pressing and lucrative work. If Saekaj were a multi-tiered cake of the sort he'd seen in Reikonos bakeries, those houses by the front gates were almost on the table, one accident of gravity away from falling off completely and being swept up by a broom with the other detritus on the floor.

Terian tried the entry door, which was stone and not wood; another sign of the humbleness of this abode. It swung under his push, and he noted the lack of a lock on it. *No one would come to Saekaj to steal from someone this far down; they'd be better off robbing from someone at the front gate of Sovar. Less dangerous.*

He stepped into a hallway that ran along the side of the first-floor dwelling. A staircase ahead went both up and down, circling in a rectangular configuration like a snake coiling itself. To his left was the path to the basement; to his right, the way up.

The door of the first-floor apartments bore a crest of an

unfamiliar house, something small and birdlike that had wings extended on either side of it. Dismissing it, Terian moved on to the staircase. *The way the Sovereign told it, my house is in greatest disgrace. Being in this building alone is certainly proof of that, but … perhaps there's even more to it.* He looked at the yawning darkness of the downward path. A single lamp sat extinguished in a sconce on the landing below, suggesting that whoever lived down there lacked the coin for oil.

Sighing, Terian walked down the stairs, listening to the supports below the stone tile cry protest at the weight of his armor. He kept a hand on the banister, almost afraid to relinquish it for fear he might be somehow stuck down in this place in a nightmare.

From the landing he could see the door to the basement dwelling. When his eyes fell on the crest mounted haphazardly on the door, he grimaced. It was slanted to one side by a few degrees, and achingly familiar.

It looked like a stylized eye with eight lightning bolts streaking out from it, four on top and four on the bottom. *So this is it,* he realized, bowing his head. *I'd long thought that if my father died, we'd be nearly out of Saekaj within the year, but this … to see it …*

His heart sunk in his chest, like a bladder of wine that had sprung a leak. He could feel his hopes deflating within, the loss of everything that he'd had pressing in on him now more than ever. *I threw it all away for … this. To avenge a father whom I hated in life. To assuage guilt over things I said to him that I didn't regret until he was dead.*

Terian held out his hand reluctantly, poised to deliver a knock to the stone door. Chips in the surface indicated that it had been knocked on more than a few times, and without regard for damage done to it in the process. He slapped a palm on it after a moment's pause, realizing quite simply—*I have nowhere else to go.*

The answer to the door came more quickly than he would have expected, as it swung open quickly to reveal a shadow in the grim, unlit darkness. "It's me," he said.

The shadow bade him forward and Terian entered the dwelling, eyes unable to discern much other than furniture in great blurry shapes. There was not a light lit anywhere in the flat, and his vision had not adapted to this utter lack of illumination, not yet. "I can't see a damned thing in here," he muttered.

He sensed rather than saw the shadow that answered the door, moving to one of the shapes of furniture. The figure walked with a slow indifference, almost a shuffle, like the body hidden in the dark had been put upon to the point of excess weariness. *So ... is that Mother ... or the other that Malpravus mentioned?*

The sound of flint striking in the darkness was followed by a spark of flame. It was a tiny glow, the wick of candle catching its end, but it shed enough light to see by. It glowed warmly, spreading its luminescence to the four corners of the small living space, and putting alight the face of the bearer in stark, orange colors.

Terian felt a gasp escape his throat before he could catch it; not that he could have kept this bottled up in any case, so great was the shock to his already wearied system. He blinked, then blinked again, trying to reconcile what his eyes were telling him with the truth that his heart had been told and believed, the one that had driven him down a harsh, broken path for this last year and more without relief or release.

"But you're dead," Terian whispered when the breath found him, and his eyes had convinced him that the face being lit by the candle was, in fact, what he had thought it was.

Amenon Lepos stood before him, his blue face paler than Terian could ever recall it seeing. His flesh hung ill on his skull, like it had been stretched over bone and then left to sag, inelastic. The candle was clutched in his hand, though, and there was unmistakable light in his eyes—he was alive, of this there was no doubt in Terian's mind.

7.

J'anda

Dearest J'anda, the letter began, *I write to inform you of ill tidings which I know will not please you. It is a burden I take upon myself in fear that word of the rumors may reach your ears in the distant lands to which you have consigned yourself by decision and fate. Though it has been too long since we were last able to renew our long acquaintance, I still trust no one other than myself to deliver this heavy blow to you, hoping that perhaps seeing it come from my quill will lessen the power of its impact.*

Less than two weeks ago, Vracken Coeltes was made the head of the Gathering of Coercers in Saekaj.

J'anda paused, the words of the last sentence like someone had taken a knife and begun carving his veins from within his very skin. His intake of breath grew sharp and hard, as though his lungs were trying to deprive him of his life. The words on the parchment blurred before his eyes, and the sharp, acrid taste flooded into his mouth.

Vracken Coeltes . . .

J'anda had not heard nor seen that name in almost a century and had hardly expected the reaction it produced. It was a staggering, sickening blow, as though someone had come along and smashed a priceless vase across the back of his head; it stung in the moment—and also later, as one came to realize that true value of all that had been lost.

"Vracken . . . Coeltes," he muttered, his breath still coming in fits, his throat tight as though he had swallowed a tough piece of meat and it had become lodged, intransigent, in his gullet.

He felt the tightness in his chest like a fist clutching inside his rib cage, and tried to ignore it, tried to push past it, to turn his still-blurry eyes back to the page at hand. *It is not the end of all things, this news. Coeltes was always a more capable liar than he was an enchanter, and head of the League is certainly a position of a politician. This is … expected, I suppose.*

Then why didn't I expect it?

It was as though the threads of a life he thought he had let loose of had thrust themselves back into his hand once more, unasked for. *Much like a slinking animal one wishes to be rid of which continues to follow. That is Vracken Coeltes, surely. I thought I was rid of him forever, and yet this letter follows me here … finds me here …*

He pulled the letter up once more, the parchment crackling as though there were bones in the paper that protested his treatment. His eyes focused once more, he continued to read.

I apologize for being the one to deliver this unkind news, but I could think of no other that I would entrust it to that could predict your reaction or soften the news to a merciful enough state to be conveyed. It is an ill turn I do you now, but I hope that it spares you a gloating one from another source, one who does not feel your wounding as acutely as I do.

With warmest regards and affectionately yours,
Zieran Lacielle

J'anda let the parchment fall from his fingers and looked for a place to sit. His bed remained in the shattered heap that Vaste had left it. He sighed and pulled the hard wood chair out from beneath his desk. He'd meant to get something softer at some point, but that point had simply never come. He lowered himself into the chair and blinked in surprise; there was indeed a pad upon it, prompting him to smile slightly. "Larana, you thoughtful lady."

J'anda sat heavily upon the padded chair, letting his back fall against its rest and his neck lean back limply, uncaring about the potential for cramps. It gave him a pinching feeling in the base of his neck, but he ignored it.

Vracken Coeltes in charge of Saekaj's Gathering of Coercers … this is …

A mournful quiet fell over him then as he tried to find a word sufficient to his purposes. Catastrophic seemed … overblown. Coeltes was competent, after all. Disastrous wasn't quite right either.

"This is a grave injustice," he finally decided, voicing the thought to his empty quarters.

And though he sat there thinking about it for some time thereafter, he came to absolutely no conclusion what to do about it.

8.

Terian

"I was dead," Amenon Lepos said, his eyes black pools reflected in the candlelight, "just as you always wished. But unfortunately for you, death was no more faithful in its charge to hold me than you were as a son sworn to obey me ... and here I am once more, as stuck with you in this place of shame as you are with me in your own disgrace."

"What sort of necromancy is this?" Terian asked, keeping himself from recoiling in horror only through greatest control.

"The extraordinary sort," Amenon said, holding still as the death he had purportedly left.

Terian felt ill, shot through with nausea compounded with disgust. *It is a great helping of revulsion that fills my belly. Once dead, supposedly permanently, the bastard did not even have the grace to stay that way.*

"I can see what crosses your mind at present," Amenon said, his voice hoarser than Terian remembered it.

"I doubt you have any notion of what flits through my mind."

"No?" Amenon asked. "Are you not ... disappointed?"

"That much is obvious," Terian said, keeping himself level only through virtue of his exhaustion. "That death would find you a morsel too unpleasant to keep should not surprise me—"

"What you ascribe to rejection," Amenon cut him off, "glosses over effort and planning. My corpse lay in state in the Halls of our honored dead for over an annum before the Sovereign saw fit to call for my revivification—"

"Not sure what he was thinking there."

"He was thinking that his Sovereignty ill-profited from my loss,"

53

Amenon said, harsh as ever. "He was thinking that my aid would help him in returning his armies to victory."

"Sounds like he misjudged that one rather badly, based on recent results—"

"Do not dare to speak that way in my house," Amenon hissed. The candle shook in his hand, the light dancing off the walls with the subtle motion. "Your disloyal tongue is of no aid to us in this, our hour of need."

Terian looked around the room, studying the carved-in shelves stacked high with trinkets from the old manor house; it was the accumulation of a life's worth of possessions crammed into a room half the size of his father's old office. From where he stood, Terian could see a door to a single bedroom and a small privy with a bucket in lieu of plumbing. "Your need appears to be rather great."

"And your aid is rather small," Amenon said. "Why even come here? You have made clear your desires in days past, your feelings about me and—"

"I tried to avenge you, you insufferable prick," Terian snapped, watching his father's face fall to skepticism. "That's right. I nearly killed Cyrus Davidon for you, in your name."

"The warrior in black," Amenon mused, voice no louder than a whisper. "He stabbed me in the back, did you know? While I was dueling that elven woman with the hair as golden as the sun's rays."

"He would have made a good dark knight," Terian said. "And you should never cross Vara in his presence. He's inordinately sensitive about her for some reason. Probably down to not getting laid, I would say—"

"Your crudity does you no credit," Amenon spat, and then his expression returned to nearly neutral, just a hint of twist in his pale lips. "So, you neatly cut off your own retreat by betraying one of your guildmates. I confess, I would not have thought it of you; I assumed you long ago had contorted yourself into eating out of the hand of your gentle and forgiving guildmaster, following his lead away from such unpleasant and boorish repartee toward insult and grievance."

"You thought I'd just talk it out with Cyrus Davidon?" Terian asked. "'Oh, hey, did you know you killed my father and took his sword?'" With that, he pulled the broad red blade and watched his father's eyes take on an aura of dark envy. "I feel certain that such a conversation would have ended in roughly the same state as the path I chose."

"I wouldn't have cared to speculate about whatever activities my former heir might care to participate in," Amenon said, "given that you and your guildmates handle things in ways unfathomable to me and mine. For all I know, you and your ilk settle your grievances with a daily *veredajh* that involves everyone in your guild in their nakedness—"

"We call them 'orgies' outside these caverns," Terian said, taking some small measure of delight in seeing his father blanch almost indiscernibly. "And that's not exactly how I would expect grievances to be settled, though it sounds better than the path of vengeance I chose."

"You disgust me still," Amenon spat, "and I can taste the lingering breath of rot in my mouth, so that should give you some idea of how low I find you and your base ways."

"It's good to be home," Terian said, smiling tightly, holding in the fury he felt building inside him.

"Amenon?" a small voice asked from the door to the bedroom. "I heard raised voices …"

"Go back to bed, Olia," Amenon said, not tearing his eyes off of Terian, "there is nothing of consequence, nothing that cannot wait until morning—"

"Terian," his mother said, "is it you?" He saw her only in shadow, but she looked thinner than he recalled, practically a crone, like a tree killed in ages past, thin, twisted limbs locked into unnatural positions.

As she came into the light of the candle, Terian felt a similar gasp drawn from him as when he saw his father. Her hair had gone from pale white as a summer moon to grey and coarse like old vek'tag hair—which was what her nightgown was made of. The wrinkles on her skin ill-suited a woman who was nearing only the century mark now, and when the light caught her purple eyes, they looked faded, almost blue, as though her sight was being leeched away. "Mother?" he asked.

"I can hear you," Olia Lepos breathed, though her eyes failed to fall on him. She came forth, hands raised to ward off anything she might run into, shuffling on slow feet, her back hunched with a weight he could not even see. "Where are you?"

"I'm here," Terian said quietly, stunned still, unable to move to her side. He watched her come at him instead, her blindness obvious now. "Mother ... what's happened to you?"

"Why should you care?" Amenon snapped. "Our problems are of no concern to you."

"Then you shouldn't have answered the door," Terian twisted to volley back at his father. "What's wrong with her?"

The resentment was etched on Amenon's sunken and colorless features. "She's ill," he said at last, as though he were parting with particularly valuable possession under great duress.

"No shit, that much must be obvious even to her eyes." Terian paused, but saw no trace of reaction on his mother's face. "What has happened?"

"It doesn't matter," Olia said, her frail hands reaching out to touch his armor as she shuffled the last steps to him. "All that matters is that you've come back to us now." Her hands shook as they slid up his armor to his face. He hurried to remove his spiked helm, and her hands rubbed across his dirty and bearded face. "You've changed."

"I've been away for a long while," he said. "Been at war for a long while."

"I heard vanished beyond the sight of this world," Amenon said. "Over that stone bridge in the east. I hadn't wondered if you might return at some ill-timed moment."

"Apparently I chose a well-timed moment to return," Terian said, "as the Sovereign has enlisted my aid in the war." He let the news slip lightly, still unsure quite how to feel about it.

"Oh, Terian," Olia said, "such excellent news!"

"This is ... unexpected," his father said stiffly.

"Try not to fall over yourself with enthusiasm at this turn of events," Terian said. "I wouldn't know quite what to do with myself if I pleased you for once."

"Well, I am pleased that you are no longer anathema to the Sovereign," Amenon managed, looking strangely discomfited all the while. "But I would not turn down a further explanation of your new role here."

"I'm working with Goliath," Terian said carefully, "But the Sovereign also asked me to tend to my house, which to my ears sounds like—"

There sounded a knock at the door that froze them all in their place. It came again, seconds later, and more insistent upon the second time.

"Who would dare at this hour?" Amenon asked.

Terian felt the heft of the red blade, still in his hand, pointed safely away from his mother. He gently brushed her hands off his face and turned toward the door, weapon at the ready. "Only one way to find out."

His father's eyes flashed anger. "Put that away, you fool. This is not some slum in the back deep where thieves come to call in the wee hours under false guise, else I'd have answered your knock with a dagger."

"I have no shortage of enemies," Terian said, loud enough that he suspected it could be heard on the other side of the door. "And I have no wish to leave myself open to death." He gave his father a once-over. "I mean, look what it's done to you."

With a noise of exasperation, his father sidled up to the door. "Who comes upon my door at this late hour? What reason do you have for disturbing our slumber?"

"I doubt there's any slumber going on," a feminine voice replied, "as I can hear you argument through the door."

Terian's eyes narrowed, darting back and forth as he tried to place the voice. "Is that ...?"

"Harken to the voice of your wife, Terian," said Kahlee Ehrest as Amenon swung the stone portal wide to reveal her there in dark cloak, her pure white hair layered over her shoulders, "for I have come to bring you home."

9.

Aisling

Aisling slipped out of Cyrus Davidon's quarters the next morning before even the first light had begun to break over the horizon. The sheen of perspiration that had dried on her flesh gave her a sticky feel, though that was hardly the worst of it. She could smell him on her skin, and though it made her slightly ill, she pushed that into the pit with all her other feelings, resolving to bury it as deep as everything else, if not deeper.

She walked down the corridor of the officers' quarters at a simple tiptoe, careful not to make noise enough to waken any of the other residents. She crept down the stairs in a slow spiral, all the way to the second floor, catching the hallway that ran the perimeter of the main building to the southeast tower. It was early yet, on the morning after what had clearly been a banner event. Silence reigned in the guildhall, soft snores audible to her ears, the sounds of an exhausted army at rest. She doubted that sleepy quiet extended to the foyer or the Great Hall, but resolved to keep clear of that as best she could. *The better to avoid that twit Verity.*

The stairs in the southeast tower were a smaller set, one that threaded inside the interior of the large circular stone structure. It rose only half as high as the main tower of Sanctuary, and her quarters were only up two landings, along with the doors of fifteen other members of the guild. There was a numbering system at place here, iron numerals mounted in the center of each door. She remembered hers by heart, pushing open the door to find the place much unchanged. She had not returned here the night before, nor in the days before that, as the siege had raged.

A simple bed and desk stood in the middle of the room, wooden furniture covered by dusty linens and little else. An armoire stood in the corner, a cloudy mirror on its outer door. She brushed past it to see her hair much longer than when she'd last looked. She opened the door and found her clothes much as she'd left them; only two spare sets and nothing else, for she had nothing else of value save coin, and she did not dare to carry that with her in much quantity. The majority was locked safely in a bank in Fertiss, at the heart of the dwarven lands.

"I don't suppose you've come with your diary already in hand," a voice came from behind her, prompting her to turn swiftly, a dagger already drawn.

Verity stood in the shadowed corner past the only window, nearly invisible in the dark. She wore a smile, and her hat was doffed, held in the hand opposite her staff. Her grey, straw-like hair fell across her shoulders in long coarse strands, reminding Aisling of a device a servant girl had used to clean her family's floors when she was a child.

"I don't suppose you thought to stay out of my quarters," Aisling replied in a growl, unsurprised but reacting the way she predicted Verity would want her to.

"Hem!" Verity said, a noise that came from her throat, deep and guttural. "Do you assume that you have any privacy at all? Because that would be a foolish thing to even consider. Shrawn owns you, part and parcel, body and soul, and allowing you even an inch of leash would be naught but an illusion."

That, too, is expected, Aisling thought. "Sometimes a good lie is better than the truth," she said, seasoning her reply with a moody resentment, barely expressed.

"There will be no space for lies between the two of us," Verity said. "You will tell me everything. I am to be your handler, the one who keeps your leash for Shrawn."

"An elf working for the dark elves?" Aisling asked. "A curious thing."

"Asking that question tells me that you are the curious thing in this room," Verity said darkly. "And my reasons are my own." She straightened. "What do you have to tell me this morning?"

"I bedded him last night," Aisling said casually. "Do you need me to go into details?"

"I will ask Lord Shrawn if he requires specifics," Verity said with a nasty grin that told Aisling the elf was not at all squeamish. "Perhaps, for now, though, you should plan to relive your encounters in exacting detail in your diaries."

"Yes, well," Aisling said, casually, "perhaps I'll run out today and get a journal, then."

"That won't be necessary," Verity said, sweeping a hand toward the plain wooden desk in Aisling's corner and a small leather-bound volume upon its pitted surface. "I've already taken care of this."

"Aren't you a helpful one," Aisling said, strolling over to the desk on catlike feet. She slipped from her leather shoes, kicking them into the corner nearest the door as she lingered over the book, opening the first page and finding blank parchment carefully bound within the book. She glanced up and saw that the inkwell had been refilled, a spare bottle sitting just beside it, a quill already in place for dipping. "You've set the table for me."

"Now eat up as though you didn't have your fill last night," Verity said, sweeping out to stand beside her. "I will be checking every day, without fail. Record everything you hear from both Cyrus Davidon and the officers around him. Include even seemingly insignificant details, and make certain you preface them in terms of your feelings about the entire matter."

Aisling raised an eyebrow. "My feelings?"

"A diary is not a straightforward recounting of events and gossip, fool," Verity said, as though she were speaking to the simplest mind in all of Arkaria. "It is a journal to one's self about thoughts and feelings. Many the spy has been caught writing missives bereft of any emotion, their intention plain to all but their own stupid selves. You are to take your time, to take pains to mask the purpose of this work."

"Are you simply going to tear the pages out once done?" Aisling asked coolly. "Because it occurs to me that a diary empty of all pages but the current one might look suspicious."

"I will copy your pages by hand onto other paper and take them to Lord Shrawn," Verity said, "so take care with your penmanship."

"I'm told I have a very lovely hand," Aisling said coolly.

"Well, keep it occupied with Cyrus Davidon," Verity said. "And take care to make everything legible. Remember, I'll be watching." She snapped her fingers, and it was as though a veil had fallen over her, the wall behind shimmering for only a moment before she was gone.

"Invisibility?" Aisling asked, trying to discern if Verity's presence was still in the room. She could have sworn she heard breathing …

"Indeed," Verity said from by the door, causing Aisling to whip around. *She moves with a quiet of her own; not bad for a wizard. Probably useful for a spy.*

"Isn't it an unpredictable spell?" Aisling asked, staring at where she thought the wizard might be. "Doesn't it tend to fade at inconvenient moments?"

"I have practiced with this spell for some thousands of years," Verity huffed. "I can remain invisible for thirty minutes at a stretch with ease. Lesser-practiced spellcasters may experience unpredictable results, but those of us who have put in the effort to learn control of their craft need not fear it. Now open the door and then look out, as though you heard something in the hall."

Aisling followed her instructions to the letter, opening the door, looking around the circular hallway that wended to her left and right, and then left the door ajar for a moment. She heard a soft footstep as Verity slipped from her quarters, gave it an extra few seconds and then closed the door once more.

That puts a wrinkle in things, Aisling thought, trying to keep from darting suspicious looks around her quarters. *She could still be in here, watching me. Well, I have a task before me in any case, might as well get it done now as later …*

She pulled out the chair from in front of her desk with a sharp scuff of the wood leg against stone floor, a short, earsplitting screech that made her cringe. She sat in the chair and scooted it back, taking greater care not to produce the noise this time. She placed her elbows on the hard wood edges of the desk and started to ponder her course.

The torches burned on her walls, the hearth lively and dancing. Its sweet smell mingled with the sharp scent of the ink, and she ignored the call of her belly in favor of at least completing something. *Verity will expect me to get right to work, thinking she's laid her intimidation upon me. Wouldn't want to disappoint her.*

Aisling picked up the first quill and dipped it into the inkwell, lifting it out and watching the excess drops drip slowly back into the well, like blood falling from a wound. The rich blackness of the liquid reminded her of the dark of Sovar on nights when the smoke of the evening's fires hung so thick in the air that it occluded the phosphorescence of the cave ceilings. She regarded it with a strange indifference, struggling to find the right note to begin on.

She rustled the pages of the diary to the first of them and considered well what she should say. It came to her in a moment, a simple disclaimer that she was voicing her tangled feelings on the matters of Luukessia and all she had seen there. She started with an encounter on the bridge, on the way to that dead and gravely silent land, putting in every last detail she could recall—and making up lies about everything she felt.

10.

Terian

"It's been a long time," Kahlee said, sweeping into the basement dwelling with her cloak trailing behind her as a bulwark against the cold. Terian watched her enter the room with measured surprise; while they had not parted on unfriendly terms, he had certainly not expected her to seek him out upon his return, and immediately at that.

"Ages," Terian said, glancing back to see his father's reaction. Amenon Lepos's face was pale but still, as though he were dead with his eyes propped open. He did not even seem to be breathing. "What brings you to us at this late hour?"

"I heard of my husband's triumphant return," Kahlee said, so straitlaced in her reply that Terian could not judge whether she was being serious or not. "Welcome news on such a dark day. As I said, I have come to bring you home."

"I can't honestly tell if you're being serious or not," Terian said, regarding her with undisguised curiosity. "You were never very good at it before, but either you've gotten considerably more proper in my absence, or you're here to make good sport of me at an inopportune time."

"Oh, is this an inopportune time?" Kahlee asked, still nearly expressionless, as she drifted toward Terian's mother. "It is so good to see you, Olia." She reached for the older woman's hand and gave it a kiss. "How are you feeling?"

"Ill but pleased," Olia said.

"Olia," Amenon said, his face showing the first signs of what almost looked like distress to Terian, "perhaps you should to bed."

63

"No, no," Olia said, her lips puckered. "I can't. Terian's returned."

"She is like this much of the time," Amenon said, stepping up to Olia's shoulder. "The healers can make no sense of it, not that they would know what to do with a natural ailment such as this."

"Terian," Kahlee said, once more, "I have come to bring you home."

"You keep saying that," Terian snapped impatiently, "as though I'm not already here."

"Your place is not here," Kahlee said softly. "It is with me, and you know it."

"For the sake of—" Terian cut himself off as the hot anger ran over. "You expect me to leave them like this?"

"What would you do?" Amenon asked with a thread of amusement. "Play nursemaid to us?"

Terian ground his teeth together bitterly. "I would—" He cut himself off, no further reply coming to him that seemed sensible or suitable to the occasion.

"Your house requires your attention," Kahlee said gently.

"I was gone too long," Amenon agreed, rather forlornly for him.

"I think you were expected to be gone somewhat longer," Terian said. "I don't even know what to say."

"A first," his father pronounced.

"You're an ass," Terian said, giving him a lashing look. "Look, I found something to say."

"Terian," Kahlee said, and her hand landed carefully upon his armor, avoiding the spikes. "We should go. You can return tomorrow if you wish."

"I suspect I'm going to be working tomorrow," Terian said tautly, "and rather a lot from here on out."

"Is that so?" Amenon asked.

"Look at the state of things," Terian said, shaking his head. "Our house is in wreckage upon the shoals of failure. In the next month, will we even be in Saekaj? Or will Mother have to deal with the crushing reality of having to drag her possessions back to Sovar?"

"Sovar?" Olia asked, head darting around in fear. "No. No, not Sovar. I haven't … don't want to go back." Her voice was a whisper, horrorstruck and thick with pain.

"I am a lieutenant," Amenon said stiffly, "in a league brigade.

Training new warriors for the Legion of Darkness. My students are not ready for battle yet, and thus there is little chance for glory in the immediate future."

"It's on me, then," Terian said, pushing his lips together as he finished speaking and casting his eyes downward. An intensity of heat burned within him, a desire to flagellate himself for his failures. *I've done everything all wrong; if I were still in Sanctuary, they'd have a place they could be safe. And if I'd stayed here and risen, they'd be in a manor house instead of this … whatever this place is. Instead, I've betrayed my allegiances in Sanctuary and shunned my responsibilities here. And for what?*

To stab Cyrus Davidon in the eye for my father's death? He glanced at Amenon, who was regarding him with a near-indifference. *What a waste that turned out to be.*

"We should go," Kahlee said quietly. The smell of some strange balm hung in Terian's nose, some cream on his mother's skin that smelled sharply of herb. "We should leave them be. You can come back."

"Yes," Terian said as his mother went to withdraw her hand from his gauntlet and pinched it against a joint. She flinched, and a small stream of blue blood welled up on her hand as she thrust it into her mouth without protest. "We should."

Without another word, Terian let his wife lead him from the basement dwelling. He took a final look back at his parents, his mother still standing there cradling her hand, while his father watched him go with a sunken face that could not contain a strange, forlorn strain of barest hope.

11.

J'anda

Six Months Later

J'anda returned from a weeklong hunt in the western end of the Human Confederation to find another letter waiting under his door. His back hurt from being ahorse for days on end, for sleeping on the ground at night, and he wasn't even sure he could cast an illusion that would dissipate the pain he felt from showing on his face. *I do not see how sitting in a Council meeting, discussing our bizarre findings regarding the Daring's disappearance, will do my back much good at this juncture.*

Stooping to pick up the letter was a difficulty in itself. *I remember with longing the days when I didn't feel these pains. When I could do something as simple as bend over without every joint from my knees to my shoulders protesting at the motion.* He snatched the parchment up in stiff fingers that protested as he coiled them around the yellowed envelope. *And you as well, fingers? You join the conspiracy against me? Be that way, then, ingrates, and after all I have done for you over the years …*

J'anda sighed and made his way over to the bed. It wasn't as comfortable as his old one, or so he thought. *Then again, I was young the last time I slept in the old one. Perhaps it is the same bed, but a far different me …*

He regarded the envelope carefully, flipping it over, expecting to see the same symbol-less seal in the wax. But it was not there, instead replaced by something far, far different.

The seal carried the symbol of an orb with a raven flying out of it to the right, with three wavy lines at the left side to represent the auras

66

FATED IN DARKNESS

of magic put forth by the orb. The raven was not obvious in the small wax indentation, either, but J'anda had certainly seen the symbol enough times to be well acquainted with it and its meaning.

It was nothing less than the symbol for the Gathering of Coercers, Saekaj branch.

He stared at it only a moment before tearing it open. The envelope and the seal were matters of greatest concern for him; it marked it as different than the last one, lacking the careful effort at hiding its origin on the outside.

And that was concerning.

He slid the paper contained within the envelope up, unfolding it and placing it before his eyes. It took only a moment for him to be able to focus on the scrawl on the page. Not nearly as elegant as Zieran's lettering, this was a hashmark of scrawl, a personal letter from someone unused to writing their own correspondence. As his eyes fell down the page, taking in more of the message, he realized that this was the sort of thing that had to be done personally, that the writer wanted to savor each word they'd written on the yellow paper.

J'anda,

I write to inform you that your last missive to Zieran Lacielle was intercepted in the course of delivery by the Saekaj Militia. Normally, I would not bother to take time out of my busy schedule to inform a traitor that his correspondence had been ferreted out before it reached its destination, but as this affords me the opportunity to close out our relationship by speaking a few unsaid things, I hope you'll forgive me the indulgence.

First of all, Zieran is resting comfortably in her accommodations in the Depths. As she is my former aide, I did of course plead with the Sovereign for some leniency on her behalf. I think you can imagine I didn't plead very hard. In fact, I might have actually gotten her sentence increased, but who knows? Certainly not me; I wouldn't care to speculate on how much influence I have over the Sovereign's judgment, after all. I did see that the matter went to him rather than a simple court. After all, they might have misinterpreted your letter as mere correspondence between former friends rather than as the very plain act of sedition that it was.

I wanted to let you know this so that you can rest assured that in spite of the fact that I won over you, gaining the role of Guildmaster here at the Gathering, I haven't forgotten you, my old rival. I could never forget you. Surpass you, obviously. Push you into exile ... yes, that was a great moment, a coup, really. But forget you? Forget your smiling, insolent face every time you proved yourself my better in the action of conjuring? No, I couldn't forget that.

Not ever. Not even after ... well, I think we both know what I did. How I beat you. I certainly know I remember; on days when I've experienced more stress than I feel is my due, I think back on the memory of your face that day in the Sovereign's throne room ... and smile. Oh, how I smile.

I can only hope this letter reaches you in the greatest of spirits, and renders them in the way that fat melts under flame. I derive much joy from imagining you clenching this parchment in between your fingers, crushing it while wishing it were me. But it is not me. For I am far beyond your reach, nestled comfortably here while you languish out there. Does it still sting, knowing that you can never come home? I imagine it does. I imagine it quite a lot, actually, and it always gives me a warm feeling near my heart.

Of course, if you'd care to prove yourself something other than a coward, you could always return and argue for leniency for Zieran. I think we both know that you won't, because I would be right there at the Sovereign's side if you did, enjoying every moment of your sweet comeuppance and the resultant downfall. That, too, is a dream I hold close to my heart, though I doubt it will ever come true anywhere but my fondest fantasies. Still, if you feel up to it ... stop by any time.

> *Wishing you nothing but the very worst,*
> *Vracken Coeltes*
> *Guildmaster*
> *Gathering of Coercers, Saekaj*

As his eyes fell over the last word, a taste like ash balanced on his tongue, J'anda crumpled the parchment in his shaking hand. *He knew just what to say ...* He shook in seething rage, keeping the parchment in his palm, unable to even muster the strength to throw it as he would have in his youth. It merely danced there, in his grasp, in the light grip of his fingers, as eventually, the tears of purest fury seeped down his cheeks.

12.

Terian

"Where the hell are we?" Terian asked as his sword sliced up through the unprotected jawline of a human soldier, knocking the man's helm asunder as he choked and fell to his knees, blood rushing out between grasping fingers.

"It's called Sarienlass," Grinnd Urnocht told him, bringing down a vicious sword on another human soldier. Grinnd sported two blades, relatively short but shaped strangely, their curving outlines formed something akin to a meat cleaver. *Grinnd would be the largest butcher in Saekaj. Actually, he'd be the largest at almost anything.* Urnocht was, in fact, wide as Vaste, and taller even than Cyrus Davidon. As the big dark elven warrior's sword fell again and again, human soldiers retreated frantically before the big man's swings. "It's a key gateway into the Human Confederation's Northlands."

"Trust Grinnd to know the name of every small town he passes through," Dahveed Thalless, their resident healer, said with a smile on his face. His white cloak's cowl was up over his head, and the northern sun shone down on him to find his sleeves brought together as he stood with a look of peace and amusement on his face, about twenty paces back from where Grinnd and Terian fought their way through the ragged human lines.

A weak sword blow spent its energy on the shoulder spikes of Terian's pauldrons, surprising him and causing him to spin his head to look at the human there, watching him with stunned eyes. Terian drove his sword through the man's neck without a thought, though he cringed inwardly as he struck the head from the man's shoulders.

Better you go like this, he thought, than fall into the hands of what follows behind us.

"You're supposed to leave the corpses as intact as possible," Amenon Lepos snapped at his son from somewhere to Terian's right. "You know this, yet still I see you constantly cleaving heads from necks."

"Old habit," Terian lied, "and you're not the boss of me, father." *He still acts as though he is, though. Doubt he'll ever stop.* He glanced over his shoulder at Amenon and saw his father tear his gaze away from Terian. *Caught him looking at the sword again. Big surprise there; of course he wants it back.*

The uneven ground sloped ahead of them, inevitably upward. They stood on a hard hill, ground above them reaching its gentle, rounded peak no more than a hundred feet up. *Unfortunately,* Terian thought, *there's a decent portion of an army between us and there.* "Where's this Sarien lass that you're talking about, Grinnd?" Terian asked, trying to break the tension. "All I see are human men in old armor!"

"Your wit never ceases to amuse you, does it?" Amenon called at him. Terian spared a glance to see his father bury his sword, a fine steel blade of good craftsmanship, in the chest of a man wearing leather armor, possibly the sturdiest set they had seen all day. Amenon's blade slipped easily through it, ripping into the chest of the human and drawing a bloody breath out of his lips as he stumbled. Amenon followed it up by pulling his blade free of the wound he'd just inflicted and running it across the man's neck to finish the job.

"If I entertain no one else but myself, at least I'm entertained," Terian said. "And really, what else matters?"

"Winning the battle?" Grinnd asked.

"That looks to happen anyway," Terian said, driving his weapon into a clash against another human, this one a blond fellow with his helm already off. *Not that their helms provide much in the way of protection; these Northmen are being cut apart like cowhide before a quartal blade.*

"Don't get overconfident," Amenon said.

"I'm just the right amount of confident," Terian said, knocking the blond man's blade aside easily and then severing his head. "Oops. Again."

"Damn you!" Amenon breathed.

"Oh, it's one less corpse," Terian said, throwing himself into the next knot of three human soldiers, crossing blades with each of them in turn as they tried to overwhelm him and failed. "We're hardly lacking here, are we?"

"You have your orders," Amenon said.

"Which do not come from you," Terian said, "and which you can go back to minding on your own. I don't report to you." He saw Amenon's hard gaze, the flare of anger in the man's already cloudy eyes. *They're always cloudy these days; he hasn't looked right since I got back. I suppose being dead for a good long while will leave its mark. Like his face—*

A flash of hot fire burned past Terian's nose and exploded into a cluster of five humans who were charging down the hill at him, feet away from where he was tangling with the three—he impaled one of the men on his sword—two men in his place on the hill. "Thanks, Bowe!" he called out, knowing that the gratitude would find its mark on the druid somewhere down below.

He caught only a glimpse of long-haired Bowe Sturrt before turning to deliver a spinning slash that cut one of his remaining foes in half. Bowe was levitating in a meditation position, legs crossed in front of him, about thirty paces back. Bowe looked at peace, eyes forward and unfocused, as though there weren't a battle going on all around them.

"And now you," Terian muttered as he faced the sole survivor of his assault. This one was barely more than a boy, and Terian hesitated as he stood there, sword in hand, while the lad regarded him with frightened eyes and a dull sword that shook so hard that the tip swung several inches back and forth.

Terian hesitated, staring the boy down, pondering his course. *This is one is but a child—*

An arrow planted itself right in the lad's forehead, knocking him over on his back. The boy dropped the sword and it clattered on a rock in the hillside. Terian looked down and saw dead eyes staring back at him, a shaft of wood planted just above the boy's right eye. Terian kept the curse he wanted to mutter locked up deep within, replacing it with a name that was almost as bad.

Orion.

"They're thinning," Orion said, his helmeted head appearing at Terian's shoulder. The helm was almost like a curved bucket, spheroid at the end atop his head and perfectly flat like a cylinder along the length of the ranger's face. Two reasonable holes were slitted for the eyes, and Terian could see no hint of the scarring he knew was hidden beneath the metal mask, just eyes watching, hawklike, up the hill, for the motion of the army opposing them.

"We've been killing them for hours," Terian said. "Sooner or later this garrison would have to run out of men."

"I expected it sooner," Orion said, bow in his hand and an arrow ready to fly with but a draw. "These soldiers are unblooded wretches, either too young or too old to be doing this."

"I'd imagine the bulk of the human armies are defending Reikonos," Terian said, "what with us throwing considerable force against it at present."

He couldn't see Orion's face, but he heard the smile in the human's voice. "They'll fall soon enough."

"I can see you're still holding a grudge against them for that exile business," Terian said, turning aside the sword attack of a man who limped down the hill at him. He swiped idly and severed the man's head from his shoulders with no more difficulty than if he'd been slaughtering some animal in a pen. He ignored the pang of discontent in his belly, just as he had done for months.

"I'll be perfectly happy to forgive them when that city is ashes and all their lands are under the boot," Orion said, and let fly another arrow.

"I doubt there will be much left to forgive by then."

"That's the point," Orion said. A nearby tree just below the crest of the hill rustled in the breeze.

Terian cast his eyes to the hilltop and counted only a half dozen more men. Three were making their way down, slowly, lamely, their legs unable to bear much weight. Three were running at full speed up, looking none the worse for the wear. "And so we reach the end of the noble battle of ..." He frowned, searching. "What was it called again, Grinnd?"

"Sarienlass," Grinnd said, easing up next to him with his dual swords. One of the last assailants came at him with a battle cry, and Grinnd cleaved him in two with a hard strike. When he caught Terian's eye, he looked vaguely ashamed. *So, he feels the same as I do about preserving the bodies of our enemies for ... that.* "The village itself is over the hill."

"I'd imagine they're not going to be getting much sleep tonight," Terian said as Orion let fly an arrow that landed in the back of one of the runners. It sent the man sprawling to the ground, and the ranger followed it up by bringing down one of the others. Terian watched the third crest the hill before Orion could get a shot off, and silently bid the man good luck. He'd certainly need it.

"If they're smart, they've already left," Dahveed said, easing up the hill along with them. The top was only twenty feet distant now.

Amenon was engaged with the last of the surviving human soldiers. Terian stood back, seeing the wild, aged eyes of the man his father fought. *Like a cornered rat, biting at everything he can.* Amenon parried a strike with surprising grace, his eyes narrowed at the maneuver. He held out a hand, his lips frozen and unmoving, and a dark light flashed around the human, who cried out in pain.

The man dropped dead, as sure as if Terian had struck his head from his shoulders. The body fell limply and rolled ten feet down the hill. Open eyes stared off into the sky beyond, his limbs askew. The human's skin was like melted wax, rippled with sudden age, as though he had melted some in the attack. *Unnatural.* Terian shuddered and turned his eyes swiftly away. "Feel better?" Terian asked, regarding his father with a careful look.

"Indeed I do," Amenon said, advancing up the hill with a little more energy in his gait. *I suppose it's better he does it this way. After all, the soul drain spell is as much a part of our arsenal as the force blast is to a paladin.*

Still … death has changed him, Terian thought. *Or perhaps it's just been his descent, and having his fortunes reversed by the no-good, misbegotten son he'd written off years ago.*

They reached the crest of the hill and Terian slowed to a halt, his legs protesting the rough treatment at the hands of the hard slope, his arms straining at all the fighting. He looked right and saw Amenon looking jealously at his sword once more, this time not bothering to hide it. "How does it feel?" his father asked.

"A lot better than my old axe," Terian said tightly. The mythical quality of the blade gave him just a hair's breadth of advantage in speed and considerable help in the realm of durability; he'd broken lesser swords against its blade. "Still, sword play is not quite my forte; if I can find a good axe with similar qualities," *or perhaps convince the Sovereign to gift me one,* he did not say, "I'll be glad to give it back to you."

"It is a symbol of our house," Amenon said stiffly, "and if not for your retrieval of it, we would not have it at present. You should keep it until such time as you find better."

"Thanks," Terian said. *Well, it's progress. Before, he wouldn't have even mentioned it, just continued to stare.*

The whinny of a horse behind Terian stirred him loose of his daydream, and he turned his head to see Malpravus threading his way up the hill, managing his path so as to keep the grade from affecting his mount. "Here comes the General," Dahveed said, a glint of amusement in his eyes. The healer stood at Terian's shoulder. "I suppose this is no great change for you from Sanctuary." The gleam in his eyes told Terian that the man was being ironic, but he had no time to answer it before Malpravus was upon them.

"Excellent work," Malpravus said as he reached the summit. Terian looked out with him across hills and valleys, green lands stretching out to mountains in the far distance. *Dwarf country.* He looked back and saw Lake Magnus gleaming in the late light of day, and in front of them, a few men rushed down the hill to a village on the northern slope. Bells were ringing, and already horses and carts were moving out of the town gates onto the road heading north. "Look at them rush away, as though they could escape their fates."

"I imagine they're of a mind to at least try," Terian said stiffly as Malpravus pulled a bag off his belt as big as Grinnd's massive head. Terian watched as the necromancer breathed soft, barely spoken words into the twilight air and red energy glowed from his fingers.

The crackle of the magics rippled over the top of the hill in lines, waving like the illusions of a desert dune in the midday heat. They threaded down the hill in swirls, following unnatural paths, racing like water caught in a drain until each line of power reached its terminus in a felled body. Terian had seen the process up close, the red light infusing a corpse as it was absorbed through the armor into the skin. He could see the dead eyes come aglow for a moment, red as a Sovarian harlot's craving gaze, as the bodies sat up in one swift, sudden motion. He wondered if his father had been jarred back to life as abruptly …

"Our army grows," Malpravus said, the crimson aura around his fingers fading as the spell energy subsided. The necromancer's delight was evident in his grin. "Our assault into the tender underbelly of the Confederation has been most unexpected."

"How could it have been expected?" Terian asked, keeping his bitterness well in check. "We've been attacking their capital with everything they thought we have left, drawing all their defense to that place." *This is like being in a fight with a one-armed man. Or carrying a mystical sword against a farmer,* he thought, looking down at the red glow of his father's blade. It looked awfully like the spell that Malpravus had just cast, but less bright.

"And that is why we shall win," Malpravus said, still grinning. "Four days' march and we will attack the keep of Livlosdald. It is the last major fortress before the north turns flat and easier to navigate. Four days, and we shall have free ranging of these reaches of the human lands. From there, we shall eddy about in their breadbasket, sop up their harvests and send them south to Saekaj, then move to join our other armies in the pitched battles of the Riverlands." He took a breath in through his nose, savoring it. "How long do you suppose it will be before the humans' will breaks?"

"Not soon enough," Orion said with undisguised glee. Terian resisted the urge to cleave into the ranger's helm, but only barely.

"You have done well," Malpravus said, looking down upon the retreating humans in the village below. "All of you." His eyes found Terian's, though, and he nodded a special sort of approbation. "But especially you, Lord Lepos."

Terian nodded to Malpravus in acknowledgement of the praise even as he caught a nearly imperceptible look from his father. *Father is not pleased; as though that should surprise me. Following here at my command must be torturous to his ego.*

"I suspect you'll move House Lepos into the last manor for this victory," Malpravus went on. Terian kept his eyes on his father and watched the flash of resentment spark there. *He still hasn't forgiven me for the betrayal of going to my current accommodation with Kahlee.*

"We have a long march still ahead of us before we finish," Terian said, standing upon the heights of the hill, hoping he could merely stand here and delay. *Just a few more minutes. Give those people time to run, a chance to escape ...*

"We move," Malpravus said, and the first of his revived army stood around him now, bringing with them the unmistakable smell of death and rot, even though the corpses were fresh. Terian thrust his gauntlet next to his nose, the oiled metal covering only a portion of the stench. "After all," the Goliath Guildmaster said, still grinning, "it would be a shame to allow all those fresh bodies down there to escape our grasp when our army still has so much more room to grow ..." He kicked his horse into motion in the descent, the gleeful look still frozen on his face.

"Move out," Terian said, swallowing his emotions as he raised his sword, urging them down the hill. He gave one glance back to see Goliath's forces behind them some ways, at the base of the hill, with the rest of the train of the army. He saw a brigade of trolls that had yet to see combat, their green skin and enormous frames a standout even in the growing dusk. The rest of the dark elven army following them was still waiting, at a distance, letting Terian and his vanguard march with the dead.

He took another look toward the valleys and forests ahead, and mentally calculated. *A month, perhaps two. That's all we have before it's over. Before we crush the Confederation's lines of supply and doom them to starvation.* He watched Grinnd start down the hill, watched his father go as well, hurrying on to destroy the village of Sarienlass below, and felt a rare dash of horror well up in him.

The Confederation will fall.

Millions will die.

He placed another boot before him, matching the step of his fellow soldiers, catching a sidelong glance from Dahveed, who gave him a knowing look, all humor gone from the healer's face. *He knows. He doesn't say anything, but he knows.*

That this plan—the destruction of the Confederation, the slaughter of all these people ... all of this ... is almost entirely my fault.

13.

J'anda

J'anda found Curatio in Sanctuary's Halls of Healing, leather-bound journals spread out before him on a desk that was piled high with spare parchment. There were candles burning on half a dozen surfaces, and night had closed in around them. The healer had a furrow in his brow deep enough to plant with seed, and a hand propping his face up on the desk as he read by the light the flickering wicks provided.

"Most of us simply use torches in sconces," J'anda said, standing in the doorway tentatively, as though he expected the calm old healer to react violently to his presence. "But you, you do things differently."

Curatio looked up at him and smiled weakly, his platinum hair practically gleaming in the candlelight. "I am rather older than you; my eyes are weaker and require more light."

"Somehow I doubt that is true," J'anda said, taking Curatio's greeting as invitation to step further into the room. A slightly greasy scent of melting wax lingered in the air.

"Do you come to summon me to Council?" Curatio asked. "For I already know that we are meeting in half an hour, and am simply trying to draw some of my search to a close beforehand."

"No. I wanted to talk to someone about regrets," J'anda said simply.

"There is certainly no shortage of members of Sanctuary," Curatio said, tiredness sketching dark circles under his eyes that J'anda could not recall seeing before, "surely you can find no shortage of regrets among our number."

"You know as well as I do that most of the members of Sanctuary are but children compared to even my years," J'anda said. "I suppose we must all seem like flies compared to your span of time."

"Keeping in mind I have married some of those 'flies,' as you put it," Curatio said with a weak smile, "and not that long ago. People are people, J'anda. One does not march through even a life as short as twenty years without accumulating at least a few regrets. And I daresay there are a few of our younger members, those who have already experienced the general wear of war, who could enumerate a few regrets that might make even an old one such as myself blanch from the telling."

"I have a great regret," J'anda said, moving to look out the window just beyond Curatio's desk. It was open a crack, and the cool night air seeped in. J'anda felt it on his face like he had dipped his chin in a basin of water from the mountains.

"I presume you wish to tell me about it," Curatio said, patient as always.

"Not really," J'anda said, looking out the window toward the great curtain wall that surrounded Sanctuary. The cracks and holes that had been gaping in its sides when he had returned from Luukessia only six months past were gone now, replaced with mortar and stone so expertly that he could not even tell where the rents in their line of protection had been. Great watch fires burned atop the wall, and men and women moved back and forth atop it, pacing the lines of their patrols. *Always on guard for the dangers that lurk in the night.* "But I want your advice on what to do about it."

"A curious request," Curatio said, "to ask my advice regarding a problem you will not describe to me. Rather like asking me to strike blindly in a direction of your choosing in hopes I will smite some unseen foe for you."

"I see the foe clear enough for both of us," J'anda said, staring out the window, the night breeze rustling his grey hair, "I merely need to know if this is a regret worth spending the waning time I have left to me chasing."

"What can you tell me, then?" Curatio asked, crisp in the quiet night. "To aid me in helping you to this decision."

"When I was young," J'anda said, staring at the movement outside as his eyes followed the natural paths of the patrols, "I was a loyal man of the Sovereignty. Of the Sovereign." He felt a tinge of shame as he said it. "I went to war for what I thought was good cause, and I fought well enough to help kill many of the enemy."

"To regret one's service in war is not surprising, especially if that service was given over to a tyrant such as Yartraak," Curatio said, and J'anda found himself jerking his head around to look at the healer. "Yes, I know who the Sovereign is."

"Few do, that are not dark elves," J'anda said with a whisper. "Even fewer would dare to speak his name aloud. A hundred years ago, I fled his service. I have not yet found the courage in myself to part with his name."

"What did he do to you?" Curatio asked. "To call into question your loyalties in such a way that you felt cause to flee all you believed in and knew?"

"Something terrible," J'anda whispered. "But he was not alone in this."

"Terrible deeds are seldom without accomplice," Curatio said. "The worst of them practically beg for it, as though they cannot bear to be done alone and quietly."

"He took everything from me," J'anda said. "In that moment, he took my belief, my conviction, my pride and my work … and he tore them all away, crumpling them the way one dispenses with the paper covering a gift. He did it all with the smug assurance that he was doing what was best for me." J'anda felt his impassive mien break into a scowl, the hatred flowing out. "And now, the architect of my humiliation taunts me. He has convinced the Sovereign to imprison a friend of mine for receiving a letter from me. One of the few friends I have left outside of Sanctuary."

"Is this truly about regrets?" Curatio asked. "Because regrets are things of the past, immutable. This sounds more like current events."

"My nemesis," J'anda said, caressing the word as it flowed off his tongue, "invites me to face up to my 'crimes.' To come back to Saekaj and plead for mercy for my friend, thinking it will be my end."

"And would it be your end?" Curatio asked.

J'anda felt the pinch of pride. "I can almost see a way where I could turn toward his, instead."

"Ahhh," Curatio said. "So now we come to it. Revenge."

"I have foresworn revenge," J'anda said, turning back to the healer, "on so many occasions as to defying the counting of them. I made my life here, and I have been content with it. What passed before was in the past. But this …" His face tightened, his hatred momentarily given expression, "I do not think I can let this pass any longer."

"You are in a somewhat unique position as compared to me," Curatio said, his face a thin mask; something waited beneath it, but J'anda could not quite determine what it was. "I have nothing but time." He stretched a hand over to idly flip a page of the nearest journal and scanned the flowing words written therein as he considered what to say next. "Yet still, I hasten to resolve events for fear that the touch of unanticipated death could be at my back at any moment. A fear I suspect you are becoming more intimately acquainted with by the day."

"It is always on my mind now," J'anda said. "I do not know how long I have—"

"No man does, truly," Curatio said. "Nor woman, either."

"But I know the limits to my days are shorter than they were a year ago," J'anda said, "and by considerable margin. I suspect I could live another five years at most; and probably much less."

"It should not change how you live your life," Curatio said quietly, "and yet I fear it must. Do you want revenge?"

"I want to help my friend," J'anda said. "I want …" He shook his head. "I don't know. Perhaps I do want the satisfaction, but I have been too much of a coward to risk my life … until now, when there is little life left to risk."

"A terrible conundrum," Curatio agreed, "and a choice I would not want to face. Still, and all—"

A knock interrupted them, and J'anda's eyes fell to the door, where Thad, a warrior in armor of red, stood, looking embarrassed at interrupting them. "Sorry, gentlemen," he said in his low, guttural accent, "but your meeting is about to begin."

"Thank you, Thad," Curatio said, allowing the briefest smile. It faded as soon as the warrior disappeared out of the door, and the healer suddenly looked more tired than ever.

"You look like you are reaching your end," J'anda said.

"What?" Curatio asked, looking up, eyes weary. "I don't sleep much these days."

"Because of Vidara?" J'anda asked carefully, waiting to see what response he might get.

"Because of many things," Curatio said, his lips thinly pursed. "Because of the guild, the weight it places upon my head. Because of this search—" His face pinched with pain, and he thrust a hand forward, knocking the nearest volume off his desk with barely concealed anger. "This fruitless, pointless search."

"Curatio—" J'anda said, surprised at the level of vehemence the usually calm healer had put forth.

"She is dead, did you know?" Curatio asked, staring sullenly off into the distance, the candles casting a gold aura on the walls of his chamber. "Vidara, I mean. The Goddess of Life, in death's embrace." His mouth twisted down in disgust and fury.

"Are you certain?" J'anda asked. "You haven't said anything in Council—"

"No, I am far from certain," Curatio said, maintaining his frown and adding a strain of petulance to his reply. *How peculiar*, J'anda thought, *to see him thus*. "If I were certain, I would not waste my time doing this, I would be devoting it entirely toward finding the guilty party and going at them with all I have." He reached down and grasped at a mace next to his desk, brandishing it as he stood. "But I have no answers in this. All I have is pressure and fury, and nowhere to direct them." He looked up at J'anda, with his lips still an uneven line. "You wish my advice? Get your revenge, while you can. Settle your affairs, especially as pertains to such unrepentant shits such as Yartraak and his various minions. If you can make a hole in their bellies and want to, do so, and I would gladly add my hand in aid, should you need it." With a flick of a button, two-inch spikes burst forth from the ball of the mace. "For life is too short, even in my existence, to continue letting those dedicated to its destruction to draw precious air while they extinguish it everywhere they find it growing."

14.

Terian

The keep ahead was called Livlosdald, but no matter how many times Terian tried to pronounce the human word, he couldn't quite seem to say it the way Malpravus did. "Live-los-dolled?" he asked.

"Live-los-dalld," Malpravus said, gently correcting him. They were both on horseback, somewhere in the middle of the growing army. The latest counts had put it at fifty thousand strong, many of them recently dead humans who had been bent to Malpravus's will. Terian tried not to think about that as the horse's gait dipped him left and right with each step. It was enough to make him nauseous without the aid of the motion. "It is the gate to the Northlands, the single most important keep from here onward."

"But no pressure," Terian said, surveying the troops before them with a serious air. They had the smell of the dead, the rancid scent of rotting flesh and purged bowel. Many of them had come from the graveyards of the towns that they had passed in addition to the fields of slaughter they'd left in the cities and towns along the way. The rest had been dark elven dead recently repatriated from the Reikonos front. "I've looked at the diagrams our scouts have provided of Livlosdald keep; it shouldn't be difficult to break."

"I don't expect it will be," Malpravus said, eyes narrowed, "but our presence in these places has surely been communicated to Pretnam Urides in Reikonos by now. I expect reinforcements, though I doubt they will arrive in time."

"He doesn't have much to give," Terian said. "He could pull them from Reikonos, leaving their capital open to our continued assaults, or he could try to marshal the men of the north—"

"Many of whom are already at arms around Reikonos," Malpravus said thinly, "or now part of our army." He smiled.

He doesn't even care what he's doing. Terian withheld a shudder and kept his tongue from saying what he might have otherwise. *I am among my enemies. I have no options left but to keep my thoughts to myself, lest my parents and Kahlee bear the brunt of my opinions.*

"You should be smiling," Malpravus said with a grin. "Our successes in this campaign and the one taking place in the Riverlands right now are all down to your urging."

"It doesn't take much to win with a vastly superior force at your disposal," Terian said, looking off to the woods at his left. "I think I was more in my element before, when we were outmatched." *Of course, I wasn't in control then. General Grennick still had strategic command of the armies then—before he lost his head.*

"I can read your thoughts," Malpravus said smoothly. "You fear the newfound position you are in. You fear you will come to the same end Grennick did for his failure."

"Some failure will happen," Terian said, trying to find a thought to soothe him, "that's a definite. We just don't know the when and the how of it, but it will happen. We have so many enemies that it would not surprise me if one of them managed to score a victory against us even in our strengthened state." He shook his head. "No, I've laid all the groundwork I could with the Sovereign on that. I just hope that after Grennick's miserable failures, he'll find room in his heart for one or two from me."

"I suspect after some of your initiatives begin to bear fruit," Malpravus said, skeletal hands on the reins of his horse, "there will be currency aplenty for trade in failures, should one come. And we have certainly begun to build—"

A cry from ahead drew the attention of both of them, causing Terian to snap his head around immediately. *What's this?* An officer appeared a moment later, one of the living ones, tromping back to where Terian and Malpravus rode two ranks back from the front of the marching column. "Report, Lieutenant," Malpravus said.

"Holes on the sides of the road," the lieutenant said, his eyes low, as though the topography were somehow his fault. "Look to have been dug." He hesitated. "Like traps."

"They know we're coming," Terian mused, adjusting his helm with a clank of his gauntlet against the metal next to his ear.

"It will not help them," Malpravus said. "Go on, Lieutenant. Narrow the columns. Keep us on the road."

"Aye, sir," the lieutenant said, bowing his head and retreating, probably grateful to still have said head.

"We haven't heard from our scouts in a while," Terian said, pondering it. "We're ... what? Three miles out?"

"Something of the sort," Malpravus said, his lips a narrow line.

"I think we should put the trolls up front," Terian said.

"Agreed," Malpravus said, nodding. "I will also have Goliath's ranks moved up in the line, remove some of the cannon fodder so that we can more aggressively respond to any army that happens to be there." He smiled, and it was an eerie sight. "Of course, when they see their own dead start to rise against them, it will probably do the trick."

Terian inclined his head slightly in acknowledgment as he gave the order to have the troll brigades brought to the fore. He barked and heard his command carried off to the waiting ears of the officers. Trollish grunts of acknowledgment reached his ears from their positions in the back, their enthusiasm obvious. *We've kept them out of the fight long enough to give them an appetite for it, I think.*

"General Lepos," a voice came from his side, and Terian turned to see a dark elf clad in the green of a ranger slip out of the woods to his right. He almost pulled his horse toward the woman, but stopped himself at the last second.

"What is it?" he asked as the ranger approached, her navy skin a clash against the forest-green cloak she wore to conceal herself when scouting.

"There's an army ahead," the scout reported.

"As we suspected," Malpravus said, sniffing. "Do you know who this army is?"

She nodded her head, but the eyes would not rise. "Anyone would, sir. It's the Army of Sanctuary."

Terian felt the ice water chill run over him, and he suppressed the thin smile that he reckoned would have come otherwise. "Well," he said, probably just a hair too fast, "I hope we've enough of that failure currency built up ..."

15.

J'anda

When he appeared out of the portal north of Saekaj Sovar, J'anda knew immediately he was being watched. He handed over the promised gold to the wizard he'd hired in Fertiss to take him here, and watched the woman disappear in a flash seconds later, obviously nervous to be even this close to dark elven territory. He could not blame her; he did not exactly enjoy being here himself.

Courage, he said to himself. *If I go to my death now, it comes but a little sooner than it might otherwise have.* He sat atop a horse he had purchased just for this endeavor, not wishing to consign one of Sanctuary's mounts to the Sovereign's wrath but also wary about walking miles and miles in his current state.

He urged the animal forward, ignoring the feeling of eyes upon him. He knew they would make their presence known eventually, that they would challenge him. It was not as though this were human territory any longer; he was surprised the portal was not surrounded by countless soldiers with spears, waiting to drive them into the heart of a traitor such as he before he could say a word in his defense.

That would probably be too good for me, though, he decided, and settled himself in for a long, slow ride. The horse was not good for much, but it did keep him off his feet, so there was that. The pace was glacially slow, not even a canter, and the sun burned overhead as it sunk lower in the sky.

I wonder if they'll come at me at nightfall? The thought concerned him little. He was one man, after all. He could have been mistaken for a trader, though it was more likely that in time of war, he'd be thought a spy and have to prove otherwise in order to keep his head. Either way, he knew without doubt that dark elven rangers followed his steps even now, as he passed under the trees strewn with rotted cave cress flowers that denoted the official beginning of the territory of the Sovereign of Saekaj Sovar.

The boughs of the trees looked like shadowed bones over him as the sun sank below the horizon. He sighed, listening to the still quiet of the woods. The chirrup of crickets was not-so-strangely absent to his left and right, but audible farther out. He considered calling out to his watchers and simply ending the charade, but like a good enchanter, he allowed them their illusions for a while longer.

The smell of the night in the northern Waking Woods was a strong aroma, night blooming flowers filling the air with their dusky bitterness. J'anda had not remembered this smell, but the memories of it came back him now, stronger than the images in his head of those days. He recalled walking these paths to war, smelling those night blooming y'algras flowers as their heavy scent floated all around, an army marching behind him.

It was a scent he remembered from the day he left, as well.

"Halt," the quiet voice of the ranger to his left whispered out at him. He tugged on the reins, which stopped his horse, probably more gently than the ranger anticipated, given his brow's quirk of surprise. Other green-cloaked dark elves were stepping out of the brush at this point, blades and bows at the ready. "Papers."

"But of course," J'anda said, taking a light breath. He raised a hand as he reached slowly for his tunic, pretended to grasp something within, and brought his hand out with a slow flourish that radiated yellow light in all directions.

The ranger in front of him blinked only once, then stared straight ahead. "I ..."

"I'm going to go along now," J'anda said, "you should stay here and guard the road for another hour. You never who could be about in the night, after all."

"No," the soldier said, voice rolling and distant, like he had not a thought in his head, "you never know."

"You're a good soldier," J'anda said, and looked at the others around him. "You're all good soldiers. You should go back to the portal and rejoin your detachment when you've finished guarding the road. Someone could be coming. Someone you would not want to miss. You should always be vigilant."

"Always vigilant," they all repeated, in time with each other.

"That's the spirit," J'anda said, and steered his horse around the lead. "Do take care."

"And you as well," the soldiers said, still in time.

J'anda watched the images that were playing in their minds flash forth in his. It was rather like an old memory; he could keep it away for the most part, let it play in the back of his mind while he considered other things in the front. It came back when he reached a point of quiet on his main thoughts, always, like water seeping up in a slow flood.

The forests opened up into clear space sooner than he had anticipated, and certainly sooner than when last he had been here, a century prior. The lands had been cleared and were lying fallow for the autumn. He could see the tilled dirt even in the light of the moon once the branches covering his head were out of the way.

The moon was rising, drifting slowly to the crown of the dark sky, and it shone down on those fields, the dark dirt tinged blue in the moonlight, like the skin of J'anda's brethren. He felt as if he were drifting slowly forward on the currents of an ocean as the horse carrying him over these dark grounds. Silhouettes stood over the flat earth, watch stations built on what looked like old trees, reaching up into the air to elevate their guards over the fields below.

Figures waited atop the towers, and he sent a subtle spell their way encouraging them to turn inward toward the watch fires that kept them warm in the night chill. Their shadowed silhouettes moved in the night, faces lit as they obliged his spell by turning from their vigil on the road. Peals of laughter reached him over the fields between them, and he felt a stirring in his heart for times long gone, of the comradeship that came with a duty such as theirs.

He carried on in a similar fashion, prompting all the guards he saw to keep him out of their sight, off their minds, as he made his way. It was a simple thing, something that the Sovereign probably expected to happen at some point. This was not the challenge; for who cared if an enchanter or twenty made his way over fallow fields of little value in the fall. It was hardly worth pledging magical defense to.

No, it was at the gate where he would begin to run across

difficulty. But that was expected, and every step his horse carried him bettered the chance that when he was inevitably captured, he would end up in the right place rather than summarily executed.

The hill with the mouth of Saekaj Sovar's entrance yawned wide ahead of him in the dark, a rounded silhouette like an outcrop sticking out of the earth. True watchtowers glowed on either side of the gate, which was wide open, and J'anda considered his approach once more. It was roughly as he had thought it would be, the same as it had been in the last war.

His eyes had diminished with his age, of course, depriving him of the ability to tell what he faced in the terms of spell casters ahead. He wore no illusion, and he counted on his aged appearance to aid him.

His horse sauntered up to the gates, and he dismounted, not needing to feign slowness and stiffness as he did so. He carried no wand or staff, merely himself. As he stood with the reins in hand, guards slowly approached, wary at the sight of his traveling cloak, which hid the vestments that identified him as an enchanter. To them, he probably looked like a trader, or a traveler of some stripe.

"Who goes there?" the nearest guard asked, as eight of them approached him in a knot, slowly breaking loose of each other until he was surrounded.

"A traveler bound for the palace of the Sovereign," he said, not bothering to look behind him as they tightened their circle. "I come with urgent news."

"Your arrival is not expected," the lead guard said with a look to his nearest companion.

"Good news seldom is," J'anda said, casting his spell sublingually, with barely a movement of his fingers. He could feel the will of the head guard, saw the man's vision of a perfect life, and froze him in place, mesmerized. He did the same in rapid order with the others in the circle, then sent the same spell in a swirling loop through the tops of both guard towers, where he snared eight more, closing his eyes to concentrate on threading the illusion through their minds.

He closed his eyes and saw sixteen different visions, most of them the same in basic regards. It was always a sensory feast when he created these illusions of one heart's desire; the crackle of mutton slow-roasting on a hearth in one vision, the touch of a dark-skinned lover in three others, fingers dancing over naked flesh, a peaceful day spent in a boat bobbing gently on the Great Sea in another, and fingers running over smooth gold, the smell of the metal wafting through greedy nostrils in yet another.

Basing them on the guards' desires, J'anda wove and crafted each of the visions as he felt the spell begin to increase in power. It was not mind reading; more like he could pick up the burdens weighing on one's heart and use the vision lighten them to the point where all the concerns of the world simply melted away. These were simple guards, not soldiers, and they had little will or desire to fight against that which he created. There were others beyond, surely, ready to spring into a battle at the slightest cue of troubles coming, but as it was, he left the guards all standing there, his horse at their center, without so much as a word spoken between them, like a stone circle in the starry night.

J'anda felt the first bite of the cave chill a hundred feet down. It was unlike the night, with the cave's stagnant air heavy around him. The slope bothered his hips, and he wished he had brought the horse a little farther. *Nothing for it now, though,* he knew. The courtyard was ahead in any case, and he could procure transport from there that would ease his bones.

He stepped into the great courtyard with mild surprise. It was quiet here, entirely too quiet for his liking. Even in a time of war, the passage of nearly all goods came through this staging area, both into and out of Saekaj and Sovar. *To see it so dead means we are exporting little and importing even less.* He looked over the circular chamber with a steady eye. Carriages sat parked with the great vek'tag spiders larger than bulls hitched to them, drivers sitting at the ready in case passengers of great import came in the night. The symbols of the houses they belonged to were draped along the sides in uncolored banners.

J'anda paused at the top of the courtyard, overlooking all the carriages. Several were for guild use, a few more were for the most noble houses, ones that might receive a visitor from the outside world and require transport on short notice. There were probably only twenty in all, and as he caught sight of the one for the Gathering of Coercers, he smiled, seriously considering it. *Too obvious,* he decided, and instead walked toward one he recognized well. A spider on a red banner, some of the only color on any of the house symbols, surprisingly crude given that use of color in clothing or banner was a thing that would be seen as low class. "Ah, Grimrath Tordor," he whispered to himself, "you have not changed, I see."

J'anda made his way to the carriage of Grimrath Tordor and sent a simple charming spell to his driver. It didn't vary too much from a mesmerization spell in the work involved, but it sent a slightly deeper twining of the magic and mind to his subject. Rather than simply paralyzing the man into inaction, as he had done with the soldiers on the surface, this required either a blunt subversion of will or a careful deception to get the subject to play along. One required considerably more finesse than the other; J'anda knew that most enchanters were incapable of this kind of subtlety.

He had practiced with the best, of course, and had bested the rest. *This is the truth that Vracken Coeltes never seemed to grasp; that to spin threads of a spell in the mind, honey is preferable to vinegar.* He'd seen the spells the way Coeltes and others did them, too harsh and blunt for the unveiling of a heart's desire. Coeltes and his ilk all preferred fear, to drive deep into the minds they paralyzed or charmed and drag out the worst aspects. It was a faster approach, he supposed, requiring less effort but their marks woke with screams rather than gently snapping to the waking world from a pleasant dream.

This was never a thing I understood. He put out his hand and slipped a subtle illusion into the now-prepared mind of Tordor's carriage driver, making him think that his master's own chief servant was in the back, that he had complimented him on his diligence at his job. He threaded the vision together as he stepped onto the running board and opened the door himself, slipping into the darkness of the coach.

The benches were padded, a curious relief. J'anda could not recall any of the seats of any of the carriages he had been in in Saekaj ever having a pad to relieve the skin against the ride. *Tordor is a most curious chap, though, I suppose, and he is likely rather old now.*

The carriage lurched into motion, passing down into the descending passage with a squeak of wheels. J'anda sat silently in the back, already preparing his next feat. The gate at the entry to Saekaj would surely have a cessation spell upon it, designed to strip any spell usage or illusion from a person as they stepped through. For most enchanters, it would be a nearly insurmountable problem; to take Tordor's carriage through, after all, would result in the mind of the driver instantly being cleared of the misapprehension that a steward of Grimrath himself was in the back. To say nothing of the guards at the gate; as soon as he began to walk through, the illusion that he belonged in Saekaj, that he had papers of any sort, would be stripped away from the minds of the subjects.

This is not a concern, however. J'anda smiled as the carriage rattled into sight of the gate. He had already felt the mesmerization spell he had cast upon the surface guards fade, leaving them with a lingering and pleasant sense of befuddlement. There was no sign remaining that he had cast anything upon them; it was long gone, and he was certain they had returned to their guard posts merely confused about why there was a horse left in their midst.

This is why you should not lead with fear, Vracken, J'anda thought as the carriage rattled to a stop in front of the gates of Saekaj. The gates were wide open, had been thrown open at his approach, probably out of respect for Tordor. J'anda peered out of the carriage window and sent a thought to his driver, a compliment to his skill and ability from the servant of his master, and then stepped out onto the cave ground, narrowly avoiding turning his ankle in a rut made by countless carriages that preceded him.

J'anda adjusted his cloak, looking into Saekaj beyond the gates. He had not seen the city in a century, but it appeared that little had changed. The Grand Palace of Saekaj was right there, on the far back wall of the cavern, and visible even from here as a sign of the splendor of the upper city.

He walked up to the gates, to the guard waiting for him, and smiled. He had no magic in mind, no illusion upon him. The carriage behind him started to pull away, turning to head back to the surface.

"State your business," the guard said politely, looking up and down his traveling cloak. This deep in the caves, he probably wasn't expecting someone to sneak down; and a citizen of Sovar would be coming from the opposite direction.

"I am a citizen of Saekaj," J'anda said pleasantly, with a smile. "And in the service of the house of Tordor, obviously."

"Obviously," the guard said with a nod. "I'll need your name and your papers."

J'anda did not dare raise an eyebrow. "I'm afraid I was dispatched on an urgent mission with a wizard and did not have my papers when

I left. You may, of course, check my identity, but my destination is the Grand Palace of Saekaj to report to the Sovereign himself."

The guard's face became a study in barely contained panic. It was the contradiction that did it, really; no papers, but the not-so-veiled suggestion of the highest authority behind him with the mention of the Sovereign and a mission. If he was turned aside and it ended up that he was actually an envoy of the Sovereign, the guard would doubtless find his head somewhat disconnected from the rest of his body. On the other hand, if J'anda were lying …

"Perhaps you should have your men escort me to the palace gates to be dealt with there," J'anda said and watched the man's face relax slightly. "I wouldn't want to cause you any trouble because of my unfortunate circumstances, after all. No reason for you to have to take this responsibility on your own shoulders."

"Right," the man said, as though he were latching on to a rope while drowning on the Great Sea. "Karnven, Rickkart, Yarwan … take this man to the Grand Palace of Saekaj."

J'anda nodded at him with a smile. "Always best to push these things up the ladder. Better they fall on the rung above, eh?"

"Quite so," the head guard said, looking immensely relieved. "Be on your way, then."

"Indeed," J'anda said, letting the three assigned guards flank him, one to either side and the third behind with his weapon not far from his grasp, surely. J'anda started forward at a leisurely pace, passing through the gates with a beneficent smile on his face, on a stroll to his destination, not a care in the world. The houses and dwellings of Saekaj lay before him, the main street turning slightly to the right as he entered the upper city.

He walked in companionable silence with the guards until just before the markets. He was on the main road and could see the start of the manors ahead, the twelve houses of greatest renown in Saekaj, lined on either side of the main thoroughfare to the palace. *Greatest in the Sovereign's estimation, those twelve. I wonder who they are now?*

As they walked through the small crowds of the market, he paused to look at a cart that was open even at this hour, selling meats of indeterminate origin. J'anda directed his hand toward the guard nearest him and sublingually cast a mesmerization spell. He let the magic drift lazily to the man behind him, wrapping up his mind in a vision of some of the high quality meats roasting lazily on a stove while he sat in a comfortable chair, and then turned the spell on the last of his guards, who was partial to something that J'anda had never quite seen before. It raised his eyebrows, but he shrugged, leaving the man in peace, staring at the meat display in the market with dull eyes, dreaming of crocheting blankets of the finest quality for everyone in Saekaj.

J'anda picked up his pace a little now, weaving out of the edge of the markets and onto the avenue toward the palace. He could see the dual waterfalls pouring out of the rock behind the palace on the walls, and put one foot in front the other as he went. He had intentionally bypassed the road that would have carried him by the Gathering of Coercers, not even wanting to see the building where it lay carved in the rock wall at the side of Saekaj's chamber. *I may see it up close soon enough, anyway.*

He walked down the main avenue in silence, stone walls separating the manors on either side of him from the road. Ahead was the gate to the Grand Palace of Saekaj, the Sovereign's own residence. He knew another cessation spell waited at the gate, one that was certain to break his hold on the three guards in the market. They were at a slightly more alert state than the ones he'd left outside and more likely to immediately report his disappearance, having been tasked with actually watching him by a superior rather than simply guarding a gate as the ones on the surface had been.

No, this was the end, this gate at the end of the road. He had evaded capture to make it thus far; while it was possible he could have lied and enchanted his way through the gate by barest luck, there was really no more need. This was the place the Sovereign dwelled, after all, five minutes walk from the entry point ahead of him. If he were imprisoned, it would be in the Sovereign's own dungeon, where word would surely make it to Yartraak if he made himself plain.

And he meant to make himself plain.

The gates were ahead, drawing closer like a doom rolling upon him. He felt no dread, however. To him, it all seemed as though the moment were here that he had anticipated and feared all at once, as though something he had been long waiting on were about to be over. It was a rush of pleasant anticipation, the idea that regardless of how it turned out, he was now committed, could not walk away. *Like an arrow flying from the bow, my course is set ... and that brings a strange freedom.*

The guards at the gate saw him coming but stood relaxed, for who could possibly be approaching the Sovereign's palace but those who were already supposed to be here? He put on his smile once more and watched them grow slightly tenser within their armor as he drew closer and passed the last manor gates before the palace without turning.

The guards lowered their halberds in front of the gate in a diagonal cross to bar his passage. He saw the stiffness of their action, so formal, their armor clanking under the ceremonial motion; a youthful jump could have just about cleared their barricade. No, this was a symbolic block. The real one was the guards hidden inside the gate, probably a battalion's worth just in the front of the grounds.

"You stand before the palace of the Sovereign," the guard on the left said stiffly, his armor less ornate than the palace guard uniforms had been a century ago. "Explain your presence."

"Oh," J'anda said, stopping just before the halberds and lifting his hands in surrender. "Very well, then. My name is J'anda Aimant ... and I believe the Sovereign would like my head on a platter."

Their reaction was almost worth the entire journey.

16.

Terian

"This battle is lost," Terian said, watching things spiral impossibly out of control.

The trolls had broken first, under a bombardment of explosions beyond anything Terian had seen before. Fire had lit the dusky skies, swallowing entire brigades in orange conflagrations. It had gone until Terian had ordered Bowe into flight to freeze one of the accursed machines that was slaughtering their trolls. That had worked, fortunately, prompting an explosion behind the Sanctuary lines that had heralded the end of their storm of fire.

Terian's next move had been to try and flank the Sanctuary line with a schiltron, a small mass of soldiers carrying shields to protect them from the rangers who were showering his lines with arrows. That had failed, though, taken apart by perfectly aimed arrows that had rent great gaps in the formation, large enough for more clumsily aimed arrows to follow.

"Godsdammit, Martaina," Terian had muttered.

As if that had not been enough, when the Goliath armies had rolled forward in a charge, all their use of magic had been completely ripped away from them by Sanctuary's use of a cessation spell upon the field of battle. No wizard, nor druid, nor enchanter, nor—Terian looked at Malpravus, whose expression was of barely contained fury—necromancer could cast a single spell. Terian watched their dead fall without any recourse. *Malpravus is less than useless in this instance, all because of that damned spell. He sits here like a dark abyss, waiting to swallow any hope I might have. Well done, Cyrus.*

"I should have anticipated treachery from your brethren," Malpravus said coldly, a touch of respect infusing his comment.

"Cyrus Davidon is no idiot," Terian said, "especially when it comes to facing a superior force. We've probably got him outnumbered at least three-to-one, and he's handing us a defeat."

"We will overwhelm him," Malpravus said, certain.

Terian studied the field of battle, drawing his gaze to the right. The lines of battle toward the back were less orderly, but he could see ... *Is that? Yes ... Luukessian cavalry. He's hiding them, waiting to deploy them until we're fully exposed. You are a clever devil, Davidon.*

"Move up the reserves!" Malpravus commanded, and the order went back, carried off by voice behind him.

Should I countermand him? Terian wondered. *He sends out more of the Goliath regulars and some of the dead out on a charge, and Cyrus smashes them with cavalry ... it'll turn this orderly loss into a rout.* Terian pursed his lips. *I'll take the middle ground.* "I'm not sure that's wise. Perhaps we should withdraw."

"And cede the field to them?" Malpravus hissed, his usual cool lost in an instant. "Ridiculous! Our superior numbers will break them down."

"They're funneling us toward them." Terian shook his head. "They pitted that path so we'd march right into their teeth, and we've obliged every step of the way. I don't like it."

"We will make up our losses once they're all dead," Malpravus snapped, "and we add the corpses of their officers to our army, with all their ability bent to my will." He said it with a touch of greed, and Terian repressed a shudder at the thought.

"You're in charge," Terian said, keeping the lightness out of his voice. *My ass is now covered; Cyrus, do your worst.*

The cavalry charge came moments later, a hard drive out of the right side of the field that cut into the dark elven formation hard, like a sword biting into a throat. Terian watched with carefully concealed glee as the lines dissolved into the chaos of horsemen slashing down on unprepared and panicked soldiers like a reaper raised and lowered upon the harvest.

Yep. That's a rout.

"We should withdraw," Terian said again, prompting Malpravus to look back at him with stunned eyes, as though he could not take in all that he was seeing. *It is rather a lot to take in—a lot of death, in any case.*

"I can't …" Malpravus murmured, raising his hands and casting a spell, red energy dancing off his fingers to no effect. "So many … lost …"

"Get us out of here," Terian said, sidling closer to Malpravus as the lines in front of them degenerated into a fracas, the cavalry channeling toward them like hard-running water loosed in a muddy rut. He pulled himself tight to Malpravus as the necromancer blanched from his touch and threw a hand in the air, his spell falling upon them and carrying them away to answer for their failures.

17.

J'anda

The guards were peaceable, if suspicious, walking him through the gates without so much as clapping him in manacles. They did, however, have him surrounded the entire way, swords a mere inch from his skin. J'anda kept his hands out and visible the entire walk, as they marched him into the Grand Palace of Saekaj. It hadn't been hard for him to guess there were no senior officers about, because a lieutenant had taken charge and his plan essentially seemed to be to take him to the Sovereign. *Probably thinks he'll get glory. Hopefully he's right, but it could easily go the other direction.*

The entry to the Sovereign's palace was hardwoods shined to a luxuriant finish, almost gleaming even in the low light. As they entered the massive foyer, J'anda went automatically toward the throne room as the guards paused, the lieutenant leading him along having a momentary freeze of concern as panic welled up on his face. "It's this way," J'anda said, and started toward the entry to the throne room.

"Hold it right there," the lieutenant said, "we need to check with—"

J'anda sighed and cast his mesmerization spell. The will of these men was stronger than he had encountered elsewhere, but he managed to slip through their defenses with relative ease. It took him something on the order of a minute to fully suppress the resistance of the last one, leaving them all standing there, exposed, in the entry to the Sovereign's house, but J'anda did not concern himself overmuch with that particular detail.

All the smart ones must have been sent to the front; these men are green as a

98

troll—and just as dumb. Forgive me, Vaste. Not checking the list to see who I was? Assuming I was not a spell caster? Not assigning a spell caster to me? They might as well have handed me a key to the Grand Palace and let me have free reign. In the days of old, this would not have been possible.

He threaded his way between the swords of the guards, pushing one of them aside to pass, opening the door to the entry into the throne room area. Here he encountered two more guards and greeted them with a smile, moving his hands as he cast his spell. "You," he said to one of them, "will announce me."

"Yes sir," the guard said, nodding blankly.

"Is he in?" J'anda asked, pulling off his cloak and handing it to the second guard. He smoothed his robes, fussing with a wrinkle in his sleeve that stubbornly refused to depart.

"He is by himself," the guard said. "He will be leaving soon for the night, but he has been waiting for—"

"Quite all right," J'anda said, as the other went to open the door for him. J'anda looked beyond and saw a familiar sight; the throne shrouded in darkness, orange lamps glowing along the sides of the hall. "Announce me as Sir J'anda the Cunning, of Sanctuary," he said with a faint smile. *Using my elven-bestowed title will certainly wake up the Sovereign.*

"Sir J'anda the Cunning, of Sanctuary!" the guard called, standing stiffly as J'anda entered the throne room, head held high. The guard withdrew and shut the door a moment later, leaving J'anda apparently alone.

J'anda did not hesitate, continuing toward the darkness in the distance. It was shrouded like a cloud around the throne, pooling around the massive wood chair as if it had been poured out of the air above. He walked at a leisurely pace down the lengthy room, feet shuffling along the thick carpet that lined the center path to the throne, and when he was roughly twenty feet away, he bowed his head low. "You'll have to forgive me for not stooping lower; my old bones aren't what they were when we last met."

The darkness bulged, crackling with energy. "No, they are not," the voice of Yartraak agreed through the shroud. "I had heard of your advancing years, your sacrifice over the sea, but I scarcely believed it. I scarcely believe it now, though at least I can see it for myself with you standing before me." The shroud of darkness began to dissolve, and

Yartraak's grey face peered out of the dissipating cloud. "What brings you here now? Did you come to end your days where you began them?"

"As your grace wills it," J'anda said, bowing again. "I think you are wise enough to discern my intent."

Yartraak looked out at him through those red eyes, narrowed with intensity. "You have personally betrayed me."

"Through my actions, yes," J'anda agreed. "I left and did not look back. I realize now that my leaving was a full betrayal all its own."

"Do you wish to die?" Yartraak asked, leaning forward. J'anda had forgotten how truly bizarre the God of Darkness's shape was. His torso was comically angled, like nothing he had ever seen before or since. Even Mortus did not resemble him.

"I am going to die," J'anda said, staring across the small distance between them. "But before I die, I wished to make my peace with my homeland. If that means dying here, so be it. But there is someone else here who, though innocent, was imprisoned for her contact with me, and I came to absolve her of my considerable crimes."

Yartraak watched him carefully. "I gave you opportunities for redemption."

"Your grace is munificent," J'anda agreed, swallowing the bile that threatened to rise in him. *It is all for the greater cause.* "You were patient with me, and I failed to recognize it at the time."

Yartraak sat in silence for a moment. "You Sanctuary fools are always so brave, as though they beat the fear of death out of you somehow. I should be interested to know how Cyrus Davidon inspires that from you people." The red eyes burned. "I tried to correct your path," Yartraak said, drawling. "The way a parent corrects a child when they step outside the bounds."

"You were certainly merciful in that regard," J'anda lied, keeping his head bowed so that the God of Darkness could not see the tightening of his jaw, the subtle flash of anger he knew crossed his own eyes.

"Indeed I was," Yartraak said. "Some thought me too merciful. I had hopes for you, for your future here, which I have maintained these long years." He snapped his grey fingers together. "At any moment, your life could have been mine. An assassin's blade in the street, a wizard's spell in the courtyard of your guild ... and I held them back because I did not wish you dead … until now, as I look upon you again and realize you were perhaps the greatest betrayal I have ever suffered."

"I am sorry to be such a disappointment," J'anda said, remorseful only for the direction the conversation was heading. *Damn. All this way, and I fail because I'm not willing, even after all this time, to wallow in the guilt he wants me to embrace like a pile of pig shit. Well, if it's to end, then I'm not going to do this quietly—*

The doors crashed open at the end of the throne room, drawing J'anda's attention away from the God of Darkness just long enough for Yartraak to grasp him by the neck and lift him high in the air. J'anda was whipped upright, legs dangling beneath him, looking straight into the red eyes of the Sovereign of Saekaj—

—and he saw no mercy there.

"Your guilt is decided," Yartraak said, "and your sentence will be carried out immediately, and with more mercy than you deserve." He lifted J'anda further into the air. "You have said your last words."

J'anda felt the squeeze as the feeling faded from his body. His eyes rolled into his head, and a darkness unrelated to the being in front of him swirled around him, dragging him into its cold and merciless embrace.

18.

Aisling

Aisling awoke on the morning after the battle at Livlosdald keep in Cyrus Davidon's arms, his hairy chest pressed tight to her back and his warm flesh leaving her feeling oddly cold. She slipped from his grasp as easily as disappearing from a market after thieving from a stand, taking advantage of the man's deep sleep to avoid stirring him as she made her escape. She'd been doing this for months and months now, and was no fonder of it now than she had been before.

Every day she sat in front of her desk with quill and ink, trying to summon up descriptions of emotions she didn't feel to couple with the events she'd witnessed and rumors she'd gathered, creating a perfect story of a girl aswirl in events bigger than herself, witnessing things she was not prepared for.

It was exactly what was expected of Aisling Nightwind.

But it was not what she expected of herself, especially since her name was not even truly Aisling Nightwind. That was a secret she kept from all, though. All except Norenn, though even he didn't know her true name. He'd never needed to, and as she'd judged by his state after her return from Luukessia, he hadn't felt any compulsion to share that information with Dagonath Shrawn. More than likely, Shrawn had never even asked. He'd decided the moment they met who she was, and everything she'd done since had been intended to play into that perception. It ran close enough to the truth in most cases that she didn't even have to try very hard to pull it off. Most of the time.

She dressed quickly and left Cyrus's tent. The cot he'd been afforded as General had been considerably more comfortable than the sleeping roll she would have used had she decided to keep to herself. But on the eve of a victory such as they'd just seen, she knew what was expected of her.

When she came out of the tent, she scanned the immediate area and found Verity nearby, lecturing a warrior on the proper care of her horse. It was a perfectly normal event in a perfectly normal place; elves were well known for their lecturing ways, their sense of superiority, and supposedly greater knowledge. Verity was not even close to the exception; she played her role as well as Aisling would have expected. The lie was only visible if one knew to look for it.

"You can't do it that way," Verity said. Aisling started to trudge past her, on the way to a different part of the camp, and caught her eyes for a brief blink before Verity continued her lecture. That was all Aisling needed to see. She knew that Verity would be along shortly, would try and catch her away from anyone. After an event like the battle they'd seen yesterday, Aisling could hardly expect any differently.

Aisling knew the expectations, played the expectations. That was the game at this point. It wasn't the game she'd been looking for when she'd left home in search of another life, but it was the one she'd been presented when she'd been caught stealing the Red Destiny of Saekaj. She imagined the massive ruby in her hands again, a gemstone larger than her head. She could almost feel the weight of it. They'd been so close too, only to have victory snatched right out of their hands by the Sovereign's own return.

Aisling dipped behind a tent, trying to find a path that would carry her far, far away from Verity and her present lecture. It was always the mornings after where it started to catch up to her, the sick feeling of what she was doing, how she was being used—

"Ah, ah, ah," Verity said, appearing in front of her from out of the shroud of an invisibility spell. "Where are you off to?"

Aisling bit back the first reply of "Wherever I damned well please" before it left her lips, but she did not bother hiding the fury that sprung upon her features. "I'm walking."

"So you are," Verity said and reached out with her slow, ungainly hand, calloused and hard and unlike a spell caster's, and wrapped it around Aisling's upper arm. Aisling, for her part, let the wizard have the illusion of control in the matter. It wouldn't be too difficult to remove the hand if she truly desired—in one way or another. "But I have a different destination in mind for you."

"Naturally," Aisling said, resigned.

Verity, for her part, drew in close. The light of the return spell glistened around them as they began to fade, the camp of Sanctuary disappearing around them. "You mustn't ever get the idea that you're in charge," Verity said as the spell's light consumed them, "else you might start to think things that will simply be the end of you …"

19.

Terian

"You shouldn't do that," Terian said to the Sovereign of Saekaj Sovar.

Even in the dim light of the throne room, Terian could see Yartraak's eyes go a ruby red, bright and hot with his fury at being challenged. "You question my will? Pray tell, why not?" the God of Darkness asked.

Terian stared at the spectacle before him. Malpravus stood to his left, a little ways back, as usual seeking to distance himself from possibly unfavorable association with Terian. *My insolence keeps saving me, at least for now. Malpravus doesn't want to walk that particular razor's edge, though, and I can't blame him. Smarter to stay off the blade entirely. Unfortunately for him, you can't be near Yartraak without some element of risk. To wit ...* He looked up at the figure clenched in the Sovereign's hand, long, clawed fingers wrapped around a blue neck that was darkening from the blood pooling in the man's head. *J'anda, you're an idiot for coming here, for throwing yourself on the Sovereign's mercy, elusive at best.*

"Dear boy, I hope you know what you're doing," Malpravus hissed at his side.

"So do I," Terian said, stepping forward to leave Malpravus behind. *You come to answer for a simple failure in battle and pretty soon you're up to your eyeballs in monster-infested waters.* "We were just defeated in battle by Sanctuary on the Northern front. It was an utter rout, and they destroyed our army beyond the capacity for easy regroup."

The Sovereign's eyes almost looked like they were coals in a fire, glowing in the dark. "Why should this make me less disposed toward tearing this one's head off?"

"Everyone has a use," Terian said, "even if it's something as humble as becoming fertilizer for the mushrooms."

Yartraak was silent for a long moment. "What would you have him do?"

Terian bowed his head in deference. "I offer only a suggestion—ask him what he is willing to do to make good on the betrayals you have suffered from him."

Yartraak considered this for a moment and then clawed hand drifted toward the ground and released J'anda, who fell limp to the floor. Yartraak extended one of the long, pointed fingers to touch the enchanter on the head, and a light glowed in the darkness. J'anda stirred, coughing as though he were about to vomit, his throat crackling as he gagged for air. Terian stood silently for a minute, then two, as J'anda massaged the neck that had just come within millimeters of being crushed. "You wish to repay me?" Yartraak asked.

Terian held his breath. *This is the moment of truth. J'anda looks like he's about half a second from giving up and dying right here on the floor. If he answers wrong, then my pleas for mercy for him are not only about to go unanswered, they're going to damage my own case rather heavily.*

"I will do as you wish," J'anda said in a scratchy voice. Terian felt a little exultation in his heart, and tried to keep from sighing in relief. "Whatever you wish."

Yartraak glanced at Terian, glowing eyes showing a brief hint of … pleasure? "You are still a member of the Council of Sanctuary, yes?"

J'anda nodded slowly. "I informed them of my intent to make things right with you before leaving, but I am still a member of the Council, yes."

"You will spy on them for me," Yartraak said, long fingers stroking the area where his lower jaw sat flatly against the bottom of his face. He had no chin to speak of, the structure of his skull was so dramatically different from any other living being Terian had ever met. *Except Mortus*, Terian thought, *but he's a far cry from even Mortus.*

"V-very well," J'anda said, voice whisper-quiet. "I will spy upon them for you."

"I will know if you are lying to me," Yartraak said, "if you are betraying me."

"Of—of course," J'anda said, fingers still clutched around his throat.

"Get him out of my sight," Yartraak said, waving a hand at Terian. "And reconstitute your army, fools. Fix your failures."

"As you wish, my Sovereign," Terian said, starting forward. He was at J'anda's side before the enchanter laid eyes on him, pulling the man to his feet and throwing an arm around his shoulder. "Let's go."

"T—Terian?" J'anda asked, eyes fluttering. "What are you doing here?"

"Saving your life," Terian said, boots clicking on the wood floor as he carried the weary enchanter along. He took care not to impale the man's arm on his pauldrons. Malpravus waited, looking at Terian with a certain cunning.

"J'anda," Malpravus said, falling in next to Terian as he rejoined them on their path to the door, "so good to see you again, though I must say you've looked better."

"And Malpravus as well," J'anda said, and Terian could tell the man was holding something back by the tautness of his body. "Such interesting times."

"Indeed," Terian said as he passed into the foyer of the Grand Palace of Saekaj, supporting a man he fully knew was betraying the Sovereign even now. *And if we're very lucky, they won't get so interesting as to result in our spectacular deaths.*

20.

Aisling

Aisling was blindfolded and led around like a child playing a game. She focused on the senses she could still use, absent her sight. There was cold cave air, which she'd known all along, since Verity's spell had brought them right to Shrawn's house. They walked for quite a while, and she could tell by her balance which turns they had her take. She'd probably only gone a thousand feet at most, unless they'd gone in a slow circle, one too subtle for her to take notice. She didn't think that had happened, though.

The scent of wood smoke was in the air here, but that simply meant she was in Saekaj, still. She'd heard the rumble of gears and levers at a couple points, as though gates were being opened for her. The sound was wrong, though, the mechanism sliding sideways rather than up, like a portcullis. Secret passages, then, carefully oiled to open with relative quiet.

She felt the tingle run along her flesh, waiting for Dagonath Shrawn. It had to be Shrawn, after all, unless she was meeting some secret interrogator. That was a thought not worth dwelling on for very long.

She sniffed again, and now she could smell something distinctly oily in the air. Faint traces of the scent lingered around her, and she tried not to make too much of a show of getting a good whiff of it. Verity's hands were on her back, pushing her. It was a disconcerting feeling, being utterly at someone else's mercy. She was used to it by now, though.

"I bring you a gift." Shrawn's voice echoed in the darkness. She could see hints of light beyond the blindfold, like torches burning in the night.

"Aw, you shouldn't have," Aisling said, channeling the words that a sarcastic, lower-class thief would have used on just such an occasion. As for what the girl she'd been before that would have said ... she couldn't even be sure anymore.

Verity hit her in the back, hard, driving her right to her knees. The pain radiated out in a spasm, blunted by her leather armor. The emotional snap Aisling took and ignored, throwing it in the pit as well. She summoned up fear and tossed it out to the front of her mind, let herself show the pain, show the concern that even worse things might be on the horizon for her. It came out with a cringe, a whimper, and coldly she added another mark against Verity in her head, then tossed that down into the pit to be brought up at a more fitting time.

"As you can see," Shrawn said, "she shows spirit. A failing, I know, but one that has been of some advantage to us in her assignment."

He's talking to someone else, Aisling realized, putting the pieces together. *His tone is conciliatory, subordinate.*

Gods. I'm in front of the Sovereign.

That calculation caused no small amount of surprise in her, but she kept it all back for later use, if or when the blindfold came off. *Let them think I'm dumb, that I'm cowed, that they have nothing to fear from me.*

"She has done well thus far," the Sovereign rumbled. Aisling feigned confusion, turning her head as though to discern the source of the mysterious voice. She'd already honed in on his exact position, though; roughly twelve feet in front of her, about thirty degrees left of her true north. *I still have my blades, but even being mystical, they'll do nearly no damage against the skin of a god.*

"Uh, thank you?" She threw out her reply as a careful, confused and thoroughly humbled thief wondering at the source of her compliment. *If I sound appropriately pitiful, perhaps they'll let their guard down and I can get through this performance with a little enlightenment.*

"Take off the blindfold," the Sovereign said, his voice high and cold. "Let her see whose presence she stands in."

"As you wish," Shrawn said, but it was Verity who took the blindfold off her. Aisling raised her eyes slowly, peering into the darkness. When her eyes met the Lord of Darkness's own, she let out a shudder of revulsion and horror that was not even close to her genuine reaction. He was a strange looking creature, that was certain, with his grey skin and bizarrely shaped body with sticklike limbs, but he was no more horrifying to her than Mortus had been.

No, in truth she took him in with an analytical eye behind the facade of the frightened thief. She saw his neck, thin for his massive size, and wondered how many good saws across it it'd take to open the artery she saw there. *Probably ten*, she decided, *if Mortus's skin was any guide.*

"Uh … huh … uh," she said, little choked breaths of horror with just a hint of shame mixed in for the god's ego. She bowed her head and refused to look up again. In her mind she was studying a picture of what she'd just seen, looking for additional vulnerabilities. The thin limbs would be promising weak points if she had something as strong as Cyrus's sword in her hand, but her daggers would make hobbling the God of Darkness problematic at best.

"Now you see me," Yartraak said, hissing into the quiet dark. The throne room around them was lit with sconces that shed silent light, more than would be easily found in the rest of the God of Darkness's own city. Then again, she'd seen his inner sanctum in his own realm, lit like a sun was hanging overhead at midday, and knew that there was more to him that met the eye. *Darkness is his shroud, but he doesn't fear the light, at least not in private.*

"I see what you wish me to see," she answered in a fearful tone, though she spoke truth through and through. She had seen him, all right, had seen of him what he wanted her to see—but she was also considering him in a way that he doubtless did not want her to, already wondering at how she could exact revenge on him for his part in orchestrating her servitude.

Just another name on the list, another mark on the wall. Though this one is a much bigger mark than the others. Harder.

"I have heard of your good works in our service," Yartraak said, "of the spying you have done for us upon Cyrus Davidon and his ilk."

"I seek only to serve," she said. "To repay my debt. To earn back what I had justly taken from me. To do whatever you require of—"

"Yes, yes," Yartraak said, brushing her platitudes off. *He probably doesn't know exactly how empty they are, though.* "And you do well at it." He leaned down. "Tell me of this battle in which you fought last eve."

This could be a sticky business, reporting directly to the Sovereign. She glanced back at Verity, making it look like she was seeking permission, and received a nod from the wizard that carried with it an evil smile. *I can't speak a word of falsehood or she'll have me on the torture racks in a half-heartbeat.* "Ah-uhm," Aisling said, licking her lips, "it was … a dismal affair for our side, with catastrophic losses …"

"I see," the Sovereign said quietly, "and how did it happen? Was your army larger?"

"No," Aisling said, struggling to find the way to approach it easily, "Cyrus Davidon—"

"Your lover," the Sovereign snapped, interrupting her.

"By your order, yes," Aisling replied, giving a nervous look that wasn't at all feigned. The Sovereign's ire was obvious, his eyes burning brighter. "Were it down to me, I would not have such an association with the man."

"Indeed?" The Sovereign studied her carefully. "Go on, then."

He hates Cyrus. Good to know. "Davidon planned and executed a strategy designed to fight the superior odds arrayed against him. He is fair at these things," Aisling said.

"He would be," the Sovereign said, with more than a little irritation still evident in the snap of his voice, "he is the favored of the God of War, after all."

Favored of a god? Aisling did not react to this in a discernible way, her mind racing with the information nonetheless. *That would be handy.* "Favored … how?"

"You do not need to know," Shrawn snapped at her, and then made a gesture with his hand. Verity cuffed her hard behind the ear, drawing a flinch.

"Come now, Shrawn," Yartraak said, looking sidelong at his servant, "she is in a precarious position at our prompting. If you were trapped against your will with such a barbarian as Cyrus Davidon as your consort, you would want all the weapons at your disposal, as the girl does. Knowledge is a weapon, and to leave her unarmed against the predations of this brute would be to fail to protect our investment of time and effort placing her there."

Shrawn looked as though he wanted to argue with that, but it passed in a flicker and was followed by only the mildest question as criticism. "But how could this be of use to her, your grace?"

"Bellarum is infinitely difficult, chaotic, treacherous," Yartraak said. "His proxy will be much the same, filled with guile and cunning and careless of the cost of lives in his battles." *I'm choking on the irony,* Aisling thought. *Does he even hear his own words?* "She should know about him, if she has not discerned it for herself."

I may have underestimated his hatred of Cyrus earlier. "I will be ever on my guard for his treachery," Aisling said, nodding. "What would you have me do, my Sovereign?"

"You will tell me in exacting detail every move of this battle," Yartraak said, settling himself upon his massive throne, "and then you will return to your duty anew, keeping careful watch on Cyrus Davidon, leaking his secrets judiciously, keeping his ear and remaining closer to our enemy than he could possibly imagine. The fate of this war rests on Cyrus Davidon, and he has landed upon the wrong side." Yartraak's teeth were bared in a grin that made Aisling feel uncomfortable. "A day may come soon when you will be able to leave this duty behind and return home. You must merely wait for that time."

She nodded at him, but her mind swirled all the while with the possibility. *He has no one else as close to Cyrus as I am, does he?* She kept her thoughts carefully concealed, as ever. *Why would he give up that strategic advantage unless ...* She blinked, as small a reaction as she could allow given the gravity of what she was thinking in the wake of this revelation.

... unless he's planning to have me kill Cyrus.

21.

J'anda

Malpravus parted ways with them out of the gate of the Grand Palace of Saekaj. Walking had become less of a chore for J'anda now, the strength gradually returning to his legs after the hard throttling that the God of Darkness had levied upon his throat. It felt pinched and bruised, and it scratched when he tried to speak or, indeed, even breathe, and thus he kept silent. He found it suited him to some extent, since, after the necromancer had left them behind on the street, J'anda hadn't truly known what to even say to Terian Lepos.

Terian seemed to have his own course in mind, though, walking J'anda carefully toward the first gate to the immediate left of the Sovereign's palace. He could see the manor beyond, a beautifully carved stone house with wooden accents to the facade. He tried to remember who had possessed it when last he'd been in Saekaj and failed. Someone important, that was sure. It was, after all, directly across the street from the House of Shrawn, which had been in Dagonath Shrawn's possession for hundreds of years, possibly even thousands by now.

"Come on," Terian said quietly, surprisingly careful about his placement of J'anda's arm. When J'anda had seen the dark knight in the throne room when he'd regained consciousness, he had been virtually certain that he'd been killed and was now in some dream after death. Then the sensory details of the throne room came flooding back in, the grain of the wood floor against his hand, the oily scent of the Sovereign's own musk, and the darkness only broken by the light of the wall sconces.

"Where are we going?" J'anda asked, taking up more of his own weight as they started down the carriage path to the house.

"Home," Terian said simply and devoid of emotion.

"Whose home?" J'anda asked, grasping further. "House Lepos?"

"No," Terian said, shaking his helmeted head slightly. J'anda had always thought the dark knight's spiked helm made him look as if a metallic cathedral rested atop his skull, ringed with spires. "They're much further down the chain, unfortunately." He seemed to shrug without moving his shoulders much. "This used to be House Lepos, though. Years ago."

"I heard of the fall," J'anda said, finally taking back the last of his weight underfoot and removing his arm from Terian's shoulder, the sleeve of his robe catching on one of the spikes. J'anda unthreaded it delicately. "But of course it only came to me secondhand, and through what I heard when last we both stood in front of the Sovereign."

"Yeah, that was a heady day," Terian said as they stepped closer to the entry to the house. J'anda's head was light and he paid little attention to the sweeping architecture of the place. It was impressive, but it left little impression on his mind, laboring as it was to keep up with his body. "Come on. We'll talk inside."

"All right," J'anda agreed as the door thumped open for him, a guard reaching for it upon their approach. J'anda gave the guards a quick glance and found them covered in livery for a house that looked familiar, but that he had a hard time placing. "House ... Burgvine?"

"Ehrest," Terian answered as they stepped inside a sweepingly appropriate foyer. "House Ehrest."

J'anda contained his frown. Why was Terian taking him into another family's house? Perhaps they were friends of his, and he didn't trust J'anda to walk any great distance? That was a reasonable assumption, J'anda concluded as he felt his legs buckle slightly.

"Come on," Terian said, "up one flight of stairs and we'll get you a place to rest." He paused at the staircase directly in front of them, as though waiting to help J'anda up.

"I am not an invalid," J'anda said, protesting more vociferously than he thought he would have given the circumstances.

"You're just a little injured," Terian said with more grace than the dark knight normally displayed. "I'm not coddling you—"

"I'll be fine," J'anda said.

"Yes, if you rest—"

"I defy you to look so good after being squeezed like an overripe grape by a god," J'anda said, staring him down.

Terian stared right back, and seemed to surrender after a moment's thought. "Fine. Why don't we go talk in private, then?"

J'anda pondered that course, tried to play it out in his head. *What is his game? I was certainly dead before he walked into the room. What did he say to get the Sovereign to reconsider?* "Very well." He swept a hand to indicate that Terian should lead on.

And lead on he did; Terian clumped his way up the stairs, boots falling heavy with every step. He led to a door at the landing and opened it, stepping inside and holding it. Inside was a bedroom, a more ornate and lovely one than he suspected most in Saekaj possessed. Wood furniture made with great skill dotted the room in a style that wouldn't have seemed out of place in the finer houses of Reikonos; the only thing absent was a window.

A wooden mannequin stood in the corner, lit by the candles and a hearth. J'anda recognized it instantly as the sort of figure warriors and knights used to store their armor on when not being worn. He judged it to be roughly Terian's size, and jumped to the automatic conclusion. "This is your room."

"It is," Terian said.

J'anda paused, frowning, eyes still flitting around. "But you share it with someone else."

Terian smiled, but it looked pained. "I'm married. Didn't you know?"

J'anda froze, and his eyebrow crept up his head. "You didn't seem the type, strangely enough. It would seem you've had a busy few months."

Terian shook his head, removing the helm and setting it upon the surface of a tall wooden dresser, ruffling a doily in the process. "I've been married for years."

"That is quite a secret to keep," J'anda said. "But then, I suppose it was hardly the only one you sprang upon us."

"Ouch," Terian said.

"Insulted?"

Terian shrugged. "Fair enough, I suppose. Sorry for not being forthcoming about wanting to kill our esteemed General."

"You say it like you did nothing wrong," J'anda said, making his way to the bed and easing down on it, unconcerned about how it might look.

"I did ..." Terian paused, searched for words. J'anda watched him labor over it, struggling to channel some feeling that writhed beneath the surface. "You know what? I just saved your life."

"As though that absolves you of what you did?"

"You're in Saekaj now, all right?" Terian stared flatly at him. "Which is a terrible place for you to be, especially at this moment in time."

"Speak for yourself."

"I feel comfortable speaking for both of us in this," Terian said, starting to pace in front of him. "I've managed to make my way into the Sovereign's good graces—"

"A curious place for you to be," J'anda said, "and, by my guess, not one in which you will live a terribly long life."

"Now who's speaking for whom?" Terian spoke in a wry tone with an unmistakable air of sadness as he looked right at J'anda. "How long do you have?"

"People keep asking me that," J'anda said with a shrug that was languid, the tiredness settling in on him like a warm blanket, "as though I would somehow know the appointed hour in which death will come for me." He leaned forward on the bed. "If I hadn't come here, I wager I would live longer than you. What is your rank?"

"I'm a general," Terian said, his face cloaked in a tangle of emotions. "In charge of the armies and strategy for the war."

"Hm," J'anda said. "And how did you come to be here, in this place and this time?"

"Malpravus found me as I walked off into the jungle after the bridge." The dark knight's manner was almost sad.

"Just happened to find you?" J'anda didn't bother to keep back the cloud of suspicion.

"He was there for the scourge," Terian said. "Said he sensed death coming."

"That's ... disquieting," J'anda said, resisting the urge to lie back and fall asleep. "So he brought you here and introduced you to his master, where you ... climbed the ladder rather rapidly, it would seem."

"I hold a special place in the Sovereign's esteem."

"How is that?" J'anda asked.

"I keep telling him the truth," Terian said, and when he caught J'anda's look, he smiled. "I know. From me, right? But I mostly do. I don't think anyone else does. It must grow tiresome after a while, being catered to."

"I wouldn't know."

"Nor I," Terian said. "But his generals lie to him, fail to take responsibility for their failures. Like the one today, for example." He sighed. "Did you know Cyrus was taking the army into the Northlands?"

J'anda shook his head, puzzling at that. "He had not mentioned it when I left yesterday."

"Don't bother to lie to me," Terian said, watching him with canny eyes, "I know you're here to spy for Sanctuary."

J'anda felt a chill pass over him. "Yet you save my life? That makes you as guilty as I, in the eyes of the Sovereign. You have betrayed him."

"Yes," Terian said with a nod, grave as J'anda had ever seen the dark knight, his voice low in whisper, "and I mean to betray him further. I just watched Cyrus and the Army of Sanctuary disembowel one of Malpravus's armies in the north. I saw the veiled dagger, the ambush, and I could have stopped it, but oddly … I found I just didn't have any interest in doing so."

J'anda kept his face free of any reaction. "Naturally."

"What do you mean, 'naturally'?" Terian frowned, keeping his eyes on the enchanter. "There isn't anything natural about the insanity I find myself in the middle of these last months. I'm up to my eyeballs in the midst of these fools, these fools who—" he looked around, as though some enemy might be hiding in the shadowed corners of the room, and lowered his voice further, "these fools who think that on the day that the Sovereign rules all Arkaria, it will be some sort of blessed kingdom ruled on high with benevolence and grace rather than the utter and complete destruction of every godsdamned land." The dark knight leaned forward. "I can guess at the origin of your reserve toward me. You hesitate to trust a word coming out of my mouth right now."

J'anda threaded his hands together. "If you were in my place, would you trust a man who has betrayed his own as you have?"

"I picked the wrong father to follow," Terian said, his face dissolving to something that looked considerably more hollow, exhausted. "When it came down it, I picked the path of the father who I hated in life. And that was just another in a long line of my terrible choices."

"Well, as enjoyable as it might be following a self-confessed maker of terrible choices …" J'anda said, making his meaning plain while letting his words drift off.

"I'm hardly the only one in this room making terrible choices at the moment," Terian volleyed back. "You had the death mark, same as I did. You could have stayed in Sanctuary. You weren't … afflicted by your own stupidity—"

"Oh, to trust an incompetent man," J'anda said, nodding his head but not bothering to hide his skepticism. "A man who cannot keep his own life in order, if you'll forgive me saying so, is in a poor position to fix the problems of entire lands. Perhaps you should start smaller, get your own house in order—"

"That's not smaller," Terian said darkly. "That's maybe the largest problem of all."

"Isn't it always?" J'anda said, slumping. "I always find it interesting how people who have little grasp on their own lives and who have made wreckage of everything closest around them are the ones with the most desire to change the world around them. Truly, the force of their opinions about how things should be is like a bellow in one's ear." He looked at Terian. "I sense you are trying to involve me in something, but you must forgive me for my lack of enthusiasm given your current condition."

"The Sovereign is raising the dead," Terian said, voice quiet. "He's somehow come up with an infinite supply of soul rubies, and he's turned loose his necromancers to raise the dead of every battle, bending their will so that even the corpses of our enemies now fight for us."

J'anda felt the tickle of a chill and the urge to rise to his feet, to cast the return spell and flee back to Sanctuary. "This is a carefully guarded secret, I presume?"

Terian nodded. "For a while longer, I suspect. If you were to leave right now, you could tell the Council, word would eventually leak back to Saekaj, and I'd be ..." He ran a finger across his own throat.

"You entrust this to me?" J'anda eyed him carefully. "You truly are a fool."

"You came back here even though you're wanted dead," Terian said. "Who's the greater fool among us?"

"Since you did the same only months ago," J'anda said, "I would not care to gamble between us on that question." The flicker of a candle made the shadows dance upon the wall. "Why do you tell me this?"

"I'll tell you more than that," Terian said. "I've got information about the troll hordes that are aiding the Sovereign. I think we can knock them right out of the war if we did things right." He glanced to the floor, lowering his eyes. "If Cyrus did things right."

J'anda felt a weak laugh escape his lips, born more of tiredness and disbelief than mirth. "If you want to use a man you've tried to kill as your sword at this moment, you're more the fool than me by quite some distance."

"I'm a dark knight," Terian said, looking away again. "I've already confessed I am foolish. Yes, I betrayed my allies. My friends. Myself, really. In some ways, in spite of ... what others might have believed about redemption being a path I could walk, I wonder sometimes if the damage done to my soul along the earlier road is simply too much to come back from. I've laid my life on the line for you today, J'anda. What I'm about to do now is place it your hands." He stepped closer to the enchanter and J'anda watched from his place on the bed, uncertain. "I'm going to find a way to kill the Sovereign," Terian said, grimly serious in a way J'anda had never seen him before. "It is likely to result in my death. But if I can do this thing, then I can die satisfied that I've given our people a fighting chance at wrenching themselves free of the weight upon their shoulders. That I've done one good thing in my life, one good thing that will count for something, that will—"

"Erase from memory all your previous misdeeds?" J'anda asked, shaking his head. "This thing ... it will not make up for what you've done before."

"This isn't about what I've done," Terian said, his eyes glistening. "That's all water down the stream. This is about what I mean to do, the last act to close the play; to sweep clear the stage and give all a new beginning. Yartraak is a tyrant, and he meddles, holds us in the palm of his hand, grip like steel and iron poured over us to keep us in our place—"

"You are out of your mind," J'anda said.

"You have nothing to lose," Terian said.

Except my life, J'anda did not say, *which I will lose soon enough in any case.*

They remained there in silence, each staring at the other, judging in the quiet what the other might be thinking. J'anda, for his part, had thoughts that whirled in his mind, too many to even number. *He means it. I believe that. He truly means to challenge the Sovereign, to plot the demise of the God of Darkness, which is an absolutely insane proposition—*

But it's not as though Yartraak would be the first god to die …

J'anda started to ask a question when a knock sounded at the door, stiff and formal. Terian started, shoulders stiff under his armor, glancing at the entry to the room with suspicion. "Did someone hear us?" J'anda asked, a small thrill of fear running through him.

"Doubtful," Terian said. "My wife and I have tested the quality of the door, in order to determine how private this room is. It would have taken a much louder conversation to be heard in the hallway." He raised his voice. "Enter."

The door opened quietly, and a tall man with a long face stood framed in it. "A guest for you, Lord Lepos."

Terian's expression changed subtly, and not at all pleasantly, at the man's appearance. "Who is it, Guturan?"

"He is here to speak to your guest," Guturan said stiffly, his vek'tag hair suit glimmering in the faint light of the flickering candle as his eyes turned to J'anda, who felt his head spin as the servant's words filled the air in the room. "He says his name is Vracken Coeltes … and he is the head of the Gathering of Coercers."

22.

Aisling

Her meeting with the Sovereign had been uncomfortable, and the revelations it had brought had been even more afflicting than she'd feared. It had left her with little desire to return to Cyrus Davidon, at least at the moment, but his attention was elsewhere for the short term in any case. Her return to Sanctuary had brought with it the news that the warrior in black had indeed placed his name into consideration for Guildmaster, along with Vara and that insufferable idiot Ryin Ayend. Aisling needed only overhear one conversation in the foyer to get the gist and another in the stairs to confirm it.

Cyrus will be Guildmaster, she thought. *Neither of the other two stands an icicle's chance in the Realm of Fire.* She locked herself in her room and summoned flowered emotions of pride and lust, pouring them into a diary entry that made her queasy. Within her mind, she considered the problem more deeply. *Yartraak doesn't want Cyrus dead, at least not yet. Or perhaps he wants him dead, but the tie to Bellarum gives him pause. Whatever the case, Cyrus's life hangs precariously in the balance, and his continued presence as a shard in the Sovereign's flesh is not likely to engender him long life and an eternal pass from the God of Darkness's wrath.*

And here I sit, utterly unprepared to extricate myself—and Norenn, especially—from the circumstances we've been in for years. She finished the diary entry and placed her quill back into the inkwell, rubbing a black smudge between her fingers. *I have only myself to call on, and killing a god with my own blades ...* She ran her hands down to her belt, letting them drift over the hilts, leather wrapped around them up to the quillons, with mystical steel jutting into the short scabbards. *I could get him if I*

121

caught him unawares, perhaps. Sleeping. Distracted, if I climbed to his shoulders, but it would take so many good sawings to open his throat ...

And that's to say nothing of Shrawn, who might be even more difficult. Constantly surrounded by bodyguards of no small skill, and doubtless he has a retinue of healers at his command to bring him back. She shook her head as she pondered it. *I've never had much interest in poison, but black lace would be practically a requirement, as I have no healers of my own to balance the scales.*

In a fair fight, me versus them on open ground, I would lose a thousand times over. She sat at her desk, the chair hard against her backside like the walls of the predicament that boxed her in. *There is no fair fight. Not for them, because they won't allow it, and not for me, because I have no allies. I am alone in this, with the entirety of Saekaj arrayed against me, and all their powers, and all their armies ...*

She took a quick inventory in her head and remembered the newly swelled coin purse at her side. *I'm carrying too much gold—again. Time to make a deposit in Fertiss, I think.* She knew, to the piece, how much she had on hand in the dwarven bank she deposited in, and it was not enough to do much more than buy a home in the country in some land away from the Sovereign's influence. *For now, anyway. If he continues trying to conquer Arkaria with the fervency he's shown thus far, the day will come when no land will be beyond his influence.*

And I'll be another corpse on the pile if I let him and Shrawn have it their way; Norenn will join me, along with most of the civilized world. She'd considered this idea to its natural conclusion more than once, wondering if she might simply enact a jailbreak of sorts, taking Norenn away in hopes that they might find some forgotten corner of the map where they could live quietly.

Shrawn is not the sort to forgive such a slight. And now that the Sovereign has made himself known to me, he would not allow my insolence to pass in any case.

The only ways out now are death or through them, then.

As it's always been.

And all by my lonesome.

She descended the stairs back to the foyer, listening to the clatter of the guardsmen on duty, their armor clanking and clinking as they stood at relaxed attention, waiting to see what the portal would bring them today. Their weapons were always at the ready, prepared for an invasion the like of which they had seen only a few months ago, but their posture was relaxed. *The axe probably won't fall on them today, but they'd be ready for it in seconds if it did.*

Aisling scanned the crowd in the foyer and then the lounge for signs of Verity, but saw not a hint of the elven wizard. Her eyes came to rest on a druid, a young one, human, whose name she did not know. "Would you mind taking me to Fertiss?" she asked, causing him to turn his dark-haired head up to look at her.

"I can't—" He froze as he caught sight of her face, on his feet in a moment, practically standing at attention. "You're her."

There was something akin to a trickling sensation of cold water dripping through her innards at his words. "Yes," she said, resigned. "Can you take me to Fertiss?"

"For him, absolutely," the druid said, hastily raising a hand aloft.

She kept the chilled irritation at his statement to herself, trying to consider how the thief Aisling would handle it. She came to a conclusion in only a second, and it matched her own thoughts on the matter. "You're taking *me* to Fertiss, not Cyrus Davidon."

The druid's jaw dropped mid-spell, and the glint of magic that had begun to appear at his fingertips vanished in an instant. "I didn't ... I didn't mean to say—"

"Just take me to Fertiss," Aisling snapped, letting her true feelings out and glancing away from the druid at the same time. She stared at the hearth as the winds of his spell swelled around her, becoming a wall of power and force, the air alive as it stripped the background from the room she was in and replaced it with another as though it were lifting her from where she was and carrying her away in a tornado.

When the winds faded, she stood in a courtyard next to the portal, the sun gleaming down on the snow-capped peaks that surrounded her. The foreign quarter of Fertiss was built between the mountains, and roads stretched off into the domes of the high swells. In contrast to those sections that had been built underground, this part of the city had been constructed here in the light of day and dark of night, suitable for guests of the dwarves.

"Wait here," Aisling said, only slightly less ferociously than when giving her last statement to him. The druid nodded quickly, cowed, and she felt a little pity for him. *At least he need not fear death from my anger, which is more than I can say for those who lord their station over me as I just did over him.* She spun and headed down the wide path to her right, passing squared buildings that were built into the side of the mountain road, the shops and cafes of the locals who wanted to capture foreign coin.

She was nearly to the entry tunnel when she felt the tickle of a presence behind her. It was a subtle thing, like a footstep on the stone walk that carried no sign of a foot being responsible. She passed the glass window of a jewel merchant's store, grand and filled with dwarven craftsmanship. Rubies, diamonds, emeralds and countless other priceless stones glimmered in the light, set in gold and silver rings, platinum necklaces, and even tiaras. She paused and looked in the glass, pretending to let a bejeweled set of earrings catch her eye.

In truth, though, she stared at the faint reflection in the glass before determining that, in fact, there was no one behind her. Fertiss was silent this morning, the foreign quarter as quiet as she'd ever seen it. The war, she knew.

Her eyes traveled along the shop wall to an alley not ten feet away, perfectly placed between the jeweler and a baker. The chimney puffed above and the smell of fresh, hard-ground dwarven bread filled the air. She turned lazily, a woman without a care in the world, and lingered close to the wall as she headed back toward the tunnel. *My trip to the bank will have to wait until—*

As she passed the alley mouth she heard the footstep again and whirled into the dark space between the buildings. She had her blade out before she dodged into the mouth of the gap herself, listening to the sound of a footstep in a puddle of still water, ripples radiating out from where her spell-clad follower splashed while regaining their footing.

Aisling pursued, blade in hand, cloak falling off behind her as she came at her follower. She couldn't entirely see them, but the splash of the puddle had covered them well enough to leave beads refracting in the dark, the shine of the sun hinting at their presence and where they stood. With a leap, she reached out and was able to grab ahold of a throat, shoving an invisible figure against the wall. "Shouldn't have followed me, Verity," she said. "You could give me the courtesy of five minutes a day without hovering over my—"

Aisling drove the blade right at the throat of her tormentor. *She can die here, in Fertiss; no one will be able to trace it back to me, and I'll be clear for a spell while they put someone else in Sanctuary to "handle" me. It'll be a bit messy, and mysterious, but at least I won't have that elven bitch breathing in my ear every—*

Her blade caught in mid air, stopped as still as if she'd hit a rock with it. It froze in plain sight before her eyes, held as effortlessly as if she were pushing against an immutable wall. It stayed there for only a second before there was a slight flash that forced her to avert her eyes, and the dagger was shoved roughly back, forcing her along with it. Her back fell lightly against the opposite wall, more the result of a push than a blow. When her eyes sprang open again, she kept the shock off her face only through long practice.

The man standing before her was certainly not Verity. In fact, he was not anyone she had ever met before in her life. "Who are you?" she hissed, at once curious and wary at how easily he'd repulsed her attack.

He was dark elven, that much was sure, and his hair was as black as the coal they'd burned when she was a child, before her family had switched to wood. It was slicked back all the way to the nape of his neck, and his features were sharp. He was thin, possessing a build that certainly did not hint at his ability to throw back a bladed attack, but his hands were covered with leather gloves. *How did he—?*

His lips were curled with amusement, but not of a scornful kind. Aisling had seen plenty of that in her life, enough to know the maliciously entertained glimmer in someone's eyes when they scorned their lessers. There was none of that here, and in fact there might even have been a hint of … kindness?

"Hello, Yalina," the man said, causing Aisling's jaw to drop at the sound of her own—real—name, one left behind years ago, one that she had not heard spoken aloud in so long. "I wonder if we might have a talk."

23.

Terian

Terian descended the staircase with J'anda at his side, the enchanter looking paler blue, almost the color of a cloudless sky, his wrinkles the only dark spots on his skin. *Who is this Vracken Coeltes?* Terian wondered. *Not that I know a great many enchanters, but wasn't the head of the Gathering of Coercers one of the Largesh family?*

"You must be Terian Lepos," Vracken Coeltes said, his hands clasped before him. He wore an ornate robe, even for an enchanter, with stitching in rectangular shapes that draped over his shoulder, unobstructed by the vestment that pronounced his style of magic. "We haven't had the pleasure."

"No one who has met you has ever had pleasure in doing so," J'anda said, whispering at Terian's side. He said it at a volume that was audible to the entire room, and Terian almost opened his mouth to rebuke the enchanter before realizing that he was speaking to Coeltes, not Terian. He raised an eyebrow but kept his thoughts to himself. *Whoever this Coeltes is, it would appear he and J'anda are not exactly old friends.*

Coeltes grinned broadly, his skin pockmarked by craters all over his face. Terian stared at him, wondering at the obvious imperfections. *He's an enchanter, but he doesn't bother to hide his blemishes; he's either confident or he doesn't care.* "J'anda Aimant. So you took me up on my invitation."

"I noticed you were not there when I spoke with the Sovereign," J'anda said as Terian stopped at the base of the stairs. "It would seem you were not good for your word."

Coeltes's smile froze then broadened. "I'm afraid I wasn't

informed of your passage through the gates, nor any stage of your arrival."

"It is certain that there will be other things I deign not to inform you of," J'anda said coolly, "now that the Sovereign has taken me into his service."

Coeltes cocked his head, lips pursed in amusement, as though he'd somehow recaptured the lead in a race. "Regarding that—you'll be working for me in the Gathering of Coercers."

"No, I won't," J'anda said, placid, a slight smile on his face. "I am a spy in the service of the Sovereign. I will be reporting directly to him."

"Ahh," Coeltes said, holding up a finger as he reached into his robes with the other. He produced a piece of parchment. "The Sovereign was concerned. As you've told your guild, whom you'll be spying on, of course, that you've come here to make amends," Coeltes's smile was barely contained by the edges of his lips, "we came up with, shall we say, an acceptable story to cover your activities. You're a spy here, a double agent." Coeltes raised an eyebrow. "Or is it triple? I can never keep track of these things."

Terian's blood cooled. *He knows J'anda's lying, too ...*

"I have yet to hear a reason why any of my activities concern you, Vracken," J'anda said, showing a sign of ire.

"Because, naturally, you require a cover story to tell your guildmates," Coeltes said, lips back to pursing in amusement. "And it is this—you are working in the Gathering of Coercers, instructing our next generation of enchanters, as only you could, you talented being, you." He raised a fist and waved it slightly, not once looking as though he were anything but entertained by their exchange. "You will be reporting directly to me in this entire endeavor." Coeltes glanced at Terian. "I trust you can keep this secret, being a General of the Sovereign?"

Terian blinked back to the present moment, his mind whirling with all the implications of what had just been placed before him. "I ... think I've already forgotten whatever the hell you were trying to convey there."

"Excellent," Coeltes said, bringing his hands together. "You'll be living in the Gathering, of course, being an instructor ..."

Terian turned to look at J'anda's face. It was frozen, utterly, and the horror beneath the sickening rage was obvious. *What the hell did this guy do to you, J'anda?*

"Do you hear me?" Coeltes's amusement was gone now, replaced by sternness, disgust. His lips twisted and his smile was rough satisfaction coupled with triumph. "You're under my command, now."

"Of course," J'anda said, and now his face was back to relaxed. His arms hung stiff at his sides, crossing where he massaged one hand with the other, the wrinkled skin smoothing out as his fingers worked over it.

"You look like the skin discarded from a piece of peeled fruit," Coeltes said, looking J'anda over. "I hope you haven't lost all your ability with your youth."

"I suppose we'll see," J'anda said. "Won't we?"

"Oh, I won't," Coeltes said, grinning again. "Don't get into the weeds of teaching, myself. I have the whole Gathering to run, after all. Always supervision to be done, especially now. Traitors to ferret out. Disloyalty to expose." He ran his dark tongue under the row of his front teeth, which were yellowed with black spotting. "Like your friend Zieran, for example. Treason is everywhere." He leaned forward, smiling conspiratorially, and lowered his voice to a whisper. "It could even be in this very room." He raised his eyebrows, and cackled. "Why don't we leave?" It was not a suggestion.

"I need to talk to this man," Terian said, looking at Coeltes, whose eyes flashed with anger as he looked at Terian, sizing him up.

"About what?" Coeltes asked.

"About the war," Terian said, "and as a ranking General in the Sovereign's service, I get to question our spies any time I damned well please, Guildmaster." He snapped the title out, and watched Coeltes scramble to hide his anger at being addressed in such a cavalier manner. "Your man will be along when I'm done with him, and not before."

"He's no man of mine," Coeltes said tightly. "Wouldn't want there to be any misunderstandings, since there are questions that have to be addressed with the Sovereign—tomorrow, I might add."

"Excellent," J'anda said faintly. "I look forward to it."

"Do you?" Coeltes asked, a most peculiar smile upon his face. "Do you, indeed?"

"I'm looking forward to you leaving my house," Terian said, his patience already worn thinner than a cheap carpet from Sovar. "Get to that, will you?"

"As you say, General," Coeltes said with a bow, far more chipper than Terian would have expected from the enchanter given how hard he'd just been thrown down in his place. "Though ... this is the house of Ehrest, is it not?"

"Of which I am a part," Terian said, gesturing toward the door. "Guturan!" he called out, and heard the motion of the steward on the landing behind him. "See this man out, will you please?"

"Pleased to make your acquaintance," Coeltes said, nodding at Terian. "I expect we'll meet again."

"I certainly hope not," Terian said as Guturan Enlas swept down the stairs, past J'anda, who stood transfixed at the base of the steps, "but I suppose I've seen worse misfortunes in my time."

"Is that so?" Coeltes asked, seemingly out of politeness only; his eyes were narrowed.

"Yes, once I was decapitated by the Siren of Fire in the trials of Purgatory," Terian said. "That was a personal low point, right there with this moment, I think." He glanced at J'anda, who was unmoving. "You want to lord your power over my friend, best do it while I'm not around, or else you'll see how the hierarchy of Saekaj works when it's used against you, for once."

"As you say, General," Coeltes said, following Enlas toward the door, which was now opened for him, "and when will you be leaving for the war again?"

"Whenever I'm godsdamned good and ready!" Terian snapped. *He's rubbing my face in the fact that I won't be able to keep him from J'anda for long.* "Why don't you—"

J'anda placed a firm hand on Terian's shoulder, drawing his attention and shutting him up. "I'll be along in a short while," the enchanter said to Coeltes.

Coeltes acknowledged his victory with a smile. "Don't be too long. You're not yet allowed to walk about without guards. Not until we've settled the question of your status."

With that, the enchanter vanished through the door, which Guturan shut behind him. Terian stared at the steward, who seemed to care little for anything he'd just seen. Probably already mentally composing his report to Dagonath Shrawn. "He's a real charmer," Terian said. "I thought you enchanters were supposed to be gracious."

J'anda answered with a hollow voice, as if stirred from a particularly troubled slumber. "It depends on the enchanter. Some of us operate from a place of peace, working our magic almost with the cooperation of our subjects, using their thoughts in harmony with our spells to create a seductive realm of imagery for their imagination."

"Right, heart's desire," Terian said, staring at Guturan, whose back was to the door, standing stiffly at attention. "I ... remember that."

"There is another way that enchanters can operate, another basis for our spells," J'anda said. "An easier way, in the short term."

"What's that?" Terian asked.

"Fear," J'anda said, hand drifting over to rest on the staircase. "To pluck the strings of the mind that wrap around fearful ideas, the things that drive us, worry us, frighten us. Every enchanter gets to choose the path of their magic early in their training. My method is ... more complicated, let us say."

"Figures he'd have chosen fear," Terian said, glancing at J'anda. "It radiates off of him, the desire to push people about with whatever force he carries."

"Indeed," J'anda said, quiet again. "Did you wish to finish our discussion?"

"I don't know," Terian said, glancing at Guturan, who was still watching them with undisguised hunger in his eyes. "Did we have anything else to discuss?" *How do I let J'anda know that Guturan can't be trusted? Oh. Right.* "Because if so, we should find a quieter place to do so." *If he's not in on this with me, I'm completely stuck. Because there is no other conduit by which I can get information to Sanctuary without his help.*

Well, it's probably impossible.

"I think there might be a thing or two to talk about now," J'anda said, nodding, and made a weak hand gesture toward the stairs. "I hate to be presumptive, but ... shall we discuss it?"

"I can think of nothing I'd rather talk about," Terian said and watched an almost imperceptible cloud cross Guturan Enlas's face as he followed J'anda back up the stairs toward his room.

24.

Aisling

"You seem surprised that I know your real name, Yalina," the dark elf said, smiling lightly at her.

"No one knows my real name," Aisling said, the chill of the mountain air creeping in through her cloak and seeping onto her skin.

"Oh, that's a terrible thing to say," the man said, grimacing. "Your parents know your real name, don't they?"

"But they don't know the name Aisling Nightwind," she replied, tension running heavy across her shoulders.

"It was a rather poetic choice," the man said, nodding. His eyes glittered, like he was in on a particularly clever jest. He stood shadowed in the alley's shade, the eaves of the shops on either side keeping the daylight above from revealing him totally. "How did you come to it?"

"How do you know about it?" Aisling asked, ready to spring. The smell of rosewater reached her nose, as though the man were lightly perfumed.

"I know many things," he said. "Like the predicament you find yourself in. I'm fully apprised of your problems."

"Are you aware that my biggest one at the moment involves a stranger confronting me in an alleyway in a threatening manner?"

"I'm not threatening you," he said, holding his hands out. "I didn't let you stab me, but I have no threats. No ill intentions."

"Is that so," Aisling said.

"That is so," he said, sincerely. "In fact, I've come to help you."

"Help me with what?" she asked, taking a sideways step, never turning away from him.

"Well, first of all," he said, with an incline of his head in deference, "let me give you my name, since I have all of yours and you have none of mine. Maybe that'll put us on slightly more even footing. You may call me Genn."

"Never heard that name before," she said, not daring to look away from him, even to blink.

"I'd never met anyone who chose the name Aisling before today," Genn said lightly. "Yet here we are, Genn and Aisling. Unless you'd prefer I call you Yalina. I could, I suppose, but it seems a bit odd since you've done everything you could to leave that name behind—"

"What do you want?" Aisling asked, feeling an uncontrollable quiver run through her body.

"I told you, I want to help you," Genn said, spreading his hands wide. He smiled. "I know it's hard for you to believe, sandwiched as you are between—oh, let's just list them—Yartraak, Dagonath Shrawn, Cyrus Davidon, Sanctuary ... This could go on for a while, actually ..."

"How can you help me?" Aisling asked. *He can't possibly know everything. He's just trying to get me to talk, looking for information.*

"Well, I think you need a friend, first of all," Genn said, "but I suspect you wouldn't simply accept my friendship if I offered, so let's put that away for a bit." He took a step to the side, causing her to mirror him, then did it again, grinning at her. "Shall we keep circling each other?"

"I could try and stab you again if you want to just get closer."

"And I could throw the attack right back at you—again," he said indifferently. "If you want to try, go ahead. It's not an illusion; your attacks are not going to find their mark with me. And ... honestly, would you want them to? I'm the only person who's offered to actually help you in years. What does it say about you that you're in a hurry to kill me if you could?"

That I don't trust you, Aisling thought. *That I don't think you're here to help me at all.* But that was not how she answered. "That I'm careful. That I've been burned before—"

"Ah, yes." Genn nodded. "Shrawn's got great big claws in you. Yanked you around for years, made you do ... unspeakable things." He twisted his lips in disgust. "And now, now you're right in the line, aren't you? Had a big meeting with Yartraak this morning? They'll never let you go now, and you can feel it, can't you?" He took a half step toward her and she did not move, though she tensed. "It's like the table odds in a game of gvarante, they just doubled against you with a move of the pieces. Now you've got to find a way to extricate yourself from Shrawn's paw with the Sovereign sticking his ugly face into the situation."

"I do as I'm told," Aisling said, ready to spring back if he took so much as another step toward her.

"The sad part about it all," Genn said, his hands fastened behind him now, a comically tall and thin statue, his sharp features perfectly carved out of blue skin, "is that if you weren't spying on Sanctuary, they would be the perfect allies for you in this situation. They're the natural enemies of your current masters, with more than a few reasons to want to give Yartraak and the Sovereignty a bloody nose, but because you're actively betraying them, it's rather unlikely they'd help you, isn't it?"

"There's not a lot of help anywhere for people like me."

"There are no people like you," Genn said, serious. "Believe me. I've looked."

She took that step back, widening the circle between them. Genn did not move to match her. "Who are you?"

"An interested party," Genn said.

"Interested in what?"

"Helping you break out of your predicament safely," he said, keeping his hands behind him. "I want to see you get out of Shrawn's grasp. I want you to have that revenge you've been hiding away in your heart, barely daring to believe in." He leaned forward slightly, stooping as he whispered. "I want to help you carve Dagonath Shrawn's head from his neck."

"That's madness," Aisling said. "Shrawn is the most powerful man in Saekaj." *Who is this ... Genn? Someone who Shrawn pissed off in the Shuffle?*

"He is now," Genn said, breaking into a smile once more. His teeth were white and even. "He doesn't have to be forever, though."

"What did Shrawn do to you?" she asked, watching him with a canny look.

"Shrawn didn't do anything to me," Genn said, straightening back up. "It's you and Saekaj and Sovar he's stepped all over."

"So you want to help me out of the kindness of your heart?"

Genn looked down the alley toward the back, where the rocky side of the mountain sloped up, then past her toward the road in front of the shops. "I see you're in trouble, and I don't see anyone else offering help. I wouldn't call it the kindness of my heart, exactly, but I'm not asking for anything from you. And I'm not asking you to do anything you weren't going to do anyway."

"You're one of Shrawn's spies," she said, shaking her head.

"If Shrawn suspected who you were," Genn said, "he'd have your family dragged into the Depths before the end of the day on made-up charges just to be sure that he had every point of leverage against you covered. You're too important to him at the moment to leave anything to chance. He's certain he has you entirely figured out, and it absolutely tickles me that he has not the slightest idea how badly he's misjudged you. It's all the more amusing because it's a mistake that Dagonath Shrawn *never* makes. The man with eyes and ears everywhere fails to realize you grew up not a thousand meters from his front door because he thinks you come from a place far from him, a place he watches but does not truly understand. A place he fears."

"Sovar," Aisling said.

Genn tapped his nose and then returned his hand behind his back. "I don't expect you to trust a stranger in an alley. You and I, though, we're more alike than you think. Let me play this out for you, because you have three choices, as I see it: first, you can ignore me and continue to do whatever you think Shrawn wants you to do, hoping that someday you'll worm your way out of his service. Perhaps he'll let you go, but I think we both know that's … *unlikely*." He put enough sarcasm into it that to tell her exactly what he thought of that option. "Second, you could turn yourself in to Sanctuary, hoping for their good graces. You could, after all, produce Verity, which would perhaps give you some favor or forgiveness, and perhaps help convince Cyrus Davidon of the sincerity of your repentance. Of course, after such an admission, he would be unlikely to help you, and thus Norenn would suffer a terrible death."

A silence fell over the alley, and Aisling looked over her shoulder toward the street behind her. No sound came from the avenue, the road quiet as it had been when she walked along it moments earlier.

When she turned back, Genn was only inches from her face. Burying her instinct to jump, she simply met his gaze. "And third?"

"Third is really two options," Genn said, his breath cinnamon and light, filling her nostrils with its pleasant scent. "You try and kill Shrawn and free your friend. Without my help, you will almost certainly die. It will not be short. It will not be kind, nor in your sleep. There will be blood, there will be torture, and pain, and agony of the sort that Yartraak and Shrawn revel in."

"How does that change with your help?" she asked, scarcely believing she'd asked.

Genn studied her carefully. "Perhaps it doesn't. Perhaps there is no help for you."

"Then I'm no better off with your help than without it—" She turned to leave, and he swooped alongside her silently, cutting off her retreat.

"I'm being honest with you," Genn said, bowing his neck to put them eye-to-eye. He wasn't terribly tall, but it still required some stooping. "I doubt you hear much of that these days. My help—it might mean your survival, or it might not. I'm hardly a seer of the future. But I know you'll have a better chance with it than without it."

"And if you're really just one of Shrawn's spies?" she asked. The mouth of the alley was only feet away; she could reach it in seconds.

"If I worked for Shrawn, he wouldn't be living in a manor house," Genn said. "He'd be sitting on a throne."

What did Shrawn do to you? she wondered again. "How can you help me?" she asked.

Genn smiled. "Well, I can warn you about some dangers you're going to face, for one. I can give you a plan, for second."

"What do you get out of being my co-conspirator?" she asked, and her eyes flicked to the mouth of the alley again.

Genn paused before answering. "Right now you're the slave of a cruel, sadistic, evil man who is the loyal servant of the God of Darkness, and they've exerted control over your will, your spirit, your life and your body. Honestly … what do you imagine that I could ask that would be worse than all that?"

I can imagine quite a lot. "You don't want to quibble over the price of your assistance?" Aisling asked.

"I will not ask anything of you, when it comes to price," Genn said. "Though when the moment comes, you may ask more of me. That will require a different sort of payment."

"The consultation is free," she said, looking toward the sky beyond, "but the help will cost me. Is that it?"

"Something of that sort," Genn said with a smile. "What do you say?"

He doesn't work for Shrawn. She chewed her lip, trying to make it look like she was trying to decide. *So, who does he work for? Or what does he represent? He could betray me at any moment, and seems to know my very thoughts, things I would never dare to speak aloud.* Her eyes flitted to the side, though her decision was already made.

"Do you wish to continue the charade of thinking it over?" Genn asked. "Or shall we get down to the business of planning your next move?"

"I could use some help," she agreed reluctantly. *And if you are who I think you are ... you might just be the kind of help I need.*

25.

J'anda

This is perhaps the maddest scheme I have ever participated in, and under the guidance of a man so singularly untrustworthy that if he had not just saved my life, I might have ended his given half an opportunity.

J'anda's thoughts ran in a continuous spiral, spinning almost uselessly in circles that grew ever tighter, permitting no thought to stray far from the track. *No chance to deviate from this spin that I am, which is rather hilarious, given that being deviant is what got me into such trouble here in the first place ...*

He walked down the main avenue of Saekaj, the luminescent ceiling of the cavern glowing softly overhead and Terian's plan rattling in his head. He had his task, and the first phase was a simple enough one. *What is the most insane part of this? That I'm taking cues from the dark knight who betrayed Sanctuary by trying to kill our General? Or that I think he's correct in his plan, in his assessment of the Sovereignty's weaknesses?*

Or perhaps it's being here, in this place, with my destiny wedded to the Sovereign once more.

He raised his eyes and saw the markets ahead. It hadn't been but an hour or two since he had last passed this way, trailing his string of guards. He wondered how that had worked out for them; hopefully not too poorly. *I would hate to think I caused their deaths.*

Though the way things will go from here on ... it is quite likely that theirs will only be the first of the deaths I am responsible for.

He looked to the Gathering of Coercers, a mighty building carved into the wall against the side of the cavern of Saekaj. It held the emblem of the guild above its double doors, and was built directly into the rock, giving it room to expand into the solid backing of the chamber. J'anda had not been here in a hundred years, had not seen this symbol above the doors, had not wanted to remember anything of it—not the swelling happiness of the best of times, of the triumphs, nor the gut-clenching horror of the last day.

You took everything from me, Vracken. Everything. And I let you have it. Now you think you will take the rest … and I have to let you.

He came to stand before the stone doors, keeping his head down, not looking up at the carved symbol. He knew every line of it in any case, and he knew it would fill him with the same disgust as looking at the wax seal on Coeltes's letter had.

We come to it at last. No more cowardly delays; no more running, no more illusions. He cracked a smile. *I have no illusions remaining, in any case. All the ones of my youth have disappeared.*

He pushed against the door and found it more solid than it had been in his youth. It moved subtly, heavy stone carved with lines to give it texture, outlines of angles and forms. It was hardly art; it was more the idle efforts of a craftsman with little imagination trying to make the doors something more than plain. The ridges felt hard against his hand, but J'anda shoved against them and entered the quiet foyer of the Gathering of Coercers.

The lamps burned with their sweet, oily smell. J'anda took it all in, allowing just enough of his memories to serve as a guide. It was larger than the foyer of the house of Ehrest and able to house over a hundred enchanters in training easily. His eyes settled on Vracken Coeltes, who waited in the middle of the room alone.

The Gathering's guildhall was quiet, ordered. J'anda sensed the hand of a tyrant at work. It was hard to imagine that anyone lived in this place. J'anda had seen more life in the dead city in the Realm of Darkness when last he had been there.

"Here you are," Coeltes said, holding a staff to his side. It was a familiar thing, the weapon. J'anda had seen it before, more times than he could count—the staff of the Guildmaster, passed from each head of the Gathering to his successor.

"Here I am," J'anda agreed, giving Coeltes what he wanted. *He wants me to see it now, in private, where he can enjoy imagining the jealousy that burns inside me at his possession of that which should have—by all rights—been mine.* And so he stared at the long staff, a hardwood that came to a tip with metal edges that clenched an orb in the middle. "I report for duty, Guildmaster."

Coeltes smiled, thinly, without a hint of genuine pleasure. "The Sovereign has plans for you. Of this you are aware, yes?"

"I submitted myself to his use," J'anda said, placing his hands into the sleeves of his robe, hiding them from Coeltes's view. The meaning of gesture was obvious—concealment, of intentions, of words. *I will give him what he wants, what he expects. Trying to convince Coeltes I am loyal to the Sovereign would be a failing endeavor in any case. Loyalty matters little to him; he would never view me as anything other than a rival to be destroyed as expediently as possible.* "I imagine he would come up with some thoughtful endeavor for me to partake of."

"And so you shall," Coeltes said, nodding. "You will return to Sanctuary immediately to listen in on them. You will stay there until tomorrow, at which point you will return for judgment by the Sovereign." At this, Coeltes appeared immeasurably pleased. "He wants to … insure that you've mended your deviant ways."

J'anda held back his immediate reaction. *I was expecting this. This is planned. It was to be, all along.*

Now I merely have to cope with the challenge.

"Repeat your orders," Coeltes said, using the staff of the Guildmaster to make a gesture at J'anda.

"Return to Sanctuary," J'anda said. "Spy. Come back tomorrow and present myself for judgment to the Sovereign, and prove myself … changed."

Coeltes chuckled under his breath. "Yes. Of course we both know that a cave cress cannot change its scent, but I imagine it will be quite the entertainment to see you try, at least for poor Zieran's sake."

J'anda caught the hint. "I will see you tomorrow, I suppose."

"I suppose you will," Coeltes said, sweeping away, his robes behind him, the staff of the Guildmaster high in his grasp, "because if you don't …" And he walked up the stairs without needing to finish. The meaning was plain enough.

Because if I don't, J'anda finished it with a surprisingly cool lack of worry, *Zieran will be killed—slowly, painfully … and it will be all my fault.*

26.

J'anda

The Sovereign's red eyes glared at J'anda out of the red darkness of the throne room. The enchanter's breath was caught in his throat, and bile hung on the back of his tongue where he'd lost the battle against his nerves less than an hour earlier, when he had been escorted through the streets of Saekaj with thirty guards arrayed closely around him, a mix of warriors and spell casters, with a few rangers at a distance, bows drawn. While it had hardly been the most humiliating experience of his life, neither had it been one he would recall fondly.

The oily smell of the throne room was pronounced, a thick, penetrating scent that wrestled its way up his nasal passages as he tried to meet the Sovereign's gaze fearlessly. "I present myself to you, Lord Yartraak," J'anda said. Coeltes lurked in the darkness next to the tall throne, the staff of the Guildmaster curiously absent. He'd seen Coeltes stalking along behind him while he was escorted through the streets as well, probably hoping that J'anda would attempt an escape that could result in his death.

"You do indeed," the Sovereign said, his voice high. J'anda maintained a respectful distance. *Let Coeltes stay close enough to crawl up the Sovereign's arse.* "I have received your message, and made preparations accordingly."

J'anda concealed his urge to smile as Coeltes's smugly satisfied expression dissolved into a flurry of blinks, his lips drawing into a straight line. *Will he dare ask? How assured are you of your place in the Sovereign's order, Vracken?*

Coeltes seemed to be at war with himself for a very long moment, but ultimately he said nothing. J'anda buried his disappointment. *Pity. It would have been fun to watch you question the Sovereign.*

"You come before me claiming to be a changed man, J'anda Aimant," Yartraak said, his sharply pointed claws scratching against the arms of his throne. "You are … prepared to prove this change?"

The bile threatened to surge forth again, but J'anda controlled it barely. "I am changed, your grace. It has been a century since I left this place, since I committed my crime. Since I wandered from the path you set forth. Truly, I did not know what I was doing, what I was thinking, when I committed my initial affront. Perhaps it was the … impetuousness of youth, misguided …" He had prepared these words, yet still found them utterly distasteful in every way, and almost as damaging to his nerves as giving voice to the phrase "deviant" had been even when he was safely within the walls of Sanctuary. "I have returned, as I told you, to save the life of Zieran Lacielle, who stands accused of treachery for communicating with me." He bowed his head. "I can claim the association only for what it is." He glanced at Coeltes, who was staring at him with undisguised loathing. "She is my lover."

Coeltes looked choked, standing small against the leg of the mighty throne of Saekaj. Was he expecting this? No, surely not, by his reaction. What was he expecting, then? "He could be lying," Coeltes said, but it came out almost a sputter.

"Yes," the Sovereign said, still stroking his chin. "You are prepared to convince us, then?"

J'anda bowed, lightly, and smiled even more so. "I am, of course, prepared to bow to your will. Anything to prove my sincerity to you, my Sovereign." He saw Coeltes once again twitch with unrestrained rage. "If I may only speak with Zieran beforehand …?"

"There are cessation spells about the entire palace at this moment," Yartraak said darkly. "You will not escape me again as you did when last you stood before this throne to answer for crimes."

"I have no more desire to run," J'anda said, shaking his head. "This is a time for proving myself to you." He kept the outrage, the horror, the disgust, buried behind the mask of a smile he wore as his illusion for today. There was no magic involved, of course, just thorough preparation and a hard realization that this was the only road.

"Bring her in," the Sovereign's voice echoed through the throne room. The doors opened at the end of the passage, the squeak of hinges and the rattle of metal knobs echoing down the long chamber. J'anda turned his head to look at saw her there, walking under her own power.

Zieran Lacielle was of an age with him, and though she had not suffered the rapid decline he'd experienced in Luukessia, she still looked unnaturally drawn and tired. *The Depths have a way of doing that to a body.* She had a slight drag in her gait, as though she'd been injured in the leg at some point and had not had it healed, or healed properly, at least. Her black hair was carefully coiffed, which was not something he'd anticipated. She also wore a full-length dress that looked as though a member of the Sovereign's own harem had surrendered it. *He truly did take time to prepare her rather than simply have her dragged up from the Depths in rags, worn and bloodied.*

Her eyes alighted with his and he saw pain reflected there, almost a resignation, and he knew her mind. *She thinks I'm doomed to die. Were I in her place, perhaps I would think the same; after all, it is not many who return unharmed from the Sovereign's death mark.*

"J'anda," she said, stopping a few feet from him, head held high. She had the cheekbones of nobility, which he knew she was. She stopped short of calling him friend, or acknowledging him in any way but formally, as though somehow it would spare him association with her, the prisoner. *If she were thinking, she would want to spare herself association with me, the traitor.*

But Zieran was never that sort of person. He turned his head, ever so slightly, to look at Vracken Coeltes.

"Zieran Lacielle," the Sovereign said, voice booming out over the room, "you stand accused of consorting with a known traitor, an exile." J'anda watched her for reaction; there was none. Zieran was as staid as he'd ever seen her. "J'anda Aimant has returned to me to make amends for his personal betrayals, and I have accepted his restitution. Conditionally."

That tipped Zieran's head slightly to the side, and her eyes found his furtively. *What have you done?* he could read there.

He smiled at her, faintly. "I've told the Sovereign about us. About how we've maintained our affections over the years, and how we—"

"That's enough," Coeltes said, cutting him off. The Guildmaster's voice lashed at him with anger, and J'anda knew he was wise to the game being played. *The Sovereign would not care if I spoke my alibi straight to her, but Coeltes is cannier … or perhaps simply cares more about the outcome of this particular lie than the Sovereign does.*

J'anda darted his eyes back to Zieran and saw the surprise there, concealed under the weariness, the fatigue. There was only one logical lie that could get him out of his particular predicament, after all, and it didn't take him spelling it out for her to make the easy leap. "My heart dances to see you again, my love," Zieran said, with all the restraint one would expect from a lady of Saekaj.

"My lips profess their sadness at the prolonged absence of yours," J'anda said, trying to sound overly poetic. *Sentiment should stir a reaction faster than anything else, if memory serves …*

"I tire of this," the Sovereign said. "J'anda Aimant, you will take your lover and prove yourself a changed man." He waved his clawed hand.

"As you would have it, my Sovereign," J'anda said, and bowed his head. He looked to Zieran and offered his arm. This was the moment, the tentative moment that he knew he would come to in this desperate gambit. He kept from swallowing hard. *Now both our lives are on the line, and truly this time; there will be no trip to the Depths should we fail this task. It will be death, here and now, for both of us—me for my lies, and Zieran for outliving her perceived usefulness.* He could see Coeltes out of the corner of his eye, stirring with interest. The guildmaster wore a very slight smile, knowing that their fates hung in the balance of Zieran's response.

"It has been so long, my love," Zieran said, taking his arm. A smile that looked sincere only up to the lines of her eyes was perched on her lips. He could see the concern there—and knew it was not only for her own life, but for what he was being asked to do—what he was being forced to do. *And she as well, truly, for we are in this together, tragically.* "I would gladly show you my happiness at seeing you here again, safe and whole."

"Then let us do so," J'anda said, feeling a strange sense of relief coupled with a welling of sorrow within. He placed his other hand upon the one she threaded over his upper arm and started to walk her out of the throne room, his stomach protesting at that which his mind knew was coming. He held his breath, trying to surrender to the inevitability of what needed to happen in the following minutes.

I need merely do this one thing—this one, agonizingly difficult thing … and the Sovereign will be assured of my … change. His brow furrowed even as her hand remained draped on his arm. *And then … then it will be time to start planning the next move, once Cyrus and the rest return from their mission in Gren.*

Then it will be time to find a way to point Sanctuary at the true menace of Saekaj, and start working to kill this tyrant.

27.

Terian

Terian stood under a tall tree, with twisted boughs, and watched from under the hood of his dark cloak as Cyrus Davidon approached with J'anda at his side. He and the enchanter had been planning this moment for weeks, trying to find the right time to attempt to win the warrior over to their cause. It had taken a fortnight before things had seemed to align properly, and word of the election of Cyrus to Sanctuary Guildmaster had reached Terian's ears only this morning, after J'anda had already set out to collect Cyrus for the meeting. *This had better work.*

It has to.

The enchanter seemed to be struggling with the walk from the gnomish town nearby, his aged body flagging with each step. "I need a staff, I think," J'anda said as he drew closer to the tree where Terian waited for them both. He'd planned this conversation in his head a dozen times, a hundred, and yet he still had no idea how it would flow. "A walking stick. Something."

"At least you can just teleport back," Terian said. "Rather than walk back to town." Cyrus was watching him, fixed on him, and the look on the warrior—the Guildmaster of Sanctuary's—face was one of mild confusion, the sort he always wore when he was puzzling something out. *Please use your reason, Cyrus. Don't make this into a battlefield. Not now. We have so little time ...*

"I know you," Cyrus said, as Terian drew back his cowl around his shoulders. "You sonofa—"

"I wasn't exactly expecting a warm greeting from you," Terian said, feeling perhaps more tentative than he had at any juncture in his entire life. "But I hope you can at least put aside your anger for this meeting ... because we desperately need to talk."

"Were you anticipating a blade to the face?" Cyrus's hand waited an inch from his sword. "I saw you fighting against us in the field at Livlosdald."

"Have you gone blind?" Terian asked. "Because I sat on my horse during that battle and never cast a spell nor drew my blade. So I find it curious you would have seen me fight against anyone."

"I know the two of you will need to sort through your warring emotions," J'anda said, "but I hope you do it swiftly so that I may be granted the grace to have the necessary conversation here before I die of old age."

"Why do I need to have a meeting with this traitorous filth?" Cyrus asked.

Predictable. At least I have something to offer. "Because maybe I can help you," Terian said.

"Help me ... what?" Cyrus laughed. "Die? I'll call upon you if ever I want to go slowly and painfully."

Also predictable, Terian thought with a sigh. "I could also do it swiftly and painlessly, if you'd like," he said, falling back into the old pattern without any effort at all. *Oh, Cyrus. I wish I could tell you how wrong I was, but the likelihood you'd believe me? Less than zero.* "But that's not why I'm here."

"You cannot believe this man has any aid to give us," Cyrus said, turning to face J'anda. The wind picked up, twirling the trail of Terian's cloak. "He offers a blade hidden in his sleeve while he proffers a hand."

"He is placed to assist you," J'anda said, "in ways you don't even know. He is also favored of the Sovereign and has the ear of Malpravus."

Cyrus's blue eyes locked on Terian, narrowed with righteous suspicion. "And why would he help me?"

"Because on the day Alaric Garaunt died," Terian said, letting his emotions rush out in a way he never did outside of his bedroom, with Kahlee, "you weren't the only one that was left broken and mourning." *Better I show him the truth of me rather than try to bluff past with false reserve. I am so close to the blade now, so near to the last cut ... one more defeat and the Sovereign's patience with me and all mine may just be ended.*

"Oh?" Cyrus asked, his cheeks turning pink.

"He may have called us 'brother,'" Terian said, "but you and I lost a hell of a lot more than a guildmate when that bridge collapsed."

"What do you want, Terian?" Cyrus asked after a moment, his curiosity clearly at war with his suspicion.

Terian grinned to keep from bursting into a wracking sob. "The son of a humble warrior leads one of the greatest armies in Arkaria. Oh, how the times do change." *It should have been me. Once upon a time, it was supposed to be—before I threw it all away for pride.*

"And have you changed?" Cyrus asked.

"I have changed," Terian said, working hard to keep his pain bottled within. "But that's irrelevant. There are forces at work here, bending and shaping the world in ways I don't care for. There are things I have seen …" Terian shuddered, unable to control his revulsion at the thought of the dead armies working their way into the Riverlands, into a circle around Reikonos, even now, "… that make me fear for the future, should I live so long as to see it."

"You're in over your head." Cyrus said, and he almost sounded gleeful about it. *And why shouldn't he be? He may have said we were done, but I declared myself his enemy still on that shore. I wouldn't be sorry to see someone out to kill me get it in the back of the neck, either.*

Terian forced a smile. "With the very, very wrong people. In so deep, I fear to open my mouth to take a breath, to speak a word. I regularly stand in the presence of a god, take his orders, carry out his wishes. And I do it all with the Guildmaster of Goliath close at hand."

"You should choose your friends with greater care," Cyrus said, but the glee was gone.

I need a chiding from you like I need an axe across my skull. "I didn't have that many options to choose from."

"Sounds like poor decision making," Cyrus said.

This is not going the way I'd hoped. "Perhaps. But how I got here is completely irrelevant. I can help you." *Just believe me, Cyrus. Just for one last time.* He kept his eyes on the warrior's, afraid to look away, afraid that he'd hint at the deception he had in mind, afraid to speak the words that were written on his heart.

I need you to kill the God of Darkness, Cyrus Davidon. Because not another damned soul in Arkaria can.

"Why?" Cyrus laughed as he asked the question. "Why now? Why risk your life, which I know is precious to you? And to help me, whom you wanted to kill not so very long ago?"

"Because …" Terian said, drifting straight back into a thought that ran through his mind over and over every single day, "'Redemption is a path you must walk every day.'"

"That is possibly the most ludicrously simplistic bit of idiocy I've ever had mouthed to me," Cyrus said. "What addle-brained moron came up with that trite bit of nonsense?"

Terian could not contain his amusement, and it stumbled out of his mouth in a low chuckle. "It was the previous holder of your august office."

"Alaric," Cyrus said.

Now I have your attention, don't I? Terian thought. *He was to you what he was to me, and now you'll lionize him more in death than you even respected him in life. Time and regret couple to make us esteem him even higher now that he's gone than we did when he was there to offer us his guidance in life.*

And oh, how I wish I had his guidance right now.

"None other. It was something he repeated to me before the bridge went down," Terian said. "He coupled it with the reminder that he still believed in me. I walked the wrong path. I followed the wrong people. It took a considerable distance for me to come to that conclusion with all certainty, but I am there now." He poured it all out, or almost, hoping it would be accepted by the forbidding warrior standing skeptically before him. "Now I offer you a choice—do you want to help me start walking back, or would you rather just watch me fall?"

Cyrus stared at him, implacable. *Please don't turn your back on me, Cyrus. Not now.* "You once taught me the lesson of facing down that which you fear, even when you can't see it. Of fighting past the legends and rumors and bullshit and striking directly at a foe. But when the day came that you considered me your enemy, you did not afford me the courtesy of coming at me straight on. Why should I believe that you're facing me head on now?"

Oh, gods, not this, you fool. Do you even know who I report to now? Sandwiched between the most terrible necromancer in Arkaria and the living embodiment of darkness? Cyrus, you're not even a threat to me; you won't point a blade at me unless I come at you. Look at you there, hand still inches from your sword. If the Sovereign were in your boots, I'd be flayed alive already. Terian kept his voice level only through immense effort. "Because you are not my enemy."

"I killed your father."

If only. "Did you?" Terian asked. "I could only wish you had killed him." *That you'd finished the job, that you'd made his corpse irretrievable, that he was gone forever and not dogging my steps presently.*

"I stabbed him to death and left him to rot on the bridge in Termina, Terian," Cyrus said.

"Of course you did," Terian said. *Can't let that particular secret slip just yet. That one could cost me my life if it came out.* "But it doesn't matter anymore."

"You spent the better part of a year following behind me as a friend until you found occasion to betray and kill me," Cyrus said. "But now it's … bygones? Water under the—"

"Fallen bridge, yes," Terian said. "Deep water under a fallen bridge, I'd say."

"You told me it wasn't over between us," Cyrus said. "At the end of that very bridge."

"It's over now," Terian said. "Unless you want to revive it."

"That easy?"

"It may only have been a few months, but I've lived a lifetime of fear since that day," Terian said. "I have other things to concern myself with now. Much more frightening things than the new Guildmaster of Sanctuary."

"You dangle under the nose of the God of Darkness and want to betray him to me?" Cyrus asked. "To what purpose?"

"To the ultimate purpose," Terian said. "I want the dark elves to lose this war. I want the Sovereign to leave Saekaj again, for good this time."

"And you think I'm the means to that?"

"You're the only one who's beaten him," Terian said. "If there were anyone else—the King of the Elves, the Council of Twelve—I'd be talking to them. But he's got them on the run. Reikonos reels under assault from our armies, and even now we make inroads into the east. The elves cower across the Perda, watching the world of man burn. The Riverlands are weeks away from a determining battle. You are the only opposition. The pebble in his boot."

"A pebble in the boot is hardly fatal," Cyrus said.

"The scorpion in his boot, then," Terian said. The frustration crashed loose. *I'm offering you a gift, fool, and I know you suspect a price. Please don't ask it, not yet, please ...* "Do you want my help or not?"

"What help do you offer?" Cyrus asked, and his shoulders relaxed for the first time.

It's a start. At that, Terian felt the first strains of relief. He didn't smile, because there was surely more to be negotiated, but it was the crack in the wall that he needed, and he knew Cyrus well enough to be certain that now—for the first time in a long while—that there was indeed hope after all.

28.

Aisling

She was bidden to appear and she did, knocking on the door at the top of the tallest stair in Sanctuary. The sound of her knuckles across the fine wood resonated within and without, her mind as numb as the sensation of her skin where it came in hard contact with the door. *An ally. I finally have an ally, perhaps.*

"Come in," came the voice from behind the door, and she heeded it, opening the soundless hinge and stepping as quietly as ever, her boots producing not even a whisper with each move she made. She looked all around her as she walked up a small staircase. As her head cleared the top she was treated to an imposing view; at each of the four compass points was a balcony, with doors swept open wide under dark eaves. White, lacy sheers drifted lightly with the breeze, something so out of step with the occupant of these quarters that it made her hesitate at its mere sight. "So ... this is the Guildmaster's tower."

"Obviously the whole central tower is not mine," Cyrus Davidon said, looking relieved, "only the top floor. Though there does seem to be a rather thick layer of stone between me and my officers." The warrior in black was in his customary armor, and he wore a look of mighty discomfort. She saw and knew that things were amiss, that trouble was astir. *Not now. Not when it's possible things could start to go right.*

She summoned her best seductive smile and put aside the pangs of worry that were starting to stir within her. "You did it." And truly, he had, not that it was a grand surprise to anyone but him. *Now I sleep with the Guildmaster of Sanctuary—hopefully.*

"I was merely elected," Cyrus said, holding his gauntlets together tightly enough that she could see the tension born out in his posture, the way he tried to put his strength to some aimless use. *No. This is not good.*

"You put yourself forward and allowed the guild to show you how much they love you," Aisling said. She felt strangely hollow, like she had to go through motions that she'd been through enough times to lose enthusiasm for them.

"I don't think that it extends as far as 'love,'" Cyrus said. "Belief in my leadership, perhaps. A lack of good alternatives, maybe." He tried to smile, but it failed to last. *Oh, no. This is it. Not now. Not yet.* "We need to talk."

"Do we? Can we do it after?" She let her hands dance around him, but it was a shallow gesture. *How many times have I tried to pull him back from this moment? Because of Shrawn.* She looked into his stark blue eyes, saw the tentativeness there. *If I had met him in another place, in a different way … I might have followed him like the rest of them.*

But instead, I follow the string around my neck.

"We cannot," Cyrus said, coming to his feet with surprising urgency.

She followed, placing fingers on his chin, moving to kiss him. "It can wait."

He leaned in for a half-second before that stony resolve snapped down on him again. "No."

This is it. She opened her eyes slowly, let them flutter, like she'd just awoken from a deep sleep. In a way, she felt she had, like the dream of playing things out for a little more time was about to end. "What?"

"I cannot do this any longer," Cyrus said.

"A tired refrain. You'll feel differently after. You always do." *This is a man who's not going to respond to manipulation forever, though to hear Shrawn tell it, every man is susceptible to that forever.*

"I don't want to feel differently," he said, shaking loose of her grasp. "I don't want to keep using you to soothe my aches while imagining you're someone else." He turned away from her. "You and I have done this dance for far too long, and I have been a fool and a weakling letting myself think that this could be more than it is. I use you selfishly, and it has to stop."

"It doesn't have to stop unless I want it to stop," she said. *In a way, this would be a relief. To have it over. To be done with this part of the charade … even knowing what it might entail.* "And I don't wish it to," she lied.

"You hold out hope for something that will never happen," Cyrus said. "My feelings for you are gratitude—for what you've done for me, for saving my life, for the guidance you've provided, and the thousand times you've been a balm. But no more than that."

"You don't know that it couldn't be more," she said. She played the role, dredged up a sense of wounded pride that she draped over the complicated feelings of fear and relief that were flooding her, and which she was redirecting into the pit as quickly as she could. *Someday, that abyss will overflow, and gods help whoever is standing nearest me when it happens.* "You haven't given it time—"

"You've given it a year," Cyrus said. "Nothing has happened. In spite of the muddling of things, in spite of the desires of the flesh, the call of my heart has not changed since the day I first took my relief in you. I respect you, I find great comfort in your kindness—that much has changed. But I do not love you, Aisling."

Of course you don't.

You love Vara.

"I wish I could," he went on. "But I do not."

"You do not know what you are saying." *Except that you do, and haven't had the balls to say it until now, either because of the job I've done on you or because of your own foolishness.*

"I know what I am saying," Cyrus said, hovering away from her. "It must be over."

"It can't be over," she said. *But it is.*

She talked to him further, listened to emotional words flow from him and posited her responses based on what she was supposed to do, on how she knew she was supposed to act, and when the moment came, she left, and in exactly the way she knew she needed to, but her thoughts were miles away, in a cavern in the dark, in the dwelling place of her race and where she now needed to return, desperately.

It is over.

Finally.

And now I have to figure out the next move … because the time for action is coming.

29.

Terian

Being in this place is surreal, Terian thought as he stared around the room. It was a study on the very top floor of the House of Ehrest, with a hearth crackling quietly to one side of the room and a massive desk in the center. He stared at the man who sat behind it, half-expecting it to be his father. *But it's not. Vincin Ehrest is not really all that much like my father, which is surprising for a man who's risen so high in the Shuffle.*

"You have a pinched look upon your face, Terian," Vincin Ehrest said, watching Terian carefully.

"I have a lifetime of unpleasant memories from this place," Terian said, shuffling away from the two chairs that faced his father-in-law's desk. His boot scuffed the wood floor, a not-so-silent reminder of the opulence of the manors of Saekaj. "The fact that they don't gut the manors and start over again with each move of the Shuffle ... Does it ever feel to you like you're living in someone else's house?"

"You forget: I've lived in this house before," Vincin said, his hair long and tucked back over his shoulder in a braided queue, looking like a gentleman of Saekaj. "I have my own memories of this place."

"I suppose," Terian said, looking up at the space above the hearth, where a portrait of Kahlee hung. He remembered a different picture there; that of his sister. *Ameli.*

"I had a reason for calling you up here, General," Vincin said, wooden chair squeaking beneath him as he pivoted on the springs.

"You don't have to call me that," Terian said absently, slowly finding his way back into the seat.

"It helps remind me that my son-in-law is so ascendant at the moment," Vincin said. There was mirth there, even without a trace of a smile. He tapped his finger on the desk, and Terian felt unspoken words. *Quick to ascend, quick to descend. He knows perhaps better than most how close I am to the blade.*

"What did you want to talk about?" Terian asked, easing himself into the padded chair. His armor jutted, spikes in inconvenient places, and he always exercised care around furniture, especially that which wasn't his.

"The future," Vincin said. "The future of Saekaj—and Sovar."

"Sovar doesn't seem to have much of a future at the moment," Terian said, watching the older man carefully. "They're about one good step from rebellion at any given moment, and you know how the Sovereign feels about that."

"I know well how the Sovereign feels about it," Ehrest said stiffly, "being in consultation with him about the matter on a regular basis. Do you know what the Sovereign intends, though?"

Terian tapped a gauntleted finger against the arm of the chair. "I'm more focused on the campaigns in the Riverlands and against Reikonos at the moment. We're closing in on Deriviereville even now—"

"Do you know what he intends?" Vincin asked again, and there was no denying the seriousness of the man's look.

"If the lower chamber rebels?" Terian asked with a shrug of his shoulders. *Everyone suspects, naturally. The trick is to make it look like it doesn't matter.* "Probably to burn it to the ground with all the fury of Enflaga on a bad day." He tried to smile carelessly, but felt it fade when he saw Ehrest's look.

"That is exactly what he intends," Vincin said, without a trace of amusement. "Do you know the composition of the lower chamber at the moment? After three solid years of a losing war? It's nearing eighty percent female. The only men left are the ones in the guard, or for heavy labor, or who are infirm or yet to come of age—"

Terian held up a hand. "I have no control over—"

"You and I spoke of this once before," Vincin said. "Of how a storm was coming—"

"We've been in a storm for a long time," Terian said. *A howling one, full of raw bitterness worthy of Tempestus, God of Storms.* "I don't see how anything has changed."

"One cannot fight against the wind and rain forever, Terian," Vincin said. "The women of Sovar, and whatever men remain— they're furious. They're starving. Their children are starving."

"This is not a conversation we should have in your house—" Terian started.

"Guturan Enlas is not here at the moment," Vincin said, waving him off. "And this is the moment we have for such a discussion. Food stores are down to nearly nothing." He picked up a piece of parchment from the desk and waved it between them. "The Great Sea is nearly finished. We're sending out our mushrooms to feed this dead army your friend Malpravus is raising. The last reasonable source of sustenance and we're stripping it bare to ... what? March on the human capital? As if they're not starving themselves at this point—"

"I don't know what you want from me—"

"I want you to get your head out of your arse," Vincin Ehrest cut him off, voice hushed. "We have a bare guard here on Saekaj right now, you know this, yes? You're effectively the General of the Armies, with your head still attached for the time being, which is a rare gift that your predecessors no longer possess."

"I am aware of many things," Terian said coolly. *Where is he going with this?*

There was a click at the door behind them, the heavy stone moving as the handle turned. Terian felt a trickle of panic at the thought of someone listening to what they'd been discussing. The door began to swing inward and he sighed, inaudibly, in relief at the flash of the white dress that appeared from behind the opening.

"Hushed voices," Kahlee said, closing the door behind her, "harsh in their disagreement. Not something I expected from my father and husband in one of their rare meetings." She strode over to the desk and stood at the seat next to Terian's, looking at each of them in turn with something approaching amusement. "I couldn't find Guturan Enlas anywhere, and the rest of the servants seemed to be away." A light sparkled in her eyes. "Are you discussing treason again?"

"That's us," Terian deadpanned. "You know how it is. If we can't discuss it eight to ten times a day, we'll never get that lovely execution we've all been aiming for. Because it's really not a good execution unless you drag your entire family into your unspeakable crimes without them even knowing a stitch about your evil, insurrectionist plans—"

"Oh, good," Kahlee said, smoothing her dress as she sat down, "I was worried you were discussing something prosaic, like troop movements, rather than the necessary matter of getting rid of the Sovereign."

Terian froze. *The mere suggestion carries the death penalty and she knows it.* A glance from her to the stricken look on her father's face suggested to him that Vincin was thinking much the same. "Kahlee ... we're not—"

"You should be," Kahlee said, head up straight and looking him straight in the eye. "You should be talking about it everywhere you think you can reasonably get away with it. You should be planning the overthrow of the Sovereign any way you can, every waking hour of the day."

"That's a tall order," Terian said, switching back to looking at his father-in-law, "and also—obviously—fatal were it to be overheard."

"A tall order but not an impossible one," Kahlee said, looking to her father. "What?" She smiled. "I know the minds of both of you. Let me be the bridge here—Terian," she said, looking to her husband, "my father has long despised the Sovereign and his system." She glanced at her father, eyes burning. "Father, Terian knows his life is short in his present role, and he has no love for Yartraak."

"Please do not say his name here." Vincin Ehrest's look of discomfiture almost caused him to shrink back in his suit.

"If you mean to be rid of him, you should not fear to say his name aloud." Kahlee's grim amusement oozed out with every word. "And you should be thinking about how to kill him, because that's the only true way to be rid of him."

Terian bowed his head and watched Vincin cover his face with a hand, the consternation falling thick on both of them. "One does not simply ... Killing gods is not exactly a cave cress harvest, with a simple plucking and the task is done."

"But you know a man who has killed a god," Kahlee said.

"A man who hates me," Terian said, looking sidelong at her. *She can't possibly know ...*

"A man you met just yesterday," Kahlee said with a certain amount of triumph. "You and your friend from Sanctuary."

Terian's blood ran cold. *If she means to betray me, I'm already dead.* He flashed his eyes toward Vincin, who was now sitting up in his seat once more, looking on with interest. "You met with Cyrus Davidon?" Vincin asked, clearly trying to smoke out the truth of the matter for himself.

"I did," Terian admitted, feeling as though he had to drag the truth out of himself. He took it out and tossed it on the desk between them, let it sit there like an offer, waiting to see if it were accepted.

Vincin leaned forward, elbows on the desk. "Would he help us?"

"Not immediately, I don't think," Terian said, shaking his head. "He'll need to see a straight line drawn between serving our need and serving his own."

"What does he want?" Vincin asked, eyes narrowed in question. "He's now the Guildmaster of Sanctuary, is he not? What does a man like that want?"

"Other than an elven paladin to call his own?" Terian threw out, rhetorically. "He wants to see his people protected. He wants to save Arkaria."

"Removing Yartraak from rulership of Saekaj and Sovar would be a very big step in that direction," Vincin said.

"But not terribly obvious nor tangible," Terian said, shaking his head. "He's laboring under the command of a father figure now dead who abhorred violence." *Oh, the irony of me saying that,* Terian thought with a rueful smile that he kept to himself. "Cyrus Davidon will need to see a direct, clear, obvious danger to Arkaria or to something of personal import to him in order to make him desperate enough to trust me in a mission like this."

"He comes from Reikonos, does he not?" Vincin stroked his white chin hair. "Our armies are close to squeezing that city unto death. Surely that would motivate him."

"Maybe," Terian said with a shrug. He caught Kahlee's eye. "I don't know. In any case, it's not as though he can just walk into the throne room and kill the Sovereign. We would have to smuggle him in, with an army as his support—"

"Or at least his sword," Kahlee said shrewdly.

Terian froze, his mouth suddenly dry. "You can't take Cyrus Davidon's sword."

"It is physically possible," Vincin said.

"If you can pry it from his cold, dead hands," Terian said, "yes. Personally, I would not rate your chances terribly high on that, and you'd make a hell of an enemy in the process in the form of the entire guild of Sanctuary, whose help we could dearly use. It's a terrible idea, and I suggest you rule it out now. The sword isn't the coup, in any case. The wielder is ..." He clenched his teeth, swallowing pride he didn't even know he had left. *Dammit, Cyrus, now I see you for what you were all along—the winner for good reason.* "Cyrus is perhaps the greatest warrior in Arkaria, even absent the sword. With the sword in his hand, he could kill Yartraak. You give it to some other idiot and run them into the throne room, they'll fail."

"What if that other idiot is you?" Kahlee asked.

Terian felt the weight of the blade at his side, the red sword of his father that he'd hoarded for his own for so long. "I'm a good swordsman, but ... I'm not Cyrus. I'm better with an axe, in fact."

"I cannot tell you how pleased I am to hear you say that," a voice came from behind the stone door, causing Kahlee to jump to her feet, Terian swiveling his head as the office door swung wide again. This time, it was not a friendly face that crept from behind it, nor one that Terian saw any hint of pleasure in.

"Father," Terian said, as Amenon Lepos stepped into the room, his helm under his arm and his face dark, the skin desiccated on his cheeks with a hint of rot set upon it. He looked humorless, as always. In his other hand, he carried a long, black axe, the blade swung over his shoulder as though he were ready to use it on all three of them, his face as expressionless as if he were stepping into a battle with his enemies.

30.

Aisling

She lurked on a rooftop in Sovar, one of the ones that didn't have a cloth dwelling pitched atop it. Her eyes fell over the whole of the town before her, down the hard slope into the back deep, the lowest part of the slum city. *I may not have been born here, but I belong here in the eyes of Dagonath Shrawn. How funny is it that he has never once considered that I came from the same place he did?*

Traditionally, Sovar in midday was a raucous, rowdy place, but now the dark elven voices were hushed. She'd walked the streets in this place for the last several weeks and been surprised at how empty they seemed compared to the days when she'd lived here. She remembered well the days when she'd disappeared into this city, rich girl hiding from her past, and every alleyway had been packed with life, teeming with people scratching by on the scraps thrown to them by the Sovereign.

At the thought of the Sovereign, she felt a very real surge of disquiet that she couldn't immediately toss into the gaping abyss inside her. She'd dealt with him for weeks, after all, him and Shrawn, asking the same questions over and over about Cyrus Davidon, trying to find a new approach to get her back into his graces. She'd felt the sting of their insults, of their desire to call into question her skills, even her motivation. They'd threatened her, they'd threatened Norenn, and Shrawn had given him a good beating right in her presence.

She'd played along, of course, murmured words of assent, but Yartraak had actually ended up being her saving grace on this one count. Two weeks into her "interrogation," he'd surrendered the idea of sending her back to Cyrus Davidon to re-ingratiate herself to him. With red eyes alight with new possibilities, he'd dismissed her, and she'd slipped away before Shrawn could have her dragged somewhere to wait for him.

Sovar hadn't exactly been a perfect solution, though, not at all. She wasn't on the run, after all, so much as she was giving Dagonath Shrawn some time to deal with other issues that were surely on his mind. She wasn't invisible here, after all. If Shrawn was worth his salt as a dealer of information, he'd have known where she was renting a room for quite some time now, as she'd made little effort to hide it. She had troubled herself to hide the second place she'd rented, though she was virtually certain Shrawn would have gotten a clear idea of her "back-up" plan as well.

And that was fine, because neither of them was really part of her plan at all.

She crouched atop the roof near the front gate of Sovar, looking down on the town below, and waited. She figured Shrawn would send someone any day now; it was bound to happen. She'd be summoned back before the Sovereign, be told what to do once more—it was virtually assured that it would be the order she'd rather reluctantly accepted would be coming.

To kill Cyrus Davidon.

She watched a string of orphans working their way across the rooftops, leaping with skill and carelessness born of youth, running and jumping from point to point. She cringed as she observed them; though hardly maternal, she nonetheless winced at the thought of a dire end for at least some of them. The tops of the buildings in Sovar were deceptive in their construction. Some were cloth, some were fired clay, and some were weaker materials covered over to look like they were either. It all made for frightfully unpredictable footing, and she knew that she would not entrust her life to that method of movement unless she had absolutely no other choice.

"Get down here, girl!" came a voice from the alleyway below, drawing Aisling's calm glance to the figure in the darkened space between the two buildings. Three floors down, a grey-cloaked wizard with a pointed hat waited, looking up so that Aisling could see her pink, fleshy face and the straw hair running out from beneath the hat.

Aisling looked down at her with a detached calm. She took a breath, taking her time getting down by jumping lightly off the roof and catching herself on a rock window with strong fingertips, then scaling her way down to the one below and finally to the alley floor.

"Look like a monkey of the southern lands, you do," Verity huffed as Aisling stood back up next to her. "Climbing around on buildings like one of those ruffians that darts from place to place stealing everything they can get their dirty hands on."

Aisling's eyes fell on Verity's hands, clean and pristine, wrapped around her wooden staff. "I'm surprised your hands aren't dirtier."

Verity reached out and hit her on the side of the head with the staff. Aisling let her, again, but this time it was hard enough to close her eyes and draw her hand to the site of the blow, prompting a ringing sound in her ears. "Ouch," she said, playing it up to be worse than it was.

"You've got a bloody cheek," Verity said as Aisling came back to upright again, blanching from the blow. That didn't take much in the way of feigning. "Think you're hiding out here? Shrawn knows about your place in the mids." Verity grinned, wide and satisfied. "And about the other one in the Back Deep, too, in case you think there's anything that escapes his notice."

Aisling kept her eyes partially closed, playing off the lingering pain of the blow to add a layer of disbelief that turned to hopelessness. She didn't speak, however, unsure of how subtle she should play the disappointment of being "caught." "What do you want?" she asked instead, croaking out the question with a modicum of pain.

"Your orders have come in," Verity said, hard and with no small amount of glee. Aisling had a vision of her as the type of person who would hang a body over a crevasse just to watch them twist, promising to pull them up if they did just one thing for her but laughing inside all the while.

"Fine," Aisling said, opening her eyes the rest of the way, letting the pain of the blow fade from her reaction to the wizard. "What does he want me to do?" She injected just the right amount of subservience, that little cross where defiance met utter lack of ability. *She doesn't need to know what I've got up my sleeve.* A little flutter filled her stomach; it had been a while since she'd seen Genn in any case, so all she had was what she'd come up with on her own.

"He wants you to go back to Sanctuary," Verity said, already preparing her spell. Her love of suffering sprang up in her expression once more, and Aisling imagined the wizard squashing a fat bug, slowly twisting with it caught on the edge of her boot, the guts squirting out from the force of the trapping. "One last time ..."

And there it is, Aisling knew, as the world of Sovar, of the dark underworld began to vanish around her, as predicted. She almost felt a pang of regret for what she knew was coming. But only almost.

Sorry, Cyrus.

The thought was all the care she had left to spare for him, and it disappeared as easily as she did, whisked away to perform the task immediately at hand, her dagger ready to do the dark task she'd been preparing to do for years.

31.

J'anda

One Hundred Years Earlier

The hated elves fled over the hills of the Plains of Perdamun, their shining armor catching the light of the sun as J'anda Aimant watched with a smile on his lips, his robe drawn tight against the winter chill. *That will teach them,* he thought with a great satisfaction as the rout unfolded before him, an army twice the size of the one he stood with breaking and running after only a minor bloodying at best.

"I doubt they even know they've been run 'round by an enchanter," General Ardin Vardeir said as he sat ahorse, watching the fleeing elves. The tingle of the southern winter was perhaps weaker than in the lands of the humans up north, but it was far colder than the caves of Saekaj or Sovar that J'anda was accustomed to. "I've never seen anything quite like that, lad—though I hope to again, darkness willing."

J'anda took the compliment in the way it was intended and bowed low as his youthful body allowed. "The pleasure was mine, General, though I must say, you should be disappointed in the rest of your enchanter corps." He glanced back at the rest of the spell casters behind him with a smile that was as smug as it was assured. "If they only held up half of what I was able to do, we could run the elves from here back to Pharesia without them ever thinking to turn around and fight back."

"And you're humble, too," Vardeir said with a light laugh. "What's your name again, lad? Amante?"

"Aimant," J'anda said, bowing a little lower. "J'anda Aimant."

"Well done, Aimant," Vardeir said, a smile of satisfaction running across his lips. "I think it's about time we pursued, turned this retreat into a rout. Wouldn't want these elves to think they've been anything less than hammered into vek'tag steak at our hands, after all." He urged his horse forward, and part of the army started to follow. The smell of horses was strong in the air, and the General turned to issue a final order as his officer corps galloped after him. "Trimane! See that this enchanter's name is recorded for special mention to the Sovereign!" He said something else as well, but it was lost under the thunder of hoof beats.

J'anda stood upon the hill, looking at the dark elven army taking up pursuit of the elves, and barely noticed when the young man on horseback came to a halt at his side. "Well done," the youthful voice came down, almost playful.

J'anda looked up into a coyly smiling face, with slight dimples in the cheeks making the young man look perhaps younger than he might have without them. His dark hair was swept over his shoulder but loose, hanging there ready to whip in the wind if he spurred the horse to a gallop. His dark blue flesh was a deeper navy tone that indicated significant amounts of time out of the caves of Saekaj and Sovar, but his manner was all Saekaj. He wore armor under his cloak, and what could be seen under the draping coat told the enchanter that this warrior was a high born.

J'anda bowed swiftly, again. He'd learned long ago as a child of the mids in Sovar that deference was one's best protection as a citizen of the lower chamber against those from the higher ranks of Saekaj. "Kind of you to say."

"It's a rare talent that can fool a whole army," the young man said with that same smile. It was delicate, even though the young man did not look delicate. He'd caught the name, hadn't he? What had the General called him? Trimane?

"I suppose I'm unusual in that regard," J'anda said, looking behind him into the corps of spell casters for the army. He caught a glimpse of Vracken Coeltes slinking behind a healer, sullen eyes nearly hidden in the shadow of his cowl.

"It's always pleasant to stray from the norm," Trimane said, watching him carefully, as though he'd said something of great significance and was watching for J'anda's reaction.

J'anda let only a flicker of emotion crack through. "Indeed," he said, replying as carefully as he could, "I find the unusual path to be the only one worth following."

"I hope to see you back in Saekaj, then, J'anda Aimant," Trimane said, bowing his head. "I'll make certain that the company secretary makes clear distinction about your role in this battle." With a last look, he moved his horse into action and rode off, over the hill, after the retreating elves.

J'anda stood watching as the cavalry rode in pursuit of the army he'd broken—well, helped break, anyway. He felt the stirrings of pride as he watched his countrymen run down the elves, and he watched, hoping to catch just one more look at one of the figures receding in the distance.

32.

Terian

Terian looked at the axe cradled in his father's hand with a growing sense of unease, his hand hovering over the scabbard of his sword. He shot Kahlee a glance and saw a similar sense of misgiving plastered upon her face, just a shade paler than it usually was. *How long was he listening out there? How much of our treason did he hear?*

"Your servants are absent," Amenon said with a crackling voice, the axe brandished high. It was smooth and a little ornate, not the sort of thing he tended to carry. *Father likes swords. What the hell is he doing with—?*

Amenon tossed the axe down at Terian's feet. It clattered across the floor with a hard rattle, settling with its wide blades almost touching his boot. He brought his eyes up to look at his father and saw the customary lack of amusement there. "I've brought you a replacement for the sword you now wear. Give it back to me."

Terian glanced at the axe, then to his father. "Say please."

Amenon's eyes narrowed. "Please."

Terian unbelted and slid the scabbard free, tossing it wordlessly at his father's feet.

"That easy?" Amenon asked, watching him with slitted eyes, as though he couldn't believe it.

"It's better suited to you in any case," Terian said coolly. "I've missed having an axe, so ..." He looked down at his new weapon. "Is it any good?"

"It's mystical," Amenon said, stooping to retrieve his sword. He snatched it up hungrily, fingers fumbling with it as though he were

167

nervous. "I took it off a dwarf in the Riverlands, some mercenary who fought better than any of the other creatures I've encountered in battle of late. It imbues you with a little extra strength, some dexterity." He placed the sword in his belt carefully, his hands almost shaking. "It's not exactly an even trade, but—"

"Your weapon was handed to you by the Sovereign, crafted by the best blacksmiths and spell-weavers in Saekaj," Terian said with a faint shrug and a sense of resignation. His eyes flitted to the red blade as his father slid it out of the scabbard a few inches. He felt no hunger to possess it any longer, just a deep regret for the choices he'd made with it in his grasp. *If only I could blame it on the sword* ... "It doesn't have many equals."

"True enough," Amenon said, sliding the blade back down to the depths of the scabbard. He straightened, and there was something satisfied in the way he looked now. "Malpravus sent me to find you on an errand of his own as well as mine."

Terian cocked an eyebrow, then looked around at Kahlee and Vincin. "Did he? Do tell."

"Our army is coming to a place called Leaugarden, in the Riverlands," Amenon said. "It's the last strategic breaking point before our armies come out of bottleneck. He expects a fight and has inklings that the Council of Twelve will attempt to buy the loyalty of Sanctuary to assist this battle."

Terian nodded slowly, his earlier sense of resignation flooding deeper within him. "Makes sense. Is there a wizard going back anytime soon?"

"The one who brought me here waits for you," Amenon said. His face was utterly devoid of feeling. "Haste would be wise."

"Yeah," Terian said, gathering himself up and taking hold of the axe at his feet, hoisting it over his shoulder. "Malpravus isn't much for waiting."

"The war waits for no man," Vincin offered sagely, prompting Terian to look back to his father-in-law. "Think on what we discussed."

"I've already thought about it, as Kahlee told you," Terian said, feigning a smile. "Be assured, I'm in full accord with you." Vincin's eyes flashed with light. *Hopefully he isn't of a mind to betray me.* "We'll talk about it when I get back, but until then—"

"Arrangements to make," Vincin agreed and looked meaningfully at Kahlee. "Contingencies to consider in all things, of course." He smiled weakly. "I'll have everything ready by the time you return."

Terian tried to hide his relief. *It's good to know that when the second most powerful man in Saekaj intends to betray the Sovereign, he's at least got the power to protect his family. Especially when he might not be the one doing the betraying …* Terian extended his hand and Vincin grasped it, giving it a good shake. "Thank you," Terian said. He kissed Kahlee lightly on the cheek, catching the full meaning of her gaze telling him more than she would have said in the presence of both their fathers. "Where did you leave this wizard?" he asked Amenon.

"Downstairs," Amenon said, with a hint of regret as he ran a gauntleted hand over the stone door. *Probably remembering the days when it was his office.* "I will be leaving you there; I need to return to the Legion of Darkness for the next phase of training our new class."

"It's all right," Terian said, shrugging it off as he began to descend a staircase he had walked more times than he could remember, his father trailing a step back. *What a curious reversal of power but a few years bring. Life can change with barely a month's notice, and spin wildly away from the expected path given more time.*

"You have a look upon your face," Amenon said, now alongside him as they came down to the first floor landing. The wood planks squeaked under the combined weight of the two men in armor. "What were you thinking just now?" His face darkened. "Unless it's something I wouldn't care to know, like one those idiotic japes you're so fond of."

"Nothing so whimsical as that," Terian said, descending the last floor in the house of his birth. "I was just marveling at how things change, and how quickly they do." He caught that look of regret from Amenon again, and sighed. "Why, who even knows how they might change between today and tomorrow?"

The look on his father's face was pure sourness, bitter feelings born of their current location, Terian knew, and he actually regretted saying it for a moment. But there was something else about it, too; an honesty he couldn't deny, and he found a strange sort of comfort in the thought, as though change, no matter which direction it took, could not lead him anywhere worse than where he already was.

33.

Aisling

She waited on the field of a place called Leaugarden for Cyrus Davidon to turn his head and look at her. She held her hands tight to her horse's reins, the instructions clear and foremost in her mind, words repeating over and over like a shameful memory that would not depart.

Kill Cyrus Davidon.

"Gods," Cyrus said, almost a whisper, as she walked her horse slowly toward him. His reticence was hardly a surprise; never a fan of high emotion in any case, Aisling had prepared herself by forcing tears, trying to make her eyes puffier to play the role. In truth, she felt strangely settled about the whole matter, which by now had begun to feel like a task she simply wanted to get over. She was numb to the moral implications of stabbing a man she'd been forced to share a bed with for the last year, or perhaps she simply did not want to consider them too deeply. *It's a little like staring into the mouth of madness when you're already on the edge. Seems such an inviting jump, if you wanted to simply take that last step and fall for a short while.*

"Can I talk to you for a moment before the battle?" Aisling asked, guiding her horse closer to the place where the officers waited.

"Can it wait?" Cyrus's expression was wary, trepidation mixed with unease, though she was not fully certain whether it was all down to her causing it, or if some anticipation from the coming battle was blended in. "We're moments from the start of a battle."

"Not really." *I have no choice but to do this now, before it begins. My instructions were explicit.*

"All right." He nodded, and she saw the decision made. He was not one to linger long on a choice, though she suspected that attribute had bitten him hard more than once. "Can we make it quick?"

"Certainly," she said and started to lead him away.

"Go on," Vara said, almost under her breath, "harken to the crack of your master's whip." Aisling could hear her victory in the statement, but she felt no sting. *Like me with Norenn all those years ago, she'll soon feel the rage and sorrow of helplessness in the face of your love being yanked away.*

"There we go," Cyrus said as he moved his horse to follow after her, "gleeful and unkind all in one."

She led him into the field, far enough away from his army that even his officers' intervention would be difficult in the short term. This was as it had been planned, and a quick look confirmed that the dark elven army was indeed in sight, far off down the road through the rolling of the landscape. She got off her horse, hesitant now as the moment drew close.

Cyrus hesitated before dismounting, finally coming off his horse and sinking into the soft ground just slightly. "Well?"

"Have you reconsidered?" she asked. The moment was coming. Even if he had changed his mind—*which he won't have*—she was without choice now. *Nothing left but to embrace him tightly and make it quick.*

"No," he said, and she could tell he was taking pains to be as gentle as possible. *I'll repay the favor to him when the moment comes.* "Aisling, it's over. Nothing is going to change my mind."

"Okay. All right." It was all performance now, and she made her slow move toward him to close the distance. Every motion was measured, careful, trying to keep from looking like she was the predator slinking toward her prey. His stiff discomfort was blatant, obvious, standing unnaturally like a statue in the middle of this field of soon-to-be battle. She approached him unthreateningly, but avoiding the seductive—more like a last kiss.

One last embrace for old time's sake.

She wrapped her arms around him as he stood there, stock still, and waited a breath. Two.

As she drew the third, he relaxed almost imperceptibly and his hands came up from his sides to wrap around her slim frame. His strong arms were without their usual strength, though, holding her lightly, as though she were a thing broken that he couldn't bear to do further harm to. She slipped her dagger out of the arm of her cloak where she'd hidden it, and the smell of the black lace wafted into her nostrils, making her afraid for just a moment that he'd smell it and *know*.

Her fingers played their way up his back plate, lifting it just enough so that she could work the blade up. Angle it just so, and it'd pierce his heart. Without a healing spell, he'd bleed to death in one minute, perhaps two since he was so large. Her head was on his shoulder, her hand in place, and she opened her eyes, tensing to make the move—

Then she paused for just a second too long as she opened her eyes and saw something quite unexpected.

Genn was standing there in the field to her side. She opened her eyes and he was there, shaking his head, almost unnoticeably, and then—

He was gone.

It took her less than another second to process it, to believe she'd seen it, and to read the message given.

Don't kill him.

She jabbed the blade into his back, angling down further, away from the heart, and Cyrus tensed in her arms. The strike was sudden, speedy, not something he'd been prepared for, clearly. She knew by the way the blade had entered his body that she'd still most likely gotten his kidney, or at least part of it. She'd studied these things in the service of the Sovereign, of course, and knew how to do the most damage.

"I'm sorry," she whispered to him as his legs buckled under his weight. "But once I told him I had lost your ear, he told me that I had to do this." A lie, but preferable to the whole truth.

He moved to look her in the eye, and she tried to keep her face implacable. It wasn't hard. "Wh-who?"

"The Sovereign, of course. He's the one who told me to get close to you." Part of her wanted to mention the other reasons, the other guilty parties. But she didn't, looking him in the eyes instead, staring into the blue chill, the unreasonable wideness of an unbelievably naïve man who hadn't predicted this, not by a long, long shot.

"Y-you," Cyrus said, the strength of his legs fading. She kept him on his feet as he stuttered his thoughts. "You were ..."

"I'm sorry," she said, "but you have no idea what he's like. What he can do. How he and his servants can compel cooperation. There's a reason you never heard his name until now."

"They'll ... heal me, you know. I'm not ... finished." He staggered in her grasp, his weight becoming harder and harder to control as his strength faded.

"My blade was coated in black lace," she said, whispering in his ear. "If there was ever a man strong enough to survive, it would be you." She withdrew the blade and stared at him curiously. *Why did Genn want him alive, I wonder? And how am I supposed to explain this to Shrawn?* "I hope you do. But your battle is over, I'm afraid, and that's what he wanted."

"You won't ... get away with this," Cyrus said, but Aisling was already looking past him to Verity, galloping toward them from over the warrior's shoulder. The wizard cast a spell of flame and it descended upon the line of Sanctuary officers like one of Forrestant's bombs, scourging fire deployed from her staff as though being spit from the mouth of a furious dragon.

Verity rode hard toward them, steering her horse in a sharp circle around Aisling and Cyrus. *This is the complicated moment; if the Sovereign and Shrawn are truly done with me, they'll have her kill me now. Or worse, leave me behind, though that's unlikely ...*

I simply know too much.

"Surprised to see me?" Verity asked, taunting Cyrus, who was barely standing.

"Serving the Sovereign? Not the usual ... choice ... for an elf." Cyrus's words came slowly, and only with great effort.

"But before I served him, I served one of his friends," Verity said and raised her staff into line with the warrior's face. She glanced at Aisling, and there was fury and yet satisfaction there, as though she were happy at the failure. "For Mortus."

Thunder cracked under the clear sky, and Verity's horse was thrown as if by a giant, the wizard tossed along with the animal. Aisling turned her head to see Vara ahorse, riding hard toward them, her hand raised with the hint of a spell still stirring the air out of her gauntlet. The fire around the officers of Sanctuary was under control, siphoned toward Curatio. Aisling watched for a second out of purest curiosity, then remembered her place was not here, and that her time was limited and growing shorter by the moment.

A flash of blue light appeared in front of Aisling, and she deciphered it immediately. *Verity cast a teleportation spell for her allies. I suppose the Sovereign and Shrawn don't want me left behind, then.* She tossed a glance toward the wizard and saw her disappear in a burst of magical energy that crackled over the sound of Vara's hoofbeats.

Cyrus leveled his gaze on her, his hand now on his sword, coming back to life after the paralysis of shock and numbness at her attack. "I trusted you," he said, voice low and gasping. Blood was trickling down his leg, his side. She felt a pinch of regret now, and not for failing to kill him.

"I'm sorry," she said and grasped at the orb of teleportation in front of her. She looked in his eyes as she disappeared, and wondered in a cold and detached way if she would ever see him again. Part of her almost hoped she did, even though she suspected that she would not survive if that day ever came.

34.

Terian

The field of Leaugarden was a rush of chaos, the Army of Sanctuary beleaguered in a way Terian could not recall seeing since the earliest days of its assemblage. Much to his chagrin, the deployment of the caltrops had stopped the charge of the Luukessian cavalry dead. He shook his head as he waded through the battle, trying his hardest not to actually kill anyone. *What were you thinking, Cyrus? You should have seen this coming and adapted, should have halted the charge as soon as you saw it going wrong . . .*

He could see Cyrus Davidon moving through the battle ahead of him. The warrior moved like cold fish guts sliding down an angled cutting board, slowly slipping through the fight. His moves were exaggerated, graceless, like he was holding himself stiff to avoid injury. The smell of blood and rot was thick in Terian's nose as he shoved aside the dark elves around him as he worked his way to the warrior, who was stuck out on his own with only one ally at his back, a human woman in warrior armor that looked flimsy as old wood compared to Cyrus's full-body plate. *What the hell are you thinking, Davidon? This isn't like you at all . . .*

The human woman at Cyrus's back took a sword to the throat and sprayed red blood everywhere as Terian closed, the surging army of the dark elves all around him. He glanced back only for a moment to see Malpravus far, far behind him. "Dear boy," the necromancer had said when Terian dismounted to join the fray, "there are always other fools to stand in front."

I guess I'm a fool for being drawn to the thick of this, then.

He watched the fight circling around Cyrus, blood streaming down the warrior's back armor as Terian parted the circle around the man in black armor. *He's been cut, and good. His sword is the only thing keeping him alive, then.* The enemies that surrounded him seemed fearful to strike forth, like dogs kept at distance by an angry master. *Even the dead fear to attack him when he's wounded. But that won't last …*

Terian shoved his way through the last of the line around Cyrus, smashing the skull of a putrid human in armor that covered his corpse-like body. He had lost patience with these dead long ago, and now wanted nothing but to be away from the stink of them; it made him want to retch, the thought of these people being used in death, their will irrelevant at the urge of Malpravus and the others who held dominion over death.

"Terian," Cyrus said, his eyes alighting on the dark knight.

"Cyrus." Terian lifted his axe above his head slowly. The warrior's eyes were dulled, their usual liveliness faded like a sky clouding over. *His sword is right there. He's too numb to stop anything at this point. I could cut his head clean off and take it, and—*

"Today, Terian?" Cyrus asked as the axe fell.

Redemption is a path you must walk every day.

Terian stopped the blade mid-fall and swept it to the side as he caught a glimpse of a soldier moving up behind him. "Gods damn you, Cyrus Davidon!" *And you, Alaric Garaunt, for preying on my weakness as a dark elf and a dark knight, for showing me a path and then not walking me clear to the damned end of it, for leaving me alone in the wilderness without guide.* "No, not today."

"I'm not sure … there'll be another," Cyrus said quietly, still slumped on the ground on all fours, waiting to be killed.

"Why did you have to get yourself beaten in battle for the first time ever today, of all days?" Terian swung his axe with a fervor; the animalistic dead had surged against him, recognizing him now for what he truly was. *I am a foe to you, creatures. I am your enemy, the enemy of the dead. The enemy of the Sovereign and all he stands for, with his tyranny, his necromancy—and for all his horrendous allies.*

Malpravus.

Dagonath Shrawn.

Father.

"Aisling …" Cyrus said, the warrior lifting up to strike at a foe coming toward him. "She ... got me."

"She was the spy," Terian said, going low against the legs of the dead sweeping toward him. "Son of a bitch. I should have seen it." *Naturally. Why wouldn't they have sunk a traitor in his bed? It's the easiest place to keep watch on him. I can't believe ...*

I guess I never thought she was the type to do that. She goes up a few notches in my estimation on that one ... Gods, I hope they didn't do that to me with Kahlee ...

"She was the ... traitor," Cyrus said, trying to get to his feet and failing.

Terian swung a hard circle, his axe flying over Cyrus's head and destroying a goodly number of the sweeping horde of the dead. Limbs split, heads broke free, and it did little to nothing to end the surge of foes around them. Terian prepared to swing around again, hoping to buy another moment for something to change, when something did.

A flash of silver plate and yellowed hair landed hard on two of the dead, splitting them asunder with a sword stroke as the paladin came to the rescue with her usual style and grace. Her eyes fixed on Terian for just a moment before she went to the next enemy, but he could see the restrained rage there, the flash of time in which she considered killing him, then passed on the notion out of expediency rather than loyalty.

"You bloody fool," Vara said as she moved into a frenzy, defending Cyrus from all comers. "What did she do to you?"

"Knife ... black lace," the warrior said, coughing up blood. "You can say ... you told me so ... both of you."

"I told you so," Terian said, hearing his voice matched in tone and cadence by Vara as he cast a look at her. He smiled at his elven counterpart, but she offered no such peace offering. *She'll kill me when I'm not helping her save his life, sure as shit.* "We're going to get overwhelmed," Terian threw out. The tide of the battle was no longer something he could even pretend could be held back. "Cyrus, on your feet!"

The warrior tried to get to his feet and stumbled back to his knees immediately. "Can't." His lips were coated in reddish-black liquid and whatever he tried to mumble out next was lost under the clangor of battle.

"Idiot," Vara said.

"He is rather a dunce, isn't he?" Terian buried his axe in another dead body that should have been resting in peace. "Any chance of help?"

Vara's answer came back slowly. "Perhaps some."

The sound of their reinforcement was a low rumble that Terian dismissed as horses at first. Then it grew in pitch and power, hard and heavy, until he was forced to turn simply to make sure that something horrible was not bearing down on them.

Ah, Fortin.

The rock giant arrived without any subtlety, crashing into bodies and sending a shower of bones and parts into the air in a fury that forced Terian to blink away and hold up his axe to deflect a flying femur.

"Fortin, get him out of here," Vara said. "He's been poisoned by that dark elven slattern."

"Poison is a coward's weapon," the rock giant said, splattering a foe. "I should like to show these cowards what I think of them."

Red magic rose over the battlefield and Terian turned his head back toward the dark elven lines. Malpravus's hand was raised high, the spell energy threading out from him to raise the fallen, and that sick pit in his stomach rose once more. "Shit," Terian said. "We need to get out of here."

"Get the General behind the lines," Vara said, and Fortin lifted Cyrus with greatest ease, the warrior dripping red down the rock giant's craggy skin as he was raised up. "We need to pull in tighter."

"You don't understand," Terian said, pausing, trying to drive home his point with emphasis in the midst of a sea of the rising dead, "you need to withdraw the Sanctuary army now. You cannot handle the numbers Malpravus has without a strong front line and a more organized spell caster front. You—we've already lost."

"A convenient thing for someone in the opposing army to say," Vara shot back. Her eyes were wild with fury—at him, at the battle, at the circumstances, at Cyrus—*and I would not care to bet on which of us is in the lead for catching her ire at the moment ...*

"It is," Terian said, "but no less true. Have you not noticed what you've been facing all along? Have you not seen what is hidden behind the armor of the dark elven troops?" *How can you miss it? They're coming back to life all around us as we fight.*

"Dark elves," Fortin said, and bones exploded from a strike he leveled against several of the dead, ripe and rotting flesh splattering like pus as he struck putrefied bodies.

"*Dead* dark elves," Terian said, swinging his axe as hard as he could. "And not the sort Malpravus is raising now, either. You face a limitless army of the dead, raised from every soldier the dark elves have lost in battle whose corpses they were able to recover."

There was a pause as he heard her do her work with a blade behind him. He waited, holding his line, fighting his foes, and a breathless gasp escaped her, audible, a moment later. "Retreat," she said quietly, then let it turn to a horrified shout that echoed over the battlefield. "RETREAT!" Others took up her call, loud voices shouting it over the splintered and faltering Army of Sanctuary. He took up his axe and ran after Fortin as the rock giant began to hew a path back to the Sanctuary line, disorganized and beleaguered as it was.

"You will answer for your crimes, dark elf," Vara said as Terian closed in with her, beating his way back to the friendliest army to him currently on the field. *Not that friendly, though,* he reflected as he caught a look of unadulterated hatred from her, swinging her sword against the legion of dead surging in upon them.

Terian had no answer for that; it should have been frightening, the threats of a furious holy knight as a superior army battered against them in the rear.

Yet somehow it wasn't.

The undead are rising behind me, trying to sweep us from the battlefield and leave nothing but our dead in the wake.

The woman fighting at my side hates me and would—will—kill me at her earliest convenience.

Kahlee and the others are in danger because of my betrayal.

I should be scared shitless, frightened beyond the believing. I should be crying in a pile in the middle of the battlefield, because—let's face it—the whole world is my damned enemy at this point.

And yet …

He felt the curious tickle within; a strange thrill of anticipation that felt so terribly out of place in the midst of the massacre, the rout, that he had to check again to believe it was real. It was warm, a tingle that twinged at his eyes as he struck down the last of the dark elves and rejoined the Sanctuary line, steadying himself to anchor it until the spells began to fly, the ones that would carry him—

Ah. That's it.

Redemption is a path we must walk every day.

I'm finally back on the path, Alaric.

"Take us—" Vara shouted, but the last word was caught in the roar of a surging charge by the dark elves. Terian readied his axe, swinging it now harder and more furiously than he would have otherwise. The word unspoken gave that strange emotion within him new life, like kindling caught hard aflame on a heavy log, burning bright as he battled to protect the Army of Sanctuary in retreat. The appearance of the blue orb glowing in front of him was mere confirmation of the truth he knew was as unspoken as the word Vara had left off.

I'm going home.

35.

Aisling

There was no light where they appeared, not even a sliver, darkness falling over her as suddenly as night, intruding in the daytime as an uninvited guest who batters down the door. Aisling took a breath as soon as she appeared, the horror of the scene she'd left behind still a stunning visual flash in her mind. The Army of Sanctuary would endure, she figured, but whether it would have its General was rather a more open question.

The air was filled with the scent of greenery, and at last Aisling spied a hint of light from somewhere above her, a thin line of it appearing in a crack like two boards were split just enough to allow a few points of illumination to come down on her. She was on her knees in this silent place, quiet save for her breathing and that of Verity next to her. The wizard was grunting in pain, and the subtle sound of bones shifting in the elf's leg told Aisling that it was likely broken.

"Where are we?" Aisling asked coolly, getting to her feet and prowling the space. Her eyes could make out the dim outline of a portal behind them, one lone shaft of light running across the top of the ovoid shape.

"Old dark elven settlement in the southern Waking Woods," Verity grunted as she shifted on the ground. "One of the abandoned ones. Built a warehouse to hide the portal before they left it, the fools." She made a noise of absolute pain that was constrained only by the elf's considerable will. "Give me a moment, and I'll take us back to Shrawn."

"Okay," Aisling said, letting her eyes dart around. There wasn't much to be seen in here, after all.

"Fool girl," Verity said, drawing a hard breath, panting as though she'd exerted herself considerably. "You were supposed to kill him."

"I stabbed him good and proper," Aisling said, pacing under the yawning mouth of the portal. Nothing was behind it but old wooden walls. She could just barely see the texture of them, now, such was the darkness. She looked up to the crack of light again and realized it must have trees growing high above it. *Utterly abandoned, then. How many people even come here?* "Why here?" Aisling asked.

"Because, you vexing moron," Verity snapped, the pain clearly diminishing her patience, "I couldn't cast a return to take us back to Shrawn's with you standing half a league away from me, and I didn't want us to appear at a dark elven portal, where they'd likely kill me right away. God of Death, what a pain—" She paused, swallowed hard, and then called out. "Come here, girl. Let's be done with this."

Aisling drifted from behind the portal coyly, staring at the wizard. "You sure you don't need a few more minutes?"

"I need a bloody healer," Verity snapped, "and I'm unlikely to find one here, a hundred miles south of Saekaj Sovar. Get over here and let's be done with this business. You have your stupidity to answer for, after all."

"Yes," Aisling said, stepping slowly back toward the place where the wizard lay, "I suppose I do."

"Grasp me tight," Verity said, sitting up. Aisling moved to kneel next to her, but the wizard made a "hem!" noise and paused. "You're going to hold tight to my legs, as though I could carry you off in flight, idiot? God of Death, spare me from this lackwit. I swear, behind me, fool. Grasp me from behind, lest you get left in this forsaken place."

Aisling shrugged lightly and did as the wizard asked, slipping behind her and kneeling, prepared to grasp her around the shoulders as expected. She pressed her front against the wizard's back, caught the scent of dry soap in Verity's hair.

"That's more like it," Verity said, voice still thick with impatience. "Now we can—"

The sound of the dagger rushing across the wizard's neck was a small thing, quiet as a footstep on stone. The sound that followed, however, was considerably louder, gasps as blood rushed out in a great flow, as Verity struggled to form words. Aisling held tight to her, pushing her head down, hiding behind her back. Verity raised her hand and hurled a silent spell backward. Flames burst just past Aisling's shoulder, a hard burst that dissipated as soon as it hit the portal's stone, the wash of heat running over her like a summer day sun had crowned and set abruptly just behind her.

"I don't like you," Aisling said, jabbing her dagger into Verity over and over with her free hand, still slumping low behind the wizard's shoulder. "I haven't liked you since we met. The funny thing is, considering the position I'm in, I hate relatively few people. You— you're close to that line." She ran the blade into the heart, again and again. "If you weren't so damned dangerous, I'd be content to let you bleed to death here, slowly." She felt the wizard summoning up one last spell and ran the tip of the dagger right into the wizard's temple, twisting as it broke through the skull. The pointed grey hat fell off Verity's head, and with a final, choked gurgle, Verity went limp in her grasp. "But that's simply not possible."

Aisling threw the body forward, off of her, pushing the dead face into the dirt and stone before slamming the dagger home one final time in the back of the skull, just to be sure. A wizard was no foe to rejoice in having, and a wizard with Verity's power was not someone she wanted to take a chance on having at her back at some point in the future, especially not given all else that was arrayed against her at present.

When the deed was done, she found the door and looked out once she'd opened it a crack. The Waking Woods had grown tall here, ancient trees reaching up to the sky, their interlaced boughs full of green life and blocking the sun almost as effectively as the caves of Saekaj and Sovar. *But not quite.* She surveyed the ruins of the old town, with weeds all overgrown and ivy covering the old buildings. Some of them had a wicked tilt to them, their wood construction overmatched by years of neglect.

She found a good site nearby, an old ditch that was filled near to brimming with small, weedy plants that were somehow surviving in these low light conditions. A few mushrooms grew in the dampness of the rocks, and it was here that Aisling dragged Verity's body. It left a trail of blood that was likely to fool no one who went looking, at least not for long, but it was far enough off the immediate trail that she felt a wizard teleporting in randomly would have to expend time looking for the body. She covered it with a few stray branches, then went over the trail with dirt with her leather boot, sweeping it clear as best she could, dropping sand in the red liquid to mop it up.

When she'd finished, she stood outside in the old town, admiring the destruction, and cast a look at Verity's final resting place. Over an hour had passed, that she was certain of, and she felt quite assured that while the body was hidden from any dark elven searchers that might wander this way, the open wounds she'd left would attract a different sort of seeker. *She'll be nothing but bones within a week,* Aisling thought with cool assurance. She took in a deep breath and sighed it out, a strange relief falling over her at the thought of what she'd done.

One less trouble on my mind. One less link in my chains. And now I can tell the story I want to, within the framework of what happened, and I've got one less voice to oppose me. She blinked. *I don't have much longer, though. That much is certain. The days of my deceits are winding to a close, and I'll need an angle if I wish to avoid his wrath, avoid his desire to dispense with me.*

Fortunately … that one's already taken care of.

Without so much as a look back at the place where she'd left the body, Aisling set her path in the direction of Saekaj Sovar, curiously relieved to face the future—and with a slightly less full abyss of emotion yawing at her feet.

36.

J'anda

When he woke in the mornings, it was with Zieran Lacielle at his side, the both of them politely uncomfortable with the arrangement they'd been forced into by their deceit. For his part, J'anda wondered which of them was the less comfortable with their sharing arrangement. Zieran bore the whole ordeal with a surprising lack of emotion, given how well she'd known him before.

"The silence is deafening," J'anda remarked one morning as they dressed, separately, as though there was a wall dividing the center of the room.

"You of all people should know how much work goes into maintaining even the most rudimentary illusions," she said coolly, her purple eyes devoid of emotion.

"Indeed," he said, taking a sharp breath in through his nose as he fastened his robe and draped the vestment of the enchanter across his shoulders. *It is far beyond strange to be in this place again, and it defies explanation to be here in this way, with this sort of ... companion.* "I suppose it almost like a real marriage, but ... without the marriage."

"The Sovereign may yet command that particular sacrifice of us," Zieran said darkly. Was it his imagination or was there more than a hint of resentment there? *I would have to imagine very hard in order to see none there; how can one live in these forced conditions without feeling some resentment?* His eyes dashed around the room at the thin walls, and the hum and buzz of the Gathering of Coercers made its way through them, a hundred voices in the dining hall somewhere behind Zieran.

"I am sorry it would be a sacrifice," J'anda said without any discernible emotion of his own.

Zieran hesitated, her youthful visage torn in sudden contrition. "I'm sorry, J'anda. I didn't mean to say—"

"I know what you meant," he said with a pained smile. *You meant that being told what to do, who to be and who to be with is an indignity. How well I know this.* "No offense was taken."

She finished threading her hair in a careful braid and threw it over her shoulder. J'anda eyed it; it had been a few weeks since she'd been freed of the Depths, and she was starting to look a little healthy again, down even to her hair. *Finally.* It assuaged his guilt at least a little over the predicament she'd been cast into, though not much. "What are you doing today?"

"Teaching new children some basics," J'anda said with a shrug. "Possibly dropping back to Sanctuary to spy, if so ordered. I haven't heard much of anything of consequence since their Gren expedition."

"Weren't you just there yesterday?"

"I was," J'anda said. "But much can change in a day."

"Are the trolls leaving us?" Zieran asked with a frown.

J'anda shrugged slightly. "Probably."

Her mouth was open to ask another question when the hammering sounded at the door. J'anda turned his head abruptly, frozen in place like he could see through it to the trouble beyond. He started to move to answer it when Zieran held up a hand to stay him. "Wait," she said. "It's my place to do this."

J'anda could not hide the flicker of annoyance. *The standards of the Sovereign.* "Very well," he said and raised a hand in a most sarcastic, faux-magnanimous gesture as the second hammering fell upon the door.

No sooner had Zieran unfastened the bolt and slid it open than the door was pushed open by six soldiers. The first of them moved Zieran aside without resistance; she kept her hands raised all the while. The rest flooded into the room and surrounded J'anda, shoving him roughly away from the bed to surround him. Swords were drawn, blades were in his back, and the points poked at his robes.

"Good morning," Vracken Coeltes said as he entered, holding the staff of the Guildmaster at his side. He was not smiling. "I hope you had a restful night."

"I have had better," J'anda said with an artless shrug, his hands in the air in the non-threatening manner. "The mattresses here, they are simply not of the quality with which I have become accustomed."

"We don't believe in human weakness in this place," Coeltes said without humor.

"But of course," J'anda said, keeping himself on an even keel. *You don't believe in weakness, Coeltes, except as it pertains to others. Perhaps someday soon I'll have a chance to illuminate for you those weaknesses you don't think you have.*

"You are ordered to appear in front of the Sovereign immediately," Coeltes said, and now he smiled slightly.

"You seem happy," J'anda said, "so I assume my execution is in order."

"Your friend Lepos betrayed the Sovereignty yesterday at the battle of Leaugarden," Coeltes said, gleeful. "Since he was the only one who saved you from death the last time you stood before the Sovereign's justice, I don't imagine you'll find another candidate willing to stand in his stead." Coeltes puffed himself up. "I, for one, plan to argue most strenuously for your death." The smile broke wider. "And without anyone worthy of note to speak in your defense," he cast his eyes to Zieran, who stood frozen in fear in the corner, staring at him as the obvious was hammered home by the Guildmaster, "I don't expect you're going to live to see tomorrow."

37.

Terian

Well ... this isn't quite so homey as I might have hoped, Terian thought, staring at the wall of the dungeon cell that he was presently occupying. *Is this the same cell that Cyrus was in a couple years ago?* He let his eyes dash around, from the hard steel door to the even stones that were the color of sand. They fit together beautifully, as everything else in Sanctuary did, and he paused for just a second to wonder at the craftsmanship of the guildhall before a knock sounded at the door.

"Come right on in," Terian said from his place on the cot. The mattress was a little flimsy for his taste, but better than the battlefield sleeping rolls he'd dealt with of late. He had a thought as he stood there; *I wonder if they've got my old horse in the stables ...*

The lock shifted in the door with a hard click and opened wide with a squeak to reveal two guards just outside, their armored pauldrons barely visible on either side of the shadowed opening while two others stood immediately across the hall, watching intently over the shoulder of his visitor.

"Oh," Terian said in surprise as he recognized the silhouette, "I have to admit, I wasn't expecting you."

"You should have," Curatio said, stepping into the cell as the door was shut by the guards behind him. "Have you spoken with J'anda recently?"

Terian slumped against the wall. "Not that recently, no. He told you?"

"He told me," Curatio said, nodding. "I have not shared this bit of information with the Council due to his insistence that it remain quiet

188

that you aided him, but he did tell me how you spared him from the Sovereign's wrath."

"Well, what can I say? I'm just saving people left and right lately."

"Saving old friends, yes," Curatio said, watching him through narrowed eyes. "I admit to being curious about your sudden desire to aid people whose loyalties you spurned not that long ago. I stood with you on that beach, after the bridge, and heard you tell Cyrus that it was not over between you. That you had chosen your father's path after his death."

"I chose poorly," Terian said. "Also, my father's not dead."

Curatio's eyebrow tilted toward the ceiling. "Indeed?"

"What was done to him was the same thing done to the rest of those lifeless sods on the battlefield," Terian said. "The difference being that he's got the soul drain spell to keep him slightly more … energized? Revived? I don't know how you'd say it exactly, but I know it gives him will beyond most of those tromping things without a thought to call their own. He quarrels, he argues, he fights, and it's not out of the sheer bloodthirsty meanness you see in the other dead." Terian pursed his lips. "If he's being controlled by them like Malpravus yanks on the other puppets, he's doing a very good job of hiding it."

"You'll need to tell the Council what you've told Vara and Cyrus about these dead," Curatio said quietly. "That and more."

"I'm not talking about my father in front of them—"

"Not that," Curatio said quietly. "I doubt it would interest them in the slightest. I mean about the army. About the dead."

"Yeah, fine, whatever," Terian said, shaking his head as he rested it in his hands.

"Why did you decide to spare Cyrus Davidon at the risk of your own life, Terian?" Curatio's question was curiously loud now, as though he were trying to get Terian's attention before he asked it.

"Because I can't undo what I've done before," Terian said, glancing up at him. "And because Cyrus Davidon is maybe the only chance that Arkaria has left at surviving."

"That's rather a lot to put on his shoulders."

"They're big shoulders, unlike mine," Terian said, shrugging for emphasis. "And it's not a large hope."

"Indeed not," another voice came as the door opened once more.

"It's a fool's hope, and all the more fitting to come from a fool."

Terian blinked, looking up. "Now this is truly a surprise." It made sense now, why Curatio had asked the question so loudly.

Vara stood in the entry to the door, Vaste shadowing behind her, hunched over so that his face was just barely visible in the door frame. "It should never surprise you to see me anywhere," the troll said. "It should merely be another joyous occasion to mark how very fortunate you are to be in the presence of—"

"Oh, shut up," Vara said in a breath of utter exasperation, her preferred emotional state.

"Yes, let us all shut up," Curatio agreed as Vara stepped into the cell. Vaste followed behind, ducking to avoid bashing his head on the lintel. "I find I cannot often hear myself so much as think over all the ceaseless bantering in this place."

"You'd miss us bantering if we were gone," Vaste said. "Especially me. My banter is so lovely. Someone should inscribe it in a book and sell it all the places where fine wit is appreciated."

"I expect that would find a small audience," Vara said, "or perhaps a very large one, as in the occupants of Gren, in all their ignorance and—"

"I have immense power of spell casting," Curatio muttered under his breath, "and yet I constantly feel powerless to affect any change in this place, bereft of the ability to even shut you idiots up—"

"Can I just point out that for once, I'm not the one derailing the serious conversation?" Terian asked.

"No," Vara and Vaste chorused. Curatio merely sighed, theatrically.

"Do I have to make my little report here?" Terian asked, looking at each of them in turn before settling his eyes on Curatio. "Because that would be preferable to a conversation with that ninnyhammer Ryin Ayend."

"At last, something we can all agree on," said Vaste.

"I don't agree with that," Curatio said. "Ryin is loyal, and he raises excellent points which are seldom refuted—"

"Or agreed with," Vara said.

"Finally, a point on which some of us can agree," Vaste corrected. "Here's another, perhaps: the dark elves are going to destroy all of Arkaria, and soon, it would seem."

"The dark elves are going to leave Arkaria under the boot of a tyrant," Terian said. "And his name is Yartraak. Make no mistake about it, he is steering this ship completely. His servants might be at the till, but he's the one giving the orders behind the scenes." He licked his lips. "You people who live in the daylight? You've never tasted darkness and despair of the sort he'll bring. Even the corruption of Reikonos's Council of Twelve is gentility compared to the Sovereign and his rule."

"If I can be his jester, I could finally entertain the whole of the world," Vaste said. "At last, I'd get the recognition I deserve."

"You'd get your head separated from your neck in about twelve seconds, I'd wager," Curatio said.

Vaste frowned. "You think that little of me?"

Curatio shrugged. "Eight seconds, then."

Impassive, Vaste stared at the healer before replying with a curious satisfaction. "Better."

"I think Cyrus is better company at this point," Vara said, and started for the door.

"I'll make sure to tell him you said so after he wakes," Vaste said. Vara, for her part, slapped him in the belly aggressively enough that he doubled over. "Or perhaps not," the troll said, slightly winded.

"Why did you come down here, shelas'akur?" Terian asked, tossing it at her retreating back.

She whirled on him, and there was no attempt to hide the rage in her eyes. "I thought, given our long association, perhaps I should at least do you the courtesy of looking you in the eye and asking you why you had taken up arms against your own."

"Because I was an idiot," Terian said, not looking away from her fury. She blinked, seeming to back down. "Because I chose the family that never really wanted me over the one that did. Because I reverted to an old loyalty of blood instead of the new loyalty of bond." He tried to put pleading into his eyes and voice. "Because I chose the wrong damned path, and not just once."

"At some point," Vara said coolly, though her eyes hinted at other things behind them, far less chill than her words, "our choices cement us into place, like a wall built with strong mortar. The things you have done ... you have a built a hell of a wall between yourself and Sanctuary, Terian Lepos."

"I'm not expecting you to tear it down," Terian said, pursing his lips. "I know that ... as much as I wish it were otherwise, I have no place here any longer. I'm not asking you to trust me as your guildmate any longer."

"How fortunate for you," Vara said, "because that would result in—"

"I'm not expecting anything other than death," Terian said, thinking of Kahlee. *I hope you managed to do what you said you would, Vincin.* "Not for myself. But if you—if *we* don't find a way to put a stop to this war before it ends in the Sovereign's favor?" He glanced at Curatio, who looked strangely impartial given the subject matter. "I won't be the only one who dies, Vara. You should know, since you nearly watched Yartraak put the claim in on him yourself through his spy—"

She swept in around his defenses with nary a warning, and when he saw what she planned to do, he did not stop her from seizing him by the throat. "Cyrus Davidon may have said that he was through with his feud with you, but I have not relinquished any such claim to vengeance on your sorry arse, Terian Lepos. If you think he was the only one you did wrong in your betrayal, you are sadly mistaken."

"Let's not be coy, Vara," Terian said, breathing only with the aid of his gorget to keep her from crushing his windpipe, "if it had been anyone else, you'd be not nearly as put out with me as you are."

"You betrayed Sanctuary, Terian," she said, voice hard like the steel-encased fingers she pressed against his throat. "Not just Cyrus, but Sanctuary. You killed our General in a foreign land when an army as green as the buds of spring was reliant upon his leadership to carry them through, and you did it at a time when the hordes of death itself were upon your very heels—"

"Your umbrage is awfully personal," Terian said. Her grip had not tightened enough to crush his armor, but the metal groaned under the pressure she applied. He kept his arms at his sides.

"You took an oath of loyalty as a member, as an officer." She looked at him under the line of her helm, the nosepiece flipped up so he could see her cheeks reddening as she grew more furious. "You were the Elder of Sanctuary for a time, for the gods' sakes. Your oaths are held unfulfilled, your word meaningless as that of a stall-keeper in Oortrais—"

"Again with the gnome hate," Vaste said. "What did those little bastards ever do to you?"

"Not nearly as much as this big bastard has," she said, cocking her head, not breaking off from looking at Terian. "You want us to trust you now. Now that you need our help."

"All Arkaria needs your help, Vara," Terian said. "All. I'm the smallest piece of it."

"We should hand you back to the Sovereign you so hate and let him have his way with you," Vara said.

"And while that would be exquisitely painful," Terian said, "you'd still be left with him on your doorstep in about six months."

Rather than diffuse her anger, this seemed to increase it. "Is that so?"

"That is so," Terian said, the pressure increasing on his gorget. The metal squealed, threatening to buckle, and pressed into his flesh. "Probably the only thing I managed to get across to him in my time as a General? Focus your attention on one offensive at a time. He'll deal with the humans first, and then he'll be right back here at Sanctuary. Unless you—"

She jammed the metal of the gorget back as she pulled forward on his breastplate, creating a hard levering action against Terian's neck. *She's going to rip my head off,* he realized as his eyes felt as if they were popping from their sockets from the pressure. *She's not going to listen at this point; I'm scr—*

"Let him go," the soft voice of reason filled the room. The pressure on Terian's neck decreased and he took a surging breath, coughing against the pain in his throat. He gulped hungrily against the loss of precious air, afraid to even exhale for fear the next breath might not arrive. The spots in his vision began to clear, and he played back what he thought he'd heard as he looked up to see both Vara and Curatio staring at Vaste with some surprise.

"Truly?" Vara asked the troll, her skepticism undisguised. "You cannot possibly believe—"

"That he's being sincere?" Vaste asked. There was a weariness about the troll that seemed not solely caused by the slump required of his massive frame to fit in the dungeon room. "Let's just assume for a moment that he's not, that he's lying to save his own neck, that he saved Cyrus's life because—oh, honestly, I can't even contrive of a reason why he would—"

"To gain our favor, of course," Vara said, as though it were obvious. Curatio, strangely, remained silent, his lips pursed in an even line.

"To what purpose?" Vaste asked, shrugging as much as the room would allow. "Now he's here, in the dungeon, but let's assume he wasn't. Let's assume we were utter fools and let him resume his place as Elder of the Council. What does that get him?"

"Free ranging of our halls," Vara said, "where he could perpetrate whatever mischief he was of a mind to—"

"What mischief could he perform?" Vaste asked. "When the day comes that the Sovereign sets his eye on Sanctuary, do you have any doubt he's going to crush us in the palm of his hand? They laid siege to us with an army of a hundred thousand and nearly smashed us to pieces. When he comes again, it will be with an army of a million or more, mostly dead, and they'll be prepared to blow our gates to pieces straightaway. They'll surround the other portals or shut them down, and we won't get a cavalry charge at their backs to save us. No, they'll encircle us like a jungle snake wrapping 'round its prey and burst through our walls, into our home, and they'll kill us all, just as they nearly did last time." Vaste pointed a long nail at Terian. "What could he do to aid them? Open our portal to them? Poison us all at dinner? Spy? Tell the Sovereign all of our secrets, like how Curatio reads his own journals until all hours of the night and that your unmentionables are pink and lacy?"

Vara flushed. "My unmentionables are not—"

"There is nothing he can do that will matter," Vaste said in a suddenly commanding voice. "Without his intervention, Cyrus would have died and this war of ours would have been cut a little bit shorter. Not by much, I might add. If it stays on its current track, we will all of us be dead or exiled from Arkaria by the end of next year." He drew his arms sideways. "This is the truth. His part in this is irrelevant."

"You accept freely as fact the grim reality he would have us believe," Vara said.

"It's going to happen," Terian choked out over racking coughs.

"Says you," she snapped back.

"I believe him," Curatio said, pushing his lips to one side pensively. "There is no other army in Arkaria that will stand against what the Sovereign has assembled. It is simply too much."

"What gain do we get out of keeping him alive, then?" Vara asked. "Why should we not strike him down now?"

"You, of all people, taking the vengeful road?" Terian asked.

"You, of all people," she said coolly, turning her head to look him in the eye with those glacially blue eyes, "should know that I once found that path more preferable than any other."

Terian felt his face tighten. "I'm sorry, Vara."

She cocked her head again. "For what?"

"For not doing what I counseled you to do when first you came here," Terian said and meant it. "For not walking the path I steered you on."

"You were only a puppet there, in any case," she said. "We all know that however your mouth might have made the words, Alaric was the voice behind them."

"It wasn't just Alaric," Terian said. "You think I never wanted revenge for anything before? I came to Sanctuary a seething mess of resentments, furious and wishing vengeance for a crime I can hardly name. He had me walk you down a path he walked me down first, and it's to my shame that I stepped off it with Cyrus."

"Yes, Alaric has counseled us all through many moments of ill temper," Curatio said, showing more than a little ill temper of his own, "but this leaves us with a conundrum. There seems to be an inevitability to the Sovereign's conquest of Arkaria. We are like the frog in the hot pot as the heat of the water rises around us."

"And now I'm hungry," Vaste said.

"I see nowhere to hop," Vara said. "Do you?"

"The lid is firmly on at the moment," Curatio said, "save for if we were to retreat."

"That's a bit of a shit metaphor, then," Vaste said. "Because the whole point of the lid being on is that the frog can't escape—"

"We are of Sanctuary, dolt," Vara said, "and retreat is not in our nature."

"Maybe not in yours," Vaste said, "but I have no problem show the enemy my hindparts in a fight—"

"That would be cowardly even for him," Vara said, whipping her other hand around to indicate Terian.

"Hey," Terian said, "you're the one who ordered the retreat at

Leaugarden—"

"And here we go, dissolving into rancor again," Curatio said, quietly cutting them all off. "Can we not come to a decision? Can we not leave aside the past for just a few minutes while contemplating the future?"

"Well, no," Vaste said, "because the past was the carriage that brought us here, after all, to this point in the ride. And like a bunch of drunken passengers, we're not really that happy with the destination at this point, because we're busy vomiting up our bad decisions and—"

"Your point is well taken, if somewhat ineptly expressed." Vara rolled her eyes as she spoke. "There are rivers of bad blood between us and Terian at this point—"

"I thought it was a wall built of—"

"Shut it, troll," Vara said. "I cannot imagine what use he would be to us at this point, nor that we could trust a word that comes out of his mouth."

"I trust him," Vaste said, and the room went silent save for Terian's heavy breathing as Vara and Curatio looked at him. "I see the line between where he was and where he is now clearly; I hear the voices of the dead sing his praises and curse his actions, and I know the specter of the evil that he fears to even whisper." Vaste leaned closer to Terian, looked into his eyes with those onyx and yellow monstrosities, and Terian saw mercy there. "Death is only a step behind this man, and he's not afraid of it for himself. He knows he's already half in its mouth, that it knows and craves the taste of him. He's afraid for others, not himself. Including us, I might add."

"Bullshit," Vara said.

"It's true," Terian said. "Though I know you won't believe me."

"I don't."

"I might," Curatio said, staring at him, trying to penetrate his mind with a gaze. "I see a regret in him, a contrition I can't recall seeing but twice before—once when he first came to these gates, and again when he returned to us."

"I imagine if I were about to be killed, I would feel somewhat contrite as well," Vara said, voice thick with loathing.

"No, you wouldn't," Terian said, drawing her gaze back to him, "because you have nothing to be sorry for in the conduct of your life." *Well, maybe that one thing ...* but he dared not mention it for fear of setting her off. "My regrets are mountains that I carry upon my shoulders."

"And now you'd have us help you with the burden?" Vara asked.

"I'd have you do what's best for your guild," Terian said, "and what's best for Arkaria. And if that happens to coincide with what's best for me … would you find fault with it?"

"Yes," she said quickly and then paused before speaking more fully. "But … I might perhaps be open to it nonetheless." She released her grasp upon his gorget. "I hope you have something of worth for us other than the desperate picture you have already painted."

Terian rubbed at his neck, almost afraid to unlatch his gorget and rub at the skin lest she grab hold of him again, this time without the protection it provided. "I can tell you what they're probably doing right now, the armies of the Sovereign, but I suspect you already know that. I've told you what they are, but that's of little enough use." He forced a smile, but it was grim. "I have counsel, but you won't like to hear it, and it's hardly the right time for it in any case. As my wife would say, all I have left is my trollery."

Vara's brow puckered. "What?"

"Trollery," Terian said. "It's her play on the word 'droll,' with—"

"No, no," Vara said, "you have a wife?"

"Uh, well, yes," Terian said. "For … years now."

There was a quiet in the dungeon as that one soaked in. Vara turned to Vaste, her face blank as a fresh piece of parchment. "Hear that? If that daft prick can find someone, even you have a hope."

38.

J'anda

J'anda was tired of the Sovereign's throne room, was sick to death of seeing Coeltes hiding in the shadows beneath the throne like some lapdog laying beneath his master's chair, waiting for scraps. *The scraps of me.*

The oily scent was in the air, heavy and bitter all the way down J'anda's throat as though he'd taken a swig straight out of a lamp. His wariness was dampened by the chill of the caves on his skin, and he stood there in his robes, hands folded in front of him in the sleeves, staring at Coeltes beneath the God of Darkness. *If only the throne would collapse, it'd crush him and I could die happy. Well, perhaps not happy, but somewhat satisfied, especially if he became a hemorrhoid on the arse of the Sovereign. There would be a sort of justice in that, the two of them bound together forever ...*

"What do you have to say for yourself?" the Sovereign asked, his clawed fingers interlaced as he leaned back in his chair. His belly looked slightly fat the way he was sitting, as though he had just eaten a particularly heavy meal and was awaiting digestion.

"I thought I was called here to answer for Terian Lepos, not for anything I personally did," J'anda said.

"He saved your life," the Sovereign said.

"You saved my life," J'anda said. "Perhaps at his urging, but ... nonetheless."

"Do you think I will hesitate to take it now?" the Sovereign asked, getting to his feet. Coeltes scrambled back, out of the way, clearly desirous of not becoming that hemorrhoid J'anda had hoped for. *A great pity, that.* Coeltes's arms pumped, and J'anda realized he did not have the staff of the Guildmaster with him any longer. *Curious. When did he dispense with it?*

And why?

"I hoped you would wait until I gave you some cause to do so," J'anda said with a shrug.

"And still you stand before me, seemingly fearless," Yartraak said, the ground thundering as he stomped his foot. *Not furiously, but for emphasis,* J'anda thought.

"I remember standing before you, filled with fear," J'anda said, looking up into the face of the God of Darkness, the grey flesh clear without the shroud about him. "It was a hundred years ago, during our first meeting. Do you recall?"

Yartraak's red eyes honed in on him. "On the day of your award for bringing us victory in the Perdamun campaign."

J'anda smiled ever so slightly. "I recall it well. I stood before you on trembling legs, and you told me how proud you were. I remember being fearful to the point of near sickness that I would say something, that I would do something that would offend you in some small way." He looked back up at the god who stood before him. "A small way, only, see, for I could hardly imagine dealing a larger slight to what I perceived as your greatness at the time."

"You were truly a hero then," the Sovereign said ponderously, slowly, as he regarded J'anda with those red eyes carefully. "A flawless example of the loyalty, bravery and spirit we wanted to cultivate. I sang your praises where all could hear."

"And they were like music to my ears," J'anda said. The Sovereign's face creased in something approaching a frown. "What? I like music. I'll admit it."

"How did you descend from such great heights?" the Sovereign asked. "What seed of disloyalty took root in your heart to grow to who you are today?"

J'anda blinked and almost told him the answer. "I feared for my very life, and so I left, vowing never to come back and face my fears."

"But now you stand before me, unafraid to die," Yartraak said, taking a step closer on his ungainly, long legs. "You have associated with the scum of other lands, have hidden in the bosom of mine enemies, preferred their lawless ways to my gentle guidance—"

"I preferred to live without fear that Vracken Coeltes would have me dragged to face my death on any given day," J'anda said, staring right into the red eyes.

"Again you blame Coeltes for your wrongs," the Sovereign said coldly.

"I was a hero of Saekaj," J'anda snapped and watched the red eyes blink in surprise, "I helped you win victories. I put down rebellions for you. I was the favored to run the Gathering of Coercers. My loyalty was unquestioned." He let his rage pour out in a white-hot heat. "When the day came that Coeltes realized that he could never overcome me through his own skill, his own victories, he undertook a coward's path to break me using your laws in any way he could. He cost you your best enchanter—and probably the war—at a moment when you could ill afford it." J'anda spit in fury at the Sovereign's feet. "What victories has he brought you? What armies has he defeated? What master enchanters has he turned out of the Gathering in my stead?" He felt the blood settled within him, leaving him cold. "What has he done for you that I could not have done better in his place, had you let me? What has he brought you of value, other than my head?" J'anda used his finger to draw a line across his neck. "Here it is, if you want it. Take it. Put it on a pike before the palace as an example of what happens to heroes of Saekaj when they come up against the ambitions of cowards and incompetents—"

"You go too far, Aimant," the Sovereign said, hissing.

"Then kill me," J'anda spat back. "Kill me and be done with it. Better that than live in fear of him always looking over my shoulder, ready to rip apart any good I can do for you—"

"Please don't," came a quiet, feminine voice from the leg of the throne, "my Lord of Darkness."

Yartraak wheeled, the carpet beneath his feet skidding as he turned so quickly. His claws scratched across the wood floor and J'anda peered between his legs to look at the woman who waited against the foreleg of the mighty wooden throne, Vracken Coeltes's unconscious body at her feet. A trickle of blood ran down his temple, but to J'anda's disappointment his chest still moved subtly up and down.

"What are you doing here, Aisling Nightwind?" Yartraak called, voice heavy with fury.

"My name is not Aisling Nightwind," Aisling said, striding out from under the throne with her hands before her, "not really. That's just what Shrawn told you because he didn't know any better."

The Sovereign cast a glance at her, hard, then stepped closer, his ire directed away from J'anda—blessedly—at least for a moment. "Is that so?" the God of Darkness asked. "And how did a little street urchin of Sovar keep a secret such as this from her master?"

"Because Dagonath Shrawn was never my master," Aisling said, catching J'anda's gaze with a look that spoke volumes about the coolness of her disposition. *The girl must have a heart of ice to stand there with him looking like that at her ...*

Or perhaps she's just another one of us, the fearless of Sanctuary, as the Sovereign would probably call us.

"Shrawn is the master of all Sovar," the Sovereign said. "All who live below are subject to him."

"And yet I am not from Sovar," Aisling said, with narrowed eyes of her own, "not truly."

"What foolishness is this?" the Sovereign asked. "I would have your name, then, if you are a citizen of Saekaj."

She nodded slowly and cracked a smile. "As well you should. My name is Yalina, of the House of Tordor." The smile grew broader. "I believe you know my father, Grimrath?"

39.

Aisling

"I am surrounded by liars, fools, and the disloyal." The Sovereign's voice rumbled across the quiet chamber a few minutes after Aisling had made her dramatic pronouncement about her parentage. She had spent the intervening time listening to Yartraak issue orders to his guards—to fetch Shrawn, to retrieve and awaken the enchanter, Vracken Coeltes, whom she'd knocked unconscious, and to fetch her father. Two of these orders she felt certain would fall to failure, but the third she was still somewhat optimistic about, though she doubted it would do her much harm if her father also failed to show up.

J'anda, for his part, seemed to be quietly listening to the Sovereign's occasional mutters of irritation. She knew the enchanter well enough through their travels together with Sanctuary and had heard of his reputation before leaving Saekaj, of course, but walking in on him in the midst of spitting a very violent piece of his mind at the Sovereign had been a strange stroke of luck. She'd entered through Shrawn's secret passage after making a circuitous travel into the caverns via Sovar before entering Saekaj, and it had involved a considerable amount of stealth. Still, the timing had been near-perfect, granting her a wonderful entrance that had probably spared the life of the enchanter.

Not that he'll be that grateful, in all probability, especially if he's heard what happened at Leaugarden.

"Liars, fools, and traitors," Yartraak muttered again as the door to the throne room cracked open. Aisling let her eyes settled on J'anda's, silent communication running between them. His was inquisitive, wondering at her game. *Let him wonder for now*, she figured. *He'll see soon enough what I'm up to—other than saving his life and hopefully mine.*

"My Lord Yartraak," a guard stooped at the entry to the enormous hall that was the throne room, "Dagonath Shrawn is not in Saekaj at the moment. His household guard issues their apologies and is scrambling to track him down."

"Hmmm," Yartraak breathed, a low rumble. "What of Coeltes?"

"Still unconscious, your grace," the guard said, bowing again. "He seems to have suffered quite the blow to the head."

And a little dose of nekref'atras in the wound to ensure he stays out for a space, Aisling thought. *He wasn't adding anything to the conversation, in any case. I could tell that much just hiding under the throne behind him.*

"You have injured one of my chief advisors, Ais … Yalina Tordor," Yartraak said, turning his low rumble toward her.

"He started to attack me as I stepped out to reveal myself to you," she said with a bow of her head. "Doubtless trying to defend you against some unseen attacker as I moved out of Shrawn's passage."

Yartraak's crimson eyes narrowed. "How did you know about Shrawn's passage behind my throne?"

She blinked innocently at him. "He led me through it last time."

Yartraak let out a low, purring rumble akin to a dissatisfied cat. "You were blindfolded."

"I may have been blind," she said, "but I was hardly insensate."

"You play a dangerous game, Lady Tordor, if that is in fact who you are," Yartraak said, "coming before me after failing to kill Cyrus Davidon."

She shrugged, tossing out the information she'd picked up in the market. "I missed the heart, but he was still damaged enough that he lost the battle." She caught a wounded look from J'anda, undisguised. She sent back a cool gaze that forced him to blink from the intensity of it. *You'd better hide that loyalty of yours, enchanter, because it will do you no favors in this place.*

"You think this is an acceptable result?" Yartraak asked, leaning toward her, his enormous frame bending almost in half to address her eye to eye.

"I would have killed him entirely," Aisling said coolly, "but Shrawn's pet wizard leapt into the middle of my attack and declared her loyalty to Mortus, trying to take her revenge by disrupting my attack."

Oily breath hit her in the face, the exhalation of a god. "How long does it take to pierce a man's heart?"

"Depends on the man," Aisling said, staring right at him. "Depends on the heart. I was told you wanted this to be a slow, painful thing. My blades were coated in black lace, and I stabbed into him under that armor of his—"

Yartraak rumbled in disgust, but she kept from flinching away. "Perhaps," he said after a moment's pause, "you are not utterly incompetent. His armor is a problem. Foolish mistake, that, letting him have it."

She caught J'anda's perplexed look for a moment before the doors to the throne room opened once more and another man entered. He was overweight, much like Shrawn, but stooped over almost into a right angle, hurrying along on his cane, his white hair now shaded grey by time. "I beg your pardon, my Sovereign, I received your summons and hurried along as quickly as I could."

Grimrath Tordor was an old man to her eyes, eyes that had not been set on him in a decade. His hair looked virtually the same, and the stoop was just like she remembered. The only difference she registered immediately was the cut of his suit; it looked new, in line with what she'd seen in the markets on her last trip through Saekaj. It was just the sort of thing that all the dandies were wearing now, and she rolled her eyes to think of him taking that particular style for his own.

"I am unconcerned about your punctuality, Grimrath," the Sovereign said.

"A thousands kindnesses you do me, my Sovereign," Tordor said as he hobbled forward. She watched him move, barely daring to raise his head, walking unseeing into something that he did not understand. "These old legs simply do not move as fast as they used to."

"Look at me, Tordor," Yartraak snapped, drawing the old man's gaze upward, carefully displayed reverence in his eyes. The old man always was a savvy player of the game; he knew how to pay just enough homage to keep being allowed to play his own.

"Yes, your grace?" Tordor asked, almost standing next to her now. His gaze was still fixed on the Sovereign, clearly paying no mind to the other visitors to the throne room. J'anda, for his part, looked at

Tordor, then back to her, raising an eyebrow as if to say, *This is your father?* She shrugged in reply. It wasn't as though she had chosen him for herself, after all.

"Do you see anyone you recognize here, Tordor?" Yartraak asked, patience clearly running thin.

She watched her father blink his eyes, start to speak, then halt, thinking over his best response. "Well, there's you, of course, my Sovereign ..."

Not smart, Father. The Sovereign made a grunting noise of fury and raised a hand as if to strike him and finally, the urgency of the situation dawned on him. Grimrath Tordor looked first between the Sovereign's thin legs at J'anda, peering at his face. "I ... think I recognize ... is that J'anda Aimant?"

"Indeed," J'anda said. "I owe you my apologies, Lord Tordor. I borrowed your carriage on the way down to visit the Sovereign a few weeks ago."

"Oh, well," Tordor said, seemingly unconcerned. "Thank you, I suppose. No harm done, I reck—"

"Do you see anyone else you recognize, Tordor?" The Sovereign was nearly bursting with anger, his eyes redder than usual.

At last—yet somehow fittingly, for him—Grimrath Tordor finally looked straight at her. And she knew, a moment after he did, that he had absolutely no idea who she was. "Hello," he said politely and looked back to the Sovereign.

"Hello, Father," she said, and watched him jerk his head back around fast enough to nearly break his own neck, eyes nearly rattling in his own head in wide shock. He blinked enough times to clear an entire desert's worth of sand granules out, and his mouth moved up and down in mute shock several times before he produced a word. "Y– Ya—"

"Yalina," she said playfully. The fright of standing before the Sovereign in this moment was oddly diminished by watching her father, one of the most powerful men in Saekaj, and certainly one of the wealthiest, reduced to a stammering idiot.

"Not p-p-possible," he finally got out. "You—you went to Sovar!"

"Well, here I am, back," Aisling said. "A little older, a little worse for the wear—"

"Is this your daughter?" Yartraak asked, leaning close to both her and her father, putting a hand on the ground and leaning forward on his claws like a predatory animal.

"She—well, I—I —" Tordor stumbled to get out. He was still clearly flummoxed by surprise, unable to sculpt an articulate thought even with time and a trowel to shape the damned thing. Aisling, for her part, tried to act as though she were bored by the whole situation and a little embarrassed. Essentially, not unlike a spoiled noblewoman might when presented with such thoroughly ridiculous circumstances.

"TORDOR!"

"I think so, your Grace," Tordor finally said. "She—well, she certainly looks like … like Yalina, though—much older, obviously and—it's—it's been some time, though, and I could be …" He cringed. "Is she in a great deal of trouble, my Sovereign?"

Yartraak's jaw clamped back into place, showing his enormous underbite. "She has just helped to secure an immense victory for our people in the Riverlands of the Human Confederation."

Tordor blinked back his surprise. "I … well … good. Her mother will be … so surprised." *Thanks for the vote of confidence, Father.*

Yartraak whirled his face to look at her. "You hid this from Shrawn."

She did not blink, looking a god straight in the face. "When he came to me, he made his purpose plain—I was to be the spy that you did not have, to be the subterfuge that you have no place for in your society." She smiled. "I was all he expected and more."

"Indeed you were," Yartraak said, low, considering. "More than he anticipated, then. Yes …"

"You didn't believe him to be the flawless spider at the center of the web of information, did you?" she asked, oh-so-coy. "I know he tries, so very hard, to convince you of his authority in these things …" She dangled the tempting morsel, waiting to see if his pride would allow for him to bite at it.

"I see the truth in the hearts of men," Yartraak snapped with such force that Grimrath Tordor took a step back. Aisling, for her part, did not even quail at his sudden burst of fury. She let him see the lack of concern in her eyes, stared him down and gave him a gaze of her own in return. "And women, lest you think yourself immune to my power, outside of my influence." He paused, composing himself. "Why do you return to me now, Yalina Tordor? Why expose who you are at this moment?"

"Isn't it obvious?" she asked, pretending surprise and knowing that he did not see it, despite his protests. "Because I've come here to declare myself to you."

"What would you have me hear?" the Sovereign asked.

"That I serve you," Aisling said and bowed to a knee for effect. "That I am weary of throwing myself uselessly at the feet of Dagonath Shrawn and having him misuse me constantly." She pointed at J'anda. "I come to tell you the same thing that he does—that your servants, so-called, have led your Sovereignty into more ill places than can properly be imagined in the realms of men and fools. They hide secrets from you, things that serve their purposes but not yours, and try to disguise their failings so you will not see ..."

"This all sounds very familiar," Yartraak said, low and suspicious, and he pointed at J'anda. "It sounds like the same lies that Terian Lepos fed me for months and years before his inevitable betrayal. Lies disguised as truth, and unpalatable either way. Interlopers from Sanctuary trying to convince me that my most loyal are least loyal, thinking me a fool all the while—"

"I'm not from Sanctuary," Aisling said. "I'm from Saekaj."

"You carry the taint of that place on you," Yartraak said, whipping clawed fingers about him in a furious gesture, "the stink of lies that Alaric Garaunt draped over him at all times."

"You've had to raise an army of the dead to win a war that you nearly had finished two years ago," J'anda said, finally entering the conversation and causing the Sovereign to whirl on him. "Which part of that is lies?"

The God of Darkness spun around to face Aisling once more. "You come to declare yourself to me? And bring me what? News that you have failed? What a kind gift."

"News that I helped you win a battle, as you said before," Aisling looked up at him, unmoved by his mercurial temperament. "As for whatever else you would have of me, I leave up to you. You know what I've done." She felt a tiny prick of shame at having her father here for this, though he likely had no idea what she'd done in the course of those duties.

"And what do you want?" Yartraak asked, surveying her quietly.

This is it. This is the moment I've been waiting for. "Only to serve," she said, lying right through her teeth once more. "Otherwise, I would have left."

"You come at a time when I have almost won the battles before me," Yartraak said, considering her carefully. "You leap upon the victor's bandwagon as it rolls through on a celebratory parade."

"Reikonos still stands," she said, looking to J'anda, planting the seed.

"For a little longer," Yartraak agreed. "How would you cure that particular ailment?"

"I'm hardly a master strategist," she said, now pulling out some of that well-traveled coyness, "but it seems to me that a hero of Saekaj is standing right behind you, a man with no small talent for helping win battles with his … abilities." She flashed a smile in the dark. "If you wanted to test his loyalty, that seems like a place where he might be of use."

Yartraak's breath rumbled in and out. He did not see the stricken look on J'anda's face. "Yes," the Sovereign rumbled. "That is a use I could have for you, J'anda Aimant." He whirled on the enchanter. "You protest that Vracken Coeltes has co-opted your life and stolen all you worked for, depriving me and yourself of victories? Prove it to me." He leaned right into J'anda's face. "Prove it to me by handing me the jewel of the Human Confederation."

J'anda's face had been impassive since he'd seen the Sovereign turn on him. His reaction was a low bow. "As you wish."

"And you," Yartraak said, turning back to Aisling. "What can you do for me?"

"I can do something for you that none of your other servants can," she said, looking right at him and ignoring the look of growing horror on J'anda's face as she spoke. "I'm a Lady of the Elven Kingdom … and I can open the city of Termina to your armies."

40.

J'anda

He stalked after Aisling down the hallway from the throne room, wary of the guards stationed around them. "Are you mad?" he asked in a barely restrained whisper, wondering how she would even answer.

She stared back at him through smoky eyes, her head turned, cool as a Northlands morning. "I just saved your life."

"Lots of people have been doing that lately," J'anda said, and he stopped in the middle of the foyer, the grand hardwoods covering every surface around them giving it the aura of some surface mansion at night. "I'm finding myself less and less grateful every time it delays me from the inevitable."

"You seem to be developing a gratitude problem," she said. "Have you thought about just saying 'thank you' and moving on?"

"I didn't hear your father say 'thank you' and move on." This was true. Grimrath Tordor had sputtered when dismissed from the Sovereign's presence, and hurried to leave, saying only two words to Aisling—Yalina, he supposed—under his breath before departing in a huff.

"He's got years of resentment and anger built up," Aisling said. "What's your excuse?"

J'anda looked again at the guards before leaning in close to her. "That you stabbed my friend in the back."

"Cyrus?" There was only a flicker in her eyes to show she felt anything at all. "He'll live."

"Perhaps it's also that you just committed us to delivering the Sovereign the Elven Kingdom and Reikonos, respectively." He pointed from her to himself. "That is a very big debt for me to pay." When she didn't react, he stepped in close. "What are you playing at?"

"Why would you assume it's a game?"

"I didn't," J'anda said.

"You said 'playing at,'" she said, "as though it's some scheme cooked up by a bored heiress or something."

He shook his head. "You're the heiress of Grimrath Tordor, the greatest collector of antiquities in Saekaj, and you've become a thief. I can't think of a reason for that other than being a bored heiress, so—"

"My reasons are my own," she said, eyes flashing in barely disguised indignation, "and this is no game. Not at this level. Not with the Sovereign opposite us."

Wariness settled over J'anda. "If he's opposite us, then truly, you are playing a dangerous game."

She hissed once more at his use of the word game. "Games are for children. Lives are on the line."

"Entire nations are on the line," J'anda replied, the quiet of the foyer making him nervous. "You should know since you just put them there."

"They were already there," she said, "I merely hastened their addition to the stakes. Anyone who's a serious observer knows which direction this army is marching, and that it's inevitable that they'll arrive there."

"And you," J'anda said, watching her carefully, "you who just professed her loyalty to the Sovereign … you're going to stop this?"

"I have my own reasons for what I'm doing," Aisling said, back to cold. "I just saved your life by bartering something that was bound to come under the hammer, since armies of dark elves surround the city. Now you've got marching orders instead of an execution. Thank me, don't thank me, it's entirely up to you. I'd simply take it as a courtesy if you don't screw things up until I've had time to do what I need to." With that, she proceeded to turn to leave.

"Why?" J'anda called after her. They were far enough apart now that there was no longer a guarantee of privacy.

"Because I serve the Sovereign," she said, turning her head back to him just enough to catch his eye. "I do what I'm ordered to do, by him and his servants. They sent me to Sanctuary, ordered me to

Cyrus's side at all times, and informed me when the time had come for him to reach his end." She smiled, and it almost looked sincere. "All glory to his name." The smile faded. "Now, if you'll excuse me … I have to go home." And she left out the front doors, opened by guards in full armor, their poleaxes stiff and at the ready, but at attention for a servant of the Sovereign as she passed.

J'anda blinked as he ran through what she'd said in his mind. *She serves the Sovereign*, she said, *but she doesn't truly. She mentioned his orders—his servants' orders. Shrawn, I have to guess* … It was a like a puzzle he was putting together, searching for the pieces that interlocked correctly. *They forced her into this course of action, somehow … had leverage over her, by the sound of it. Made her fearful … like me*, he though ruefully. *Now she smiles at them and speaks the words of their agenda while following one of her own …*

Perhaps I'm not left alone in this fight against the Sovereign now that Terian is gone, he concluded as the guards shut the door with a clatter behind her. *Though I'm not sure I could call her ally, given that there's absolutely no telling how she wants things to play out …*

41.

Aisling

She walked into the front doors of her parents' house as though she owned the place, though in fact neither she nor any member of her family did. Every one of the twelve manors that lined the road leading to the Grand Palace of Saekaj, as well as every other home in the upper chamber, belonged to the Sovereign, and was let out by his favor alone. The high ceiling of Saekaj was like the limit upon the opulence of the place, with nobles rising and falling in the Sovereign's estimation and moved about in the great Shuffle with every change in their position.

The House of Tordor had maintained a residence in the top twelve for over three thousand years. She stared around the carved stone of the entryway. An opulent chandelier hung from the ceiling, lit with a thousand candles that shed their light all day and night. It had been imported from an iron-and-glass works in the free city of Aloakna before that town had been destroyed at the Sovereign's decree. It was permissible to make alterations to one's house, though if one were shuffled down to a lower manor, they had to remain. Her father had been very careful to keep his little collectables mostly out of sight, things that could not be argued to be part of the house, should such an occasion come about. And it had in the past, she knew, though not in her lifetime.

"I'm home," Yalina Tordor said aloud, though not at all loudly. There were servants standing at attention against the walls, two men in long coats of the sort that were preferred by the serving class, tails down almost to their knees.

"You are expected, madam," one of the servants said, bowing his head at her. She didn't bother to disguise her smile. She was clad in leather armor from head to toe and wore a great cloak over the top of it all, cowl back and her hair loose around her shoulders. It was doubtless the first time the servants of the House of Tordor had had a true rogue as a visitor in their house, a ranger bent toward the delicate craft of thievery and stealth. *There's not exactly a guild for us, after all, at least not an accredited one.* "This way," the servant said, pointing toward a sitting room hidden behind a well-carved door that Aisling suspected had not come with the house.

"I'll see myself in," she said, brushing past the servant, who tried to disguise his shock and failed. She entered the sitting room with a simple push of the swinging door to see her father on a plush, red-padded couch, clutching his walking stick between his fingers. Her mother, looking aged and weary, sat next to him, worry etched in the lines of her face, which looked to have deepened in the years since last Aisling had last seen her. "Bet you didn't think that you'd be summoned before the Sovereign on the day of my return," she said, opening grandly with a smirk, "to hear about how well I turned out, and what excellent service I'd provided to the Sovereignty."

"Uh, well, no," her father said, pushing up to his feet, his back crooked from being hunched over. "I must confess, I thought for certain that if ever we were called to account for you, it would be a summons to Sovar to identify your body."

She made a disgusted sound deep in her throat. "You assumed that because I became a thief, I'd simply become a common one, with a common destiny, and end up dead in a gutter. Your faith is truly the buttress that holds me aloft."

"Well, you have to admit, dear," her mother said, eyes sad, "there are not exactly a great many thieves that live to a ripe old age, or that become accredited in the eyes of the Sovereign. Most of them endure slow death in the Depths—"

"I'm not common, I keep telling you," Aisling said, pacing slowly around the small table that separated her from them on the couch. "You should have known that, of course, because I told you when I left that I didn't aim to be gutter trash."

"All Sovar is gutter trash," her father said darkly.

"All Saekaj is gutter trash as well, actually," she replied. "In Sovar they know it and embrace their calling with pride. Here it's all appearances and balls, trying to put on airs to hide the stink of our cave-dwelling nature. We're a low people, preying on each other. And Saekaj is the worst of all, feeding on the carcasses of those below, lording it over them."

"I trust you didn't return like some dark horror from the Back Deep simply to preach a revolution," her father said, leaning hard on his cane, "because I think you'll find it causes more than a fair amount of alarm up here."

"As well it should," she said. "No, I didn't come home for that. I came because it's expected, after I revealed myself to the Sovereign." Her eyes fell on a series of sculptures from around the world, displayed on a high shelf. She did the calculation in her head; they were worth six million gold pieces to the right buyer, probably; only a million or two if fenced. "Appearances need to be tended to."

"So ... you're not staying, then?" her mother asked, with undisguised relief.

"I wouldn't worry, Mother," she said, now smirking again. "Remember, you get credit for my successes, not just my failures, and I've pleased the Sovereign to some degree recently. Perhaps it'll move you up a rank or two in the Shuffle."

"I worry more about what happens if you decide to embrace those thieving ways you left us to pursue," she said.

"I'm a bit too busy to thieve at the moment," Aisling said, and her eyes fell over a gold-inlaid chair that was perched in the corner. The gemstones crusting it were probably worth at least a few hundred thousand gold pieces; once removed and melted down, the gold plating was probably another hundred thousand by itself. The chair, though, was almost worthless without them. "And I never truly had great need of the proceeds, did I?"

"Then why?" her mother asked. "Because of that man?" She struggled. "What was his name? Northen?"

"Norenn," she whispered. A trace of sadness ran across her face.

"Was it all for him?" her mother asked.

It may have started that way, she thought but dared not say, even here, *but it certainly isn't turning out that way.* He felt like the habit she couldn't break, the tether she couldn't snap even to save her own neck. "I owe him," she said, and spoke the truth in this, though not all of it. She gathered her cloak about her and turned to leave.

"Will we see you again?" her father asked, as close to plaintive as she'd ever heard him. She turned at the door, looking at his stooped-over figure. Time had not been kind to him, his back worsening in her absence. He looked at her through worried eyes, focused on her at last. She saw a matching gaze from her mother, though buried under a layer of reticence born of years of rift between them.

Aisling Nightwind opened her mouth to answer, but could not find a reply that she wished to give. And so instead she turned and left the house of Yalina Tordor, her cloak swishing behind her, almost certain that she would not return but harboring one last hope that perhaps, someday, once the thing was done, her answer might change.

42.

J'anda

The road to the front was a long and laborious path, a dirt road trod hard by horse and wagon and man, threading through fields that might once have been green but were now mud and shit, blood and gore turning the ground soupy but empty, all traces of corpses removed as the army of Saekaj and Sovar marched forth to their ultimate goal.

The city's walls were visible on the horizon, a day's ride from the hilltop that J'anda rode across, his horse cantering beneath him at a leisurely pace. His back hurt, his legs hurt, and the rest of him was along for the painful ride. The signs of life were there under the walls of Reikonos in the distance. He could hear the faint roar of an army at siege, could see the trebuchets firing hunks of rock and bombs that looked like birds at this distance but which were probably the size of horse-drawn carts. Occasional explosions rumbled like thunder to his ears, and he watched it all with a heavy heart, knowing the end was nigh.

The sun set and he slept on the side of the road, in the dirt on his bedroll, the occasional dark elven patrol rousting him out of bed as they passed. For convenience's sake he used a spell every time to convince them to move on and leave him be, and every time it worked, giving him as much peace as he might find in such a barren place, with the sound of siege and horror on the near horizon.

When he reached the edge of the army the next day, the smell of death was thick in the air. It hung heavy with the aura of rot, of flesh turning soft and falling off bone, a smell he drank in through his nose and wished he could spit out like a bad bite of meat.

He passed a corps of knights that had vek'tag as their steeds, saddles giving away their purpose to any with the eyes to note and the minds to decipher the curious meaning of the spectacle. The spiders hissed at each other, wilder than the vek'tag put to use in hauling carts in Saekaj and Sovar, he supposed.

J'anda rode on, toward the front, the walls of Reikonos growing taller as he went. The projectiles flinging back and forth were close at hand, now, though it all seemed very half-hearted to him, as though neither side were trying very hard. It was as though the humans knew that a simple lobbing of rocks would not turn back the tide of the advance, and the dark elves were saving the city for something else, a darker fate, perhaps.

He was directed toward the General's tent and found himself face to face with Malpravus a little before the evening hour. His bones ached, his muscles were weary from the long ride, and he stood in front of the necromancer feeling almost as dead as any of the Goliath Guildmaster's subjects. Still, when the skeletal gaze fell upon him for the first time, he made himself bow as he performed the perfunctory greeting. "I report at the order of the Sovereign, ready to make good your assault however you might use my skills."

Malpravus did not answer immediately, though his thin smile grew broader as he stared at J'anda with a disquieting satisfaction. "The Sovereign sends me the greatest non-elven enchanter in the land. Where from springs this sudden desire to use you in this service, I wonder?"

"It springs from the recent betrayal of my benefactor," J'anda said, cutting to the quick. "Apparently, spying for the Sovereign was no longer sufficient to prove my loyalty after Terian's turn."

"Yes, that was unfortunate," Malpravus said, though he seemed little concerned with it. "Not entirely unpredictable, but then the Sovereign and I have never seen eye-to-eye when it comes to loyalties. I have long argued that they are far more flexible and situational than he believes, firmly stuck in his everything-is-treason modality."

J'anda raised an eyebrow at the admission. "I'm afraid I … don't understand."

"We all seek our own ends, dear boy," Malpravus said, waving his long, thin fingers in trails through the air as though weaving some

217

spell, "and to believe otherwise is mere childish foolishness. Loyalty for the sake of loyalty is the greatest delusion of all, as though you can compel fastidious service with no promise of reward. It is in our natures to always be seeking the better deal, more favorable terms, and the Sovereign misses this under the mistaken assumption that religious motivation can keep his entire kingdom in a tight line." The necromancer shook his head, *tsk-tsking* as though he were commenting on a child's naiveté. "That is a blind spot, a weakness that even his closest advisors can do little about, though they certainly try to exploit it as often as possible." He steepled his fingers. "I believe you had such an experience, yes?"

"It sounds as though you already know the answer to that question," J'anda said, watching for reaction.

Malpravus merely smiled, shrugging his narrow shoulders as though caught in the act of some minor indiscretion. "Rumors do circulate, naturally, and it would take less sensitive ears than mine to let pass so juicy a tidbit without parceling it away for later consumption. Still, though, I think you know well the flaws within the system that keep us ... constrained."

"Perhaps," J'anda conceded. "You'll forgive me for not indulging fully in this conversation given the current thin limb I find myself out on with the Sovereign."

"But of course," Malpravus said, fully understanding. "And allow me to reassure you—you need do nothing here at present." The necromancer's smile was disconcerting in an obvious attempt to be comforting. "The situation is well in hand. I have arrangements in the works that will deliver this city to us in a matter of short months, with no illusory tricks necessary." He pulled his fingers apart. "I am not the Sovereign, and I do not demand you surrender all fidelity in this instant, merely that you keep an open mind for what is in your best interest when the moment comes to make your next choice. This city will fall, because the Sovereign commands it. Sit back, watch, take credit ... save the lives of as many of the beleaguered humans as you wish." At this Malpravus grinned. "I promise I won't tell. Because whether we want to or not—for now—the Sovereign's will must be done."

43.

Terian

Months in the cell beneath Sanctuary had done little to improve Terian's disposition. Oh, certainly, he'd been accorded every courtesy and was fed better than he'd eaten with the armies on the march. Still and all, the cell in the dark was not exactly home, and the overwhelming silence was hardly the place he would have preferred to spend his days.

Especially now that we know the Sovereign has kidnapped Vidara and is using her to make his infinite supply of soul rubies to power that undead army. If we could just eliminate that single support from him, the platform that he stands upon would at least become unsteady, if not collapse utterly. Terian looked at the sand-colored walls. *But instead, I sit here, wondering why I didn't stay in a place where I might do at least marginally more good. Like, say, for example, leading a gnomish army in battle against the tides on the Sea of Carmas.*

A low rumbling noise reached his ears, commotion carried along the stones of the ceiling from somewhere above. Whispers at the door to his cell followed moments later as the guards discussed whatever business was occurring, and Terian got up off his cot to try and listen. He walked softly without his armor, which was stacked in the corner.

"... sounds like they're going to war," one of the guards said, more than a little excited and youthful, Terian figured.

"I heard something about Reikonos," came the voice of another, this one female but just as excited. "Did you hear that?"

"Maybe," came a third. "Couldn't tell over the ruckus. Why couldn't there have been one of those grates near us? You know they're not going to send anyone down to tell us squat until after it's all over—"

"Greetings, guards!" Vaste's voice bellowed down the hallway. "I have exciting tidings for you."

"Whaaa …?" the young man asked, then lowered his voice. "You were wrong. They sent an officer to tell us."

"What's going on?" the woman asked.

"Reikonos has been invaded by the dark elves," the troll pronounced. Terian could almost imagine the energetic delivery that the healer seemed to put into his words, see the half-smile he wore almost all the time. "The Guildmaster is putting together a squad to go into the city to scout things, get some eyes on the ground." He paused. "Err … eyes in the city. No eyes literally on the ground, unless they were to be ripped out of the dark elves."

There was a pause as the guards seemed to process the news. "Can I go?" the young man asked.

"We're on guard duty," the female guard hissed at him.

"You should go volunteer if you're of a mind to," Vaste said. "It's not as though the prisoner is going to come bursting through the door at exactly this moment, after all. He's got a solid several inches of steel between him and the cool, underground air of freedom, after all."

"I want to go with the Guildmaster," the second man said. He sounded older, his voice low and rough. "I went with him to Luukessia, you know. Once, when we were on the front lines north of—"

"Oh, shut up," the young man said. "We all know about the time Cyrus Davidon called you by name. You never stop telling the story."

"Well, it was special," came the slightly chastened voice of the storyteller. "It's like he knew me—"

"Ughhhhh," the woman said. "Forget it, I'm going. You'll watch the prisoner's door, won't you?" Terian struggled with trying to figure out who this was directed at, until the answer came a moment later.

"I'm not getting left behind," the young guard said. "I want to make sergeant someday, you know. I got left out of the fights at Livlosdald and Leaugarden, and I wasn't even here during the siege. If I can make a good impression, maybe I can—"

"Forget sergeant. Lieutenant is where the gold really starts, and I'm not that far from being there if I can just—"

"But he already knows your name, apparently, so—"

"I'm not getting left behind—"

"Gentlemen," Vaste said, booming voice drowning them all out. "And lady. Why don't I just watch the door for a few minutes while you all volunteer, and then whoever isn't chosen can come back and resume their post? Problem solved, and you all get a chance to weasel your toward lucrative advancement without having to fight each other to the death right here in the hallway for the opportunity."

"You'd do that?" the woman asked.

"As long as you don't leave me here all day," Vaste said.

There was an uncomfortable pause. "That's damned decent of you," the older man said. "You know, for a troll."

Terian flinched, imagining the look on Vaste's face through the door. "Yes, it's almost like I'm a person," Vaste agreed, surprisingly calm. "Now run along and make your mark, all of you. And try not to make it a bloody mark, either, crushed under the terrifying power of the dark elven army. Shoo, shoo." Sounds of footsteps retreating down the hall at a run made it through the door, followed by Vaste's loud sigh. "Idiots. I'm surrounded by idiots."

"At least you know it and can work around it," Terian said as he heard a key slide into the lock. The door opened wide and Vaste stood there, staring at him. "Imagine if you were too dull-witted to make it work for you."

"Then I'd probably be stuck in a cell not unlike this one," the troll said, leering down at him. "Why aren't you dressed?"

"Didn't know I was supposed to be," Terian said, glancing at his armor in the corner. "It's not like anyone sent me a formal invitation to anything, and I have been down here for a couple months now without any cause to think—"

"Oh, it's been a lot longer than a couple months since you've thought," Vaste said, making the motion toward the armor. "Come on, then. It's time."

Terian stared at him with suspicion. "Time for what?"

Vaste did not blink away, just stared right through him like he could see to the heart of the dark knight. "Time for you to do what you came here to do."

Terian stared back. *What do you know, Vaste?* "Which is?"

"Time to show Cyrus what's happened to his homeland," Vaste said, holding his staff to one side. "Time to convince the Guildmaster of Sanctuary to kill the God of Darkness."

44.

J'anda

The streets of Reikonos were in pandemonium, the armies of the Sovereign moving through at will. If there were defenders behind the walls, J'anda did not see them, but then, he had not seen much in the way of defenders atop the walls in the months that he had been watching, either.

This city has been ripe for the plucking all along, and now plucked it is. Malpravus said he had a plan, and damned if he did not. A knight riding a vek'tag leaped across a building above him, burying a spear in a human man as he passed, the screams lost in the chaos of the street.

J'anda wore the illusion of a dark elf in armor, figuring it was his best defense in the current setting. Only a few people were moving about on the street, the majority of the dark elven army still situated on the main thoroughfare to the city, spreading out like ants leaving the mound, but slowly.

The smell of fire was already in the air, but it had been that way all the time J'anda had been on the siege. Reikonos had burned in segments, a bomb of dragon's breath powder lobbed across the wall every single day by the dark elven army—whether they needed it or not, he'd heard some crass trebuchet soldier joke while drinking.

J'anda recognized the building ahead of him as one of the shops of the slums. It was a butcher shop, actually, one where they sold cheap meat, proclaimed usually by a cryer that stood outside the doors. He knew this area from his prior travels here, and figured that what he was looking for had to be nearby.

Ah. There it is.

A stream of five soldiers ran past in front of him, screaming bloody murder through at least a few rotten jaws, barely taking notice of him as they smashed through the window of the butcher's shop, seeing the weakness and kicking their way in as the bandits they were. He knew their kind; he'd been supping with them for months, after all. The dead were a fearsome enemy, all milk of compassion bled out with their life's blood. Whether Malpravus intended it that way or it was simply a natural side effect of the army being what it was, an undead legion, he knew for a fact that they were more base and vile than most of the soldiers he'd been acquainted with in any army.

A loud clacking noise echoed over his shoulder as one of them smashed his way back through the door to the butcher's shop. Loud screams punctured the air, causing J'anda to blanch as though they were a knife thrust into his ear. They were far closer than the other screams, the low keening that hung over the city in a repetitive state.

One of the undead was dragging a woman in a dress out of the shop. His soulless, rotten face was exposed, bloodless cheeks and sunken eyes rotting out of his head as he dragged her with a bony hand from her abode. Her cries were loud, frantic, panicked.

J'anda considered his course carefully before deciding to intervene. He decided upon a spell of charming first, to be followed by illusion if that failed, and finally mesmerization. He threw up a hand, weaving together the threads of magic as he spun it around the undead soldier. It pushed into the mind of the wraith with surprising ease, and he decided it was a product of their lack of will. It was, perhaps, the easiest spell he had ever cast.

And then he saw the heart's desire of the thing holding the woman in its dead hand, and he nearly vomited in his disgust, almost stopping his spell and retching there in the street.

"Gyah," he said, barely keeping it back, holding tight to the threads of the spell, solidifying them, pushing the illusion of what the thing wanted right into its head. It craved flesh, truly, this far gone, driven by Malpravus and unnatural need. It was like a lesser version of the scourge in its appetite to consume life, but it had not the massive maw nor the teeth for it. It was governed by the nature of the man who had once been at the heart of the mind he now twisted to his own benefit, descending along the primal lines of its progenitor's basest instincts from a time before civilization. *But unlike the scourge, at least the minds of these dead are not unfathomable...*

The woman from the shop fell out of the grasp of the wraith, its hand loose around her as it halted under his command. J'anda spun the last threads into its mind, completing his hold over it for now. The creature in his thrall saw its desires fulfilled. J'anda saw them, too, and again barely kept down his most recent meal, the stark horror fresh in his mind. "Come with me," he said to the woman, whom he now realized was wearing a butcher's apron. "Unless you want those things to do their worst to you."

She looked up at him and found his eyes with her own, dull and full of barely contained panic. Her mind was nearly shut down; he could tell simply from looking at her. She had seen the impossible, had it grab hold of her and prepared to sink its teeth into her flesh, and she was not prepared for it in the slightest. She blinked at him, and he dismissed the illusion of the dark elven soldier and replaced it with a human guard's visage, just for her. "Come with me," he said and beckoned her forward.

She responded slowly, getting up off her hands and knees, scrambling toward him. She said nothing as he turned, expecting her to follow as he made his way toward his destination. He ignored the shouts down an alleyway and focused on what needed to happen next, on getting his rescue to the safety he was prepared to provide.

He paused in front of the old barn and looked at the chain across its entry. A chain was hardly the sort of thing that would keep him back, naturally, especially in this moment, and especially because he knew where they kept the hidden key to the old guildhall of the Kings of Reikonos.

45.

Terian

"My gods," Vaste said from where he stood next to Cyrus Davidon on the balcony of the Citadel in Reikonos. The troll's voice was small, far smaller than his frame would ever have suggested, almost tiny enough to have come from a gnome, Terian thought.

The air stunk with the smell of flesh—burning, rotting, or perhaps mingled with the simple stink of waste, Terian could not tell. It permeated his nostrils as he stared at the back of the warrior in black armor as Cyrus stared at his city burning. *And here,* Terian thought, *in the ashes of his old world, perhaps we find the redemption for all my failures.*

"Cyrus," Vara said as she came to the warrior's side. "It will do you no good to look upon this. There is nothing to be done here."

"Nothing?" Cyrus's voice was low, anger threatening to spill out of him. *He's about one good second from snapping and leaping down thirty stories to try and fight that entire army himself.* Terian could see the dark elves streaming through the streets below, the hordes of the undead spilling through and wreaking their havoc.

"That's not entirely true, is it?" Terian asked, sensing his moment was at hand. He caught a slight nod from Vaste that only encouraged him further. "You know it. You can't defend this city now, that's sure; there's no wall you can put up, no bridge you can guard and let them run against you, match their power against yours in a futile, foolish grind to their death. They are inside, they are everywhere, and wild with the taste of blood and slaughter, these dead."

"Because of you," Cyrus said, and that fury edged closer to the surface.

"Not only because of me," Terian said. *Don't be dumb now, Cyrus.*

"They like the taste of blood and slaughter?" Cyrus asked, and he smiled like a psychotic. "I'll drown them in it."

"For once," Terian said, trying desperately to speak sense to the barely contained madness he sensed in the man before him, "don't be the fool warrior who thinks with his gonads that I always—falsely, I might add—accused you of being." *He's desperate, angry … I can't let this get out of control.*

"It wasn't that falsely," Vara said.

"Use your shrewd mind," Terian said, "calculate the odds against you in this fight." *Don't be stupid. Please don't be stupid.*

Don't give the Sovereign Arkaria. Not like this.

"And let my city burn?" Cyrus said, staring off the balcony.

"You can end this," Terian said, getting around to it at last. "But you won't end it here, and not by throwing yourself into a battle you can't hope to win. If you want to turn this army around, you need to provide them with a reason to walk away so compelling they cannot possibly stay for another moment of pillage."

"You magnificent bastard," Vara said, and she sounded almost respectful.

"Pretend for once I need you to do my thinking for me," Cyrus said, turning to look at him, the madness passed. "What would you have me do?"

"We go to Saekaj," Terian said, the nerves of the moment rushing in on him. *This is my last chance.* "You have a dagger matched against a sword. Saekaj is the exposed neck. Open it and watch the sword lose its menace."

"You want me to invade your own home," Cyrus said. "To stomp down your doors, settle your scores—"

"I want you kill the God of Darkness!" Terian said, months of pent-up emotion escaping in a rush. "I want you—you wielder of that," he pointed at the warrior's sword, "I want you to free my damned people—because no one else can. I want you to turn loose your rage and set us all free in one stroke of the sword."

"Killing Yartraak will take more than one stroke of a sword," Curatio said, interjecting at last. Terian spun to look at him, wondering if he faced friend or foe in the healer. The elf's expression was distinctly neutral.

"I want you to save my home," Terian said, trying to put aside any hint of deceit and letting his true feelings spill forth. "I want you to save us, Cyrus Davidon ... to save *our* people. Mine and yours."

The warrior looked out over the balcony, across the horizon, and Terian wondered what he saw. *Is it just the destruction of a place he has long held dear? Or is it something else?* Terian's eyes flicked down, seeing a spider-knight crawl across a building somewhere far below as screams wafted their way up to him. *Does he only see the moment at hand? Because I see the future as I look out across this tableau of horror ...*

Saekaj's future. Sovar's future. Intertwined in death, crushed under the weight of the mad tyranny of their own god.

"We go," Cyrus said, tearing Terian from his reverie. "Mendicant ... take us back to Sanctuary, if you please."

"And?" Terian waited for the answer, his last hopes reaching out for it like a thirsty man trying to grasp a skin of water before him. "Then?"

"And then ..." Cyrus said, voice low, determined, "we go to Saekaj ... into the halls of infinite darkness that Yartraak calls his own—" He turned and looked Terian in the eye, and the dark knight saw the thin veneer of the warrior's rage, hiding below a veneer of civility only, "—and I stab that godless son of a bitch right in the eye until he's nothing but a shrunken corpse. Just like the last one we killed."

There was a rush of relief in Terian's mind, tempered with something else, as the spells began to run across him and whisk them back to Sanctuary. It was the dim realization that in spite of all he had hoped for, the man he had turned to in order to free his people had darkness of his own lurking beneath those blue eyes, something Terian had only caught glimpses of before.

At some point, Cyrus, he thought, trying to grimly focus on the task at hand and failing, *we're going to have to deal with the darker forces that are trying to sway you, that have free reign of your mind in the face of the horrors you've seen. And I only hope that the day we need grapple with them is not today, because we have other work to do first.*

46.

Aisling

"So this is where you're hiding yourself from Shrawn these days," came the quiet voice out of the corner. Aisling's muscles tensed all at once, the near-silence of the room in the mids of Sovar that she was squatting in broken by an utterly unexpected voice. She spun to find him there, in what should have been an unsurprising moment, but it was, nonetheless, worth a start.

"Genn," she said, staring him down. He was standing sedately with his hands behind his back, looking around the rocky room as though there might be someone hiding in the corner. He'd caught her sitting on the unpadded seat carved into the rock, pondering her next course of action. She'd been fully ensconced in thought, unprepared for company, especially of the sort that appeared without so much as a knock.

"I love what you've done with the place," Genn said, sweeping his hand around to encompass the small room. "Which is to say, nothing. Very clever, not leaving a trail for Shrawn to follow."

"I need to be out of his sight for a time," Aisling said. "So I can—"

"Can hopefully avoid the tragic death of Norenn when he realizes that he's no longer got a hold over you." Genn's eyes lit in the dark, shining in the light of the single candle with a gleam that seemed brighter than what the lone flame should provide. "Yes, I got that."

"What are you doing here?" Aisling asked, coming to her feet.

"Well, I came to warn you that your moment is about to arrive," Genn said, taking an exaggerated step. The man was nothing if not excessively showy, his smooth voice and dry delivery a strange contradiction, as though he were unserious about anything and unconcerned by all that was before him. "Your chance to rescue your friend is at hand."

"Why?" Aisling asked, viewing him with no small amount of suspicion.

"Because that's what allies do," Genn said with a smirk. "Help each other out, see."

"No, I got that," Aisling said. "But why are you my ally?"

"Well, surely I must be sympathetic to at least some of your aims," Genn said with that same insincere smirk. "Have you guessed which?"

She stared at him. "Freeing my … friend?"

"That's part of it," Genn agreed, nodding. "Let me just spell it out. I want you back in control of your own destiny. I want you to throw off the yoke of Dagonath Shrawn."

She stared at him. "On that much we're agreed."

"We're agreed on more than you know," Genn said, though now the smile grew tight. "Shrawn is in Saekaj at the moment, but you should not try to find him."

"I thought you said you wanted my destiny back in my own hands," Aisling said.

"Going after Shrawn right now guarantees nothing but your death," Genn said. "He's hidden, surrounded by more danger than you can safely sneak past. No point in confronting him until you both have to and you're ready."

"And I'm not ready," Aisling said. "Is what you're saying."

"Dagonath Shrawn is a powerful wizard," Genn said, hints of concern peeking through behind his eyes, "in addition to being the most powerful mortal in all of Saekaj and Sovar. Challenging him on his home ground without a plan to deal with both his magic and allies is simply suicide. Remove his influence from you, get that dagger away from your throat by taking back Norenn, and then you can start worrying about the rest."

She blinked at him, pursing her lips. "Do you know where Norenn is?"

Genn smiled. "It just so happens I do … but," he said, and she detected the first hint of canniness from him, some hidden intent in his bearing, "I have one other task for you to perform, one other soul to liberate as you do this thing ..."

She listened as he told her what to do and felt both a thrill of satisfaction that she'd guessed his identity early on ... and a nearly all-consuming fear at what he asked of her now.

47.

J'anda

The slums of Reikonos were aflame before him, and J'anda watched from the roof of the barn where he hid with five dozen others, all his energies focused on maintaining the illusion that the barn was also on fire, his dark elven features no longer hidden from the humans who shook in fear all around him.

"Who are you?" one of them asked, a man who looked as though he were ready to soil himself.

"My name is J'anda Aimant," he said, threading an illusion into the mind of a passing patrol of the undead on their way to tear apart the nearby markets as he snared a human child from their sight and directed the little boy toward the barn with a spell of charming. "I am a member of Sanctuary." He pulled his mind out of the illusion long enough to look his questioner in the eyes. "I am here to help."

He ignored the murmur of conversation that his admission spawned as the door opened and the little boy he'd saved wandered in out of the streets, quickly seized hold of by one of his other "guests," an older woman far beyond her childbearing years. She soothed the boy, and J'anda helped idly, devoting only a small amount of his attention to them, enough to keep the calm in the old barn as he put all his other efforts on what was going on outside, reaching his spells out as best he could, and trying to save as many of them as he could from the death that worked in the streets all around.

48.

Terian

The onslaught of dark elves down the tunnels of the Sovereign's palace was almost too great to count, almost too many to believe. *He must have an entire division of guards in here,* Terian thought as he drove his axe into the skull of a still-living dark elf. *And they're all live ones, too! Women and mere teenagers, it's just about all he has left, I suppose.*

"Where the hell is Cyrus?" Martaina Proelius asked, arrows flying from her bow down the stony corridor, each striking unerringly into the gaps of the armor of the palace guard, bringing them low.

Terian focused only on the task at hand, knowing what the answer had to be. A rumbling shout of fury came from the other end of the corridor as Fortin, the rock giant, smashed his way through an advancing patrol of the guard with little in the way of mercy to hold him back. More and more of the Sanctuary army was being delivered into the Grand Palace's dark and twisting corridors by the minute, far outpacing the arrival of dark elven reinforcements.

"I don't know," Menlos Irontooth shouted, turning loose his wolves on a bevy of dark elves that entered out of a room mid-way down the hall, only a few doors down from where Terian had seen Cyrus disappear. "But he's missing a hell of a fight!" The Northman paused. "Lady Vara, too."

Terian simply swung his axe, trying to pretend he was not even here. *They're not the ones missing a hell of a fight,* he thought, the bare darkness shattered by the sound of axe and sword, spell and shield. *I just hope they survive the fight they're in ... because if we don't hold back these reinforcements, the likelihood that they'll win against him is ... impossible.*

49.

J'anda

He was running out of dead to turn back; the slums were completely consumed, the fires burning out of control in a circle around the place where he'd made his stand. He could see through the eyes of others, through the eyes of the last of the humans, whom he guided into the barn now, a young lady that he'd managed to slip away from four undead soldiers before they tore her to pieces in a frenzy. She'd climbed to the top of a roof at his command, let him see the flames climbing skyward, and when coupled with the spells he'd drifted about, looking for minds to snare, he knew that there was an empty zone stretching in a few hundred yards around the slums that he deemed clear.

J'anda let the spells he'd sent around the barn disperse, feeling assured that they were safe for now. He remembered that last vision from the young woman's mind, though, of the rest of the city consumed in violence and flames, and it made him sick in the heart, in the stomach. As the last person he saved joined the crowd thronged around him, J'anda stood and looked them over with a bone-deep weariness born of exerting all his magic once more. "I'm afraid I have to leave for a time," he told them, staring into the frightened faces before him. "Stay here until it is over."

"What ... what if they come looking for us?" a young man asked, no more than fifteen. His face was dirty, the smudges of smoke looking like he worked furnaces all day for his wage, though J'anda knew he did not.

"They won't," J'anda said. "They believe this entire section of the

233

city to be in flames. They'll be looking for their entertainments elsewhere." He stretched, listening to his old bones crack. "Stay quiet. Hide here. You will be safe."

He glanced once more around the room. There were over a hundred people here in this little space, crammed in from end to end of the barn that had been turned into a barracks. "It will be all right. I promise." And he lit the return spell that would carry him back to Saekaj—*and, perhaps, some end to this madness ... for there is no end to be found here in Reikonos.*

50.

Terian

The sound of a rock giant bursting through the wall into the foyer was enough to keep Terian scrambling after him, trying to stay safe in the shade of the massive, craggy-skinned beast. *Keep trying to overwhelm him, you tin-plated idiots. See how well that works.* Pieces of corpses lay strewn in the rock giant's wake, and Terian tried to avoid looking at the parts that seemed to have been chewed through by unstoppable jaws. *Not a fit end for anyone, really.* The rumbling sound of the rock giant speaking to someone ahead made its way back to him through the dust.

Cyrus, he realized, recognizing the voice that came back in reply, though he missed the answer itself.

He's alive.

"Cyrus," Terian said as he stepped out of the rock-giant sized hole in the wall. He found the Sanctuary Guildmaster standing there with Vara at his side, blood trickling out of his nose. "Did you do it?"

"It's done," Cyrus said, catching a hell of a look from the elven paladin at his side. "Well, she did it. But it's still done."

Relief washed over Terian, almost a year's worth of nightmares, of planning, of scenarios wrought in blood and torment finally let loose of their hold over him. "Good. You should go."

"Go?" Cyrus blinked at him. "Go where?"

"Home," Terian said, moving toward the throne room doors, laid open and broken behind the warrior.

"How do you intend to get the dark elven army out of Reikonos?" Cyrus asked. *For a man who just killed a god, he doesn't exactly seem relieved. Certainly not as relieved as I am, but then, his home is still under the hammer.*

"I can't yet," Terian said, making his posture as docile and yielding as possible. "You killed the Sovereign, but he has servants that do his work for him. I can't control the army until I've dealt with them."

"We can deal with them together, then," Vara said, and he saw the trap waiting there behind her suspicious eyes.

"You could," Terian said. "You could run through Saekaj, destroying every great house in turn, killing every soldier, inspiring fear and making them flee before you."

"Sounds like fun," Fortin rumbled.

"*But*," Terian said, "afterward there will be little or nothing left, and no one to command the army to return from Reikonos."

"I had better hear a plan take flight out of your lips swiftly," Cyrus said. "I came here and did your damned bidding—"

"And you did it beautifully," Terian said. "But the rest of this? It's not your fight. This battle is mine, now."

"I want your word, Terian," Cyrus said. His temper was clearly rising, his eyes narrowed. "That you will fix this. That you will deliver what you promised."

"I will do it or die trying," Terian said, meaning every single word of it.

"You will need help, I think," J'anda said, appearing out of the shadows. Terian almost did a double take at the enchanter. *How long has it been since I saw him? He looks even more worn, if that's possible.*

"Aye," Terian said. "We will."

"Do I even need to say it?" Cyrus asked. The wariness was settled over him like a spare set of armor.

"If I don't get those troops out of Reikonos," Terian said, "you won't need to come looking for me. Believe me on that." *Now all I have to do is go through Malpravus and Shrawn and whoever else to get it done. Piece of cake. Piece of rock cake, maybe, that I have to eat entirely.*

"Because there will be nothing left of you?" Vara asked. She didn't sound sorry to hear it.

"There are still powerful people invested in keeping Saekaj and Sovar under control," J'anda said, stepping in to answer for him. "They will already be moving to exert that control now that he is dead. Fortunately," he said with a smile, "I have set a few wheels in motion myself." He glanced over at Terian. "Which we should now attend to."

"Fine," Cyrus said. The warrior looked like his fury had subsided. "We will leave it in your hands."

"That's all I ask," Terian said and tried going just a little farther to see if it would take. "Brother."

There was a long pause. "Brother," Cyrus said, and to Terian's ears it almost—almost—sounded like the voice of his predecessor, and in the moment before he began to plunge into the aftermath he'd planned, he felt a hard pang of regret knowing that he'd never hear Alaric say it to him again.

51.

Aisling

She'd managed half of Genn's request with some difficulty. She had
the Red Destiny of Saekaj in her hand, the two guards left behind to
defend it having giving her a hell of a fight considering she'd tried to
bluff her way past. The young kid, he hadn't been a problem. But
there'd been a woman warrior at the door, too, and she'd had an ill-
favored look that reminded Aisling of Sareea Scyros, that dark knight
who followed Shrawn around on his leash. This woman, she hadn't
folded as easily as the kid, and now Aisling had a bloody lip and the
female guard had considerably worse. But at least the guard was still
breathing.

The air was thick with the smell of walls destroyed and wood
smashed to splinters as she crept into the throne room. Aisling found
them where Genn had said they'd be, and she heard the muffled
question without knowing who asked it. "How is she?"

She heard the answer clearly, though, spoken by Curatio.
"Drained. Though I am at a bit of a loss to explain how exactly this
was performed."

"Using this," she called out as she tossed the Red Destiny of
Saekaj. It hit the wood floor and wobbled as it rolled across to where
they stood, those officers of Sanctuary. It was surprisingly easy to part
with the thing, as though years of her nightmares about it made it
unpleasant to so much as hold.

"Slattern," Vara said, more than a little nonplussed. Her blond hair
glowed in the torchlight, and she looked like an angry cat the way she
held her body stiff and near-ready to strike.

"What are you doing here?" Cyrus asked, his eyes tracking her as she stood in the shadows.

"Heard the hubbub," she lied. "Came running."

"Were you already here?" Cyrus asked, seeming to unconsciously draw closer to his elven paladin. Aisling watched the Sanctuary members move, especially that ranger, Martaina, angling to get a clear shot. *Best to hold still for this; if he means to have me plugged with arrows, there's not much I'm going to be able to do to stop it right now.*

"Does it matter?" Aisling asked, her eyes falling over the aged and crone-like form of the Goddess of Life. She looked frail and worn, just as Genn had said she would. "Take the Red Destiny. See if you can restore some of the souls to her. It might aid her recovery."

"Do you think a pretty bauble will make us forget what you've done?" Vara asked. She was a second away from drawing her weapon, if that.

"Why would you forget it?" Aisling asked. "It's not like I can." In truth, she felt little remorse now that she saw Cyrus Davidon here, in front of her, seemingly unharmed. She'd smelled blood and black lace on her blade for what felt like months after Leaugarden, and it had barely registered as anything other than a prick of guilt occasionally in an otherwise occupied mind. *I didn't used to be this way.*

"Why?" Cyrus asked, and she realized that to him, this was the only question that mattered.

"He took someone dear to me," Aisling said. She poured her feeling out, letting it bubble up from the abyss in a way she wouldn't have dared with Shrawn, not unless she needed to appease him. This was real, it was genuine, like heartbreak too hard to contain. She could have contained it, though, if she'd been of a mind to. It was more useful this way, though.

Just like Genn had told her. *Absolution,* he said. *Seek it. You'll need it later.*

And who was she to argue with a god?

"And you very nearly took one dear to me," Vara said, all the accusation bearing down.

"Did you just say …?" Cyrus asked, always the last to be in on a joke.

"Hush," Vara said sharply, admonishment always delivered after compliment. *That is her way.*

"I could apologize, but I'll be honest—" Aisling started.

"For the first time ever?" Vara asked.

"I didn't mind beating you for him," Aisling said. *And using vicious truth as well as vicious lies? That's my way.* "Of all the things I was told to do, fighting with you over him was the sweetest, because you don't normally lose. How did it feel?"

"How will it feel when I kill you?" Vara asked.

"Like nothing," Aisling said, and she began to withdraw. *Play the remorse again, now …*

"Wait," Cyrus said. "Your … love? Your friend? What happened to them?"

She froze, the shadows of the doorframe all around her, shrouding her. Norenn was still out there, where Genn had told her to go, waiting for her to finish this moment, this confrontation. "I don't know." *Yet.*

"You can't think you're just going to walk out of here—" Vara said.

"Let her go," Cyrus said.

"You cannot be serious," Vara said, spitting irritation at him. "This is the second person who has attempted to kill you that you have let walk away in the last year. Any more and I will start to suspect that you truly do wish to die—"

"You killed the one who tried to kill me," Cyrus said, settling his eyes on his elf. *You win, Vara.* "She was no more than the hand of Yartraak, else she'd have finished the job. She certainly had the chance."

"Do you expect me to thank you?" Aisling asked. *Because I would, if that's what it took to get out of here. To get to my next appointment.*

"I'd say you've shown me your gratitude over the last year in every way I could possibly handle," Cyrus said. He meant it to hurt her, but it was clumsy at best. *I've been taunted by more vicious and skillful than you, Cyrus. You're not that sort of man—purposefully cruel.*

And hopefully you never will be.

With almost nothing else left to say, she listened to his last remark on the subject. "I don't ever want to see you again."

As she drifted off into the shadows of Shrawn's passage back to his manor, she let float a gentle reply, so quiet that she doubted anyone but the elf would hear her: "I promise you never will."

Because if you ever see me again after this, Cyrus, it won't be as Aisling Nightwind, that much I can guarantee you.

240

52.

J'anda

"Where is Dagonath Shrawn?" Terian asked, staring down the guards at the front entrance of Shrawn's manor house. They were clad in the standard garb for those of their station, plate metal around the vital organs and looser chain at the arms and legs, giving them more mobility in a close fight. J'anda watched the scene of interrogation unfold under a portico that perfectly aped that of the Sovereign's own mansion. Terian stared down the men standing between him and an answer on the current whereabouts of the most powerful man left in Saekaj.

"He is not here at present, Lord Lepos," the head guard said, hand hovering about his sword's hilt. Terian had his own hand nowhere near his axe handle, J'anda realized, either because the dark knight did not suspect the direction this discussion was heading, or because he was unconcerned. "If you'd like, I can have him contact you as soon as he returns."

"I need to know where he is, right now," Terian said, taut, still standing stiff without a hand on his weapon. *This may turn out to be a bad decision on his part; preparation is always a good guest.* "Either part with the information or move aside."

"He's not here," the guard said again, and now his hand drifted to his sword. "I'm going to have to ask you to leave—"

"Are you kidding?" Terian asked. "The body of the Sovereign of Saekaj is in the street behind us!" He tilted to point at the main avenue just beyond the wall at their backs. "You idiot! Shrawn is in charge, and we need to know where he is."

The guard shook slightly but drew his blade, holding it in front of him like a shield. "You won't find him here." The other two guards at his back drew their swords as well. "You will have to depart."

"Morons," Terian said and murmured something before he waved a hand at the lead, who grabbed at his throat and let his sword clatter uselessly to the ground. "This is not a moment to quibble." He stared at the other two, the subservients. "Where is Shrawn?"

"We'll die before telling you," the first of them said. The second nodded agreement.

"Well, duh," Terian said and shook his head. His pointed helm shook with his motion, and the axe came out, striking the first of them across the blade of the sword as he brought it up. The second started to attack, but Terian spun and hit him squarely across the neck, chopping into the chainmail at his throat and ending his offensive with a gurgle. The threat at his back dealt with, the dark knight came back at the remaining guard and hacked at his sword, overpowering him until he was able to plant the blade firmly between the guard's eyes. His work done, Terian drew back his blade and hefted it over his shoulder. "Can't get an honest answer out of these people, I swear ..."

A clatter came from the street behind them, and J'anda looked back to see the Army of Sanctuary moving past outside the gate. They were on the march, toward the market square, most of the soldiers visible only as they clomped past the gap in the wall of the Shrawn estate where the gates yawned open. A rocky head bobbed past at the top of the wall, Fortin somewhere in the middle of the column. He turned and looked at them, and waved with the exaggerated enthusiasm of a child as he passed the manor.

"Nice to know we have some friends left," Terian said as he mopped up the blood splatter on his face with a handkerchief. He waved back at the rock giant, nodding politely with a tight smile as he did so.

"I don't know that you could call any of them friends of yours after what's happened," J'anda said, looking at the corpses before the door of the house.

"What are you talking about?" Terian said, putting the handkerchief away. "Cyrus just called me brother. We're clear."

J'anda cocked an eyebrow at him. "Do you expect you would be welcomed back to the halls of Sanctuary at this point, were you to want to return?"

The dark knight's face clouded over. "That's ... we don't need to talk about that right now. We need to find Shrawn." He turned and headed for the doors to the manor as though pushed along by a titan.

"What are you aiming for at this point, Terian?" J'anda asked as the dark knight hefted his axe once more, clearly intent on smashing his way through the doors of the manor house.

"I'm aiming to find Shrawn," Terian said, lifting the axe, "and I'm aiming to separate his head from his shoulders. Once that's done, we need to find a way to consolidate power in Saekaj, get everyone in a line, and get control of Yartraak and Malpravus's undead army so we can get it the hell out of Reikonos—"

"There is no one more committed than me to the idea of removing that particular torment from the human city," J'anda said, trying to be the voice of reason as Terian brought down his axe with a hard blow on the wood of the front door, "but I think perhaps you are misguided in your approach. You are not thinking this through."

"I'm thinking just fine," Terian said and brought the axe down again, cutting a massive gash in the ornate wood door. "Control is the name of the game, now, and we're not going to achieve it unless we can get Shrawn out of the way." He brought the weapon down again. The door shuddered under his assault but did not yield or break. "The sooner we get this done, the sooner we can get about the business of ending this damned war—" He raised the axe to attack again when the door was thrown open suddenly, causing the dark knight to dodge aside to avoid being struck with it as it swung out.

"For the sake of a—" Aisling said, standing framed in the rectangular outline of the door to Shrawn manor. She looked at Terian with irritation. "What are you doing, you idiot?"

Terian, for his part, looked merely stunned, his axe back up, at the ready. "I'm ... opening the door. What are you doing?"

"It was unlocked, fool," Aisling said, shaking her head as she rolled her eyes.

"There is always another way," J'anda said softly. "We have but to see it."

"Well, I'll tell you what I see now," Terian said, hefting the axe again, "I see a traitor to Sanctuary—"

"That's ironic, coming from you," Aisling said.

"Stop it, both of you," J'anda said and watched as Terian lowered his axe. "Aisling, why are you here?"

"I'm about to rescue a friend," she said, looking at him sullenly. "You?"

"Here to kill Shrawn," Terian said, putting his axe back over his shoulder. "You want to stand in the way of that?"

She laughed loudly. "I'd help you swing the axe if I wasn't sure you'd still find a way to botch it." Her face tightened, the lines around her eyes furrowing deep as rage came to the surface. "Shrawn's mine."

"Step aside," Terian said, his own countenance darkening. "He needs to die—"

"At my hand, yes," she said, a blade suddenly visible in hers, "but he's not here in any case, so this argument is presently pointless."

"What's your problem with Shrawn?" Terian asked, frowning.

"Who do you think was pulling my puppet strings at Sanctuary?" she fired back as Terian nodded. "What's your complaint?"

"Mass murder," Terian said. "Starving the poor. Butchery. I don't know; there are scads of them. Pick one."

"Well, you're not going to get anywhere swinging your axe about at me," Aisling said, folding her arms over her chest but keeping her dagger visible.

"We need to find him," Terian said and started to push past her.

"Don't take my word for it?" Aisling said, spinning to look at him.

"You're in his house when I come knocking, so ... no."

"You call that knocking?" She pointed at the axe.

"It's a euphemism," Terian said, stalking through the foyer and opening a door under the stairs. "What's the likelihood he's hiding in here?"

"Somewhat low, I would have to imagine," J'anda said, looking at all the woodwork. "Unless he was particular confident of how things would shake out in a Saekaj without the Sovereign, I believe he would have been highly motivated to come rushing to Yartraak's defense when Cyrus and Vara killed him just outside Shrawn's own manor. He is a wizard of some skill and could doubtless have made a very great contribution to the battle, as it was."

"He might have been able to kill them both," Aisling said, looking suspiciously at J'anda. "I'm actually surprised the Sovereign didn't."

244

"I didn't see the fight," Terian said, stepping into the ballroom open under an archway to their left, "but it sounded like he didn't use much in the way of spellcraft. Like he decided he wanted to beat Cyrus to death and worked hard to make that happen, failing merrily all the way until his head left his body."

Aisling made a face. "They cut off his head?"

"Vara did, I think."

"Figures," Aisling said, in disgust.

Terian cracked a grin at her. "You're not jealous of losing to her, are you?"

"I'm only sorry I lacked the means to do the decapitating myself," she said, smiling bitterly at him.

Terian's eyes swept the ballroom. "Well, he doesn't appear to be hiding in this room. Only nine hundred thousand more to go, I assume—"

"Shrawn's not here at all," came a voice from behind them, prompting J'anda to whirl. A woman stood there in a white gown, simple, covered in a traveling cloak and cowl that covered the top of her head. She stood with another man at her side, a healer by his vestments, red dye coloring his goatee and long hair.

"You're Dahveed Thalless," J'anda said with a shock of surprise. "Head of the Healer's Union." Another man, massive as a mountain, lumbered into the Shrawn estate behind him, followed by a druid drifting through the air a foot off the ground. "And … I have no idea who the rest of you are."

"J'anda," Dahveed said with the smile that J'anda remembered from when they'd made acquaintance long ago, in the wars before he left in exile. He'd become reacquainted with the man in passing these last months in Saekaj, now that the healer was head of his guild. Dahveed pointed to the large warrior behind him. "This is Grinnd Urnocht." He turned to the druid. "Bowe Sturrt." His eyes glimmered as he went to the woman in the cowl. "And this is—"

"Kahlee," Terian said, surging past J'anda to wrap the woman up in a tight embrace, lifting her off the ground, careful of his spikes. He lifted his faceplate and kissed her, and, most surprisingly, she kissed him in return.

Aisling sidled up to J'anda, footsteps so soft he did not hear her until she nudged him. "Who's that?"

"Terian's wife, I believe," J'anda answered, watching as the dark knight set his bride back on the ground in the quiet of the manor's foyer.

"Terian's married?" Aisling's voice run through with genuine surprise. "I guess there's hope for Vaste, after all."

53.

Aisling

"This is all a very touching scene," came a voice from the door, a dark knight shouldering his way through the small throng gathered there to stand ahead of the healer Dahveed, "but utterly pointless. What are you doing here?" His armor was angled, and his attention was directed at Terian.

"I'm looking for Shrawn," Terian said, placing himself just between his bride and the new arrival, ushering her behind his shoulder as though the man were some threat to her. "What are you doing here?"

"I saw them cutting through the square with your wife in their midst," the man said. Aisling looked him over, realized he was a dark knight, puzzled at the rough familiarity, the seeming baggage between the new arrival and Terian, and came to a quick conclusion. *This is Amenon Lepos.*

Wait. Wasn't he dead?

"I presumed they were on some mission for the Sovereign," Amenon Lepos went on, undeterred. "I came following behind as soon as I heard the news about the Sovereign. Barely avoided running head-on into the army of that guild you ran off to."

"That would have been a poetic ending," Terian said, lips puckered in plain agitation, "you coming up against Cyrus and Vara again. They could kill you a second time, maybe make it stick this round."

"You brought them here," Amenon said, drawing a very familiar red sword blade and clutching it in both hands. "You killed the

247

Sovereign."

"I did not," Terian quipped, reaching for his axe, "being neither a wielder of teleportation magics nor able to presently smite a god. But I did have a hand in it, no doubt."

"You're a traitor," Amenon said, voice low and hissing. "You have betrayed—"

"I didn't betray him half as hard as he betrayed you—"

"This is not the moment to fall to discord," Dahveed Thalless said, stepping between the two of them. "Amenon, old friend … surely you must recognize that with the Sovereign dead, certain things must be done out of necessity. Sovar will likely rise—"

"You have done terrible things this day," Amenon said, not taking his eyes off his son. "You have unleashed a torrent that could destroy us all—"

"I can think of no group more worthy of a good destroying than the people of Saekaj—" Terian spat back.

"Well, this is pointless," Aisling said and turned her back on the whole scene and left, drifting toward the exit at the back of the ballroom with quiet steps. She ignored the voices of escalating rage behind her, and the attempts to calm them both down. She came to the back of the ballroom and looked at the alcove where the Sovereign had sat, a perfect match for the one in his own palace, and stared at the dimness within. It gave her a sense of deja vu, a sick feeling, and she plunged forward to the edge of the darkness and found a light sheer curtain of dark cloth that she pushed aside to—

"Gyah!" she said in a frustrated whisper as she entered to find a familiar face staring at her, Genn sitting on the plush bench seat at the back of the alcove. "You scared the hells out of me!"

Genn picked up a goblet in front of him. The scent of a very bold wine filled the air as he swirled it around in his hand before bringing it up to his lips. He smacked them together afterward, as though trying to decide what he thought of it. "Yartraak and Shrawn certainly have excellent taste."

"Approve of the vintage, do you?"

"Oh, I wasn't just talking about the wine," Genn said, getting to his feet and sweeping a hand to indicate the décor and furniture. "Exquisite wood paneling, imported delicacies, first-rate padding." He ran a hand over his derriere, which was neatly covered by his leather pants. "They truly did have a grasp of the finer things."

She listened carefully. "'Did'? Does that mean Shrawn is dead?"

"Oh, heavens no," Genn said with a shake of his head. "He's still set to be quite the thorn in your side. I wouldn't get too embroiled in matters of little concern at the moment if I were you. You might want to focus on your task at hand and worry about these other people later, if ever."

"You read my mind," Aisling said, ducking out of the alcove and heading toward the door at the back of the ballroom. The shouting in the foyer had ceased, but she did not stay to see why that might be the case.

She threaded through tunnels carved in the side walls of Saekaj, stumbling across servants who huddled in fear, the news of the God of Darkness's death having reached their ears. She ignored them, opening every door, plunging ahead blindly in the warren of tunnels. The air was dank and still as any dungeon she'd ever visited, carved as deeply into ground of Arkaria as the Sovereign's own manor.

She found a staircase at an intersection and followed it down, wondering if Shrawn would have built his manor in the style of the surface ones; living quarters up, dungeons down. *This might have even preceded Shrawn*, she thought as she came to iron doors with stone blocks lining the walls, opulence itself to import the artisanal objects rather than simply suffice with the existing stone. *Even the dungeons are overwrought here, monuments to the richness and self-importance of this man.*

This man I will kill.

She found the keys on a hook near the entry, wondering at the unguarded nature of the place. It occurred to her that guards might not have been quite so cowed as the servants into hiding, or else might simply be doing it in a different place, far from their respective duty stations. Either way, she seized the key and began unlocking doors, throwing them open. She took a candle off the wall and used it to shed light in her search.

The first three rooms were empty; the fourth held a madman who rambled as he looked at her, beard long and with a fiercely awful smell. She left him to his madness, swinging the door shut but not locking it, figuring the sound of it opening would warn her if he decided to attack her.

It was at the fifth door that she found him, peering out the small, barred window in the door. "Aisling!" he hissed when he saw her. She fumbled for the right key as she thrust it into the lock. "How?"

"The Sovereign is dead," Aisling whispered, as though fearful of being caught. "Shrawn is not in the city. Quickly, we must leave."

"All right." Norenn stumbled out of the dungeon cell on unsteady legs. He wore rags only, cloth so tattered she did not know what form it had started its life as, only that now it was not fit to be so much as a sack for rotting vegetables. The smell of him was nearly the worst she had ever caught a whiff of, and he was so thin and emaciated that she feared he might fall apart.

"Come on," she said, putting his arm around her shoulder. "We need to get out of Saekaj."

Norenn nodded, letting her take up some of his weight. "Sovar. We have to get to Sovar."

She blinked at him in surprise. "Sovar? Why?" *Not that I wasn't planning to go there anyway, but his fervency given his state is … surprising.*

Norenn smiled, revealing that several of his teeth were missing. "Because the Sovereign is dead, yes?" When she nodded, waiting for him to elaborate, his smile broke even wider. "Because it's time. The moment we've been waiting for."

"Norenn," Aisling said, "we're thieves. The only moment we wait for is the one where someone leaves their door unlocked."

He shook his head. "No, no. That was never the point, and you know it. All our talks. All our conversations—you know. Because of your upbringing." He had the sound of the madman, just a touch, ranting now without reason, though she suspected now she knew where he was going with this. "We have to get to Sovar. Have to."

"But why?" she asked, not sure she truly wanted the answer. *He's been imprisoned for years. Let him just want to get out, to breathe the air of his home, to see the familiar sights roughly unchanged. Let him be broken and need time to heal, to come back to himself. Don't let him be …*

"Because, don't you see?" He was grinning uncontrollably now, urging her forward, back toward the stairs, out of this place. "Because now that he's dead, there's no one—no god—to stop us. The revolution is about to begin, Aisling—" Norenn's face tightened with a fury she had not seen outside of her own, the one she hid in the abyss, and this, somehow, frightened her far more than even Shrawn did, "—and we have to be there when it does."

54.

Terian

The timing of this encounter is as piss-poor as any Back Deep resident of Sovar, Terian thought as he stared at his father, the red sword up at high guard and his new axe up, prepared to block the coming attack. The smell of sweat and death was in the air, on his tongue, and it was as bitter a tonic as ever he'd tasted.

"You are a traitor to the Sovereignty," Amenon said, "and to the Sovereign who has taken you in after you were cast out by your supposed friends—"

"After I betrayed my friends," Terian snarled, "for you—"

"—you have wrought immeasurable harm—"

"—I've secured a brighter future for our people, free from the darkness that is choking us—"

"ENOUGH!" J'anda shouted, and flashed Nessalima's light hard enough to draw every eye in the room to him. "Truly, if you two intend to murder each other, let us get on with it, please. For if not, the Sovereignty is presently without guide, though I doubt it will remain so for long."

"Shrawn will move to consolidate his power the moment he hears about the Sovereign," Amenon said, voice thick with accusation and resentment. "If he is not already."

"You say that as though you'd rather not see him continuing to squat atop the structures of power here," Terian said, darting a hard look at his father.

Amenon's pale face did not flush, though his emotions came out in the baring of his teeth. "I would rather see you atop the Sovereignty

251

than that treacherous dog who has so often attempted to feed my entrails to the spiders."

"Well, that's unlikely to happen," Terian said, catching a hint of amusement from Kahlee, "so let's instead think about how we want this to shake out. If the Sovereignty is going to go into chaos—"

"Saekaj will be under threat immediately," Dahveed said, stepping into the circle of argument. "Sovar is starving, the spark of insurrection already poised to light the tinder of the lower chamber. It will not take much to start the blaze."

"What can we even do?" Kahlee asked, throwing back her cowl to reveal blue hair – exactly as she'd had it when he'd encountered her in the markets years before, showing it as a sign of her rebellion to any noble with eyes. Terian did a double take. *Where have you been hiding, wife of mine?* He had already been surprised by the forceful nature of her greeting, the sincerity of her kiss; this was like a return to the old ways for her. "What can we do? Saekaj is some fifty thousand nobles while Sovar is some two million."

"Less, now," Terian said, "thanks to war and starvation, but still, the size of that gap is daunting, is it not?"

"They could sweep the upper chamber in a great mob," Amenon said, looking rather sick about it for a dead man, Terian thought. "It has always been the worry—which is why the Sovereign has always been the currency that backed any action—"

"That kept the rabble down, you mean," Terian said, letting his anger out in a slow hiss.

"You would prefer to give them free reign in Saekaj?" Amenon asked, eyebrow up. "Let them burn and plunder and steal, tear down the edifices brick by brick—"

"It's mostly stone," Terian offered in retort. "I'd put my gold on them burning out the wooden innards after carrying off everything of value."

"And ravaging the women," Amenon said.

"Sovar *is* mostly women at this point," Kahlee said. "Women and the infirm. I expect they'd leave off ravishing, though I wouldn't be surprised to see mobs burning their social betters out of sheer resentment and anger at the countless years of mistreatment."

"Wonderful," Amenon said, throwing up his hands. "Thousands of years of civilization, of order, and it should be torn down and surrendered in the face of a screeching mob—"

"There was always going to be a reckoning," Terian said. "For what we did, how we held them down—"

"There was not going to be any such thing," Amenon snapped, "until you removed the block that kept that particular cart from rolling down at us—"

"It's really more like a waste pond," Grinnd said in his low, cultured tone, "with the dam removed, I think—"

"However you want to order the example," Kahlee said, shouting them down once more, "Sovar will rise. That seems inevitable. Force of arms will be the only thing that keeps them out of Saekaj—"

"We should cut them off from the surface as well," Amenon said, voice hard and unyielding. "If they have to starve for another week or two, that'll take the starch out of their desire to murder us all—"

"My urge to murder you is rising by the moment—" Terian said, fury spitting loose of his mouth.

"This is getting us nowhere," Kahlee said, shaking her head. She began to walk away, and for a moment, the clamor between Terian and his father died down. She turned to look back at them. "Don't you see? When Shrawn returns, he won't be arguing, because he has no one to argue with. He'll march whatever troops are loyal to him right into the mouth of these caves, block access to Sovar and do what Amenon's suggesting. They will starve Sovar."

"Unless they rise in insurrection," Grinnd suggested, "before Shrawn can position his forces."

"Which is a distinct possibility," Dahveed said. "These resentments have simmered for more years than I can count. Many in Sovar have been waiting for a moment just such as this."

Terian felt a tightness in his temple and looked to J'anda, whose face was drawn in pensive thought. "What the hell do we do?"

The enchanter shrugged. "The problem is one of two chambers, two cities. Saekaj has always been the one atop the ladder, content to toss its garbage and shite down upon the rungs below with the Sovereign's blessings. Sovar has not taken that abuse with grace, and with the Sovereign out of the picture, I imagine they will awaken to possibilities they have not seriously considered before—"

"Such as a eating a good meal," Dahveed added.

"Saekaj wishes to remain atop the heap," J'anda said. "Sovar wishes to not remain at the bottom, in plainest terms. Force of arms would be used by Saekaj to preserve the status quo, force of mob would be Sovar's answer to change it." He shrugged again. "As you said, a reckoning, one way or the other."

"Is anyone under the illusion that a mob turned loose on Saekaj would be a good thing?" Amenon asked.

"The citizens of Sovar probably think so," Terian said without any heat whatsoever.

"It will ultimately gain them nothing except a few meals and some trinkets," Amenon snapped. "There isn't that much food hoarded here, certainly not enough to feed two million people. The granaries will be empty in a week, until the new production by the slaves above—" He halted as he caught the quickly exchanged look between Terian and J'anda. "What?"

"I wouldn't count on there being any slaves," J'anda said. "The Sanctuary army was on their way to free them."

Amenon stepped closer to J'anda, breathing death at the enchanter. "Without slave labor working the crops … we will all starve."

"Don't get dramatic," Terian said. "It's the middle of winter. No one's even thinking of putting down a harvest at the moment."

"Are you—?" Amenon put his fingers over his eyes.

"Somewhat sick of seeing people squashed and squatted on by this nation?" Terian asked. "Why, yes. Yes, I am." He took a step forward. "Why can't we build something new here? Something that doesn't lean so hard on Sovar and slaves to prop up the nobles?"

"Because you'll never get the nobles in line to do so," Kahlee said, almost apologetically.

"Then maybe they should content themselves with dying under the flailing fists and feet of pissed-off, starving citizens of Sovar," Terian returned.

"I have no time for debate," J'anda said, sweeping his cloak behind him.

"Apparently neither did the other one," Kahlee said, frowning. "Looks like she snuck off."

Terian caught J'anda's eye and saw the weary resignation there. "It's her way. But not yours. Where are you going?"

"I came back to this place for two reasons," J'anda said, gathering his robes around him. "One was to end the Sovereign's reign and threat to the world. The other," his face grew dark, "was to enjoy revenge on Vracken Coclies, who twisted the Sovereign against me. One part of my mission is finished." The enchanter headed for the front door, passing around Grinnd, who bowed his head politely as J'anda passed. "The other remains yet to be done." He disappeared out of the manor house, as quietly as Aisling.

"So it's back to us again," Terian said, turning his gaze to look back at his father, the pale, dead flesh on his face showing none of the rot he'd seen on the other undead. "And arguing over the same ground."

"We need a plan," Kahlee said, imploring. "One that takes into account what will come from both chambers, what is going to happen here. One that figures Dagonath Shrawn's inevitable machinations into the game—"

"We might not want to do it here, then," Dahveed said, smiling as ever. "Perhaps somewhere less attached to Shrawn?"

"We should return to my house," Kahlee said, and Terian saw the fire of anger smolder in Amenon's eyes at the mere suggestion. "My father should be there. We need to include him in this matter. He can help."

"Many could help," Terian said, looking around the fine wood of Shrawn's entryway, up the steps to the second floor that he had never gotten around to searching. "But finding people who want Saekaj and Sovar to come out of this fight without one ripping the other to pieces ... now that is going to be more than a little challenging."

55.

J'anda

The streets were crowded with milling people, and loud noises still made their way down the tunnels and through the gates of Saekaj. J'anda listened as he walked, but the bustle of the mob was enough to drown out all but the loudest clamor from the caves beyond the upper chamber. People were panicking in the streets, rejoicing in the streets—every emotion along the spectrum was on display, even a small amount of looting, though the predations of a servant's child were ended quickly under the canes of a dozen dandies. J'anda spun a spell around them to stop the rapid rise and fall of their blunt instruments as he passed, silently exhorting the boy to go home, and watching him rush off into the crowd, surprisingly unrepentant.

The dark blacks and whites of the attire of Saekaj's citizens were a surprising contrast to each other. He figured the fashion trends must have been squarely in the middle of reversal, one of those colors gaining favor over the other in a struggle as old as the Shuffle, since there was no universal consensus to be seen in the market. The stalls were closed, nearly nothing was being sold, and it seemed more like a noble social gathering than anything else. Men in suits, women in gowns, and children playing madly as the concerned buzz of conversation filled the cool, damp cave air.

J'anda skirted the edge of the throngs, passing between groups as easily as a horse threading through an army. No one took notice of the enchanter as he made his way to the Gathering of Coercers. Once outside the guildhall, he pushed his way inside with no effort at all. He was greeted by the scared faces of students just inside, watching the entry as though something terrible—a rush of criminals straight out of the Depths, perhaps—was sure to follow him.

"It's all right," he said gently as their eyes took him in. "Nothing to fear."

"We heard the Sovereign had been killed," Zieran said, drifting out of a pocket of students at his side. They all looked so young compared to her, their ages somewhere in the teens. "We assumed—"

"The Army of Sanctuary did kill him," J'anda said and watched the reaction. It was mostly stunned silence, though he would have felt comfortable betting that anger would follow in some cases later. "They marched through to the surface some time ago to go free the slaves."

"Are they ..." a young man asked, his navy complexion whitened with pustules on his cheekbones, "... are they coming back?" He sounded almost afraid enough to faint. "Will we have to fight them?"

"They're not coming back, no," J'anda said, shaking his head. "Nothing to worry about. Their business here is concluded."

He drifted toward Zieran, who was now separating herself from the students she'd been knotted with, moving toward a far corner of the Gathering's entry, one more secluded. J'anda held up a hand to implore privacy as he followed her, and made his way to speak with her without anyone following.

"What are you doing here?" Zieran asked, twirling a bit of her loose hair around her finger. "You were supposed to be in Reikonos."

"The city fell," J'anda said. "I came back. Became ... embroiled in events." He let his eyes flick around. "Where's Coeltes?"

"I don't know," Zieran said. "He disappeared after the news came through. Got that look in his eye—you know the one, always showed up after someone got the best of him—like he had some new consideration in mind. Took the Staff of the Guildmaster and left."

"He didn't say anything?" J'anda asked.

Amusement lit her features. "He wouldn't. Not to me at least, would he?"

"I suppose not," J'anda said and looked over the foyer. *He's the last thing. The last bit of business I have in Saekaj.* He grimaced. *I was so hoping to be done, right here, right now—*

"Sir J'anda," one of the students asked, tentative, as though she was intruding on him in a most private moment.

ROBERT J. CRANE

He blinked out of his thoughts, and settled his gaze on her. "Yes?"

"Are you ..." she licked her lips, "... are you staying?"

He paused, taken aback. He wanted to answer the question on the basis of Coeltes's lack of presence alone. *I want to find him, to settle the score.* Something, though, held him back from that. Something in the way she asked.

"For now," he said, and he smiled gently, "I'm not going anywhere right now." And he listened as the malcontented buzz that filled the room subsided, returning to something almost comfortable for the crisis that they were in.

56.

Aisling

The road back to Sovar was not a road at all, but a passage in someone's basement that was hidden by an old armoire. Aisling had been able to shove it out of the way all on her own, the crashing of the furniture echoing through the empty house. She neither knew nor cared where its masters were, only that she could drag Norenn along the passage by herself, threading down the spiral of the tunnel into the mids of Sovar, where they came out in a cave in the midst of a very surprised gathering of women.

"Sorry," she said as she dragged Norenn through the meekly protesting women, who seemed cowed either by the sight of the daggers in her belt or the ragged man on her shoulder. "Apologies." She pushed through the door and found herself in a cave avenue, one of the tight passages carved out of the main chamber of Sovar.

"Toward the mids," Norenn said, nearly breathless. He had not protested the walk one iota, which worried her. He seemed exhausted yet invigorated, a warring of emotion and body which seemed strange for one who had spent so much time in captivity. She worried that his enthusiasms would wear his body to an early end, but still she followed his counsel rather than trying to find her safe house, the place she had so carefully picked out to hide in when this moment came. "Take us to the square of Uru'kasienn."

Aisling bit back her protest, the urge to tell him he needed rest. It wasn't hard, burying her emotion and sentiment; in fact, after hiding from Dagonath Shrawn and Sanctuary for all these years, it was almost habit. It wasn't as though she didn't want to see what might be happening as well; it was more of a hope that there would be nothing happening, that it would be peaceful, at least for now.

She pulled him through the tunnel and past half a hundred doors as they looped back and entered the main chamber, leaving those carved living spaces behind and entering the more open air of Sovar's mids. The streets sloped down prodigiously, the natural contour of the caves a misery for those who wanted to get out of the Back Deep with a wagon or pushcart. Norenn's weight was not an easy thing for her to absorb on this journey, but she managed it well enough, reaching the Square of Uru'kasienn in ten minutes of walking.

The gathering Norenn had predicted was well in force by the time she was six cross streets back from the square. It had been a dull roar on the echoing cave walls when she'd first become aware of it; by the time she was that close, it was impossible to ignore, tens of thousands or more voices raised in unison every few minutes in response to a speech someone was giving.

"It's started," Norenn said with a satisfied smile, as though he'd just had both bed rest and bed unrest to satiate his every need.

"Something has," Aisling muttered, reaching the edges of the crowd. Gone were the people walking singly or in pairs. Now the streets were filled with groups that kept merging with one another, becoming larger and larger the nearer they drew to the square's center point. It was the only place in Sovar large enough to accommodate even a reasonable sized crowd. She looked up and saw people hanging out of the windows and looking through flaps in the cloth tops of buildings, children sitting on the rooftops three stories up.

She shoved her way where necessary, Norenn seeming to draw strength from the proceedings all the while. The smells of the people around them convinced Aisling that change was, perhaps, necessary, but that it was change involving baths for everybody, and not the sort that involved blood. She caught the first hints of the rhetoric now, and it was seasoned to enrage. Hard words, charged and angry, inciting the people to hurl themselves at the source of all problems (Saekaj, naturally) flew through the air. Invective went along after, to the cheers of the crowd. "This is not going to be good," she muttered to herself, unheard under the chaos.

"But it'll be fun," a voice said from her side, and she caught a glimpse of Genn, hiding under a hood. "Cleansing, I think." And then he was gone, vanished into the crowd.

"What was that?" Norenn asked.

"Nothing," Aisling said, biting her lip. "Nothing at all."

They broke to near the middle of the square and saw a platform erected. It was exactly the sort where the annual summoning of the dregs took place, the sad parade of the children of Sovar in front of their magical betters from Saekaj, where the farmers tried to discern if the pigs had any magical talent. She'd seen it twice and remained disgusted by the spectacle. It looked gross and profane to her eyes, parents and children throwing aside their last shreds of dignity to kiss up to the spell casters who would "judge" them, as though there was any sort of latitude in magical talent.

The stage used for judging was crowded now, but not so full that people were falling off. She could see a half-dozen at the fore, but one before them all, standing tall at the front of the stage and spewing his anger across the crowd like some temple elder in the presence of Enflaga's faithful. It was a man, she could tell that much, and when she saw his robes, it told her a little more. Spell caster. The vestment triggered another easy judgment: enchanter. And when the voice fell clear on her ears, something else. Familiar.

"... For years they've sucked on your blood like a tick, like an insect that burrows under the skin and causes paralysis, using our very muscles against us. They commanded our bodies, our souls, and took everything they could—wives, husbands, daughters, sons, even the food out of our mouths!" This produced a roar of approval, and drowned out the speaker's next words.

"—knows what it's all about," she heard Norenn say in her ear as she felt a little sick. She was close enough now to see him, to put all the pieces together and recognize the man who was, quite simply, about to start the insurrection.

She knew his features, knew his voice, knew his robes, and knew that furious temperament. *J'anda is going to be so very, very angry*, she thought as her blood ran cold.

The enchanter on the stage about to stir the mob to war was none other than Vracken Coeltes.

57.

Terian

"Sitting back and watching the entire population of Saekaj—men, women and children—be massacred is completely unacceptable," Kahlee said, her eyes focused across the top room of the old manor house—Amenon's office, Terian still thought of it, even though it was Vincin's now.

"I don't think anyone here is advocating that," Terian said, glancing at Grinnd, who stood with arms folded, deep in his own thoughts, then to Bowe, who meditated with his eyes shut, floating three feet off the ground with his legs crossed before him.

"They may not be advocating it here," Dahveed said, standing next to the fireplace, which crackled in the quiet, "but I can assure you there are voices advocating it in Sovar right now."

There was a subtle noise of crowds outside, and Terian looked out to see a few curious onlookers poking at the Sovereign's corpse, which still rested in the middle of the avenue. Someone had the head and was staring into the eyes, then dropped it and ran away screaming, the sound of terror stripped away by the thick window separating him from the cavern of Saekaj.

"We should—" Amenon began.

"No," Terian said.

"You didn't even hear me out," Amenon said with the bite of impatience eating into his voice.

"Was it going to be something about stomping on Sovar right this moment?" Terian stared at the fire without looking at his father. "We need to help those people. Your people, I might add, since you did come from Sovar originally."

"Aye, I did," his father said, "and I know how they think. I know their wild and ranging moods, I know the lack of discipline, the craving for revenge over imagined slights—"

"Starvation isn't a slight," Terian said.

"We've been arguing this for hours," Kahlee said, and Terian turned to see her rubbing her eyes. "We don't have time for this."

"We don't have much of anything else," Terian said, shrugging his shoulders. "It's not as though we have an army at our disposal. House Lepos is disgraced. Other than a few guards, all we've got is House Ehrest's commercial interests, and the head of it isn't even here." *Which is concerning*, he thought, his eyes finding Kahlee's and finding worry there. "Anyone fancy fighting a war against whoever comes in here to assert control with nothing but a bunch of merchants and trader convoys at our disposal?"

"That's not going to keep Sovar at bay," Amenon said roughly. "You'll need an army."

"And yet I have none to give," Terian said, staring harder into the fire. He glanced at the portrait of his wife above the fireplace, remembered the one of his sister that used to hang in its place. It made a curious hole inside him, a strange reminder that the world was changed all around him. "Where are our armies now? Besides Reikonos, obviously."

"The hordes of the dead, you mean?" Dahveed asked, sounding none too pleased about it. "Running rampant through the Riverlands, of course, scrambling to capture arable land and stores of food."

"We need the assistance of necromancers to control them, to bring them under our sway," Amenon said. "We need them here, now."

"I only know one necromancer," Terian said, "and his loyalties are decidedly unpredictable in this matter. For all I know, Goliath has thrown in with Shrawn." He threw up his hands in despair. "If Shrawn even knows what's going on. Where the hell is the man, anyway? You'd think, given how intimately tied he is to this place, that he'd—"

"Dagonath Shrawn is never far from where he needs to be," came the voice at the doorway, the muffled by the faceplate of the knight who spoke.

Amenon was the first to name her. "Sareea Scyros. How interesting to find you at our door again at this late hour."

Sareea Scyros entered the room with a subtle swagger, her armor clunking as she moved. "What I find interesting is that years after I left your little group, I find you predictably in exactly the same spot. You stand in stasis, waiting to die."

Terian unslung his axe, feeling the hard hilt in his hand. "If there's to be a fight, I don't think we're the ones who are going to die here today."

Her eyes glimmered through the faceplate, and he could hear the hint of a smile as she spoke. "You sound so assured."

"What do you want?" Terian asked, looking carefully at her.

"I do not come here for myself," Sareea said, hand resting on her weapon's hilt, "but because I am bidden to do so by the Sovereign of Saekaj and Sovar."

There was an audible gasp in the room, and Terian knew its source. "She's talking about Shrawn, not Yartraak. The bastard has already declared himself successor." Sareea inclined her head in mild respect. "The only question I have is whether he even waited until the corpse was cold before seizing power."

"He waited until the deed was done," Sareea said. "But now it is finished, and there is no longer a reason to wait. Dagonath Shrawn is the new ruler of Saekaj, and all your debate is pointless. Whispers of Sovar's disloyalty and insurrection are already reaching our ears through the Sovereign's spies. He moves an army into Saekaj even now to prevent this uprising."

Terian felt a thin thread of hope slipping away. "He's going to put this place even further into siege, squeeze it until it vows loyalty to him."

Sareea smiled. "Look out the window."

Terian turned his head to look past the desk and saw the army in the street already. There were more than a fair number of them. They did not have the look of the dead, but rather solid armor and chainmail of the sort given to a fast moving army fit to be a front line. They were lined up in the street past the manor's wall, and Terian sighed as he looked upon them. *The only consolation I have is that there was nothing more I had to give in this instance, because trying to assert authority over this city with the Army of Sanctuary at my back would have been … ruinous.*

Perhaps to all involved.

"Well, that's a definitive statement," Grinnd said, looking over Terian's shoulder.

"They're still going to be facing down a revolution from Sovar," Terian said, looking back at Sareea. "Is Shrawn truly ready for that?"

"Are you?" she asked, staring at him evenly. "Because last time, you tried to save them."

Terian's jaw tightened at the memory. *She swore she'd never tell, so naturally she trots it out at a moment when she can jab me with it like a spear.* "His plan, on the other hand, is to kill them all. We're like light and dark, he and I."

Sareea cocked her head at him. "And you're the light, I presume? Because no self-respecting dark elf would ever profess to be anything other than darkness, but you ... you've lived in the light entirely too long."

Amenon eased up to the window, putting his shoulder against Terian to look out at the army in the street. "How many soldiers?" he called back to Sareea.

"Several thousand," she said without care. "More will come, but this should be enough to hold the mob back, to push them into Sovar and keep them there for the time being."

Enough to leave a trail of bodies in the tunnels, to flood Sovar with blood, Terian thought as he glanced out the window. *Enough to guarantee that anyone who doesn't embrace the Shrawn regime will come to a messy end.*

"I don't expect you'll be seeing much in the way of resistance from Saekaj," Dahveed said, coming off his place next to the fireplace. "They'll all fall into line behind Shrawn gladly, especially when rumors of insurrection drift up."

Terian heard the truth of it and looked to Kahlee to see her reaction. Her head bowed, dipping down enough that he knew she saw it, too. *They'll gladly bow to Shrawn if it keeps the mob of Sovar from our gates.*

We've lost this fight before it truly began.

"I suppose you've come here seeking loyalty," Terian said, turning his head to look at Sareea, still standing in the entry to the office.

"I have," she said, and she flipped up her faceplate. "But not from you." She looked just to his left. "Amenon?"

Terian's father did not even turn his head, and the lockjaw spell crawled down Terian's throat like a hard-scaled snake had slithered into his open mouth. He held onto his axe only by long training, and his other hand came up to his throat out of desperate reflex the moment before the blow landed that drove him out of the window.

Glass shattered around Terian as he pitched out and slammed into the ground three stories below. It was hard rock that greeted him upon landing, and he bounced once before coming back down, his throat still obstructed by the lockjaw curse. He felt for his axe and failed to find it, blood dripping into his vision, obscuring it. When he went to mop it up, one of the small, blunt spikes on his gauntlet stabbed into the wound, drawing a gasp of pain from him.

"You never did belong here," his father said as he landed a few feet away, filling Terian's ears with that hateful, rasping voice as he dragged Terian to his feet by the collar. He pulled the spiked helm from Terian's head and it clinked against the ground. "You never should have been a dark knight." His father ripped off his gauntlet and Terian batted at him ineffectually, still trying to free his throat from the curse that afflicted him.

"Maybe you should have spared your daughter to be heir," a voice came from behind Terian, and he tilted to look with his eye still clouded. *Shrawn.* "It seems she would have been a more fitting one than this ... disappointment." Shrawn's cane clacked against the rock.

Amenon ripped the back plate off Terian, and his chest plate fell off in the process. Terian started to turn to face his father, but a sharp, gauntleted punch landed in his gut and bent him over. "You are not wrong, Dagonath."

Terian tried to blink the blood out of his eyes, the dark haze over everything stubbornly refusing to yield against his efforts. A sharp blow to his kidney sent Terian to his knees, and when he recovered enough to look up, he saw Sareea there, staring pitilessly down at him. She kicked him in the face and forced his nose into the dirt, where the crack of bone and rush of blood told him she'd broken it.

Where is ... Bowe? He brought his head out of the rocky dirt to see Grinnd standing with Bowe and Dahveed behind his father. *I suppose ... they were never my allies to begin with.* He spit a clump of blood into the ground as Sareea grabbed him by the boot and ripped it off of him, followed by the other. When he tried to kick her, she stomped him in the stomach with her own plated foot, driving all the air out of him.

"All your jests and quips," Shrawn said, watching his humiliation with a certain amount of glee, "and you can't come up with one now, Terian Lepos? All your schemes, your plans, your cleverness ... you really were the best thing to happen to Saekaj Sovar, did you know that?" He leaned over as Sareea stripped the greaves right off of Terian's legs, leaving him utterly unarmored, his underclothes the only thing between him and the cave night. His father stared down at him pitilessly with dead eyes. "Without you, this place might never have known the Sovereign it deserves." He smiled. "I cannot thank you enough—though I am about to try."

He gestured with his cane and the pile of Terian's armor burst into flame. The fire crackled and burned, hard and intense, the heat forcing Terian's blood-drenched eyes to close. It felt like someone holding a desert day close to his face, like the burn of his skin after being exposed to unshaded sun for too long. When he opened his eyes, he saw his armor, with all its points and spikes, melting before his eyes. Great rivulets of the steel ran down it as the breastplate lost its shape and the smaller pieces went ahead of it, sloughing into the rock of the front garden like water poured out onto the stone.

When the fire subsided and the remnants steamed, Terian was left staring at that which had protected him from countless slings, swords, arrows and blows, in a pile, steaming, formed to the rock like clay shaped by unskilled hands. *My armor ...*

He was kicked down into the dirt, his face buried in the rocky dust. He caught a glimpse of motion, of his axe in Sareea's hands, raised up. *So this is how it ends,* Terian thought, the blood dribbling out of his lips. *I should have gone with J'anda. Should have gone with Cyrus. Never should have come back here, because this place is definitely not my h—*

"Wait," Kahlee's soft voice drifted over them, and he turned his head enough to see her make her way over to him. She stood over him for only a moment before getting on her knees. *Not you too, Kahlee ...*

"He shouldn't go alone," Kahlee said, and the last breath of hope fell out of Terian. He'd been prepared for some last insult, a final betrayal, anything but this. She knelt next to him and lay in the dirt beside him, her face opposite his, looking into his eyes. He saw a smile of reassurance there and swallowed the bitter disappointment and guilt, knowing that soon it wouldn't matter if he held it back. She wrapped her arms around him and pressed herself against him, warm against his skin even through the cloth.

"I'm sorry," he whispered as he saw the axe raise out of the corner of his eye. "I'm sorry it ended like this."

The axe came down as the light of a return spell twinkled in his blood-clouded vision, and his wife—*that sneaky little minx*—carried him away with magic he'd never even known she had.

58.

Aisling

Aisling had never felt so uncomfortable as she did when Norenn brought her into the place where the insurrection was headquartered. She could not even recall feeling so out of place in Shrawn's dungeons, nor on any of the occasions when she suborned her will to do the things to Cyrus Davidon that Shrawn had ordered her do. It boggled her very imagination that such a place as this, a headquarters of insurrection, could have survived long in Dagonath Shrawn's Sovar, so obviously under a paranoid nose, watched by all. These thoughts, though, she kept to herself, especially as she was introduced to Vracken Coeltes.

"A pleasure to meet you," he said, without a trace of recognition as he nodded his head to her. There was no reason for him to recognize her, of course; she'd hit him from behind and rendered him unconscious without him ever laying eyes upon her. He took in Norenn with a similar look, a fiery charisma she'd seen come from the stage. "And you, as well. A political prisoner, eh?"

"She just rescued me from Shrawn's dungeon," Norenn said, leaning hard on the stone wall of the building two blocks off the square. There was a buzz of energy that had followed them after the rallying, something that had lingered and trailed back to this place. The roar of the crowd was still in the air, still obvious even now, waiting as they took a brief rest before the next speeches.

"Did you indeed?" Coeltes asked, looking at her evenly through careful eyes.

"It's so good to see you again, Norenn." Strong arms grabbed him around the biceps, causing Aisling to swing her attention around to see who had approached so unexpectedly. "And out of Shrawn's grasp, no less."

She blinked at the sight of him in his fine silks, looking not nearly as worse for the wear as when she'd seem him last, with a spear through his heart. "Xemlinan Eres," Aisling whispered.

"Aisling Nightwind," he said, meeting her gaze with his own. There was something going there, something behind the eyes that hinted at depths of knowledge while his tone was all enthusiasm coupled with playfulness, like a young man who'd just received every gift he could ever have imagined. "I'm pleased to see you outside Dagonath Shrawn's clutching fingers. I trust you're well?"

"Better than ever," Aisling said, not feeling it one bit. She took Norenn's arm and pulled him to the side, finding a quiet corner of the room as Xem and Coeltes chatted personably with two others, watching her with him out of the corner of their eyes. "What are we doing here, Norenn?"

"We're here to join the fight, of course," Norenn said, standing a little straighter than he had earlier. She wondered if he was simply regaining his strength or if it was false hope given by the locale that was galvanizing him to action. "Can you imagine it, Ais? After all those years, after all we've seen, all the dirty spiders like Shrawn ... Saekaj is about to get its due."

She glanced at Xem, who caught her gaze and smiled knowingly— *at least to his mind, probably.* "Norenn ... we've been their prisoners for four years." She made her voice plaintive. "But we're free now. They may have taken these years from us, but they need not have the rest. Let's just leave, please."

"I will not leave," Norenn said, pulling back from her, his face darkening. "How can you have gone through ... what we've gone through ... I can't even imagine, on your end, the things you've had to do to survive ... how can you possibly want to leave Shrawn alive after all that?" He looked wounded, hurt. "How can you let him win?"

She buried her true reply within, as per usual. *Shrawn always wins.* "Because we don't owe these people anything, and staying here means going straight into his teeth again after we've just pried ourselves free of his jaws. This is insanity, to go forward again. We should leave. The Sovereign is dead; Shrawn is going to take his little kingdom here, and he's going to pit it against itself while trying to stomp down on Sovar." She tried to run a hand down his front, to soothe him as she would a babe. "This is the worst place in Arkaria to be at the moment."

"This is my home," he said stiffly. "But I suppose yours is a chamber higher."

She stiffened. "You don't see me running back to Saekaj, do you?"

"I just see you running," he said, eyes narrowed. "Of all the things you've become in our time apart, I didn't suppose 'coward' would be one of them."

She pretended it stung her, but in truth it was of little practical consequence. Norenn had never been much of a fighter, and neither had she before Shrawn and Sanctuary had made her one. "I've seen battles beyond counting, Norenn. Too many. More dead than you can imagine. And I fear I'm about to watch the worst of them yet." She leaned toward him, whispering. "These people are more or less defenseless, and Shrawn has armies at his command. Weapons. Trained troops. We have starving people and anger, a poor combination against a wizard with the fury of fire at his disposal."

"We have passion," Norenn said, and his eyes flickered with the righteousness of his cause, sending another tremor of worry through her, "we have justice at our backs! We are the wronged, and we have been held down for so long—the fury of our rightness is true and resonant in our souls." He looked around him. "With people like these on our side, how can we lose?"

Under armored feet and ten thousand spears, she did not say. Instead, she smiled weakly. "I only worry for you," she said, knowing that this battle was lost. She turned her head enough to catch a glimpse of Genn in the corner, walking through the headquarters as though he belonged here with the others. In truth, she knew, he did. He caught her eye and smiled, but not reassuringly. "I can't blame you for wanting to fight for your home." Her voice cracked, as she intended. "My home is with you, and I would not see it destroyed. Not after all this."

"It will be fine," he said, taking her into his arms. She found no reassurance there, either, strangely numb after gaining at least half of what she thought she'd worked for these last years. "We have the numbers. We are the righteous. We will win."

"Of course," she said, mopping strained tears onto his rags. She produced them while thinking of the oddest of things—Sanctuary's defeat of Mortus, and the fear that had come hard with that battle and the chaos in the realm that followed it. It was one of the clearest occasions when her true emotion ran close to the surface, so close she could not hide it in the moment. *Now it comes back to me as needed, as I hide myself and my intent from the man I've worked to free all this time.*

Norenn pulled back, looking her in the eyes with his own, warm and caring in spite of the argument—or perhaps because of it. "It will be all right," he told her again, and pulled away from her, making his way on wobbling legs back to Xem and Coeltes, wearing a smile of wolfish delight.

Now I am not even myself with the man I sacrificed everything to save, she thought dimly as she watched him go. *Now I hide even when I could be me, could tell him how I truly feel because … how do I truly feel? And why?*

Who am I?

"Worry not," came Genn's whisper in her ear as he slipped past her, unnoticed, just another dark elf in the headquarters of the insurrection, speaking so low that his voice was lost in the chaos being planned around them, "I like the new you." And he disappeared while she stood there staring at the man she had given up everything to save—and the one she could no longer even bear to be herself with.

59.

J'anda

The summons came for the Gathering of Coercers' Guildmaster, and J'anda took it because no one else would, not even Zieran, the cold footsteps of the messenger still ringing across the entry as he ran to depart, more missives in hand.

J'anda had read it, had looked around, waiting for someone else to take the initiative, to ask about its contents, and when no one did, he felt the same flash of surprise as when Alaric had informed him that he was an officer of Sanctuary by fiat rather than vote. *You are in charge because no one else wants to be. Same old story.*

He'd departed immediately, vowing to return and mostly meaning it, having them bar the guildhall door as he left, just in case. The trainees were quiet, fearful, their worry as obvious on their faces as a smear of jam on buttered bread. He left them with a smile of reassurance and heard the heavy wood bar thunk into place behind the stone doors as he left, walking through the surprisingly quiet streets of Saekaj with nothing but an envelope in his hand.

He was stopped twelve times from the guildhall to the front gates of the palace—on nearly every street and in the quiet market. The guards were out in force, and they all bore the gauntlet identifying them as House Shrawn rather than Saekaj militia. J'anda supposed it was going to be the new insignia, and he found he did not care. The streets were packed with them, the soldiers crowding the area in clusters and clumps, watching him with suspicious eyes. He saw not one other civilian anywhere during his journey, and by the time he reached the Grand Palace of Saekaj, he was well and truly tired of presenting the crumpled letter that he carried unwanted in his hand.

When he was ushered into the throne room, he realized with some surprise that the corpse of the old Sovereign had already been moved out of the street. He hadn't even realized it as he walked by, so great was his irritation with the constant supervision of the soldiers.

The throne room looked the same as when he'd last seen it a few hours earlier, though it was more guarded now than it had been when Yartraak had sat the throne. There were men hammering and chopping at the old throne, tearing it down with axe and hatchet, the front legs already brought low, the high back sloped at a forty-five degree angle forward, like a horse down on its front legs. *And so passes the days of Yartraak, the Sovereign of Saekaj, the only of his name.*

"J'anda Aimant," Dagonath Shrawn said, announcing the enchanter himself from his place in a padded seat placed in the middle of the long carpet that stretched the length of the room. "So you are the Guildmaster of the Gathering of Coercers now?" He nodded, once, inclining his head slightly to the side as if it were obvious. "As it should be."

J'anda glanced behind him at the destroyed doors through which he'd just entered, and saw the hole in the wall where Cyrus Davidon had been flung not a day earlier. "I see you are in the process of redecorating?"

"I suspect some carpentry will have to be done," Shrawn said, getting to his feet, staff clutched in his hand. "I confess a slight degree of surprise in seeing you here; I did not expect Coeltes, of course, but I assumed Lacielle would take up the mantle of leadership after his flight."

J'anda cocked an eyebrow at him. "His flight? So you know that he has left us?"

"The rat leaving the ship before sinking, I am afraid," Shrawn said, watching him carefully. "Do you know where he has gone?"

J'anda did some careful watching of his own. "If I did, I can assure you I would be after him swiftly, looking to settle some business left open between us. Do you know where he is?"

Shrawn laughed, a deep, resonant sound that hurt J'anda's ears as it bounced off the walls of the throne room. "I had heard that the two of you had a long and unpleasant rivalry that required resolution." He tapped the cane against the carpet, producing a muffled thump. "I do, in fact, know where he is. And I would tell you, save for the fact that he is presently deeply mired in trying to inflame the masses of Sovar into insurrection."

That is an answer in and of itself. "And yet you just told me."

"I have told you only that he is in Sovar," Shrawn said, waving away the statement as though it were a bothersome pest humming about his head. "Should you go after him now, you will find yourself in the midst of an angry mob looking for citizens of Saekaj to turn inside out and eat alive. You are truly a wondrous enchanter, but I wonder at your ability to survive in the face of such breathtaking odds."

J'anda smiled. "They are better than even, I would say."

"Well, let me have my say, then," Shrawn said, smiling, "and see if it fits your purposes better than an even chance." He stepped toward J'anda cradling the cane but not actually using it to walk. "Sovar is preparing to rise, the years of resentment bubbling to the surface as surely as water boiling on a fire. The angriest elements will come to the fore, will spur them into action, into internecine war. There will be blood. There will be 'revolution,' as they call it. And they will come surging up through the tunnels into our own, intent on spreading death and killing everyone whom they perceived has wronged them."

J'anda watched him, keeping his face straight. "I sense you have a plan to stop this. But why should I care?"

"Why are you in the Gathering of Coercers even now?" Shrawn asked, stepping to his side and not looking at him, staring at the far end of the chamber.

"I am waiting for Coeltes's return, of course."

"You are a skilled enchanter," Shrawn said, "and a charming fellow. You could surely have followed the trail that Coeltes left behind, like a ranger after a wounded animal. If you'd been of a mind to hound him, you would have found his lair by now, settled your business, and returned to your beloved Sanctuary, I think." At this, Shrawn tilted his head to look at J'anda. "Your loyalty is still to them, and we both know it. Something else holds you in place, something that had you sitting a vigil at the Gathering all night. Loyalty of a different kind, not simple revenge. You care for this place, or your students, at least. The months you have spent here have not been coldly focused on only one thing; you have bonded, you have cared."

"So what if I have?" J'anda asked, shrugging. "You intend to use that as a lever to force me to fight for you?"

"I force you to do nothing," Shrawn said with a shrug of his own. "If you mean to leave, do so with my blessing as the Sovereign. Indeed, I owe you and your friends much for coming to this place and doing what you have done. Go, and come again if you'd like, after the so-called revolution. We will endure in Saekaj, I can assure you." His face went expressionless. "But it will not be an easy fight, especially with Coeltes at the fore of the enemy. I will need to counter him, and for that, I will require enchanters of my own."

J'anda felt the cold slide of a single droplet of sweat down the hair at his temple. "You wouldn't."

"I would prefer not to," Shrawn said. "They are the future of the Gathering, after all, and need time to grow into maturity and their full strength. But without them, I face the old head of the Gathering against my soldiers, ill-prepared for his spellcraft. I will need your students, there is no way around that." He angled his head, and there was almost a quality of mournfulness. "It is a waste, but it is the only option I have against a powerful enchanter, for we have so few of our own with the other armies now under other control."

J'anda caught the hint in Shrawn's voice, but declined to pursue it to its conclusion. "And if I help you?"

"Then I will help you," Shrawn said, smiling now, though faintly. "I assure you that I will do everything in my power to steer Vracken Coeltes into your path so that you may deal with him however you choose. If you wish to capture and torture him, I will provide whatever assistance you nee—"

"Thank you," J'anda said, cutting him off. He paused, a thought coming to the fore. "And my ... past problems with the Sovereign?"

Shrawn looked him over with amusement. "It seems unlikely to be of great issue in your current condition, but rest assured I give little care about your proclivities. I care only for stopping this insurrection and turning it back on the unrestful. To save lives, as it were."

He's a liar, J'anda thought. *A murderer. He's been responsible for more death than anyone I know, other than the Sovereign and Malpravus.* "You will have my help," J'anda said, ignoring all his other thoughts and taking the hand proffered to him by the man who now ruled Saekaj.

60.

Terian

The light was low in the place where the spell took them, almost reminding Terian of the darkened building where Malpravus had carried him after the return to Arkaria. The floor under his naked back was wood, and it squeaked as he moved, pain lancing down his sides. He bent a knee, drawing it closer to him so that he could look at it, swollen already, and dabbed at his nose, coming away with thick, blue blood. "That's going to leave some scarring."

"You look terrible," Kahlee said, sitting up and producing another squeak from the wooden floor.

"Thank you, wife," he said, trying to sit up himself and failing after a surge of pain from a broken rib. "I should have transferred my torment to Shrawn before I left, but I was too busy choking on a lockjaw curse." He rubbed at his throat; the curse had mostly passed. "Speaking of magic ... I didn't know you were ..."

"Mmm," Kahlee said, getting to her feet, leaving her cloak to puddle on the floor next to him, an invitation to cover himself in it, he thought. "It was my father's doing." She turned to look down at him. "What do you get for the rebellious daughter who has it all and wants none of it?"

"Lessons in heresy, apparently," Terian said, trying to adjust his nose and drawing a grunt after pain shot up into his skull at the attempt. "Oh, gods. I haven't been beaten like this since ..." He blinked, and the image of his father ripping him out of his armor came fresh to his mind, a wound that stung all the more for his surprise at the care he felt for it. "Ever, actually."

A door opened behind him, casting bright illumination into the darkened room, scorching his one open, unbloodied eye. "Well, there was that time that the Siren of Fire ripped your head off," came a familiar voice from beyond as the light flooded in.

Terian's eye adjusted quickly and he felt the breath of a healing spell tickle over his flesh. "Curatio?" He blinked and looked around the room, which was a simple wooden quarters, a building unlike anything he'd seen on the Sanctuary grounds. "Where am I?" Another figure stepped into shadow behind the healer, this one feminine, long hair hanging around her shoulders, her outline obvious in that she wore pants and not a dress. "Vara?" Terian asked, squinting at her in the blinding daylight.

"Not exactly," the woman replied, almost laughing in her amusement.

It only took him a moment more to remember where he'd heard that voice before. "Baroness Cattrine." He looked past her and saw a dusty street. "I'm in the Emerald Fields, the new settlement."

"I'm sure you wondered where my father hid me," Kahlee said, picking up her cloak from the ground and draping it over Terian. "Now you know. The last place anyone would think to look for a scioness of a dark elven family."

"In the Elven Kingdom," Terian nodded, getting to his feet, his wounds healed save for a little residual pain. He wrapped the cloak tight around his shoulders. "What are you doing here, though, Curatio? Don't you have a goddess to heal, or something?"

"My work in that area is done," Curatio said, with a twinge of regret. "No, I have other matters to attend to, I think. Obligations that require my attention elsewhere, such as here."

"I almost feel as though you were waiting for me," he said, looking at the healer. He shifted his gaze to the Baroness. "Both of you, maybe."

"They weren't," Kahlee said softly, drawing his attention back to her. She ran a hand over his shoulder and it tingled, bereft of the protection of his armor. Even with the kindness of her touch, he felt the loss of the armor very acutely now, and the sharp strike of inner pain was such that he couldn't keep from blanching, just a little. She did not pull away, and her face had a pain of its own. "They were waiting for my father ... and if he hasn't shown up by now ..." The worry caused her cheeks to sag, her eyes to fall in despair, and suddenly the worry of his armor was lost to Terian, "... then he is mostly likely dead."

61.

Terian

"What were the last words that Alaric said to you?" Curatio asked, a bolt out of the blue, breaking the silence of a dour moment. "To you, personally, not to the expedition on the bridge."

Terian needed to think for only a second. "'I believe in you' ... and that redemption is a path we must walk every day."

Curatio pursed his lips at this. "Indeed." He nodded his head as if it settled a matter. "Very well, then."

"'Very well, then' what?" Terian asked, more than a little perplexed.

"You have problems," Curatio pronounced.

"Tell me about it," Terian said dryly, "I'm exiled from my homeland and practically naked in the middle of a town of people who are probably still carrying a grudge for what I did to their hero, Cyrus."

"Those are minor and easily dealt with," Curatio said, waving off his concerns. "Well, at least the second and third."

"May I suggest we deal with the nakedness first?" Cattrine asked, cringing. "For I have no desire to see it—no offense."

"None taken," Terian said, pulling the cloak tighter around him.

"Perhaps some," Kahlee interjected, draping herself on his arm.

"Only a little taken, then," Terian amended. "What are my problems, Curatio?"

"Come along," the healer said, and began to walk away, prompting Terian to follow, Kahlee at his side. Cattrine waited for them to pass by her, entering the wide, dirt avenue of the town, Terian's bare feet finding every coarse and troublesome pebble along the way.

"Ouch," Terian muttered under his breath. "Curatio, where are we going?"

"Do you have anywhere else to be?" Curatio asked, not turning back. He did not await an answer. "No? Then what does it matter?"

"You're becoming alarmingly Alaric-like," Terian said, taking in his surroundings. "And I assumed that came with the post of Guildmaster."

"I was the acting Guildmaster for some time," Curatio said, wearing a very slight smile. "It does not take long, I assure you."

Ahead was a square, and he could hear the laughter of children as they darted around a statue. He watched, catching a hint of something peculiar in their movement, the way they leapt to avoid the thing. *That's not a statue*, he realized as the enormous stone thing ham-fistedly made a high swipe at one of the children. It went wide above them and came slow, and was followed by another peal of laughter from the children. *Fortin*.

As they entered the square, the rock giant swung his head around and caught sight of them. Pausing immediately from his game, he turned and carefully stepped clear of the children, leaving them behind in a matter of a second and a half, thundering across the square.

"Oh, look," Terian said, watching the rock giant approach with growing unease, "one of the people who is carrying a grudge against me."

"I imagine you meet them everywhere you go," Cattrine offered.

"It's becoming a real problem," Terian agreed as the rock giant skidded to a stop, Curatio stepping out of his way to allow the enormous creature passage.

"Give me one reason," Fortin rumbled, stooping to look into Terian's eyes with his own enormous red ones, "I should not tear you limb from treacherous limb, now that your business with Sanctuary is concluded."

"You were waving at J'anda, then?" Terian asked, staring back at him, calm as though he'd just wandered into the same game as the children had been playing with the rock giant. He sensed the tension grow in the air and watched Fortin begin to raise a hand, and formulated an answer. "Because I'm pretty." Fortin paused, and

Terian could almost see the question mark pop into the air above the creature. "You don't kill pretty things," Terian explained casually, "because if you do, eventually you'll be left with nothing but ugly things to look at."

"Hold, Fortin," Curatio said, causing the rock giant to look at the healer. "Terian is not our enemy."

"Perhaps not yours," Fortin rumbled, and looked at him with red eyes, cheerfully murderous, "but I feel certain that the General might feel at least some residual annoyance at the betrayal he suffered from this one."

"He called me 'brother' in the palace," Terian said, shrugging.

"But you tried to kill him," Fortin said.

"What, you never had a brother you tried to kill?" Terian asked, playing a desperate gambit and throwing more than a little flipness in at the same time.

The rock giant looked at him, and the sound of rock grinding against rock came out of his jaws as he appeared to consider this. "That … is not a social nicety among your kind, though, I was told."

"I'm not nice," Terian said, "or social."

"Mmmm," Fortin rumbled and finally nodded. "Proceed, dark knight." The thick ridge of rock that ran across Fortin's eyes moved into something akin to a crooked line. "Where is your armor?"

"Lost it in a fire," Terian said, taking up the walk to follow Curatio once more.

"Unfortunate," Fortin called after them. "You should get more. You would be a soft target in that cloth."

"I'm a soft target anyway, right now," Terian said, shrugging, Kahlee still walking beside him. *And there's not much I can do about it, unfortunately.*

62.

Terian

They made their way into a wooden building with a hearth that crackled aflame, the heavy smell of wood smoke keeping the light winter cold at bay. Terian wrapped the cloak tighter around his shoulders as Cattrine Tiernan ushered them in and had them sit on old furniture, a plush couch that looked as though it had been rescued from an elven living room set aflame. It bore scorch marks on either arm, and the Baroness shrugged when Terian looked from it to her, frowning.

"Do you want to know your problems, Terian?" Curatio asked, settling next to the fireplace, standing next to the heavy wooden mantel that was nailed into the wall so artlessly Terian could see the nails sticking out of it. *What kind of idiot carpenter built this place?* The answer came to him suddenly. *No carpenter at all, probably. Skilled tradesmen are likely lacking in this town, after all.*

"Sure, might as well lay them at my complete lack of a doorstep," Terian said as the Baroness disappeared back down the stairs to the outside, shutting the door behind her as she went. "Or my borrowed one, perhaps?"

"First," Curatio said, "what do you mean to do?"

"Well," Terian said, smiling brightly and without any actual enthusiasm, "when we last we saw each other, I meant to crush the Sovereign's allies and cast them out of Saekaj so that I could give my people a reasonable chance at something like the freedom the humans and elves and dwarves and goblins and gnomes—pretty much everyone but my people—have enjoyed, without a tyrant sitting on them. Since then, though, I've been beaten, betrayed, and nearly executed, so ..."

"So he's free of obligation at the moment," Kahlee answered helpfully. "What did you have in mind, Curatio?"

"I have very little in mind, in point of fact," Curatio said. "Tiny seeds of ideas, really."

"Well, my damned idea tree got ripped out of the ground and turned into firewood," Terian said, "so I guess I'm open to hearing from you, since at the moment my course of action runs to 'procure clothing' and not much farther."

"Your problems are three-fold," Curatio said neatly, like a lecturing teacher at the Legion of Darkness. "The first is that Dagonath Shrawn has asserted himself over Saekaj with the mailed fist of a tyrant stepping into the role of Sovereign."

"Yay," Terian said, "it's like the good old days—or like yesterday, I suppose, but without all the religious iconography."

"The second problem," Curatio said, "is that there is a long-brewing revolution taking root in Sovar, one that will doubtless expand into violence and come to blows with Shrawn's forces above. Their intentions are surely to take their vengeance with fire and rage."

"Fun," Terian said. "I'm sure when they're done with tearing Saekaj into shreds and burning all the nobles, the mob will calmly set up a peaceful government, ruled by the people, that'll feed everyone and ensure tranquility in both caverns."

"And the final problem," Curatio said, "and perhaps most distressing—Malpravus has seized control of the armies of the dead and is moving them toward Saekaj and Sovar at the moment, along with Goliath and the remainder of the dark elven forces."

Terian felt his stomach drop at the news. "Well, that's a new one to me."

Curatio raised an eyebrow at him. "I doubt his intention is to, as you put it, set up peaceful rule by council, either. He is another who desires to make Saekaj his personal power base, to become the new Sovereign. Thus you are faced with three distinct threats, with three separate visions of the dark elven peoples' future, and the possibility that any two of the three may in fact combine forces to deal with the third—or you, should you enter the fray."

"Me?" Terian laughed, a sharp bark. "Curatio, I don't even have a weapon or armor. To go up against Shrawn or Malpravus's army, or the mob that is Sovar's survivors is a type of suicide I don't regularly contemplate."

"And yet you want to walk the path of redemption, do you not?" Curatio eyed him.

Oh, he's getting a kick out of this little twist, isn't he? "Does the path to redemption lead right into the jaws of death?" Terian stared right back at the healer.

"It led us to Mortus, did it not?"

Point for point. "Cyrus Davidon led us to Mortus," Terian said.

"At some point," Curatio said, looking a little tired, "you should put aside this obsession you have with Cyrus."

"I don't hold a grudge anymore, okay?" Terian ran a hand across his hair, catching his fingers in the blood matted there. "That's over with."

"I do not speak of your foolish desire to kill him, which I am thankful has passed," Curatio said evenly, "I am talking about this perpetual sense that somehow Alaric favored him over you because of who he was or who you are."

Terian glanced at Kahlee and saw a cloud of emotion on her face that she was keeping back. He laughed, mirthless. "Alaric favored Cyrus. I don't think I'm imagining it. He set him up as successor."

"Oh, yes, he gave him the keys to the kingdom," Curatio said dryly. "Or the pendant, at least. But that came after a long race, filled many choices that each of you made that led you in different directions. There were others in that race as well, ones you did not take notice of because you were too focused on your perceived rivalry."

"I didn't see him as a rival," Terian said, casting his eyes down. "Not until I'd lost. He was like—like the older, better brother that I knew I never had a chance against. At least, not after I left."

"After the choices you made," Curatio corrected. "For I assure you, Alaric held no ill will against you. You became the person you aimed to become, choosing to direct your efforts in less serious ways than Cyrus did, to better the guild less than he did, to build credibility with the members less frequently than he did."

"He was the General, Curatio," Terian said, shaking his head. "I couldn't compete against that."

"You did not even try," Curatio said. "You chose to cede the race, you chose the easier path. You were an officer, and once the Elder, and you absolved yourself of doing the work that Cyrus did. And it was a fine choice, but you cannot complain after the fact that the result was unfair when you never took it as seriously as he did. If redemption is a path that must be walked daily, you must factor your detours into account when the time comes to tally mileage."

"What would you have me do, Curatio?" Terian asked, throwing his arms wide. "What? What *can* I even do?"

"Fight," Kahlee said, leaning toward him now, her eyes burning. "As you have never done since the days of old, when you chose to partake in the soul sacrifice. Fight for the glorious society you naively believed in before the death of your sister burned it out of you. For the days of the Sovereign and that sort of sacrifice are over, and will be over for all time, if we prevail against Shrawn and Malpravus and all the rest of the would-be tyrants."

"I would," Terian said, looking at his wife, "if I but stood a chance. But it's me, now, Kahlee. Me alone, against three factions with armies and anger and weapons." He looked down at his chest, and it looked sunken in the V where the cloak met below his pectorals. "There is no chance, not for me." He tasted bitter defeat, and it was like old brew gone sour on his tongue. "There is no hope."

The door to the office opened then, and Cattrine Tiernan re-entered, two men following behind her. They struggled under the weight of the burden they carried, draped in cloth, and Terian peered at them, curious. *It almost looks like a corpse.* They set it upon the wood floor with a hard thump, and it settled with a sound of clanking metal. It stood upright, the cloth still covering it, and Terian looked at it as though he could see past the cloth cover. *What the …?*

"'Hope,'" Curatio said, "to borrow a phrase from someone of our mutual acquaintance, 'is a light that shines in the darkness when no others can be seen.'" He sidled over to the thing that Cattrine's workers had brought in. "I can give you hope, Terian—but just a small one. The start of the path, if you will. Where you go from there … well, it's entirely in your hands." With a flourish, the healer tore off the white cloth, and Terian sat, breathless, chills unrelated to the weather running down his skin. "Well?" Curatio asked. "What do you think?"

Terian swallowed, hard, unable to take his eyes off the spectacle before him, a nearly complete tableau that lacked only two small things. "I think ... I have nowhere else to walk, so ... I might as well go the way a seasoned guide tells me to."

"Then you can walk your path with the aid of this," Curatio said, and only glanced at the armor of Alaric Garaunt at his side, complete save for the helm and the sword of the old knight, "and may it protect from all the harm that will come your way ... just as the Ghost of Sanctuary would have wanted it."

63.

J'anda

One Hundred Years Earlier

He awoke to the sound of Trimane dressing, the warrior's armor clinking at the side of his bed as he fastened it on, his dull, colorless armor such a contrast to the man who wore it. Trimane had flair, had humor, personality that bulged at the seams. His armor, on the other hand, J'anda thought, was everything that was wrong with the Sovereignty—*no differentiation, just a people who walk in lockstep, afraid to look or act in a way that doesn't fit with the crowd.*

"You're staring again," Trimane said, voice ripe with amusement as he slipped on his gauntlet. "Best not look at another man too long, lest someone get the idea you're a deviant."

"I have no idea where such a notion could come from," J'anda answered him, not half as entertained by the concept as Trimane. That was part of the warrior's draw, he figured; others he'd known in this way were frightened, afraid to so much as jest about the secret and forbidden ways in which they partook. The threat of the Depths was a joke to Trimane, a man as fearless as any he had ever met. *He takes this serious matter and makes it funny in his way. Or is it simply gallows humor?*

"I'm off to war," Trimane said, finishing with his other gauntlet. "Or possibly court, today. Hard to tell the difference, really. What are you up to?"

J'anda rolled over, the silken sheets of his small cottage at the edge of Saekaj entrapping him in his bed. It was a luxury, an extravagance he would not have been able to even consider were he still a simple instructor at the Gathering. *Being a war hero and the current favorite of the Sovereign carries a special set of rewards, I suppose.* "I may be at court. I may not. I am not certain. The Sovereign chooses peculiar times to have his consultations about the war, and they always come at a moment's notice."

"Agreed," Trimane said, leaning in close to him. "I look forward to seeing you at court, if I see you there. And perhaps, if not, I'll run across you on the battlefield, if we end up going to one on this day. And failing any of that …" Trimane smiled. "Dinner tonight?"

A glimmer of nervousness twinged through J'anda's stomach. *So bold, this one. Not even afraid to eat together in public, keeping up the facade we are mere friends.* "Are you not … afraid?" He caught the hint of hesitation in Trimane's eyes. "Of being caught? Of being … known?"

"One should not live one's life in fear," Trimane said with a smile. "Even for us, our lives are too short to dwell in such a place." He stood, nodding at J'anda. "Right?"

J'anda smiled weakly. "But of course," he said, going along with it. "Of course you're right." The smile faded as soon as Trimane was out the door, quietly, into the dark of Saekaj, and the silken sheets picked up the chill of the caves once more. But he was not entirely sure that Trimane was right, when he thought about it further, and it left him with that same sense of unease all the day long.

64.

Aisling

So this is what an insurrection looks like, Aisling thought as the crowd roared again. It was not a quiet thing, that much was certain, and she did think of the crowd as a thing. It was not a gathering of people, not anymore. It had taken on a life of its own at the steering of the people on the stage—Xem, Coeltes, and now Norenn. They told stories, they rallied support, and the crowd—the thing that was alive—grew hour by hour, and even minute by minute as word of the Sovereign's death faded from shock into a feeling of "What's next?" that was punctuated by hunger.

"They have spared not a thought for us in all these years," Norenn shouted, voice still sounding a little thin from his weakness. He had not slept; he'd had no time. He carried on with a fire in the eyes, driven by something that his newfound freedom had let loose along with his body. "No one in Saekaj has worried about us in the years of war or the years before, has worried about our children starving in the streets ..."

"He really does have a delightful manner about him," Genn said, drifting next to her at the base of the stage. She stood at the base and watched the crowd, afraid to watch Norenn do his talking. When she heard Genn's voice, she did not even turn to face him. "I can see what drew you to him."

"And I can see what draws you to him," Aisling murmured, sure he would catch it even if she hadn't spoken at all.

"Am I that transparent?" Genn asked, sounding mildly offended.

"Yes," she said.

"Well, let me ask you this," Genn said, amused again, "why are you still here?"

She didn't have to ponder to find an answer that worked. "I have nowhere else to go."

"See, I don't think that's it," Genn said, slipping in front of her, smile reaching up to his eyes. "We both know why you're here."

"Do we?"

"We do," Genn said, "one of us is just a little afraid to admit it to herself."

"Oh, do tell," Aisling said, glancing behind him into the crowd. It roared with approbation at some exhortation from Norenn, and a look over her shoulder revealed him basking in the adulation. When she turned back, Genn had circled to her left ear, giving her an unobstructed view of the continually growing crowd.

"Let's be honest," Genn said. "Just put it all out there, since you already know me, and I already know you. You enjoyed the work that Shrawn put you to. You enjoyed learning how to watch, how to fight, how to kill. It was like the nectar of life poured across dying lips. You were bored as a socialite; it's why you followed this thief to Sovar. You loved playing the people, playing the game, even worming your way into the hearts of Sanctuary's members was a thrill. You found adventure of the sort you didn't know you were seeking, and backing it all was a mission that no one even guessed at, threaded with enough deception, danger and threat to keep even the quickest mind entertained."

"I don't know that 'entertained' is the right word for it," Aisling said tightly.

"Oh, but it is," Genn said. "You thrive on it, the chaos. It's not like with Cyrus, where he throws himself into battle and adores it, whatever the cause. No, with you it's the subterfuge, the deception. You'd be just as happy getting all the money and glory and the goal without having to actually fight at all. It's the dagger in the night, the whispered word that turns the army in the direction of your choosing. You may have started out pushed and manipulated by Shrawn for his sake and that of his master, but damn if you didn't up mastering it on your own account and twisting it against him for your own ends."

She shrugged the accusation off lightly. "Shrawn's still alive."

The grin was obvious in Genn's words. "For now. But it doesn't even matter if he dies, and you know that."

"It doesn't?" she asked coolly. "Why not?"

"Because it's the chaos that counts," he said, "that delivers the desired result, that keeps it interesting. Don't get me wrong, I'm sure that Shrawn, dead, bleeding in front of you would be a fun little scene, but … what would you do after that?"

"I'm sure I could find something."

He laughed as the crowd roared, covering it, full of genuine glee. "I'm sure you could, too, and I'd love to watch it happen. But where you and I diverge on this is what we both think you'd be doing, because I think you still entertain this idea of some sort of glorious return to the days before you stole the Red Destiny the first time, as though that were a bridge you could simply cross to get back to who you were. It's not, and you can never go back to who you were."

"Who said I wanted to?" she asked, pushing more feelings into the abyss unexamined. *Not now. Not with him watching.*

"You do," Genn said as she caught a hint of strange movement in the crowd. "It's in your head. It's a lingering doubt. Part of you thinks it could be that simple again, that you could go back to being that … dull. A simple thief in a simple place, with a complicated mind bored by all she sees."

"Do you know what I see?" Aisling asked, as the crowd roared again, hands thrown in the air—save for one. "Right now?"

"Of course," Genn said. "What I'm interested in, though … is what you'll do about it." She glanced to the side and he was gone.

Aisling turned back to the crowd, feigning nonchalance, as though she were kicking at the dirt at her feet. Her eyes, though, flicked up and focused on the man snaking his way through the crowd with a purpose, ignoring the speech and absent the emotion of those surrounding him. His face was blank, focused, on the mission to get closer to the stage. *A spy or an assassin—which are you?*

He drifted closer to the edge of the stage, creeping through gaps in the crowd that even she would have had trouble getting through. He shoved a little, pushed a little, and managed to work his way up to the fore, against the wooden platform and at Norenn's feet. He looked up as he had the entire time, focused on his target with unblinking eyes as the crowd roared at his back once more, but the man himself showed no more interest in the crowd than if he were merely in an evening bath rather than an ocean of hostility.

She watched him watching Norenn, and wondered when he'd act. If he struck him down, how would it play out? Norenn would die, right there on stage, delivering his message, his story of being a prisoner, of being in the deprivation of Shrawn's dungeon in front of half a million angry people. That would certainly move them in a direction, but only one—fury.

Shrawn didn't hire this assassin, assuming he's a professional. Her eyes darted to the stage where she caught Xemlinan's gaze and he nodded at the man in the crowd as if to suggest what she should do.

Dammit, you bastards.

The man leapt as she moved, and she slammed into him just as he brandished a knife and nearly landed it in Norenn, who was standing there blinking in surprise at the unexpected attack. She hit him with her shoulder and knocked the knife clear of his grasp, sending him toppling into the crowd unarmed. She managed to preserve her own balance and stay atop the stage, placing herself protectively between her quarry and Norenn.

It proved unnecessary.

"Assassin!" Xem cried in the stark and stunned silence, in a voice that carried across the crowd. A ripple ran through them after a moment's pause, and a roar of their fury, unleashed, came a moment later. The mob surged, ocean upon shore, pushing toward the stage. Aisling watched the would-be assassin disappear under a flurry of blows originating from all around him as they fell upon him like dogs on a starving meal.

"It had to be this way," Xem said, whispering in her ear. "We wouldn't have let any actual harm come to him, you know. There was never a chance this fellow was going to get close."

"What if he talks?" Aisling asked, turning her head just enough to feel his breath on her neck. "What if he—"

"I don't think he's going to get the chance, do you?" Xemlinan nodded and Aisling turned her head to watch, unflinching.

The man was already being torn to pieces, the mob shoving and fighting to get their chance at him, to vent years of fury on a symbol of that which they hated utterly. The roar was deafening, louder even than the cheers, and she could not hear the swearing of the assassin's attackers even as the blood started to fly through the air.

"This is just the beginning," Xem said, pulling away from her ear to bask next to Norenn, who was smiling at the sight of the first of their many enemies getting what they so richly deserved.

"And oh, what a beginning," Genn whispered, unseen, in her other ear. "Can you even imagine how it will end?"

She didn't even need to ponder it for a second to answer. "In blood and chaos." She drew a breath as the mob continued to rip apart the body of a man just feet from her. "Just like you want it to ... Terrgenden."

65.

Terian

"How do I look?" he asked, feeling decidedly uncomfortable in the armor. It was a fear born of self-consciousness, of knowing that the armor had its dings, its flaws, that it showed its age, and also brought with it a clear recollection of its last wearer. *Whose sword I am not fit to carry, nor whose helm am I fit to wear.*

"Very fine," Kahlee said, looking him up and down. "Having your hair out and your face visible is a ... bold choice that I hope you'll remedy before going into a battle." She wore a somewhat impish smile.

"Alas," Curatio said, back to standing next to Cattrine Tiernan's hearth, "the helm is not so easy to come by. It rests in a shrine behind Sanctuary, whereas the rest of the armor was ... misplaced, let us say." The healer smiled, all enigma and no explanation.

"When do I start to get the good secrets?" Terian asked. "Because I hoped they'd come with the armor."

"The only thing that comes with the armor," Curatio said, "is the weight of responsibility."

"And a very slight smell of mustiness and salt air," Terian quipped, taking a few steps experimentally. "It's a little tighter in the crotch than I expected."

Curatio harrumphed, drawing Terian's attention back to the healer. "Are you ready to begin?"

"As ready as I'll ever be," Terian said, straightening up in his new armor. "But I have to ask, Curatio ... do you have a plan to fight an army? Because I don't. I mean, you can put me in front of them in

ROBERT J. CRANE

this armor and I'm sure it'll hold up reasonably well, but eventually I will get overwhelmed and die under the weight of the dead's crushing numbers."

"Agreed," Curatio said, nodding. "And I am taking steps to aid you in this regard."

"You know when I said that this was not Cyrus's fight?" Terian asked. "I only meant it until I got my ass kicked. This can absolutely be his fight now, because I could really use the help of someone with his particular skills—"

"No, it cannot," Curatio said, shaking his head. "The stakes of the game you now find yourself playing are too high to have someone else come in and do the thing for you. This is your fight, and you will win it."

"I find it alarming to hear you say that," Terian said, "if only because I've yet to hear where I'm going to get an army to do the fighting with, absent Sanctuary ... or the humans ... or the elves ..." Curatio shook his head with each suggestion, "Dwarves? Gnomes? Goblins—Curatio, there's no one left." Terian threw his arms up. "I mean, I can't command the dead myself." His face twisted as he pondered it. "Unless I can."

"You cannot," Curatio said, shaking his head. "Nor do you need to. Those poor souls need to be put to rest, not commanded by anyone mad enough to wrest them away from Malpravus's clutching hands. I have outlined for you three great challenges, three tests, essentially, that you must pass to come to the end of your current road."

"And then, I shall be redeemed wholly and totally," Terian said with no small amount of sarcasm, "and shall never, ever sin again."

"When one has erred as badly as you have," Curatio said, glancing at Kahlee, "the road to return becomes somewhat rockier as you attempt to come back."

"Yeah, yeah," Terian said, moving around in his armor. "All right. Fine. So, I need a plan." He gave it a moment's thought. "I'm not coming up with any ways to defeat two armies and a furious insurrection."

"Why don't you start," Curatio said, sounding a little impatient, "by pondering how you can make yourself stronger. Because before you defeat an army, you will need one, and even before that, you should convince yourself that you possess the ability to lead one of your own. As it stands, I doubt you have the confidence to do much more than quake in your new greaves should you find one at your back right now."

"Nice," Terian said, pursing his lips. *But he's right. Even Dahveed and Grinnd didn't back me when my father and Shrawn started to tear me apart. Only Kahlee did.* He turned to look at his wife. "What do you think I should do, my dear?"

"I think you should consider carefully all that you know about Arkaria," Kahlee said, chewing on her own lip, "all the places where you might find some aid, and swiftly."

"Woo," Terian said without enthusiasm. "I doubt I'd be very welcome in Reikonos at present. The Elven Kingdom would have no use for me. Nor would any of the other powers." He glanced around Cattrine's office. "Frankly, I'm amazed that I'm even welcome here."

"Well, that's more down to me," Kahlee said, "and Father." She frowned. "Surely there must be somewhere that your travels have carried you where you could find aid. Some hamlet or village where they would remember your name fondly."

Terian felt the prickle of memory nearly forgotten, shame creeping up his cheeks with navy heat. "Maybe one place, sort of. But I don't know what I'd find there other than ..." His voice trailed off. "It's a faint possibility. Extremely faint. Pale as death, on the threshold of—"

"You will need a wizard or a druid, I trust?" Curatio asked, strangely cool.

"I will indeed," Terian nodded. "But this is ... I mean, it's a long shot. This may be absolutely nothing, and I mean nothing. It could be less than nothing."

"It's all you have," Kahlee said quietly. "Best to pursue every thread to its end. Perhaps it will lead you to another."

"Yeah," Terian said with a nod, pursing his lips, as a rueful sort of dispirit fell over him. "I guess so." He looked up at Curatio. "All right, I better get started. Did you have a wizard in mind, or are you taking me yourself?"

Curatio kept his face shrouded in a strange aura of mystery. "I'm afraid I can't, but there are a small band of mercenaries available for hire that have made their way into town. I'm certain we can engage their services to aid you in this."

"Mercenaries," Terian said with a slow nod of disappointment. "Great. I can't pay them, but ... great." *I truly am at the bottom. I would say there is nowhere to go but up, but this quest I am about to undertake is likely a very great waste of time.*

"I think their leader might be willing to pass on coin from you, in any case," Curatio said, with the hint of a smile. Terian felt a certain amount of discomfort at the healer's amusement.

"Nobody does anything for free, Curatio," Terian said. "And definitely not when it comes to helping an outcast like me."

"I believe he thinks he owes you a favor," Curatio said, his smile broadening, "and as you well know ... you can use any help you can get at this point..."

66.

J'anda

It was hardly the first council of war he had attended, nor even the first in the throne room of the Grand Palace, but it was certainly the most surreal. J'anda stood in a semi-circle with the others around him, feeling quite out of place next to Dahveed Thalless, standing for the Healers' Union in his white robes. Grinnd Urnocht stood for the Society of Arms in his massive armor, with his mighty swords tucked into his belt. Bowe Sturrt seemed to represent the druids while Amenon Lepos stood in his place for the Legion of Darkness.

Whether Dagonath Shrawn was speaking merely for himself as Sovereign or also to represent the Commonwealth of Arcanists, J'anda could not decide. The division of the new army down league lines had confused him at first until he realized that Shrawn had no practical military experience and most of his fighting force was mere guardsmen.

"The current threat comes from below," Shrawn said, "though we expect Malpravus of Goliath will be battering his way through the great gates of the surface within days."

J'anda blinked and watched Amenon Lepos sputter out his response first. "The gates?" the dark knight asked. "Is there no one defending them?"

"We have little left in the way of defense," Shrawn said. "The Sovereign, in his wisdom, sent all but the guards off to war, and even many of them, in fact. He had troops in Sovar, of course, but their loyalty at this moment is hardly assured. I have placed loyal guards in the tunnels below the Depths, and at the Front Gate of Sovar to block any movement out of the lower chamber, but they are not numerous enough to withstand assault, and so their orders are to withdraw immediately upon contact with a serious offense."

"You need spell casters in place down there," Amenon said, recovering his voice. "Something to stem a tide of hard resistance, to take the starch out of them and make the weakest run scared."

"I agree," Shrawn said, and J'anda caught a strange sense of victory from the wizard pass between them. *Where is Terian, I wonder?* "But there are few wizards, and I suspect we have lost an equivalent amount to what remain to Sovar. I believe the same goes for all our spell casters, save for the enchanters." He smiled at Terian. "Only one enchanter appears to have left to go to Sovar."

"I should point out," Grinnd said quietly, "that the ones who left were doubtless from Sovar to begin with. It isn't as though they've defected, merely gone home in the absence of clear order here."

"The result is the same," Shrawn said dismissively. "Perhaps they will stay in their homes, out of the fight, or perhaps they will join their brethren when the moment comes. My spies assure me that the rage is building in Uru'kasienn Square even now. They have torn a purported assassin apart, hung pieces of him from the buildings nearby. They are working into a frenzy that will galvanize them to action when the minds that steer them will it. Our course is but to oppose it, and swiftly, so that we may be on about the business of dealing with the assault from without undistracted by this other matter."

"What would you have us do?" J'anda asked.

"Prepare your people for the fight," Shrawn said, thumping his cane as he walked in a circle around them all. "Warn them of what they are up against—the end of their very lives. For none shall escape this mob, should they break through our lines. And they will be swiftly followed by Malpravus and his guildmates—and I suspect, the remainder of the Sovereign's soul rubies, ready to claim all of the dead of Saekaj and Sovar into the service of Goliath."

67.

Terian

"I can't believe it's you," Terian said, shaking his head. He stifled a sigh, his thousandth of the last few hours, as his party swept over the low peak of a mountain under the influence of Falcon's Essence, their feet poised magically off the ground.

"I admit," Brevis Venenum said, his crumpled gnomish face the epitome of everything Terian despised about his life at the moment, "I was surprised when Curatio inquired about us lending you a hand in your efforts as well. But it's a pleasant surprise all around, I'd say. Always nice to be given a chance to do a good turn to a friend, isn't it?"

The wind blew past his face, not quite at a howl. Terian drew the cloak around his new armor tighter, trying not to let it in. *Not having a helm is making this a hell of a lot colder than it should be.* "I have to admit, I'm surprised your sense of gratitude is that strong toward me."

"How could it not?" Brevis said, surprisingly cheerful. "You gave me a chance to say things to that scheming bastard Orion that I never would have had opportunity to, otherwise! Alaric wouldn't hear it, and look what happened. He was wrong!" Brevis jabbed a tiny finger at Terian, the gnome looking bizarre framed against the breathtaking vista of mountain peaks all around them, a tiny little crumpled figure in layers of cloak and cape, wrapped up almost like a baby.

"Indeed," Terian said, choosing to take the very high road rather than engaging with Brevis on that particular disagreement. *Alaric may have be wrong about Orion, seeing as he was scheming with the Dragonlord at the time, but he wasn't wrong to tell you to get the hell out, you cancer of a person …*

301

He blinked and looked to either side of him, watching his small party walk on air above the mountainous terrain. Gertan and Aina were Brevis's companions, but fortunately they were nearly silent compared to the chatty gnome. Kahlee caught her husband's eye, only a few steps behind him, walking alongside the last member of their party. *And another perpetual pain in my ass.*

"I think we should slow down," the final member of the party huffed. She was clearly winded, even more so than the gnome, though she was taller by quite a bit. Her pale blue skin was closer to the cerulean shade of the sky than the darker navy of Kahlee's, and she looked like she was about to drop right down the side of the mountain. "Yes. We should slow down," she huffed, decidedly. "Sit. Everybody sit. Now."

"You're so accursedly bossy, Erith," Terian said, trying not to roll his eyes at the only healer he had with him. *Curatio, why couldn't you have just come with me instead of vaguely protesting you had things to do? As though being Elder of the largest independent guild in Arkaria takes time or something ...*

"I prefer to think of it as 'commanding,'" Erith said.

"And a Sovarian prefers to think of his mother as something other than a whore."

"I don't care for your inference there," Erith said, propping back on her haunches in mid-air. She floated as though there were a bench under her, keeping her from dropping out of the sky and rolling down the peak below. *That would be a sight to see,* Terian thought, unable to control a grin at the thought. She looked at him with suspicion. "Or the way you're leering at me."

"Sorry," Terian said, stifling the laugh that threatened to bubble up. "Just ... something came to mind."

Erith glanced at Brevis, who was hiking along without them, clearly oblivious to the break the healer had called, his two compatriots behind him. "I hope it was a thought of that damned gnome skiing down the mountain on his face."

"Close." Terian kept his expression carefully guarded. "Very close."

"Hm," Erith said and looked at Kahlee. "What's your part in all this, Lady Lepos? Please tell me you're not just the loyal puppy dog that follows her husband around in all his mad efforts."

Kahlee's face flashed amusement. "Is that not what a lady of Saekaj is supposed to do?"

Erith gave her a look with no small amount of suspicion. "Yet you're aware enough of it to say so with irony." She smiled at Terian. "Oh, I like her."

"She's my counterpoint in that regard," Terian said, and then looked at his wife. "The lazy healer does raise an excellent point, though."

Kahlee stared back at him coolly. "What? That it seems peculiar that I, of all people, would not play the doting and supportive wife role well?"

"So you admit it's a role?" Terian asked, smiling slyly.

"I admit nothing," Kahlee said, shaking her mop of blue hair and mussing it as she pushed it back over her shoulders.

"I'm liking her even more," Erith said.

"Great," Terian said, not taking his attention off Kahlee, "join us in a veredajh later."

"Ewwww! And…no."

"What are you playing at, Kahlee?" Terian asked, keeping careful eye on his wife, who did not react to his question. "Is this some … guilt for your father? Some desire to follow in the path he started on?"

"Perhaps I simply see the best chance for Saekaj and Sovar along the road you walk," she said, but put no more emotion into the reply than she might have a query about the price of apples in Pharesia. "Has anyone asked you why you've walked the mad path that you have, zagging where most would have thought you'd zig?"

"I don't think anyone's seen most of the mad path I've walked," Terian said. "They've just noticed the erratic moves."

"And now she raises an excellent point, making me like her even more," Erith said, "though not enough to do what you suggested earlier. Why are you doing this, Terian? This looks like suicide."

"This specific mission?" Terian asked, shrugging. "It's not suicide. It's very low risk, in fact, visiting where we're going."

"Not that," Kahlee said, taking up station next to Erith. "Why are you doing all of this? You keep talking about redemption as though it's something you stumbled into."

"No," Terian said, "it's something I was led to."

"Terian," Erith said, gawking at him, "I've heard the stories. You were *led* to an altar where you murdered your sister at your father's command. You were Elder of Sanctuary and took off like you'd been exiled when that thing—" she waved at Brevis, receding further into the distance, "—got into a verbal bout you sanctioned that lost half the guild at the time. Then you came back but decided that when your father died at the hands of Cyrus, you should avenge him in the most horrible and secretive way possible." She shrugged. "Yes. Mad path, agreed. But it seems like you've made all these decisions and then … how do I put this? Scrambled from bad one to the next bad one?" She filled her words with a great abundance of humor, but the edge persisted beneath that. "When someone goes to the Great Hall looking for dinner, their motivations are clear—they're hungry. When I watch an argument, I can see when someone gets angry at the verbal lashings they take. It's as obvious as the nose on your face, no offense." She kept her eye on him, now suspicious in a different way. "Curatio asked me to come along on this because he said you were trying to do right by Saekaj Sovar. But I've got a serious question about you, Terian, because I have no idea what the hell you're all about or where this sudden surprising virtuousness will even last."

Terian looked to Kahlee, who still seemed indifferent to the whole matter. "Do you see it?"

Kahlee stirred as she answered, as though she were waking from a deep slumber. "A little more than she, but not to the extent I would like to."

He nodded slightly. "If I tell you, if I draw the map—will you tell me what's causing you to follow?"

"Perhaps," she said.

He pondered that for a second. "That's a better deal than I'll get anywhere else, I suppose. All right. I killed my sister, you got that right. I did it because my father ordered me to, even though I knew it was wrong. Seventeen years of absolute faith was shattered to tiny pieces, like shards of glass in my soul." He paused, thinking about it, pursing his lips as he did. "Have you ever had a moment when everything you knew about who you were was ripped away?" He looked around. The only response was silence.

"When Alaric found me, I was one of the first to come along after the founding of Sanctuary. I was so cut up inside … some of the others were, too, don't get me wrong—" He stopped, shaking his head. "When Alaric called that place Sanctuary, I wanted to shake my head and laugh. A sanctuary for what? Losers?" He laughed, but it was bitter and caught in his throat. "Far from civilization, we hid. I was the heir apparent, I thought. Then Cyrus came ... and he changed everything."

"Oh, wow," Erith said, dry as overcooked chicken. "I should have known it'd come to this. Did he take everything from you?"

"No." Terian shook his head slowly. "But for a long time I thought he had. Because when I came back, everything was different. But I believed in Alaric, so I swallowed my worries and tried to feel like I was at home. See, when I was standing at that altar, with my sister pleading for her life ..." He ran the back of his hand across his eyes. "That memory never got easier to bear. My father said it would. Said that sacrifice was the price of greatness." He sniffed. "They call it a soul sacrifice, but I felt like I was the one who lost my soul."

"What the hell does that have to do with Sanctuary?" Erith asked, clearing her throat. "With losing your damned mind over and over?"

"If my father's instructions for the first seventeen years of my life were broken glass," Terian said, "then Cyrus Davidon was the last bit of push I needed for them to cut me up inside. Because when I heard he killed my father, it was like he became the perfect scapegoat for everything I hated about myself. He was the catalyst that grew the guild, the man that took the accolades and the comfort away, the one that Alaric bestowed favor on. And when he killed my father, it was like all that glass just went right to the heart.

"But Cyrus wasn't responsible," Terian said. "I was responsible. He moved forward and I held back." He held up his hand, wiped his face, and stared at the wet droplets running their way down it. "I blamed him when I should have blamed myself. Hated him when I should have hated my father. Stared at his light and worried that my darkness was too great. If redemption is a path we walk every day, I tried to walk it in darkness half the time, traveling at night, being true to the teachings I held dear as a child, even though they were broken glass in my bleeding fingers. I never let it go, no matter how much damage it did."

"You gonna let it go now?" Erith asked, somewhat somber for once.

"I want the light," Terian said, sniffing in the high mountain air.

"I've seen the darkness. I've seen what it does—to Saekaj, to Sovar. The darkness isn't just the failure of light to penetrate the caves down there—it's everything in that place. It's hiding who you are so the Sovereign and his servants won't drag you out for having a doubt, a fear, a disloyal thought. It's being afraid to stand in truth, having to bow to those who want nothing good for you, only what's good for them. Alaric was the light for me. He believed in rule, in law, in principle, in things that you could see, that were like a lighthouse on the promontory when you lost your damned way." His voice cracked. "The Sovereign was will over all, force over those who disagreed, obedience over truth, and damn anyone who disagrees to pain and torment. The only ones that thrived in the light were the ones he allowed to step in it, and they were all arrayed around him at the center. Alaric was never like that. I know who I want to be now, and it's not my father. And I know who I hate, and it's not Cyrus."

"Funny thing for a dark knight to say." Kahlee broke her silence but barely, with a voice he had to strain to hear.

"Maybe I'll be a new kind of dark knight," Terian said, mopping at his eyes again. "I mean, I'm already in a position where I'm going to have to fight my battles without the aid of a weapon or an army." He glanced at Brevis. "Except you and them over there. Which is worrying."

"Which?" Erith asked, hauling herself to her feet, bobbing in a breeze. "Us or them?"

"I'm amazed anyone is following me at all, at least on this fool's errand," Terian said and started forward again, feet on what felt like solid ground, even though he knew they were anything but. *This is a strange position to be in—as though I finally know the path, and the path is truly insane.*

Erith fell in beside him on one side, Kahlee on the other. "Where is this we're going, again?" Erith asked, huffing slightly less now.

Terian took a deep, cold breath and felt like he'd stuffed his face into the snow on the peak below before breathing it in. *To the most insane place I could possibly imagine showing my face, that's where.* But he did not say what he thought, instead keeping it as simple as the name of a town he'd never thought he would see again. "Aurastra." His mouth was dry from all his talking, and his lips smacked together as he said it again reverently, almost in a whisper. "It's called Aurastra."

68.

Terian

He could see the village below, and every fiber of his being called out for him to leave, to turn back, to ask Aina to cast the spell of teleportation and take them far, far away. His muscles were tense beneath his armor, and he could still feel the puffiness around his eyes from the telling of the story earlier. He sighed, the thin air requiring him to take another breath. He stood in a copse of pine trees with his party, staring at a village that still bore the scars of burned roofs and a graveyard visible with more makeshift headstones than he could easily count.

"What the hell happened here?" Brevis asked, surveying the place, his knobby features even more furrowed than usual.

"It was a massacre," Terian said, growing strangely accustomed to the sick feeling that permeated his belly. *I expect I'll be feeling this way quite a bit, given both what I'm up against and what I have at hand.* "The Sovereign sent my father and I here with a team to seal a mine. We encountered … trouble."

"And destroyed everything?" Erith asked, her mouth slightly agape.

"I didn't," Terian said, "but I might as well have. I don't even know how many people died here. Men, women and children."

"And you brought us here why, exactly?" The healer's voice was higher than it had been a question earlier.

"The Sovereign wanted the mine sealed for some reason," Terian said, gaze catching on the blackened ruin of a house, only a few timbers remaining to jut out of the earth, snow piled within. "There was a portal down there."

"So you've brought us here to investigate that portal," Erith said, as though she were trying to piece it all together, "because … you have no other idea what to do."

"That … is accurate," Terian said, and felt the breath leave him. "I have nothing else. And I knew this was insane. Truly. I mean, if we walk through that village, they're going to attack us, and we're going to have to flee, because I'm not doing to those people what was done before. I just won't." He sighed again. "But I needed to see. And like you said … I have nothing left to do."

"I always did enjoy the smell of desperation on a man," Erith said, and he could not tell whether she was joking or not. "Lead on."

He looked sideways at Brevis, who shrugged. "We're here. Might as well look at your mine. Not as though I've got anywhere else to be. Mercenary contracts for our band are a bit sparse at the moment."

"Reikonos got sacked," Terian said, "I would imagine that's somewhat dampened their enthusiasm for hiring mercenaries, being without much in the way of a government in the moment."

"It's a problem," Brevis agreed, "and one I hope they surmount soon."

"Yes," Terian said, hoping the sarcasm would pass his ally—*one of the few I actually have at this point*—by, "it's a real shame that city getting sacked affected your business." And he pushed forward through the trees, the fact that his feet were off the ground the only thing keeping him from making untold racket as he went.

The wind whipped through the valley as Terian tried to skirt the edge of the village. He estimated that half the number of houses stood here that had been here before. *Who would want to settle in this place after what happened?*

There was movement on the road through town, though little enough. It was quiet and the day was drawing to a close. The sun was low in the sky, orange highlights against white clouds as it shone just behind a nearby peak. The thick-knotted trees around the village gave the area a dim look, shadowing the approach to where he knew the mine lay. *That's to our advantage*, he thought, plotting out their course. *This should be simple; we can go invisible for a moment, cross the road, and once we're in the pines, we'll be able to get to the mine and away from the populace without them being the wiser to our approach.*

"Why are you hiding like that?" Brevis asked, voice cutting through the still quiet of the night as Terian held himself against the solid log wall of the side of the building.

Terian whirled on the gnome, who stood just behind him at face level. Terian barely restrained his fury, holding a finger up to his mouth. "Shhhh," he whispered, but knew it was too late.

The sound of movement in the cabin at his side was clear. Feet hammered on the floor at the sound of the motion outside and the door at the front of the building was thrown open as Terian peeked out, his heart already falling in his chest. Another door opened at the rear, cementing that sensation of everything dropping around him.

No. Not like this.

"Prepare to get us out of here," he hissed at Aina, who stared at him blankly as though she'd not heard him. Footsteps against the snow crunched around the sides of the building, the sound of people approaching. "Are you listening?" he asked, voice rising. "We need to—"

He spun as the first of the villagers came around the corner with an axe in hand. It was raised by a young man with a thin red beard, not even enough there to braid. Terian caught the fury in the dwarf's eyes, saw the rage flash there in a second, the commitment to action—

And watched the axe drop a second later as the fury was replaced by ... recognition.

"It's you," the dwarf said dully, letting his weapon fall, the blade dropping into the snow. "It's ... it's really you!" He looked Terian up and down. "Your armor—it's—it's different, but I'd recognize that nose, that face anywhere. It's *him!*" he called out into the night. "He's back! He came back!"

"He doesn't look like he hates you at all," Brevis said as doors began to open all over the village of Aurastra. The residents flooded out, and the call was taken up—"He's back!" Terian watched it all unfold, feeling a strange kinship with a woman he'd once met who viewed everyone who approached her with a preparation to flinch, as though the whole world meant to hit her given half an opportunity.

In short order, Terian found himself surrounded by dwarves and even one human woman, who looked upon him without fear, and listened as they spoke to him, calm, quiet and full of a reverence—a relief—he never could have expected, not in this place or any other he had known.

69.

Aisling

The Sovar barracks fell without a fight, the guards dispersing as soon as the mob appeared, running, screaming, their purpose plain. She saw helms discarded and men throwing armor aside as quickly as they could pull it off, hoping to appease the beast snaking its way through the streets toward them. She would have told them not to bother had she not been firmly in the belly of it, but there was no hearing her, not in its midst as she was. Instead, she watched as the guards were beaten mercilessly and then held aloft, limp as cloth dolls, their features not even recognizable as faces.

The seizing of the armory's weapons was an undramatic thing, quick and ugly, with squabbling and fights among the writhing mass that flooded into the barracks. She watched it all without comment, saw someone die in the internecine quarrel, but no one else seemed to care and so she didn't either. In her own mind she was screaming once more at the edge of the abyss, but she let her stricter nature shove those feelings down as always.

There was no leading this thing she was a part of, but Norenn was trying, standing at the front of the mass always, with Xem and Coeltes beside him. She watched him with that detached, sick feeling continuing to grow inside of her. The chaos that Terrgenden had predicted and wished for was certainly being made manifest, though she did not have any idea how to feel about that, other than concerned.

As it turned out, concern was plenty enough to be getting along with, at least from where she sat in the middle of it all. She did not dare to put her cowl up, to try and be a stranger in the midst of this mob, for fear of where that might lead. Instead she stood in their midst and mimicked what she saw around her—expressions of anger on thin faces, spittle-shot rage flying from her lips along with chanted imprecations. Hate, that was what she saw, injustice turned round against those who had purveyed it, though she suspected that the counterbalance was not going to result in any justice of its own.

"To Saekaj!" the call carried back to her. She missed it coming from Norenn, though she saw his lips move, and when it reached her on the voices of others, she knew that it was what he'd said, what Xem and Coeltes had said, what all of them meant.

As for her, she was sure that it meant something else entirely. *It means death to everyone above*, she figured, but she struggled with the emotions she buried, and kept summoning up a rage to display, even though she had a hard time feeling any of it any longer.

70.

Terian

"You saved our lives," the young dwarf said, standing at the head of more of his own people than Terian could number. *Half as many as there should have been,* he figured. "That man that was with you—the shadow knight—he ordered deaths, we heard it. We huddled," he said, wisps of his beard like little red clouds trailing out of his cheeks, "afraid, because so many of our men had already been killed."

"We thought we were all dead, for sure," the human woman said. Terian locked eyes with her for only a moment, and then flinched away. "When you burst into the house, with me and the children—"

"We thought we were dead," the young dwarf said, and Terian had to look up. There were mutters of assent, and he found himself blinking hard. "All of us, dead. Our whole town, dead."

"You saved us," the woman said. "Spared our lives from certain end by blade and fire."

"I came here first, though," Terian said hoarsely. "With them."

"And would they have come without you?" the young man asked.

How can they be this forgiving? Terian wondered, not daring to look them in the eye. *Though the true villain in this is Shrawn, for ordering us exposed to those people—and Xem, for doing the deed.* He blinked again. *Plenty of villains to go around, not surprisingly.*

"Aye, they would have come without him," Kahlee said. "The Sovereign himself ordered your village's mine shut. Once someone had seen, survivors were absolutely forbidden." She spun on Terian. "You saved these people, by your hand."

"I ..." Terian froze, that choking feeling at his throat again.

312

"Kahlee ... so many of them died ..."

"We were dead," the young dwarf said again, "and you saved us. Would any dark elf have done it other than you, dark knight?"

"I'm not a ..." Terian blinked hard, again. Seeing the evidence of his past dredged up was a fresh burn in his chest, as though someone had kindled the memory of what he'd done to Ameli, forcing him to relive it by every moment, to savor every jagged emotion it brought with it. "I look around this place, and all I wish ... is that I could have done things differently."

"Why have you returned to us?" the human woman asked, moving through the crowd to the front. She came to stand by the wispy-bearded dwarf and placed a hand on his shoulder.

"I don't know," Terian said, looking at them for the first time. "I came to see the cave. The Sovereign ... he's dead. The people in Saekaj and Sovar—they're in turmoil. I came here because I'm ... searching for something."

"What are you looking for?" the young dwarf asked, his eyes drawn.

"A way through the portal we sealed off," Terian said, sighing. "A fool's hope? I don't know."

The young dwarf looked to the woman next to him before answering. "The way is sealed. It was blasted shut."

"I know," Terian said, resignation falling over him, "I just needed to try anyway."

"Can you smell the desperation?" Erith asked, sniffing. "Smells like pine."

"The only way down there," the dwarf said, "is air vents tunneled to keep the miners breathing while we mounted rescue in the event of a cave-in. They're small. Too small for you, that's certain. And the way the tunnel was blasted closed, if you try and dig through, it collapses. We tried." He blushed a little under that wispy beard.

"Fool's hope lost," Terian said, nodding, embarrassed. "I understand ... and thank you. We'll leave you be—"

"Well, that's hardly the end," the dwarf said. "Like I said, we have the emergency shafts, and they're tunneled by the children of the village." He puffed out his chest. "I dug one of them myself when I was a lad a few years younger."

Terian stared down at him. "Uhh ... well ... I mean, I'm not the biggest man you'll ever meet, certainly, but I'm not as small as you probably were when you squeezed down that ..."

"No, you're not," the dwarf said and turned his eyes to Brevis, who was watching the whole exchange with disinterest, through squinted eyes beneath a thick brow, "but if you perhaps had someone who was small, who could cast the return spell ..."

71.

Terian

Brevis protested, he squealed, he had a small fit and a large one, but ultimately he allowed a rope to be tied about his waist so that he could be lowered into a dark shaft in the mountain that had been covered over with old boards. Once removed they had a smell about them, something like Saekaj and Sovar, actually, and Terian found himself leaning in to take a deeper sniff while they waited for Brevis to do his work.

He fussed all the way down, then fussed all the way back up, squalling like a tiny storm, echoing up the long, dark rock tunnel that was plenty wide enough for him to fit inside with room to spare.

"Smells terrible in there!" Brevis said as they pulled him out. "Like dust uncleaned for a thousand years, like goblins nested in it."

"I don't care if they moved out of Enterra and claimed it for their very own," Terian quipped as the gnome came out of the earth, face covered in a thick layer of brown grime, "so long as you cast your binding spell down there."

"Yes, yes," Brevis said as they sat him back on the pitch on the side of the mountain. It was a narrow space, hidden behind a patch of bushes, a hundred and fifty feet up the slope of the mountain. Terian could see the village below when he stood, chimneys smoking quietly in the night, lights burning in the windows.

"Aina, did you bind here?" Terian asked, glancing at the druid. She stared at him blankly, and he turned to Erith instead. "Did you?"

"Done," Erith said, shrugging. "I'd prefer to have kept my return point at Sanctuary, but ... what are you going to do?"

315

"What I've asked, thankfully," Terian said, picking Brevis up off the ground and cradling him beneath an arm. "Come on," he gestured to Erith, who blanched and closed her eyes. He held out an arm in invitation. "Let's go."

"I'm still not interested in your veredajh offer, no matter how desperate you smell," she said, letting him pull her close. "Brevis, quickly, please."

Terian glanced at Kahlee, who watched the entire exchange with some trace of amusement, her blue hair framed against the dark rock of the mountain face behind her. She disappeared in a swirl of light as Brevis's return spell carried Terian to the bottom of the shaft below and dirt crunched beneath his feet.

"Gods, it's dark," Erith mumbled. "Like home."

"I will never come visit you," Brevis said. Terian handed the gnome to Erith, who accepted him as though she were taking hold of a baby who'd soiled itself. She murmured a few words and the light of her return spell carried them away, back to the surface.

Terian stood in place, looking around the chamber. It was dark as any cave in Saekaj or Sovar, perhaps more so. When his eyes adjusted, he could see the portal in the center of the chamber, radiating blackness out of its ovoid structure. "Huh," he marveled to himself, "I guess it worked."

A flash behind him jarred him enough to make him spin, where he found Kahlee standing sandwiched between Brevis and Erith. "Yes, it worked," his wife said, "and let us hope that your plans continue to do so."

"I'm highly in favor of that," Terian said as she handed Brevis back to Erith, who by now simply looked completely disgusted. "Want to step inside?"

"Shouldn't we get Gertan and Aina first?" Brevis asked, twitching as Erith held him cradled in her arms.

"Probably," Terian said, "but are you sure they won't run if we encounter trouble?"

"What kind of trouble are you predicting here?" Kahlee asked.

"Portals come from the gods," Terian said, staring into the ululating blackness coming out of the structure, "so ... a god, I guess? Of some sort?"

"I am not loving your plan at this point," Erith said, "in fact I may be less sold on this than before you entrusted your tragic life story to me."

"I can't blame you," Terian said, nodding. "And I can't ask any of you to follow me on this. I should go alone."

"Into a god's realm on your own?" Brevis asked, voice high. "Yes. Seems like a very brave idea. I commend you. Be safe. Let us know how it turns out, if we should run, you know. Fair warning and all that."

Terian nodded. "Will do." And before he could hear an argument on the matter, he plunged headlong into the portal at a run.

The world distorted around him, twisting and writhing, and he felt pressed through a hole too small for him, as though he'd traveled through the shaft with Brevis with a titan pushing him in. When he popped out the other side, the light was blinding, forcing him to squint and blink to try and clear his vision.

The smell was oily, familiar, like something he'd caught wind of that could invoke memory, given time. He forced his eyes open and found himself in a chamber that was perfectly round and called to his mind the Citadel in Reikonos. The walls appeared to be white marble, gleaming and bright, and he saw a door with a staircase that led down against the wall in front of him. He circled the portal and looked behind it, finding another staircase, this one leading up.

"Hmm." He shrugged, and started toward the down staircase, catching movement out of the corner of his eye as he did so. He spun and saw Kahlee emerge from the portal, the darkness it emitted wafting off her cloak like smoke as she separated from it. "What are you doing?"

"Following you," she said. She took in his direction and moved to beat him to the staircase. He hurried to catch her but she slipped in before him. It was a wide stair, broad enough for them to walk together side by side, and it ran along the wall of the circular tower. He charged down as she giggled while outpacing him, and stopped when she did, hitting a solid wall where he figured there would have been a door.

"A staircase that goes nowhere," he said, reaching out to touch the marble wall in front of him. Kahlee stood there, waiting, watching what he did with a peculiar look upon her face. "That's just ..."

At his touch, the wall disappeared, vanishing as though it had never existed, and revealing a most curious spectacle.

Terian stepped through the door into a room filled with pedestals, a chamber that looked as though it were set up for the display of objects. He saw books, golden goblets, jewel-encrusted treasures and more. His eyes swept the room and landed on an item in the corner, one which he could not quite tear his gaze away from.

"Where are we?" Kahlee asked, stepping into the treasure chamber behind him.

"It's ..." Terian let his words drift off as he walked across the room, unable to complete his thought as he moved toward the thing that he had seen. Long strides carried him toward it, and the whisper of Kahlee's cloak ensured that she was following behind him. "It's ... that."

"And what is *that*, Terian?" she asked. "And where are we?"

"Treasure chamber of a god," Terian said, threading his way around a pedestal holding a book written with a script that he couldn't read.

"*Which* god?" There was urgency in her voice, well justified to his mind, save for the thing that he knew which she did not.

"Don't worry," he said, flashing her a smile that was at least a little cocky, like a piece of his character, his old confidence rushing back to him. But it was coupled with something new—or something very old, he thought.

Hope.

He stopped before the pedestal, looking at what floated above it, dancing on air as surely as if it had had Falcon's Essence cast upon it. "This," he said in quiet awe, "is a lot more than I expected."

"Can you ..." she looked around nervously, head practically on his shoulder, her body pressed against him from behind. "Can you just take it?"

His mouth was dry as if his father had just rubbed his face in dirt and kicked it all down his gullet, but there was a thin thread of belief upon him. "I think so." He paused and extended his hand tentatively.

"Is there a barrier?" she asked. "Shouldn't there be something to protect it?"

"Not this time," Terian said, suddenly very warm, very hopeful that he was not wrong. His hand neared the edge of the pedestal ...

... and passed through all the way to the thin, rounded hilt of the battle-axe that waited there, a double-bladed beast of a weapon with two heads that were larger than any he'd ever seen before.

He seized it by the grip and pulled it down, the power surging through him like a rush of cool relief across his body on a scorching day. It ran through his muscles and into his mind, and he spun on Kahlee as she appeared to move as slowly as if she were trapped in hardening amber.

"What ... is ... it?" she asked, impossibly slow next to him.

"This ..." he said, savoring the feeling that yes, dammit, he finally was good enough—*like Cyrus*, "is Noctus ... the Battle Axe of Darkness ..." He swung it once, at his side, and it hummed through the air with the power of a god, even though its master was now dead. "And it is mine."

72.

J'anda

One Hundred Years Earlier

The darkness of the throne room was broken every twenty feet by the lanterns hanging atop the pillars. For J'anda, it was a strange thing to see, at odds with God of Darkness's proclamation that everlasting night should be observed in the caves, the illumination as low as possible to stay in line with his way.

After the brightness of fighting out of doors, though, it was hardly a difficult adjustment to J'anda's eyes, and he took this strangeness in stride as another enjoyable part of being in the court. And it was enjoyable, being in the court—for the spectacle, for the feeling of power that came of being at the center of decisions. All the rule in the Sovereignty radiated outward from this place, and J'anda felt acutely the sweetness of it and the sense of slight danger as well, like the warmth of holding one's hand close to a burning wick without getting too close for too long. It was balance, all of it, an exercise in care.

The Sovereign sat atop the throne at the far end of the room and everyone catered to him in the small crowd. J'anda estimated there were fewer than fifty people in the throne room at the moment, and he could name almost every one of them. The biggest power players stood in the front of their own respective retinues, and for his part, he stood one step behind the Guildmaster of the Gathering of Coercers, Ebridgen Varlenn. She was an older woman, hard-nosed and free of warmth, an enchanter who knew her way around fear in her spells and outside of them.

320

Vracken Coeltes stood only a step behind J'anda, to his left, and his teeth could practically be heard grinding up where the Sovereign sat, J'anda was sure. It was distracting, knowing that the enormous, gaping hole in the world where Coeltes stood was just at his elbow. *Couldn't he be an insufferably disappointed vek'tag's ass back at the Gathering?*

"Come forth, Ebridgen Varlenn," the Sovereign called, voice clear but high. "And bring your new protégé along with you."

Varlenn, for her part, looked back at him with no sign of approval. This was simply her way, and he knew it by now. She did not show any sign of pleasure when things went well, but she certainly did not hold back the pain when things did not. "Come," she said simply, and he followed her, leaving the black hole of Coeltes behind with some relief.

"Yes, approach," the Sovereign said, gesturing them forward. He was shrouded in his darkness, but some elements of his strangely shaped body were obvious. The claws were visible, at the top of the long fingers. His size was not a surprise, of course. He was a god; height seemed practically a requirement. Who would worship a god that stood only as high as your knee, after all?

Varlenn stopped some twenty feet before the throne, at the edge of her comfort zone, J'anda suspected. She executed a bow at the waist, deep and formal, as though she'd run into an impregnable rope stretched across the middle of the room that hit her flush with her navel. She returned to standing and turned her head to offer J'anda a look of reproach. He bowed, more deeply than she.

"It pleases me to see you again, J'anda Aimant," the Sovereign said, "to have such a dedicated servant in my presence, one who has delivered victory after victory to me in this righteous war."

"It pleases me to deliver these victories to you and your army," J'anda said, bowing once more. It seemed the thing to do.

"Step closer," the Sovereign said, gesturing him forward, and J'anda obliged, moving into the shroud of darkness as he was beckoned ever forward. He looked up and up to the Sovereign's face, seeing for the first time the strange shape of it, the tusks jutting from either side and across the top of his skull.

J'anda lowered his head out of respect, glancing involuntarily to the side when he caught motion. He locked eyes with Trimane through the thin veil of darkness that clouded around him, the warrior standing behind General Vardeir. Trimane arched his eyebrows in amusement, and J'anda swiftly returned his own gaze to the floor, nervous tingles running through his body and causing him to quiver. *Not smart, Trimane. Not here.*

"Look at me," the Sovereign said, and J'anda brought his head up slowly. He looked into the bizarre visage of the God of Darkness and caught something akin to a smile, albeit so much stranger than the one he'd just seen on Trimane's face. This one seemed more grotesque, bizarre, and bereft of any warmth. "You are my servant, and with you I am deeply pleased."

"I thank you, my Sovereign," J'anda murmured, loud enough to be heard.

"You are the hero of this war," the Sovereign said, "and your name is known to all our people. Now stand at my side."

J'anda swallowed heavily and did as he was bade, stepping into the shadows of the Sovereign. The shroud of darkness covered him but did not blind him; it was surprisingly easy to see out of it, to see the whole room spread before him. It was certainly there, a veil over everything around him, one which the light could not penetrate from outside, but here, in its depths, he could see out of it with ease.

"Watch them squabble over favor," the Sovereign whispered, so low that he realized it was only for his ears. "Fighting each other with words as though their petty struggles will gain them anything."

J'anda blinked and watched as one of the Sovereign's high advisors, a man in the fifth largest manor in Saekaj, stepped forward with a bow and began a speech that was so droolingly obvious in its attempt to beg for a morsel. "It is ..."

"Disgusting, is it not?" the Sovereign asked, and J'anda looked up to find his red eyes fixed on the enchanter's own, ignoring the subject speaking to him. "This is how it is all the time. I have considered ridding myself of a court entirely. I sit here in the shroud of darkness—my own little illusion, you see—waiting for something other than pettiness to entertain my interest. But this is it, all day, every day. It bores me, J'anda Aimant, this sameness. I long for anything different, new, unique, praiseworthy. Like yourself."

J'anda swallowed. "I am ... pleased to oblige." He tried not to look at Trimane, but failed. The warrior was watching the cloud, just as everyone else in the room was, but J'anda could not shake the feeling that he looked at it differently, not the same, that he gave himself away in the process.

"The darkness is what matters here," the Sovereign said, and J'anda hurried to nod along. "Keep a man in darkness, and none but the foolish question you when you are the light." J'anda's eyes widened at the sound of what seemed like blasphemy, but he did not speak his mind. "Now watch as these fools debase themselves before us."

J'anda did watch and kept his mouth shut all the while, his heart beating a steady rhythm, wondering just what he feared when it was obvious that he was living his life in exactly the manner his own god had just advised—in utter darkness.

73.

Terian

He held the axe tightly in his hand in Administrator Cattrine Tiernan's office (he didn't quite know what to make of that title), almost afraid to let it go, as though it might puff into dust or smoke if he surrendered it even for a moment.

"Perhaps that should be your wife," Kahlee said from her place on the old sofa next to the hearth.

"It doesn't talk back as much," Terian said, not taking his eyes off the smooth lines of the double blades.

"Though if it did, I imagine it'd be able to back it with something more than a paltry fire spell of the sort that barely lights tinder," she added.

"It is an impressive find," Curatio said, back to the hearthside, his white robes shaking lightly as he moved to angle his head, looking at Terian's new weapon with undisguised interest.

"I just wonder," Erith said, her lips pushed together, "I mean … is it a good thing that he's going to be carrying something called the Axe of Darkness while he's walking this supposedly new path?"

"I'm still a dark knight," Terian said, looking into the gleaming blade, which stared back at him, revealing his face in the curve, his features exposed without the helmet belonging to his armor. "Can't change that."

"Besides," Curatio said with a light tone, "the last wearer of that armor carried a weapon known as Aterum—the Edge of Night. It is the bearer that matters, their intent. And this bearer needs a weapon, lest he be forced to attack his enemies—of which there are no shortage—with his own gauntlets."

"I never had a talent for fisticuffs," Terian said, staring at his scuffed gauntlets for only a moment before looking back at the axe. "With this, though ... it's not an army, but I can do some damage with it."

"Yes, but can you do the right damage with it?" Curatio asked. "Merely bearing a godly weapon is hardly a guarantee of success."

"Well," Terian said, letting the axe fall to his side, "that's the question, isn't it? Where are Malpravus's armies?"

"Gathering, I suspect," Curatio said. "They have not begun to appear around Saekaj Sovar yet, presumably because he has heard the whispers of dissent within the walls of those caves. The more dead that he can sway to his control ..." The healer held out a hand as if to shrug.

"He means to let the rich and poor fight it out until they're all equal in death," Erith said sourly, "and then he'll unite them under his magnanimous rule."

"Sounds like him, doesn't it?" Terian asked. "I have to stop this ... this mess in Saekaj and Sovar. Before it comes to that, and he really does end up mopping up all the corpses with his remaining soul rubies."

"Yes," Curatio agreed, "you do."

Terian looked straight at him. "Well, I could use a little help. I mean, this threat—"

"No," Curatio said firmly.

Terian let out a long sigh. "Fine. It's on me, then." He raised the axe. "Me and this."

"What about us?" Kahlee asked, looking vaguely insulted.

He looked toward the couch. "This is going to be a fight, and you just admitted you can't cast offensive spells very well. I mean, maybe I'd take Erith, because who cares if she dies—"

"I sense you're going to need a healing spell at a critical juncture and I'm going to totally 'whoops' on it and cast return instead," Erith said sourly.

"Don't forget your gnomish friend," Kahlee said a little acidly. "And his two tagalongs that don't say anything."

"Yeah, that's a real band of true power," Terian said. "Look, this is madness—"

"Fitting for you, then," Kahlee said.

"We don't even have a way into Saekaj unless Curatio teleports us in," Terian said, pointing the axe at the healer, "and he's saying he's not helping."

"Well, that much at least, I could do," Curatio said.

"Marvelous," Terian said, nodding slowly at the sudden reversal. "So, that's settled." He put the axe over his shoulder. "Erith ... want to come die with me?"

"Uh ... not really?" Erith looked at Curatio. "But ... I suppose I can come with you until it gets really bad, and then just—"

"Erith," Curatio said, somewhat sternly.

"Fine," she said. "For the homeland and all that."

"I'm coming as well," Kahlee said, standing up. Her expression suggested she would brook no argument. "I won't be up front with you, but I need to be there for this. If things get out of hand, I can leave too, as well you now know."

"And I hope you will," Terian said, looking her in the eyes as she inched closer. "Though I still have no idea why you're doing this."

"We all have our reasons," Kahlee said with a smile. "Though not all of them are as clear as yours."

"His still aren't clear to me," Erith said under her breath. "What is it again? Redemption? Death wish? I forget."

"Do you want to ask Brevis for his assistance or are you ready to leave?" Curatio asked.

Terian thought about it, and felt that weariness slam down on him again. "I can't ask anyone else." He glanced at Erith. "I wouldn't even blame you if you didn't come. I'm not exactly a proven leader, and you're right, the reasons I'm doing this can't be clear to anyone who's watched me weave back and forth down my road like a drunken longshoreman." He held the axe up. "But I'm doing it because I have to. Because it's the right thing to do."

"A noble cause," came a voice from the door, and he spun to see who spoke to him. Her hair shone gold over her silver breastplate, and the cynical bent that was usually found in her voice was strangely absent on this occasion. "And reason enough to enlist an ally or two to your side, I would think."

"You'd be about the only one to think so, Vara," Terian said with a rueful smile. "Did you hear me talking from halfway across the village?"

"Indeed, I heard you from three-quarters across the town, over the sound of amateur carpenters doing something truly terrible with a saw of the like I have never—" She bristled as she stepped into the room and closed the door with her leg, a smooth motion that kept her from freeing her arms from behind her back. "It matters not. I am here now, and I come to help you."

"It's not your fight, Vara," Terian said softly.

"I didn't say I was coming with you," she chastened him, "I am not stupid enough to show my blond locks in the city of the dark elves without an army at my back—nor to face off with an army with my head and neck exposed for the cleaving."

He felt for his throat with his free hand. "It's not so much the neck, because I've got the gorget, it's more that without the helm it doesn't really do its job properly—"

She pulled her hands from behind her back and tossed something at him, something round and roughly melon-shaped, though larger and lighter, and he caught it easily with the aid of his axe-enhanced reflexes. "Don't lose your head," she said, and he saw a hint of sincerity break through her cool facade, the hints of a smile tugging at the corners of her lips as she left, closing the door behind her.

He stared into the helm she had tossed him and felt the chill run over his flesh as he pondered the emptiness within. *I am not worthy to wear this ... but perhaps someday I will be.* He took a deep breath in through his nose, taking in the smoke of the hearth, and placed it upon his head, staring out through the eye slits of the helm that completed his armor.

"Are you ready now?" Curatio asked, not quite succeeding at stifling a smile.

"I'm ready," Terian said. He felt his two traveling companions step close to him as the magic of Curatio's spell began, and he realized that indeed, he was as ready as he could possibly make himself.

74.

J'anda

Shouts echoed down the tunnel and J'anda shuddered, trying to suppress the desire of his body to shake in the chill. This was not always a thing that had bothered him, and he partially attributed it to the ravages of age, of the spider-veins and wrinkles all over him. He pulled his robe closer around him; never a terribly effective bulwark against the cold, here it felt even less useful, the thin fabric and elaborate stitching designed to magnify his magical power with the runes embroidered on it, not to protect from the elements.

"Do you think that's them?" Zieran asked, the sounds growing louder ahead.

"Probably our guards retreating," J'anda said. "They were set around the Front Gate of Sovar and further down; if the revolution is beginning, I suspect that we'll see them first as they retreat to us."

"Oh," Zieran said, her face close to blank. He'd seen in her battle before, and the look she wore was strange, not what he'd ever noticed her wear in those situations, nor in any other. "It feels different this time, doesn't it?"

"Because of who we're fighting?" J'anda asked, staring down the dark tunnel ahead, looking over the shoulders of the soldiers in the front ranks. The slope of the tunnel allowed him some view over the heads of the taller soldiers before him.

"Yes," Zieran said, and her voice shook slightly. "It's different, don't you think?"

"You weren't there for the Sovar riots during the war, I forgot," J'anda said with a slow nod. "When the revolutionaries rose up."

"They didn't want me to go down to Sovar for that," she said with a trace of resentment. "Said it wasn't a fit place for a woman."

"There were women aplenty in the insurrection," J'anda said with a little amusement of his own. "I almost got run through by one with a pitchfork as I ran a charm spell into the residents of her building. Coeltes saved me from being impaled by sending her screaming into a nearby oven." He blanched at the memory of the heat from the woman's clothing catching fire, the smell of her flesh burning, her screams as loud before she dove in as after.

"Coeltes saved you?" Zieran asked, her eyebrow raised. "Truly?"

"He was commended for it," J'anda said with a shrug. "It was before my successes on the battlefield, back when I was not a rival for his ambitions, so …"

"Ah."

A raw scream echoed through the tunnel, the dull roar that followed sounding like a crowd in a market square gone wild. "I remember thinking as we put down that insurrection," J'anda went on, staring at the curves of the tunnel wall, "that what we were doing was righteous. We were enforcing the Sovereign's will over a place that needed it firmly laid down. That the rebels were truly like … insubordinate children stepping out of line. And it was a hell of an insurrection, Zieran. A full-fledged food riot, the starving people packing the streets, their clothes hanging limply on their shriveled frames, unable to even really fight back against the soldiers with their spears …" He shook his head and looked around. "Never imagined I'd be sitting here again, doing something damned similar."

"Why are we here, J'anda?" Zieran asked, leaning in to whisper to him. "You're a child of Sovar, I'm a rebellious one of Saekaj, I've got no loyalties there. We could take these students and leave."

"Have you ever seen a mob have their way?" J'anda asked quietly as the screams beyond died.

"No," Zieran said. "But I've seen a tyrant who said he was a god step on enough people to make a mob. Now I feel like I'm watching another one do the same without even bothering to claim the godhood."

"A mob is a thousand tyrants," J'anda said, not taking his eyes off the darkness ahead. "The anger of the people, once roused, without law or order, turned loose like a reckless, wrathful river when a dam breaks." He glanced at her, and he could feel his heart full. "There are children in Saekaj, even younger than the ones we brought with us." He looked at his students, quivering a few rows back. "That mob down there is angry, furious. They have a right to be, and one could say that they are even justified in what they would do to the parents of those children, the ones that benefited from the last tyrant, helped prop him up, ate his largesse like pigs at a trough. But their children ... they don't know any better, and while they may have gone on to do the same as their parents ... they may not have." J'anda blinked. "A mob would kill them anyway. Dash the brains of their babies across the floor in absolute fury as they stripped everything of value out of a house. A mob is the tyranny of the many, unrestrained by law or decency." Another shout echoed off the cavern walls, louder now than ever before, the sound of trouble drawing closer and closer to the reckoning. "And they are coming ... and soon."

75.

Aisling

She found herself squarely in the middle of the madness, which didn't bother her at all. There were men and a few women on the leading edge, wirier, stronger than the rest, or perhaps just more angry, and they charged ahead. She watched a few of them tangle with guards on the retreat. They killed some, were killed by others, and just generally started the bloodshed a little early.

And there was bloodshed. Aisling could see the raw, seething fury in the crowd, like a spell in the air, writhing and undulating with an energy all its own. Whenever one of the enemy was brought down, a ragged cheer rang in the winding cavern road to Saekaj. A guardsman would fall from being struck in a weak spot, bleed out over a few minutes of hard run as he tried to escape, and as he waned and the jackals of the crowd caught up to him and brought him low, she inevitably saw the fall as the body disappeared under the weight of their numbers. Pieces of armor and body would emerge from where the oceanic swell of people surrounded the fallen form, and it didn't take long until entrails were held aloft as a sign of their victory. Judging by the noise, it was all excitement.

For her part, the excitement was still ahead, and it was not the sort that she thrilled to. Watching the seething anger resolve itself by ripping foot soldiers to pieces disgusted her. At Livlosdald the ground was red and blue and soaked with bloody mud; at Sanctuary's siege it had been the same, as though it had rained gore from the skies. It had been enough to leave her sick of it.

That, at least, was combat among soldiers, even ones that I knew, that would have called me friend.

And yet this display is the one I find more horrifying.

She watched a child of no more than ten stream past her, screaming rage at the top of her lungs with a severed arm grasped above her head, watched the girl trampled unknowing by a crowd that didn't even realize she was there. *This is madness. Absolute madness.*

"Yes," Genn whispered in her ear, "it truly is."

"Are you enjoying yourself?" she asked, glancing to her side to see Norenn a little further along in the crowd, huddled with Vracken Coeltes and Xem, cheering at the violence to the fore. *Why aren't they up front?* she wondered.

"I don't really enjoy the violence part of it, no," Terrgenden said, shaking his head as he appeared. "I was merely trying to begin the upheaval process that's so very necessary in this place."

"Fitting for the God of Mischief."

"Most people say Chaos, actually," Terrgenden said, almost indifferently. "Mischief is what children get up to when left unobserved."

"I saw a bit of that, too," Aisling said, and tried to look back to see if the girl who'd been trampled was still visible. She was gone, either dead or pulled up too far back for her to tell.

"I don't even really like the chaos part of it, though," Terrgenden said. "Mischief, chaos, that's just everyone's interpretation. That's the party line, see, what you hear from the others."

"From your peers?" Aisling asked, not all that interested. "Your pals in the pantheon?"

"I have so very few friends," Terrgenden said. "Only one close one, really. Probably the one you'd least expect. Do you want to know what she calls me?"

"Genn?" Aisling asked, feeling a push from behind as someone expressed their irritation at the slowness of the mob's pace.

"God of Justice," Terrgenden said, and she looked back in time to see him smile. "Because chaos and mischief when introduced into an unjust world such as ours? Well, really, they're the instruments of justice."

"And here I thought it was law," Aisling drawled, the roar of the crowd nearly drowning out her reply.

"Different goddess, that one," Terrgenden said. "Different

department. Like word and deed, separate things. Do the laws of Saekaj and Sovar seem just to you?"

"They were set by a tyrant," Aisling said, "so no. They don't. But how is your version of justice any different? Because if it's this?" She waved a hand in front of her. "I don't see justice. I see furious retribution about to fall on a hell of a lot of people, some of whom deserve it badly and some of whom don't deserve it at all."

"And now you've come to the key problem," Terrgenden said with a grin. "Justice and vengeance get all tangled together when the law is written by a tyrant and ultimately overturned by the forces of anger and resentment."

Someone shoved against Aisling and she shoved back, ramming a leather-armored elbow into a nose and dropping the person that had shoved her under the shoes of those that followed. "Lot of that going around."

"Do you know the solution?" Terrgenden asked, and Aisling turned her head to look at Xem, Norenn and Coeltes. They were talking amongst themselves, shouting out hectoring encouragements to the mob as the snaking crowd of people turned another corner and a guardsman disappeared beneath the fore. A blood-soaked helm was lifted up a moment later, navy dripping from the front edge enough to tell her that it had been used to murder its wearer.

"I don't see much in the way of solutions from here, no," Aisling said as the helm made its way across the crowd, lifted high as another symbol of victory.

Something hard was slipped into her hand and the world around her slowed as it did. She looked down in surprise and saw Genn standing there, moving like normal while the crowd appeared to have slackened to a crawl. "You give Justice an advocate. A champion, if you will, and you arm her so that she can do her good work."

Aisling stared at the object in her hand, a dagger longer than the ones she carried before, with a blade stretching from her elbow to the tips of her fingers. It was pointed and jagged, with a decorative hole in the middle of the blade, and quillons that were turned in a half ovoid, sharp points coming off them in angular lines. The hilt came to a pommel with a little orb centered at the base, and it glowed yellow as though someone had cast a spell that was caught within. "What the hell is this?"

"An evener of odds," Terrgenden said, but his figure was blurred, as though he were disappearing into the ether. The crowd around her had the same look, a faded quality about them, as though they and the world around them were turning to smoke. "It's not the first aid of its kind I've given, and indeed not even mine to give, originally—but I trust you'll use it better than was the last I tried to hand out here."

"I—" she started to make her reply, but he was already gone, disappeared from her sight, leaving her holding the blade, the world around her like a shade of itself. By the time she looked up again, the screaming and shouting at the fore had grown to a fever pitch, and she knew that the battle was upon them.

76.

Terian

Terian made it out of the Grand Palace of Saekaj without killing anybody, though it was a narrow thing. He wasn't even huffing, though he had his new axe firmly in hand, the guards looking at him with undisguised surprise as he went past. They didn't challenge him, save for one who offered a half-hearted query, which he ignored. *They probably aren't expecting to have to stop anyone from coming out of the palace, after all; it's those going in that are the worry.*

Erith and Kahlee followed in his wake, looking a little like members of the old Sovereign's harem, he supposed. He kept this thought to himself, of course, knowing full well that with Curatio now gone, there was no one else to heal him should he let that thought be birthed from his lips. Though he knew he could run faster than both the women who trailed behind him, he didn't care to press his luck in moving ahead without the assistance of the lone healer now on his side.

"Quiet out here," Kahlee said as they paused upon the bridge, looking out down at the front gates and out into Saekaj. There were minimal guards, and all of them wore the symbols of House Shrawn.

"I'm guessing the revolution has begun," Terian said, feeling a certain tension run through his body.

"How do you think that will go?" Erith asked.

"It'll be a massacre, one way or another," Terian said, "but I don't know which way. And it doesn't matter, because it leaves Saekaj and Sovar open to Malpravus's army of the dead, so whoever the winner is, they won't have an overabundance of time to enjoy their victory."

"Do you see a path to your own victory?" Kahlee asked quietly.

"A very narrow one, perhaps," Terian said, chewing his own lip. He started to adjust the helm and realized he didn't truly need to. *That's new. The old helm required constant movement when the faceplate was down to keep it from obstructing my view.* "If I can turn both sides in common cause against the outside enemy ..."

"You think you're going to convince Sovar to let go of their millennia-old grudge with their rulers and Saekaj to let go of their ancient suspicion of their lessers and get them to fight together?" Erith asked, incredulous. "Good luck."

"Thanks," Terian said, starting forward in a jog again, "I'll need it."

"You'll need a miracle, too," Erith said, huffing as she fell in behind him, "and that I don't have to give you!"

Much as he hated to hear it, he knew she was right. *There's nothing for it, though,* Terian thought, and instead he just ran faster toward the gates, hoping that he could get there in time, and wondering what he would do if he did.

77.

J'anda

Dagonath Shrawn's shouted orders grated in J'anda's head, like the screams of a wounded animal channeled right into his ear. The mob was in sight, running headlong into the front ranks of Saekaj's guard, and Shrawn's orders did nary a whit of good, like drink poured out in a waiting gutter as the lines dissolved in chaos when the two sides met. Spear points met targets or were pushed down into the dirt. Screaming citizens of Sovar met their end on the point of blades or jumped screaming into the fray, dragging down guards and overwhelming them with rage and numbers. It was a slaughter, J'anda had to concede after the battle had been joined only two minutes, but not of the sort he was used to seeing.

"This is ..." Zieran breathed next to him, horror ripe in her voice.

"Yes," J'anda agreed, though not entirely certain what he was agreeing with.

Screams and cries of rage and anger mixed with those of fear and pain, groans mingled with exhortations, fury with exhaustion. It was an unpleasant sound, battle of a kind he'd never heard before, and he caught only glimpses of what was going on as the line between him and the front dissolved.

"Should we cast something?" Zieran asked. Her question was jarring. J'anda watched an angry, weaponless woman in threadbare red clothing hurl herself onto a guard and meet a blade straight in the chest. She looked down at the mortal wound as dark blue blood seeped out, staining her ragged tunic, and she punched the guard in the face and rained hammering blow after hammering blow on him until he was pulled down under the tide of the mob.

"I ..." J'anda paused mid-thought. Over the shoulders of the soldiers and on the other side of the fight, he caught sight of a familiar staff, the purple glowing globe within its metal framing held aloft. Shrieks of fear radiated out to its right, the sound of soldiers losing their courage from magical ends.

"Coeltes," he whispered under his breath, eyes narrowing to slits as he caught sight of his quarry.

"J'anda—" Zieran shouted, but he was already pushing his way through the crowd, casting spell after spell to ensnare the minds of those in the mob, to mesmerize them for just a moment, creating a small wave of forward momentum on his own side that let him walk ahead as though the sea were pulling aside for his sake.

All thought of sides forgotten, J'anda moved ahead to confront his enemy—the only one he truly felt he had left.

78.

Aisling

She could move in the crowd like a shadow, unseen and too fast by half for those around her. She deftly dodged through holes where they appeared and slipped past the pointed spear of a Saekaj guard without even needing to worry that he'd stab her. Her alacrity was off the charts, and she could sense that the perception that others had of her was somehow altered, as though the tinge of darkness that had appeared the moment Terrgenden had thrust the blade in her hand made the eyes of others more likely to slide right off her like water off a slippery rock.

She tried to decide what she should do about it and resigned herself to following the crowd for now. It wasn't a place she wanted to be, not truly, but it felt like where she needed to be. *An implement of justice? An advocate for it?* She watched another guard torn apart, this time up close and slowly, and wondered at the man's story. Was he some deep, dark Saekaj villain, spending his every day glorying in the pain of those beneath him? Was he some sainted soul who tried not to hurt anyone as best he could while doing his job? No, more likely he was somewhere in between, but it bothered her to think of him as a person while the crowd ripped him to pieces and left only shreds of him, as though they'd been turned into some undead scourge.

She glanced around her, unhurried now that she had a weapon in hand that made her feel secure. It was a strange thing to stand in the middle of a battle for once and feel not totally wary. She'd crept in behind lines of enemies before, but now she was in among those she supposed were almost her own—though she did not feel that way about them. She was watching them slam into a line of forces directed by Saekaj, by—

Yes. There he was.

Dagonath Shrawn.

He sat up the slope, his staff in hand, barking orders that were lost to the roar of the mob overwhelming his guards. He was far enough back not to be imperiled, yet, but she suspected that would not last, especially since she was now at the front of the crowd surging through. She glanced back to see Norenn behind her a ways and started forward, threading her way through the opposition nearly unseen, wondering exactly what she'd do when she finally got to Shrawn.

79.

Terian

The battle had been joined, and it was utter havoc. The guards were absent their position at the gates of Saekaj, and Terian had passed through the empty streets fearing the worst. When he'd found them all in lines snaking their way down toward Sovar, he'd known that it was bad. This, perhaps, was worse than he'd feared, though, this narrow and frightening hell that seemed as though it were a cauldron ready to boil over. He could see the battle down the way, sensed the guards at the back of the line already nervous at the sounds coming from ahead, the clamor and clangor of a fight that did not sound remotely civilized.

"Oh, my," Terian said, and looked back at Erith, who trailed behind him. He blinked, looking for— "Where's Kahlee?"

"Huh?" Erith turned her head, looking along with him, as though his wife would materialize out of the air. "I ... didn't notice she was gone until now."

Terian frowned, glancing about. "Should have known she had her own plan when she refused to square with me about her motives." He shook his head. "If this gets ugly, make sure you have your return spell ready to run."

"Oh, I will," Erith said, plunging in behind him as he started pushing his way through startled and frightened guards who seemed only too happy to let him pass, as though his movement toward the front would somehow keep them from having to advance. "But what's going to happen to you if you get overwhelmed?"

"I'll die, I reckon," Terian said. "Don't want to join me, do you?"

341

He shot a grin back at her, not letting his nervousness show. It took a second, but she shook her head. "Run if you need to. No point in both of us going down if it turns sour."

"You're a real hero, Terian," she said, and for the first time he didn't hear sarcasm in her voice.

"Well, let's hope I live long enough to have someone other than you tell me so," he said then froze as he heard a shout from behind him. As he turned his head and took in what he saw, he felt his stomach drop precipitously.

"Wow," Erith said, and the sarcasm was back. "The odds on that one just got a hell of a lot longer, didn't they?"

"They did indeed," Terian said, and he could feel the color draining from his face as he began pushing his way back through the line of stunned guardsmen, making his way back up to the fore of the army, which was now back the way they came. "Very, very long."

Up the slope and descending toward them quickly, Amenon Lepos stood shoulder to shoulder with Sareea Scyros—and an entire legion of the dead followed just behind them.

80.

J'anda

The soldiers around him were breaking and running, but J'anda kept his eyes on the purple orb fixed atop the Staff of the Guildmaster of the Gathering of Coercers, watching it rise and fall with each spell that Vracken Coeltes cast. Fear permeated the air around him—the squeals of terror, of the worst horrors that could be imagined, the absolute lowest thoughts a man could conceive of—they were paraded around in the minds of those Coeltes afflicted, made manifest in their heads and poured out in a self-fulfilling prophecy as grown men panicked and fled, causing even those unaffected by the spell to lose their nerve and run.

J'anda kept his course, throwing out the spell of mesmerization in front of him, pacifying those in his path and pushing them aside as he worked toward Coeltes. He caught glimpses of the man, grinning as he did his work, glorying in the spread of fear, the application of terror, the near-viral propagation of it amongst his enemies—

He's always enjoyed it.

J'anda could feel the cold rage fire hot, burning up from within his belly where it had taken refuge these last months, stoked by what he saw, by the bastard's sheer joy in afflicting others in that way. Grown men fought to run, faces plastered with anguish and horror as they shoved into the lines behind them and were grasped, stabbed, impaled, torn asunder by the mob that followed. J'anda cast his calm upon it as best he could, but it was like trying to hold back the tide with only a bucket.

He loves fear.

The trailing edges of purple magic spun through the air as Coeltes cast another spell, broke another mind, and J'anda watched a man ripped to pieces in front of him with rough implements, screaming as blood sprayed from his mouth, more terrified of the vision placed in his head than of his flesh being torn apart and his eyeballs gouged out of his face—

J'anda's hands burned, his heart burned, his soul was aflame with anger of the sort he normally did not allow to bubble up within him. It was a righteous fury, fueled by a hundred years of shame, of feeling exposed and humiliated and broken and burned all in one—

It ends now.

J'anda summoned up the last of the calm he could find within himself and let it rush out in one good burst, sending a dozen men in front of him to their knees, then to the ground, nearer to asleep than dead, spun into an unconscious state by his reckless, emotionally charged casting.

"Vracken Coeltes!" J'anda shouted, and the Guildmaster's staff bobbed as its bearer paused to look at the falling ranks before him. He saw the hint of panic in Coeltes's eyes, and raised his hands to cast against the man just as the purple staff moved—unfathomably fast, faster than youth alone explain it—and its orb pointed right at him.

The swell of magics burst forth at J'anda, the purple light filling his vision, swirling around him, and dragging him within himself as he heard nothing but a silent scream fill his ears, one that sounded all the more familiar because he knew it was his own.

81.

Aisling

She could have killed a hundred by now if she'd wanted to, they moved so slowly. As it was, Aisling had yet to kill a single person, she simply balleted around them, dancing past unnoticed save for the breath of air in her wake. She'd moved to the side of the tunnel for the sake of perspective, and it was giving her a good view of everything, the battle passing her by nearly unnoticed.

She stood apart and watched J'anda drop some twenty men between her and Coeltes as Coeltes moved to engage him. He moved fast enough that he seemed to be operating at her speed. She caught a glimpse of the staff in his hands and nodded in understanding. She did not, however, move to assist the enchanter. *I think this is his fight ... even if it goes against him.*

Her attention was elsewhere, in any case; Shrawn was standing fast, holding his ground as he raised his staff and dropped an enormous fire spell that hit both his own soldiers and the racing front rank of the mob. It exploded like a barrel of Dragon's Breath and when it receded, ash and melted metal were all that remained of men and armor. His own line failed to re-form where he had done it damage, and the fury of the mob raced in like water to fill a hole in the earth.

Shrawn's grimace was obvious, his lack of art in battle even more so. He cast again and again, his flame burning more and more enemies out of his path but doing little good save to delay the inevitable surge. The ranks of guards in front of him died in quantity, some to his own increasingly panicked spells, others to the rush of angry citizens of

Sovar with their stolen and makeshift weapons.

It was Norenn who got to Shrawn first, who battered him as he burned alive the last man in front of him. Aisling was already moving when she saw him get there, saw him club the wizard—Sovereign of Saekaj, if that was what he wanted to call himself—and dropped him to the floor of the cave.

Like a river rushing around a rock, the mob rolled around Norenn, something she thought was curious until she saw Xemlinan and two others steering them from a few feet back. It gave Norenn the room he needed as he pulled the staff out of Dagonath Shrawn's hand and held it aloft before bringing it down on Shrawn's head. She was close enough now to see the old wizard's head rock back, his eyes close from the pain, then snap open again in fear, fully aware of what was about to happen.

"... tortured me for years," Norenn said as she edged through the crowd. She made it behind him just as he struck Shrawn again, drawing a quiet cry from the pudgy old bastard. He looked helpless on the ground before Norenn, like a fat baby who wanted to curl up in a ball. "You thought you could do whatever you wanted to whomever you wanted, and that there'd never be anyone strong enough to make you answer for it." He raised the club again. "But your day is over, Shrawn, and I will make you—"

She stabbed Norenn in the back and watched his mouth gape open from the side. She stabbed him again, and again, and again, through the heart, never letting him turn around to see it was her. She laid him out, letting him fall face forward into unknowing death.

When she was done, she took Shrawn's hand and brought him to his feet. He blinked, trying to see her in the shadow, and she realized she wanted him to. In an instant, the shadowed sense of the world dropped away, and she knew he could see her plain.

"It's you," he whispered, dark blood running down his face. "You saved me. I'll see you rewarded for this. You've done a great service and—"

She ran the new blade across his neck wordlessly, fast enough to interrupt his ability to so much as speak. He just stared, stunned, as the dark blood sprayed right into her face. Then she stabbed him in the belly, slower, opening him up, letting all that cold fury that had settled in her own guts over the years pour out as she opened up his.

She didn't say a word the whole while, just gutted him, and when she was done, let him drop, still choking from his slit throat, to the cavern floor.

He stared up at her, unable to speak, eyes offering up a desperate plea that went ungranted; she simply showed him her blade, navy with his blood and Norenn's. "This is justice," she whispered as Dagonath Shrawn died before her eyes, and she wondered if what she'd said had any element of truth to it, or if perhaps it was just another in a long line of lies she'd told herself these last years.

82.

Terian

"Is that your—?" Erith asked from just over Terian's shoulder, her eyes fixed on Amenon in his hard-angled armor, his glowing red blade close at hand.

"Yeah," Terian said, realizing the Goliath army was mingled with the dead, coming down the tunnel in front of the gates of Saekaj, ignoring the open target in front of them in favor of the army ahead. *Knock aside the hand with the sword in it first, then deal with the exposed neck.* "That's him."

"And he's part of Goliath now," she said, "great."

"He's dead," Terian said, pushing his way through the last rank of guards to the front of the fight. "You can't even blame him; he's Malpravus's puppet now, through and through." The last part he said loudly enough that he was sure that Amenon heard him. If his father had any reaction, it was not obvious, at least not like Sareea's. Hers was to draw her curved, sharp-edged sword and hold it in front of her.

"What is this?" Sareea called in the intervening space between them as the army of Goliath came to a halt with a raise of Amenon's hand. "Do mine eyes deceive me, or do I see a dark knight clad in the ragged armor of a fallen paladin?" She sneered and hissed as she spoke, full of jeer and insult. "Have you gone back to your old ways, Terian, trying to pretend you are a dragon that flies when really you're a snake that crawls the earth?"

"I'd rather try and fly than be content with letting my belly drag the dirt," Terian said, clutching his axe and stepping out from the lines of guardsmen all around him. "Which, incidentally, is a great way to describe associating with Goliath."

"You do not know that of which you speak," Amenon said through his helm, his voice low and impatient.

"I see you're working for Malpravus now," Terian said. "Tell me, was it because you wanted to, or because he controls your thoughts?"

"I have all the same thoughts as before," his father answered with the same irritability as ever. "That my son is a disgrace, a shame, and your new attire proves once again that you are no child of mine."

"I'm carrying Noctus," Terian said, brandishing the axe high, "surely that's got to count for something."

"It will count for nothing," Amenon said, "save for that I will take the weapon from your dead hand and use it for my own good."

"That'll be two of your own children that you'll have killed for your own self-aggrandizement," Terian said. "I'm sensing a pattern."

"Do you sense your own death?" Sareea called out, breaking from her line to match his father's steps forward. *They're going to attack me as a team. How novel for dark knights.* "Because that approaches more swiftly than any 'pattern.'"

"I sense that it's going to take some time and effort to shut you up," Terian said, sighing with impatience as he let her come forward while his father circled to his left. "Luckily, I have both to spare."

"You have very little time," Amenon said, and moved into his blind spot. *Or at least, where it would have been on my old armor—I can see him perfectly.* Sareea moved in the opposite direction, forcing Terian to fix his gaze on her. "You are a piteously bad dark knight, waiting for your enemies to strike at you—"

Terian saw the move from his father and swung the axe low, knocking aside the red blade and sweeping back around in time to catch Sareea's hooked edge and throw it aside. He retreated a few steps to put them both in front of him, standing at the third point of their triangle. His father's hand danced up, and he felt the clawing of the lockjaw curse upon his throat. It felt like fingers clamped on his neck, pushing into his skin and restricting his breath—

"Not so fast," Erith said, and the pressure released. Sareea and his father both turned their heads to look at the source of the voice, audible over the sound of battle down the tunnel. "Oops," Erith said, backing up into a line of soldiers that was already doing some backing up of their own. She was exposed, at least a half step in front of a group of guards that did not look eager to fight.

Terian swept forward and attacked, knocking Sareea's weapon aside and then striking his father from behind with a hard axe blow that knocked him sideways, but stopped on his armor. Terian stepped between them and Erith, holding his axe up defensively. "I'm the one fighting, and I'm over here."

"Look at him," Sareea said with a piteous laugh. "Thinks he's a white knight, some defender of the helpless."

"Hey, I'm hardly helpless," Erith said, annoyed.

"Then protect yourself against this," Amenon said, extending a hand toward her as his fingers glowed red.

"NO!" Terian called as the spell magic leapt forward. He swept down with the axe blade and it clanged off his father's armor, directed into the nearest chink in his armor, a gap at the forearm. The axe sunk in, blood squirted out, and his father dropped to one knee.

"AIEEEE!" Erith's scream filled the cavern and Terian whirled to see her with her arm hanging free, blood shooting out in a perfect re-creation of the wound he'd just inflicted on his father. Her skin ran with boils, with stagnant, curdled blood opening in sores, and when she opened her mouth the air stunk of rot, of powerful horror, and her eyes went white and sightless.

"Erith!" Terian called, but she wobbled then fell to the ground, unmoving as black blood oozed into the dirt in a slow wash, and his last ally in Saekaj and Sovar died where she lay.

83.

J'anda

One Hundred Years Earlier

He'd received the summons and come as quickly as he could, the Sovereign's note warning him to present himself immediately. It had caught him at the Gathering, working with students, on a rare day when he did so now. He'd received his orders to return to the front lines in a week, in preparation for a battle that would take the fight to the elves over the river Perda, and he found little anticipation in that idea. *To be away from court is to be away from the Sovereign's favor, and more than that, to be away from …*

… Trimane.

He was allowed into the palace in the customary manner, with none of the pomp or circumstance of court days, but that was expected. It was how it always was when he came for a private audience. It had happened frequently of late, the Sovereign summoning him to talk, to converse, to share counsel, and it was such a strange sensation, standing in the presence of a god and offering opinion.

He was not kept waiting long in the anteroom before the throne room; just long enough to suspect that whoever was currently having counsel with the Sovereign was someone of great import, like Dagonath Shrawn, perhaps, or that dark knight that everyone was talking about. What was his name? Amenon Lepos, that was it. Soon to be a general, to hear the court tell it.

When he came in, J'anda was not announced. That was not

351

unusual, even on court days, though. What was unusual was finding the Sovereign enshrouded in the veil of darkness, looming on the throne like a black cloud of coal smoke hanging on the ceiling of Sovar.

"J'anda Aimant," the Sovereign said, so formally that it caused J'anda to slow his pace.

"You summoned me and I have come," J'anda said, taken slightly aback. "What service can I provide for you this day, my Sovereign?"

"What service indeed," the Sovereign said, still shrouded in the darkness, his voice high and bereft of the warmth J'anda had come to expect from it of late.

J'anda approached the throne and found himself increasingly wary as he did so. *Is he in a mood, or have I done something to offend him …?* "My Sovereign—" he began, but did not manage to get it out.

"You have been hiding something from me, J'anda," the Sovereign said from out of the darkness. "Hiding something from everyone, it would seem."

J'anda froze as though an ice spell had hit him, penetrating his stomach, seeping into his bowels, chilling him inside and out. His head felt suddenly weightless, as though it had been ripped free of his body. "My Sovereign—"

"Do not offer your excuses," the Sovereign said, and the cloud grew as Yartraak got to his feet. He towered overhead. "You have been caught engaging in deviant behavior with Trimane Hareminn. I have seen it with my own eyes."

Now the ground felt as though it had fallen out from under J'anda, as though he were suddenly very high up and spiraling to the earth below. "I … I don't …" Words did not come, thoughts did not come, and it was suddenly both warm and hot, as a trickle of sweat crawled down the back of his neck, the oily scent that hung in the room overwhelming him, crawling into his nose and lingering there, making his already queasy stomach feel sick.

"You cannot even deny it," the Sovereign said, in a cross between crowing and fury, "and you do not try."

J'anda let the accusation hang hard in the air. His skin crawled as though a flight of insects had come over him, shame running over his flesh, horror at being exposed as strong as if someone had kicked down his door while he had been in the act. "I don't … know what to say."

"You have broken our laws," the Sovereign said, cold contempt causing J'anda to recoil at every word as though it were screamed in his ear rather than delivered with quiet fury. "You have shamed us and yourself."

Do I dare deny it? He did not look up, afraid to stare into the darkness for fear that the red eyes would catch his. *He is certain. He does know. But ... how?* "I am ... sorry," he said, and the mere words made him feel even sicker, as though he'd just been forced to agree with a particularly appalling sentiment, such as that innocent children should be a perfectly viable food source for Sovar.

The darkness shifted, and J'anda could see the hints of red as the Sovereign stared down at him. "You are contrite, I can see that. Ashamed, as you should be for your ... disgusting behavior."

J'anda kept himself from shaking at the knees, though only barely. He felt as nauseous as any illness had ever made him, and his mind raced with thoughts of Trimane. *Did the Sovereign find out from him? Is he ... all right?*

Please let him be all right. Let him have merely betrayed me ... been tortured into betraying me, even ... son of an important house, surely they'll merely send us both to the Depths together for a spell. Or perhaps just me ...

"I feel nothing but shame," J'anda said, telling the lie only through great effort. "I am sorry to have been such a disappointment to you."

"And indeed you have been a disappointment," the Sovereign said. "I favored you, promoted you, sought your counsel, and here I find that behind my back you have been engaged with this sort of depravity." The Sovereign made a sound of disgust. "I will have several of my harem sent to your home immediately, and you will absolve yourself of these gross and disturbing allegations by curing yourself of your deviancy with them, do you understand?"

J'anda felt his eyes flutter involuntarily. "You ... are merciful, my Sovereign." His head bobbed inadvertently. He felt as though it would float away, or perhaps split open, or simply disgorge the contents of his stomach, he was not sure which.

"I truly am," the Sovereign said, and the shroud of darkness departed, leaving Yartraak standing before him, his disproportionately skinny body tall and gangly next to the small figure of a man who stood only to his hip, smiling with a grin so wide that J'anda could scarcely recognize the man for who he was.

Vracken Coeltes? But ... why—

J'anda's eyes fluttered again as Coeltes stepped forward with a box. It was cradled delicately in his hands as though it were important, something so delicate he could not possibly bear to see it come to harm. Coeltes offered it to him, still grinning wider, with more satisfaction than J'anda had ever seen from him.

"I have taken steps to insure that you do not stray from the path I have set before you again, J'anda," the Sovereign said as Coeltes offered the box to him again. "It troubles me that a Hero of Saekaj could be so easily swayed into deviancy. Take my good faith in you as a sign, and go forth with my blessings, remembering always that I have been firm but fair in my treatment of you."

J'anda's eyes locked on the box, a simply carved wooden affair, as it was thrust toward him. He took it almost involuntarily as it was shoved roughly into his midsection, his hands catching it so as to keep it from plunging through him like a knife in Coeltes's hands. When Coeltes seemed certain he had a firm grip on it, he relinquished his own, still grinning with those even teeth, and his deft fingers slipped to the top and opened it wide before J'anda could do much more than look down with his dull eyes, trying to digest what he was seeing—

"Take this as a sign of my mercy," the Sovereign said, and waved him away with a single flick of the wrist. "And expect no more tolerance for this sort of behavior. Remember that I am as a parent with you, always guiding you back when I sense you stray."

J'anda stared down in quiet horror, his mind screaming at him from somewhere within, but it was buried so deep inside under a flat and hollowed out facade that he could scarcely even hear it. "Of course," he said.

"Go forth and prove yourself reformed," the Sovereign said, "or next time I shall take Coeltes's recommendations to heart and punish you severely." He waved his hand once more. "Go, and look upon my reminder as frequently as you need to in order to cure your tendencies. Seek me again after you have done the penance I have asked."

J'anda's body was practically weightless as he nodded, feeling as though his head would fall off his shoulders. It wouldn't, though, damn it, even as he turned on his heel and walked out, putting one foot in front of another, moving like an empty shell of himself. He stared down into the box as though it contained something he should know, but it didn't. Just another shell, really, like he was now. Or at least part of one.

Later that night, he would wear the first of his many illusions, draping it over himself and imitating a guard, slipping out of the gates and into the great wide open of the outdoors that he once feared. It held no fear for him now, though, and he kept his illusions firmly upon him until well after he reached the city of Reikonos.

But for now he simply put one foot in front of the other and stared down into Trimane's empty eyes, his butchered head staring up at J'anda's out of the box that Coeltes had handed him. And one foot in front of the other carried him off, nearly as bereft of life as what he carried in the box, save for the specter of fear that had settled in his heart like an unwelcome guest, placed there by Vracken Coeltes, to linger like an uninvited guest for every day of the rest of his life.

84.

Terian

He used the axe to guard against the swords that came at him, one after another, but even with his speed he was overmatched, two great knights against his flagging strength and failing will. The front rank of the dead closed around Terian, and he could feel fear starting to overtake him as the guardsmen at his back panicked, surging away, and the army of Goliath closed ranks to kill him.

"Do you feel the change in the air?" his father asked, swinging low with his red blade glowing in the darkness of the cavern. "Do you sense your defeat at hand?"

"I sense a whole lot of death about to sweep through Saekaj and Sovar if I don't stop them," Terian said, ripping three corpses apart in a single swing and knocking Sareea off her feet with a hard swipe as he did so. "Once upon a time, you might have cared about that."

"And once upon a time, you would have done what you were commanded," Amenon said, striking hard at him. His sword caught upon the axe blade and bounced hard, the harsh clang echoing in the cavern. "You were such a good lad, such an obedient child. Where did you start to fail? Where did your reckless disregard for authority spring from?"

"Probably from that time that you told me to kill my own sister," Terian said, throwing the blade back at Amenon and knocking him off balance.

"Yet you passed that trial," Amenon said as Sareea came at Terian from behind. He thrust the bottom of the axe handle at her and hit her squarely in the chest, knocking her backward. Her fall was broken by three soldiers of the dead. "But like a true failure, you never stopped whining about it, dwelling always on what was asked of you instead of what you gained through that test—"

"Always focused on what I lost," Terian said, feeling the sweat rolling over his upper lip. "On what I chose to take out of this world, on what the soul sacrifice really meant to me. I lost the one truly decent person in my life, the one who joked to escape her horror at what transpired around us." He attacked his father, striking the red sword with his axe overhand, driving the old man back. "She saw clearly what Saekaj was, the blight it brought, the leeching effect it had on the less fortunate. Everything the Sovereign built he did with an iron hand so strong that it survived his own exile, allowing you and Shrawn to keep rolling on in his absence, ignoring every person you crushed beneath you—including me."

"You are the same as every failure I ever met in my ascent," Amenon said, rolling back to his feet with an alacrity Terian found surprising from the dead man. "Always desirous of success until the price became too high. Then the complaints began to issue forth, always talking to justify your failures."

Terian looked at him with absolute fury. "You are my constant, did you know that? You are everything I have never wanted to be. All I need do is look at you and I know who I desire to be simply by going in the opposite direction of you—"

The strike to his back knocked Terian over, the blade catching him under the back plate and by surprise. His shoulder planted into the tunnel dirt and his head rattled inside the helm. The pain was close to the worst he'd ever felt, writhing inside like someone had set fire to the veins in his back and let the blood within boil.

"And yet you threw away everything you professed to care about to avenge me." His father dropped into his sight, looking him in the eye as Terian came back to his feet, caught once more between the pincer of Sareea and Amenon. They both wore the looks of satisfaction now, the knowledge of the lions that the sheep was doomed. "As failures do. You never committed to the darkness, always thinking you could run back to the light—and that is why you will die here, unremembered by anyone."

Terian stood, just barely, the axe of darkness wavering in front of him, and watched helplessly as the two dark knights closed on him, death in their eyes, murder writ large enough for him to read it coming, and helpless enough that he could do nothing to stop it—

85.

J'anda

He threw off the spell of fear like it was nothing, because it was nothing. It was a pale shade of something he had lived with in his heart for the last hundred years, and it was like bitter hemlock poured in his mouth; he spat it out without a drop passing into his gullet. He let the spell pass over him defrayed by his fury, soaked up by the magic he turned in his fingers even now, and a flash of light burst through Coeltes's own woven spell as J'anda turned it around.

"Do you know why I never used fear in my spells, Coeltes?" J'anda asked, seething fury as his old rival backed up a step. The Staff of the Guildmaster quivered as he hesitantly brought it upright. *He's never seen one of his spells fail like this before.* "Because every once in a while, you run across someone who simply has no more time for *fear* in their own life."

He brought his hand up with all the darkness he could summon from within, drawing deep on a feeling he had vowed never to inflict upon another soul. "But I somehow find it eminently reasonable to give you more than a fair helping of it by throwing a pox of it into your life."

For the first time since the days of his training, J'anda Aimant drew upon a lifetime of the bitterest taste he could recall, of the insecurities of hiding, of worrying that someone would see him for what he was and the shame of knowing his cowardice when they did—

And heaped it all into one grand spell that he flung into Vracken Coeltes's face like a punch.

His enemy's face crusted over as the spell hit home, weaving into the tightest parts of his mind and entwining itself into his nightmares, dredging them to the surface. J'anda felt the man's torment, his agony, his insecurity at watching himself—he, Vracken Coeltes, a good lad from a good family, humiliated and beaten in every competition by some rat from Sovar, some less-than-nothing pulled out of the Depths, some pathetic creature named J'anda Aimant—

And J'anda had not a single ounce of pity left.

He tightened the spell, dragging it around Coeltes' neck like a noose, circling him with a vision of everyone the guildmaster had ever met laughing at his humiliation, watching him brought low, attacked by those around him, closest to him—people that truly, probably, did not even think about Coeltes—watched them humiliate and shame him in the burning way that J'anda himself had felt on that day in the Sovereign's throne room. It was a rich spectacle, and in his own mind Coeltes was racked with sobs, burning with tears, reduced to nothing—

When J'anda was sure there was no more insecurity left to seize upon, no more inner torment to work loose with prying fingers, no further humiliation left to inflict, he felt Coeltes start to slip away. It was a curious feeling, and he wondered about the efficacy of his spell in an almost detached way. He was new to it, after all, this particular type of spell weaving, and with Coeltes feeling like he was drifting out of it, at first J'anda thought he was simply breaking loose.

Then he looked upon Coeltes's face, across the space between them, and knew that it was not so.

Vracken Coeltes's face was twisted in pain, his hand tight upon the V where his robe met, clawing at his heart as though he could dig it out of his chest, as though it had betrayed him. J'anda moved closer, torn between continuing the spell even as his foe drifted out of it, or stopping the pain before he had finished the task at hand. He watched Coeltes sag against the Staff of the Guildmaster, leaning hard on it before he collapsed to his knees amidst the fallen guardsmen and insurrectionists all around, his bright robes obvious even next to the dyed colors of the citizens of Sovar.

J'anda reached him as Coeltes collapsed to his back, and dropped down to look his old enemy in the eyes as he released the spell's hold. Coeltes's eyes swam until they focused on him, like those of a waking man coming out of a deep dream, and his face was creased with pain as he clutched at his chest.

"I ..." Coeltes said, looking at J'anda, lips parted and barely able to form words.

J'anda held him lightly, almost afraid to touch Coeltes. "Yes?"

Coeltes stared right at him and blinked. "I thought ..." he said, struggling to speak, "... for sure ... you'd die ... first."

J'anda stared into Coeltes's open eyes, pain creeping in, his face knotting up. "Are you afraid?" J'anda asked him.

He looked back into J'anda's eyes, dulled, the pain the only thing keeping him from passing out. "Yes."

"Don't be," J'anda said and wove the spell of mesmerization with but a thought. Peaceful calm seeped into Coeltes's mind for the last seconds of his life as his mind went to a place where he had all he ever wanted—and it was less than J'anda would have believed necessary.

Vracken Coeltes's neck went slack, and the Staff of the Guildmaster fell out of his hand and bounced against J'anda's chest. He caught it as it rolled against him, more out of from the surprise than intention.

And as the shock of what he'd done rolled in his mind, giving him once again that weightless feeling, another sensation spread through him in that instant from the staff, one far stranger, one that was akin to the world slowing to a crawl around him, the battle coming to something approaching a halt as magical energy surged through him in a way he'd never felt before.

86.

Terian

"You are not fated to die in darkness."

Terian swallowed hard, the bright light around him like a sunny day shining through closed eyelids. He felt strangely out of place, as though he'd been standing somewhere a moment ago—somewhere dark, yes—and now was somewhere else entirely, as though he'd been picked up by a Yartraak-sized figure and placed in a different position.

His eyes adjusted to the brightness and he found himself surrounded by blue skies ahead, blocked only a little by the shade of something keeping the light from overwhelming him. It took a second for him to realize that it was a roof overhead, that the light was shining in sideways, that the skies were only visible around him through white sheer silky curtains that blew in the wind, which was cool and passed through his armor as though it weren't there. It took him another moment to realize that it actually wasn't.

"What the hells?" Terian murmured as he looked down to find himself draped in white robes that matched the sheer draperies.

"Not the hells," the voice spoke again, drawing his gaze to a figure wearing his armor—well, his armor now—standing between him and the blue skies beyond.

Terian blinked again. "Alaric?"

The figure in the helm—his helm, dammit—took a step forward, and the shadow drawn by the light around him allowed his face to clarify. "Indeed," the old paladin said, taking his own look around. "And it would appear we are in the Tower of the Guildmaster, back in Sanctuary."

Terian's eyes darted around. "So it would. Umm … isn't this Cyrus's tower now?" He paused. "Also, aren't you dead?"

Alaric shrugged at the query. "Suppose I am. Does that mean that you are also dead?"

Terian thought about it. "I was certainly heading that way."

"Even with that?" Alaric gestured toward Noctus, still clutched in Terian's hand.

"I was … overmatched," Terian said, looking a little forlornly at the axe. "I always thought that the sword made Cyrus who he was, at least since he got it. I guess I forgot that he was pretty good with one before he laid a hand on Praelior."

"You're not bad yourself," Alaric said, nodding at him. "I am curious, though—why not use your spell, the one that reverses your injuries on your foes?" Terian blinked in surprise. "You know the one, yes?"

"You were watching that?" Terian asked. Alaric merely shrugged again. "Well, I couldn't on my father, because he's dead. No vitality to take. As for Sareea …" He looked down. "I don't know, I … I suppose I'm a fool, but I'm surrounded by two dark knights and realizing that I don't want to be anything like either of them."

"Mmm," Alaric said, nodding as he walked toward one of the balconies where the sheer drapes fluttered in the breeze. "And so you fight them as a warrior, without an ounce of magic. It certainly is noble."

"You mean stupid," Terian said, trailing behind the paladin. "I'm taking on two spell-casting knights while injured and refusing to use the one means at my disposal that could save my life." He gritted his teeth. "It is stupid. And yet—"

"Stealing the essence of another to save your own life carries a certain unpleasant connotation to you, does it not?" Alaric turned to face him, hands clipped behind his back. "Stirs unpleasant memories?"

Terian's throat constricted, almost as though he'd had the lockjaw curse inflicted upon him. "You know me too well."

"Just well enough, I'd say." Alaric kept his hands behind his back and looked at the dark knight evenly. "You chose darkness before, Terian. *Chose* it."

"I know," Terian said, and his throat felt dry as dust.

"But redemption is a path we must walk every day," Alaric said, with a twinkle in his eye, "and you can choose to walk in the light … as you have proven."

"I don't know if I believe in redemption, Alaric," Terian said, letting loose the feelings that had hung heavy upon him for days and months. "I don't see how I could."

Alaric's face was inscrutable, save for his smile, which had not moved one bit. "I have faith in you."

"Faith in me to what?" Terian cried, looking around him. "I failed, Alaric. I failed, and countless people will die because of it. I may have walked in the light, but I didn't bring any of it to Saekaj or Sovar, where they needed it at least as much as I did." He squeezed his eyes shut and felt once more the burning of failure, of fear, of emotion in the corners of them as heat streamed down his face.

"Terian," Alaric said, and Terian opened his eyes to see the paladin standing in white robes, his armor gone. He had his hands crossed in front of him now, and suddenly Terian was aware of the armor back on his body now, the helm only obscuring his vision a tiny bit. "Repeat after me: *Lacherone, a'shay, metiiree.*"

Terian blinked at him but did not hesitate in following the knight's command. "Lacherone, a'shay, metiiree." Light swelled, glowing around him as if the sun had moved to shine in his eyes, and when it disappeared, he was back in the darkness—

And his father stared at him with his mouth slightly open, Sareea like a statue next to him with her sword frozen in place, her own look of astonishment perched upon her lips.

"How …?" Amenon asked, the shadow of the caves lying upon him as the light from the healing spell faded.

Terian blinked into the darkness as the army of undead rattled behind them, unease rolling through them as though they'd seen something—*clearly not a ghost*, Terian thought ruefully—that had frightened them all.

"Impossible," Sareea pronounced, still lingering back, keeping her distance.

Terian kept the axe level and twisted his back just enough to tweak the spot where his wound should have been.

It was gone.

"You were a knight of the shadows," Amenon said, his surprise twisting to disgust. "You were supposed to thrive in the dark, to live in the dark, fated to die in the darkness—"

"No, I am not," Terian said, and he felt a small thrill of excitement run tingling over his scalp. "I choose my path, you don't choose it for me. I may have been born in the darkness, but I don't choose to live here, and I damned sure don't choose to die here—"

Ayliiron, harajann, epishee.

The words sprang to his mind and he spoke them like an incantation, and the axe in his hands burst into flame as the army of the undead gasped in front of him, fear lighting their dark eyes at the sight of—

—of—

"No," Amenon gasped, staggering back in horror.

"*Yes*," Terian said and stepped forward with his axe on fire with the holy light of a true paladin ...

... a white knight.

87.

Aisling

"Well, that's a hell of a thing," Aisling said. It was certainly not a thing she had expected to see, Terian Lepos in Alaric Garaunt's armor, wielding Noctus, the Battle Axe of Darkness, on fire from a paladin spell and up against Goliath's undead army headed by his father and that wench Sareea Scyros. It was almost too much to take in with a single look, in the midst of a battle, but fortunately she seemed no longer constrained by petty details such as fighting when she didn't want to.

She slipped through the crowd of guardsmen toward the front of the battle and nearly tripped over Erith Frostmoor's corpse, which looked like it was already festering from some sort of spell, she assumed. With some effort and without fully knowing the reason why, she dragged the carcass toward the side of the tunnel. Guardsmen looked down as she passed, the corpse making a skiffing noise she pulled it across the dirt of the tunnel floor, the sound of Terian's battle not quite drowning it out.

Once she was sure that Erith was out of the way, she stood to watch the proceedings again. She stepped out of the right-side line of the guardsmen that were at least no longer retreating, even if they weren't fighting, and watched a white knight take the battle to two dark ones.

88.

Terian

The Battle Axe of Darkness sang as he whipped it through the air, bringing it down hard on his father's sword. Chips of the mystical steel flew through the air, tinging on his armor as he spun swiftly and batted aside Sareea's attack at his back as though she were moving at a trot rather than a run. He pointed the head of the axe at her and whispered *"Sae-aro, pho-ashon!"* under his breath as the voice of Alaric bade him, and a burst of force shot forth from the hilt-tip and sent Sareea flying back into the Goliath army, bowling over another six dead men.

"My son ..." Amenon said as Terian turned his attack back to the dark knight.

"I am no son of yours!" Terian shouted as he brought the axe down again, chipping a quarter inch of metal out of the already damaged blade just above the sword guard. "I failed you and you forsook me, I chose a different path and you denied me! I want nothing to do with you—and you will pay for what you have done to me and everyone else in this place!"

Amenon's face crumpled as though life left him, and his sword sagged in his hand as he raised his other hand to desperately strike at Terian. Terian could sense the spell coming, like with Erith. *Going to take the soul of your last child to save your own life, Father?* Amenon's fingers jutted forth at Terian's chest, and Terian knew there was no chance he could strike fast enough stop it in time, not even with Noctus—

The spell shot forth as Terian brought his axe down to shield himself, and the flame running across the weapon guttered slightly, as though a strong breeze had just blown through. It stayed afire, though, and a sound like screaming filled the air as hints of light shot forth from the axe, following a trail back to Amenon's hand, still extended in the casting of the spell—

His father's eyes went wide, stricken, as the spell he'd sent out to take Terian's soul drew something else entirely back into him. His red irises grew somehow redder, angrier, and then orange—

Amenon Lepos burst into flames from the eyes out, a fast-running fire that shot out of every crevice of his armor as his flesh lit. The scream was potent but short, lipped with yellow and red as it flew forth from his mouth in a fiery exhale, and it completely consumed the dead man in seconds, burning him up and leaving nothing but an empty suit of angled armor that came clattering to the ground, still smoking.

Terian held the fiery axe in front of him, staring at the flames as they burned, dancing on the weapon as though inspired by the sight before them. "He should have known that my soul would disagree with him utterly."

"A most intriguing notion," came the thin, reedy voice of Malpravus as he stepped out of the ranks of the dead army of Goliath. "I confess, my boy, I thought we'd cured you of such sentiments, and yet here you are, standing before me a white knight, in the raiment of Alaric himself, no less." The necromancer seemed to drift across the ground on air, as though he wore a Falcon's Essence spell to lighten his passage. "I must admit disappointment; I had such high hopes for you."

"I'm not sorry to disappoint you," Terian said, keeping his axe in front of him like a bulwark to protect his soul. "The path you offered is one I'd never care to commit myself to—power for the sake of power, shunning all decency when the moment arises, forgetting any bonds of fellowship if the chance comes to betray them for greater strength—"

"You're all fools," Malpravus said, shaking his head. "Noble fools, you Sanctuary idiots, but fools nonetheless." He swept a hand forward to encompass the army of guards behind Terian. "Look at these people. During your battle, they feared for their lives, yet watched you struggle in a fight for yours. Watched. Did nothing. They fear what comes for them, and they should. Death marches the way of all the living, and the only way to turn it aside is power. Yet what do most people do? Chase coin? Fight for scraps? Seek minor influence over others? Aim to breed with someone whose face is beautiful for but a day in the scheme of things?" He shook his head as though casting his words of wisdom before a swinish audience. "No, no. Power endures. In fact, it is the only thing that does." He looked to the dead, lined up next to him, and the front snapped their jaws as one, at his command. "All else fails, but power endures." Malpravus's thin hands came to rest upon his chest as though he were crossing them to meet there. "As I endure."

"Yeah, well ..." Terian nodded, "... let's see what we can do about that." He breathed the words of the spell again, his axe pointed at Malpravus, and was rewarded with a rush of force that burst forth and hit the necromancer squarely in the chest. The black robes billowed as Malpravus was launched over the front row of his army, and the second, and the third. The black cloak fluttered as he fell down in their midst somewhere, like a stone dropped to earth with a handkerchief to trail it.

The army of the dead quieted in shock, bony jaws open in utter surprise. There was no sound, not from the Goliath army nor from the guardsmen behind Terian, just silence and amazement, and the distant sound of water dripping somewhere far away.

"You will walk your dead asses out of my city," Terian said, breaking the still, "or I will exorcise every last one of your empty shells and leave you a pile of burning bones." He pointed his axe straight ahead, taking a breath that flared his nostrils as he did so. "I will fight you to your second death in the name of the united Saekaj and Sovar, and you will spend the last moments of your servitude burning with holy fire."

He thrust the axe forward again and breathed the words, and his blast of holy force hit the center front rank of the undead army and sent bones flying in a storm. It bowled through at least six rows of them, and Terian twisted to his left, firing again with his new spell. He could feel the magic drain, but he cast again, this time to the right, and watched rows of skeletal enemies, barely held together by the rotted remains of flesh, torn asunder by his power.

Pieces of his foes showered down on the infinite rows of dead behind them, and Terian felt his magical energy beginning to wane.

He twisted his lips in fury, again shouting loud enough to be heard through the entirety of the caves. "Now get the hell out!"

For a moment, he thought it might work. They seemed so tentative, the frightened dead, at the sight of a holy knight standing his ground against them. But then Sareea's armor clawed its way out of a pile of bones, and further back, he saw Malpravus's hand do the same, the cowl-shrouded face rising out of a ribcage, wearing a skull as an unintentional hat.

"Strike him down," Malpravus hissed, in a voice that sounded amplified by spellcraft, high and horrible, "kill them all!"

89.

J'anda

The fighting had stopped between the mob of Sovar, now quivering at the sound of shouts that J'anda knew originated from Terian, bellowing at the top of his lungs about a "united Saekaj and Sovar" and "holy fire," and who knew what else. J'anda was barely listening, the Staff of the Guildmaster clenched tight in his hands as he shoved his way through the Saekaj guardsmen, who seemed to be doing a fair amount of quailing in fear at the mere sound of the raised voice.

With the staff in his hand, J'anda felt as though he could move faster than he had before. It was a curious sensation, akin to the one he'd felt when he'd had Cyrus Davidon's sword in his hand once upon a time, when he'd asked the warrior if he could merely hold it. He used the staff as a cane, even though it reached slightly over the top of his now-stooped height, and it gave him strength. His speed was much improved as well, and he shouldered his way through the guardsmen with an alacrity he couldn't recall enjoying even as a young man.

And so, he concluded, *the Staff of the Guildmaster is a godly weapon of some stripe, it would seem. Which might explain why Coeltes never carried it in the presence of Yartraak; I would imagine he'd find that sort of thing threatening.*

Skeletons were dissolving in what looked explosions of bones by the time J'anda reached the last few rows of waiting guardsmen. They were bunched tighter here, and he used the staff to sweep them away at will, pushing them sideways so that he could move to the fore. By the time he reached the front, Malpravus's hissing voice was filling the cavern with its unnatural sound, invoking the dead to "kill them all!"

J'anda already had his spell prepared before the first rank of the dead began to charge. He snaked the casting through the front row with ease, tangling the minds of the dead men with all the simplicity of tying a knot with a piece of string. *The dead have such simpler minds than those of the living*, he thought, remembering the facility with which he had deceived them into avoiding the Kings' Guildhall back in Reikonos. He charmed the front rank, pulling them easily out of Malpravus's grip and halted them, causing the second row to smash into them while charging. Three of the skeletons dissolved in that moment, breaking to pieces as their minds discorporated.

J'anda seized on what he had left and grabbed firmly onto more. *I doubt this will last once Malpravus realizes that someone is taking hold of his prizes; it is unlikely an enchanter can hold the minds of the dead better than a necromancer, after all, but for now ...* His small undead army raised their swords and hacked into the second row along with a few of their fellows that J'anda had seized in the second row, ripping into the third—

"J'anda," Malpravus hissed as he discovered the treachery, "I offered you a vision of power, of freedom from the fear that haunted you for so long. Now you throw my decency back in my face, I see."

"There are many words I would use to describe you, Malpravus," J'anda said, moving to stand next to Terian. He nearly did a double take at the knight, now clad head to toe in Alaric's armor. "You look good," he said, meeting Terian's eyes, and the knight held out a flaming axe in salute. *Is that Noctus ...?* He shook the thought away for later. "'Decent' is not one of the one of them."

"Once again, you Sanctuary fools prove yourselves unable to change," Malpravus hissed from the front row of the army that stretched off around the corner behind him. Up the slope, J'anda could see movement as officers of Goliath fought their way through. The helm of Orion was obvious to him as he shouldered past undead legions, a bow in hand, and Sareea Scyros stood a few steps in front of Malpravus and to his right. "More the fools, you are, for your lack of vision."

"I think we see just fine," Terian said, "and that includes seeing you for what you are—a charlatan who would do anything, say anything, kill anyone and sacrifice an entire people in order to get what he wants."

Malpravus stood carefully, his fingers templed in front of him, but there was no mistaking the cold fury in his eyes of a man denied what he'd sought. "It is convenient that these cities are built into tunnels and caverns," he said, taking a step forward, something rattling as he did so, "for the work of digging the grave is essentially already done."

"Shit," Terian said and brought his axe high. "He's going to—"

But there was no time for him to finish before the red power of spell magic shot forth from Malpravus's hands and flew through the army behind J'anda, aimed at the dead that he knew were waiting at their backs, behind them at the site of the battle between Saekaj and Sovar. "He's going to flank us!" J'anda cried, "he's going to raise the dead and bring them sweeping in to crush us—!"

The moan and cry of dead rising at their rear rattled its way up the tunnel to reach J'anda's ears, and he felt a horrible sense of defeat twisting down upon him. He inched closer to Terian as the guardsmen behind him seemed caught in a circle of fear, looking from the army before them to the unseen but loud threat behind them, as though the jaws of a great beast were prepared to swallow them whole.

90.

Aisling

"Shit," she breathed as the dead began to rise from the battle down the tunnel. She could see them a little from where she stood, but not too much—tops of the heads, mostly, as they threw themselves into the ranks of the guardsmen who had been on the leading edge of the battle between Saekaj and Sovar.

She spun her head around and looked straight up the tunnel slope. It was all bad news that direction, too, from Malpravus on back, into ranks of the undead that probably stretched to the surface and beyond.

She blinked as she found the obvious answer, obvious as hell, really—

She moved without thought, creeping forward in the way that only she knew how to do, more careful now than she might have been otherwise, legs bent and steps light, trying to keep from betraying her intentions. She moved up the tunnel at speed as the undead army surged down in a charge, and she was almost to Malpravus with her dagger drawn when his head snapped around to look directly at her, as though somehow he could see through the effect of the blade, could see her—

"KILL HER!" Malpravus screamed, louder than even his order to annihilate the city, and she heard the note of panic in his voice. *Cares nothing for his army, only for his own self,* she realized for certain as the undead came at her. She fell back unashamed, using her dagger to cleave head from neck, spine from body. It was the only way to be sure to finish the dead, and it was clumsy work with such a short blade, but she was proficient and fast, and her speed kept her alive long enough to retreat behind the swinging blade of Terian's axe, which brought holy fire to every undead creature it touched, as though it were literally burning the evil out of them.

"Nice of you to join us, Aisling," Terian said, his weapon moving in a fast circle, cautious of his swing within the arc of J'anda's safety on his left.

"Damn, you can see me, too?" Aisling asked, stabbing an undead human in the faceplate and breaking through. "I thought this dagger made me invisible."

"You're wispy and shadowed," Terian said, driving his fiery weapon across the middle of eight undead soldiers in a line, "but I suspect my axe gives me license to see through whatever illusion you're hiding behind."

"I see you much the same," J'anda said, swinging his long staff into the head of an undead, knocking it clean off as purple spell magic spun from it and washed over the undead in front of him in a wave. They paused, some sixteen of them, simply stopped, clotting the forward flow of the attack on that entire side of the tunnel as the waves behind them slammed against their waiting fellows and crashed into chaos. "And I agree, it is good to see you—however lightly we might be doing it at the moment."

Never thought I'd hear them say that, Aisling thought as she spun to evade a thrown axe. "We're going to get overwhelmed here, you realize that, right?"

"Against an infinite legion of the dead?" Terian shot a force spell from his axe that broke the line of attack. "Can't imagine how that could happen."

"Because the enemy is surging behind us?" J'anda asked, blasting out another round of spell magic that resulted in undead soldiers up the slope turning against those around them.

Aisling kicked an approaching foe that tried to attack Terian from the side, sending him shattering to pieces through the air. "That's what I was thinking of, yes."

Another sound of dark doom rolled over them, then, and red magics shot past once more. Dead started to rise at their feet, and Aisling stomped hard on a skull, smashing it to dust as it tried to bite her. She could hear it taking effect down the slope, though, down among the dying guardsmen that were already besieged by undead and were now facing a second wave of their fellows rising against them. There was movement far down there, a writhing, almost living, soulless army of the undead throwing themselves into the shrinking force of guards and defenders of Saekaj.

"This may end up being a short battle," Terian said and brought his axe down again, sending bones flying in a hard arc in front of them. "You two should get out if you can."

"I am not leaving," J'anda said, and with his staff he broke cleanly a skeleton, shattering it to pieces. "I will not flee this place in fear. Not again."

Aisling felt her jaw tighten. *I could leave. I could slip quietly right into Saekaj and hide, or cross into the tunnel up the way and out one of the secret entrances to the surface. I could leave this place behind and the undead wouldn't follow me, Goliath wouldn't follow me, no one would.*

I'd finally be free.

But she felt the abyss within, looked down in it, and found some cold anger, some hot fire still burning unsoothed. *Malpravus. He's like Shrawn. He's like Norenn—what Norenn became.*

Norenn.

Whatever she felt, she pushed back into that abyss, knowing that the time she'd have to deal with it, to feel any of what she'd long held back, was drawing quickly to a close.

This is it. This could be the end.

"I'm not leaving," she announced, cutting the head off another undead, watching six more coming running up to replace it. She dealt with them swiftly, and the ones that followed, and still there was no end in sight.

This is it.

Never have to feel again. Never have to hide it again.

This could finally be the end.

At last.

91.

Terian

"So this is what it felt like on that bridge in Termina," Terian muttered to himself as he caught a glimpse of his father's empty, burned-out shell of armor. The smell of death and fire hung in the air as he struck another undead and sent it aflame, running up the slope into its brethren. The fire spread to a few others, and the rest gave it a wide berth, afraid to join their fellows in final death, apparently. "Now I know, Cyrus." He felt a strange sense of relief at that, like all the weight that he'd carried for so many years was gone from his back.

"Jeesh," Aisling said, spinning into an attack against an undead soldier that separated his head from his body, "J'anda and I were both there, we could have told you what it was like if you were that keen to know, spare you having to fight an undead army like this—"

"I don't think that would have spared us from this moment," Terian said, feeling the sadness close in on him. *This is a matter of time and numbers; we have only so much time, and they have all the numbers.*

As if to punctuate the point, J'anda cried out and stumbled, and Terian turned his head to see the enchanter with an arrow sticking from his shoulder. He grimaced as another shot past, just barely, as J'anda dodged. He pointed up the slope with his staff. "Orion."

Terian spun and pointed his axe at Orion, who stood with bow drawn and arrow nocked, ready to deliver another point of death to J'anda. Terian let fly another burst, feeling the magical energy drain him dry and take a trace of life as it did so. This time the burst was different, carrying an edge of flame at its tip, like a cone of fire shooting up the slope. It consumed the dead in front of it as it went, and hit Orion squarely, knocking him into a hard flip that turned him over for a rough landing.

"You all right?" Terian asked as he spun to check on J'anda.

The enchanter wore a pained expression, a peculiar sight on a man he'd always known to wear illusions, at least until Luukessia. "Not really. I'm bleeding quite severely."

"And us without a healer," Aisling muttered.

"Not without," came a sharp voice. Terian raised his head to see Dahveed striding forth, Grinnd and Bowe at each side. Dahveed's fingers twinkled in the tunnel's dark, casting everything around him in a soft, white light.

"Good to see you, I think," Terian said as Grinnd strode forth to stand next to him, massive swords out and hacking away at the dead. Bowe unleashed a burst of spell fire and lit up six of the undead, giving Terian a subtle look as he did so. "Okay, I know it's good to see you."

"Damned right," Dahveed said with an easy grin.

"What, were you waiting until the situation was at its grimmest before casting your lot with me?" Terian asked, bringing his axe around again and again, hacking his way through the never-ending attack of the undead army.

"Not exactly," Grinnd shouted. "We were fighting against the undead down the slope, but it wasn't going anywhere very fast. Decided grouping together might be a safer course, especially if we can fight our way to Malpravus."

"He's warned when we come at him," Aisling shouted. "Like the dead whisper it in his ear. Saw me sneaking toward him from a mile off. He'll just retreat up the tunnel."

"We can fly," Bowe offered in his quiet voice.

Terian looked at the druid and felt a smile crease his lips. "That might work …"

"And then what?" another voice, more commanding than Dahveed's, shouted across at them from just outside the gate to Saekaj. Terian whipped his head around to look at who spoke, trying to penetrate the veil of their cowl, pulled low around their face. "Even without a leader, an undead army continues to survive, to pillage, to burn and destroy—you should well know that from Reikonos, Terian."

"Who the hells is that?" Terian asked, squinting to see through the darkness of the cloak. There was a second figure behind the first, triangular cowl pulled down even farther, and a third beyond that.

"I am astounded at your unfamiliarity and ingratitude," the first cloaked figure said, sliding back his cowl to reveal pointed ears and a face both serene and amused, as well as ageless.

Curatio, Terian thought with a smile. *Then that means the other two are* ... "Nice to have your help, Vara and—"

The second figure pulled back her cowl, revealing female features and the pointed ears of an elf, but that was where any resemblance to Vara ended. This woman's hair was dark and lustrous, and her skin looked pulled slightly taut, as though she were somewhat aged. Dark circles hung beneath her bright green eyes, and she wore a circlet of withered greenery around the crown of her head. She looked serious and angry, and Terian got the very distinct feeling that he did not want to stand in the direction of that anger. "Not Vara," he said quickly.

"Vidara, actually," Curatio said as he brought something gleaming out of his sleeve, something red that glistened in the light of Terian's axe. "So not terribly far off, as these things go—"

Without a word of warning, Curatio turned the giant, shining gem—the Red Destiny of Saekaj—that was cradled in his hands toward the army of the undead. A light shone from within as the healer's hands glowed brightly, like daylight bursting into the cave, and red energy burned spots in Terian's vision both in front of him and behind as the undead howled loud enough to drown out almost all other sound in the tunnel.

"No!" Malpravus screamed, barely audible over the cries of the dead. "NOOOOOOOOO!" The necromancer's high voice was absolutely panicked in a way that Terian had never heard from the Guildmaster of Goliath before. There was a smell of something akin to rain drying off the cobblestones of a street, and a sizzling sound ripped through the air. Terian forced his eyes open, forced himself to look as red spell magic burned through the undead legion, souls torn from their vessels and channeled into the giant ruby in Curatio's hands.

The magic pitched, reaching a fantastic glow, the most powerful spell Terian could recall seeing, and the energy drew to its close and stopped, the Red Destiny shining like an orb of crimson in the darkness. Curatio's anger was stark in the light of the massive gem, and he handed the stone to Vidara behind him, her face glowing in the light of the souls ripped straight from her flesh.

She drew it in like a breath, the magic coursing up her hands to be absorbed within. The Red Destiny glowed bright and then guttered out, empty of its power. In its place, the Goddess of Life glowed, her face brought back to youth, flawless skin agleam with something like daylight, her hair shining with inner light like the rest of her.

"Perhaps you should not gawk," J'anda said, rapping gently on Terian's helm with the end of his staff, "you are married, after all."

"You're not even interested in women," Terian replied, not daring to take his eyes off the goddess.

"Neither am I," Aisling said, low and amazed, "but for her I might make an exception."

"Might I remind you," Dahveed said with the air of someone only mildly amused and very tired, "we are in the middle of a battle here."

"Right," Terian said, ripping his eyes off the Goddess of Life and looking back up the bone-strewn slope to where Malpravus stood next to Orion and Sareea, and no one else. "Well, Malpravus ... looks like your army's gone to pieces."

"There are other, living bodies up the tunnel," Malpravus said, his voice a furious hush. "Wizards, enchanters, healers, druids. I have warriors and rangers aplenty as well, numbering in the tens of thousands, and ready to march down here to battle you few—"

"I dare you," Terian said, and took a step forward. "I dare you to come and face us, Malpravus, because all I see in this moment is you, a scared-ass ranger, and a dark knight who's been too afraid to attack me for the entirety of this battle." Sareea bristled at his insult, but did not move to strike at him. "What's the matter, Malpravus? Can't find your courage?" He hefted the still-burning axe. "Care to try to re-power those rubies of yours with my soul?"

"I think I would find your soul ... unpalatable at this point," Malpravus said, thin face etched with a silent fury. "As for courage ... yes, you have it, of course. All of you fools do, you fools of Sanctuary—"

"We take none but the brave," Curatio said, sweeping his way over to stand next to Terian. "But you already knew that."

"And at some point very soon," Malpravus said, waving his thin hands as he gathered a spell before him, "you will learn—bravery is irrelevant; only power matters." The light of a return spell glowed around him and Sareea seized one of his arms as Orion grabbed hold of the other, the three of them disappearing. A cry from up the slope followed behind the retreat of the necromancer; shouts of Goliath members to follow his lead echoed as wizard magic flashed up the twisting slope of the tunnel to the surface.

"Courage always matters," Terian said, almost more to himself than anything. "Though you'll never see it that way, Malpravus."

Curatio slumped as the light of teleportation magic lit the tunnel ahead like lightning, receding as it signaled the retreat of Goliath. "No. No, he won't." Terian moved to catch the healer, who looked desperately weak, his normally smooth skin showing signs of creases, his eyes wearier than the knight could ever recall seeing him. "But that won't stop him from being dangerous … and from seeking revenge for what has happened this day."

Terian held the healer's weight against him as he let the flame on his axe die, smokeless, returning to a smooth, black polish of the metal. "Let him seek his revenge; we'll be ready." And he turned his head to look at Aisling, at J'anda, at Dahveed, Grinnd and Bowe. But as he turned to look at the scared army of guardsmen quailing at his back, he had to wonder if they truly would be.

92.

Aisling

She followed in their wake as Terian helped Curatio into Saekaj, leading him forward to the first house in front of them. The healer was barely able to walk, unable to stand without aid, and the silent procession was followed by the army of guardsmen, who seemed to have no idea what to do with themselves now that Shrawn was dead.

"You did well," the third cloaked figure whispered in Aisling's ear, and she glanced over to see Terrgenden beneath the hood, smiling at her. "Just enough chaos, just enough justice to get the thing done."

"So this is what you were after all along?" she asked, muffling her words so only he could hear her. "Vidara renewed?" She caught a glimpse of the Goddess of Life trudging along behind Terian and Curatio, and the woman turned her head to look straight at Aisling in acknowledgment of her name being heard. "Saekaj and Sovar in … what? Shambles?"

"The tale's hardly been told on that one yet, wouldn't you say?" Terrgenden asked with that same smile as Terian threw open the door to the first building he came to, moved down a staircase and pushed through stone doors into an apartment in the basement.

"Where are we going?" J'anda asked, leaning heavily on his staff. The enchanter looked uncomfortably weary.

"Finding him a bed," Terian said, looking around the small basement apartment. "Empty enough," he said before dragging the healer into the bedroom and settling him upon the bed. "You going to be all right, Curatio?"

Curatio looked frailer than Aisling could ever recall seeing him.

"I'm a bit ... drawn, shall we say, but I shall manage in time."

Aisling glanced back through the narrow stone doors to the basement, wondering why she'd followed along. The guardsmen seemed to have followed behind to the building like soldiers on the march, but unable to figure out what to do without an order. "Someone should probably lead these people."

"Why not you?" J'anda asked, giving her a wan smile.

She smiled at him through thin lips. "I'm not exactly the type to lead an army of Saekaj. What about you? I saw some enchanters in their midst."

"Not my specialty," J'anda said, shaking his head, "commanding armies and such. I am but a lowly child of Sovar, already elevated far above my station—and I am not staying."

"I'll deal with it in a minute," Terian said, leaning over Curatio on the bed and running a glowing hand over the healer.

"Look at the General," Aisling said, more to poke Terian into reacting than because she opposed his sentiment in any way.

"I have a suspicion," Curatio said, "he's about to be more than that."

"Hush," Terian said. "Save your strength."

"I meant to ask you three," Curatio said from where he lay, "you do know you're holding godly weapons, don't you?"

J'anda held his silence and she could see by the look on his face that he wasn't about to speak first. "Yes," she answered for both of them. "And Terian obviously knew; who wouldn't recognize Noctus?"

"Do you know what each of you holds?" Curatio asked, eyebrow raised in genuine amusement.

Aisling lifted the blade out of her belt where she'd hung it. She glanced at Genn—Terrgenden—and saw him nod slightly, perhaps some small note of approval. "I don't know its name, no."

"It is called 'Epalette,'" Terrgenden said from beneath his hood, drawing the gaze of all of them, "The Point of Atonement."

"Not justice?" Aisling asked, staring straight at him.

"I'm afraid that title belongs to J'anda's weapon," Curatio said, his voice a bit raspy as he looked at the staff with the glowing purple orb. "It is called Rasnareke, the Ward of Justice." He glanced at Terrgenden. "I had wondered what happened to it."

"Hmm," J'anda said, staring at his weapon. "Justice."

Aisling looked down at her own blade, wondering for the first time at its strangely white glow. "Atonement." Her eyes found Terrgenden, and he smiled thinly.

"And here I am with the darkness," Terian said, looking at his axe, which almost glowed with blackness, of the sort one might have seen emanating from the portal to Yartraak's realm. "Apparently I can't escape it, no matter how hard I try."

"Now, now," Curatio said, clucking his tongue, "you should know better than anyone that darkness is hardly a permanent or defining quality. Especially since not five minutes ago that axe shone brighter than even Nessalima's own weapon. It is what you do with the weapon that defines it. The weapon does not define you."

Aisling stared at the blade in her hand a little forlornly. *Such a shame. I could have used a little … atonement.*

"Don't be that way," Curatio said, catching her eye. "You're hardly locked into the opposite course, no matter what anyone," he looked pointedly at Terrgenden, who raised his hands with a look of feigned innocence, "might tell you. Your destiny is in your hands … Is that not right, Terian?"

Terian was staring at his axe and looked up, drawn out of what had clearly been a reverie filled with deep thought. "That's the absolute truth," he said quietly, looking straight at Aisling in a way that left her feeling strangely sure that he knew exactly what was on her mind. "Redemption is a path we must walk every day, after all … and there's no better day than to today to start that walk."

93.

J'anda

This was a most improbable meeting, J'anda thought as he stood in the throne room, wishing he were shrouded in the darkness of the days of old one last time. *This is perhaps not a wall I wish to be a fly upon,* he thought from his place in the middle of the room, the torches burning even brighter, driving back the old shadows that lingered in the room. It cast every figure in the place in stark relief, not only the trio of former Sanctuary members that he was part of, but also the three members of Terian's old team—Dahveed, Grinnd and Bowe, as well as the new arrivals that stood across from them, looking extremely nervous to even be here. At the center of it all, between them both, stood Kahlee Ehrest, the broker for this particular arrangement. *This is what she was doing while her husband battled for the survival of Saekaj and Sovar.* Terian looked at her warily, as though he were not quite sure what to say to his own wife.

"You know what happens if anything happens to us, right?" the leader asked, a thin man in fine silks.

Terian sighed audibly. "Xemlinan, if I wanted you dead, you'd be dead. I didn't agree to Kahlee's request to meet you up here just to lop your damned head off." Terian's eye twitched, and J'anda could see he held something back akin to desire, perhaps to do the thing he had professed he would not. "No one is going to kill any of you, no matter how this turns out. At least not here."

Aisling stood directly opposite J'anda, arms folded around her, but her hand not-so-subtly resting on the hilt of her dagger. She, too, scanned the faces of the visitors to the throne room, looking for threats that were not presently there, not even on the face of their leader.

"So you've invited us to Saekaj simply to talk," Xemlinan said, nervousness obvious on his face. He squinted against the new light of the throne room. "How curious, since that has never happened before."

"The Sovereign's never been killed before," Kahlee said.

"And Sovar has never risen so hard as to force an army up the tunnel between our cities," Xemlinan said sharply, turning to look at her. "Is it coincidence that you offer an invitation to us after that happened?"

"Sovar would have been a mass grave if we hadn't halted your little revolution before it had a chance to feed Malpravus even more dead bodies," Aisling shot back at him. "You very nearly gave our enemies the tinder with which to burn us all."

"The people are starving," Xemlinan said, eyes flickering. "They have been trod on by you lot—"

"Not all of us," J'anda added.

"Not any of us, actually," Terian said. "I've been gone for years, in case you forgot."

Xemlinan blew air out through faded blue lips. "You sit in the seat of he who oppressed us for millennia—"

"I'm not sitting in his seat," Terian said, chucking a thumb over his shoulder at the empty space where the mammoth throne used to rest. "I mean, even before Shrawn had it hauled off in pieces, that sucker was way too big for my ass—"

"I should have known I'd get nothing but jokes from you," Xemlinan said, a man whose patience seemed exhausted along with the rest of him.

"You don't know what you're going to get from me, Xem," Terian said, "just as I don't know what I'm going to get from you. Will it be another betrayal that results in the deaths of women and children?" Xemlinan flinched slightly at the strength of the accusation as the man's allies on either side gave him the eye. "Or will we be able to work together to prevent a pointless war between Saekaj and Sovar that will only result in more starvation, more rage, more anger, more hate—in a giant wall of bodies marking the tunnel between the two cities—"

"That wall has been built over more years than either of us can remember," Xemlinan said.

"Then let's tear it down together, dammit!" Terian said, letting the words spill out with a passion unusual for the former dark knight. "Let's give Sovar what they've been wanting—equality."

"You can't eat words," one of Xemlinan's allies, a man in ragged clothing, said.

"We'll give you bread, too," Terian said. "Conjured to start with, but bread. It's about what we've got in Saekaj at the moment, too, frankly." *The war has not been kind to any*, J'anda thought.

"How can we trust you?" Xemlinan asked with narrowed eyes.

"How can I trust you?" Terian asked. "The answer is ... I try it, and if you don't turn on me, I assume it works. You try trusting me as I start bringing in food to Sovar, and some self-determination for its people, and we see how it goes."

"I—" Xemlinan started.

"He saved our lives, you know," another one of Xemlinan's allies said. "In Sovar, a few years ago." The young man looked around at those surrounding him. "Came into the house when some of our number rebelled. We were women and children, waiting up the stairs at the top of the place, hiding under an invisibility spell. He looked right at us and told us to keep hiding, then led his allies away and left us there, alive." The man glanced around. "You know insurrection is death, and he let us live. I say we throw in with him, at least for now."

"A familiar tale," Kahlee said, giving Terian a look that J'anda couldn't quite decipher.

A low mutter ran through the small crowd of representatives for Sovar as J'anda looked sidelong at Terian, who appeared flushed with surprise. *It would appear that our knight had a few surprises in him even before he shed the dark* ... "I will do everything I can to see that the people of Sovar are fed and given a fair shot," Terian said. "I think we all know it's not going to be easy to overturn thousands of years of mistrust between the two cities—"

"But you're the one to do it?" Xemlinan asked, looking wary. "It wasn't that long ago that you were a good for nothing drunk, Terian. You've wobbled your way in more directions than I can count, and now this is your route? Are you sure?"

"I'm sure," Terian said, taking a step forward, his paladin armor clinking with the movement. "Look at me, Xem. I'm not the man I was when last we met. I have no interest in doing what the Sovereign or Shrawn did; you know I've hated these people and that attitude as much as you did. I left and went back to Sanctuary, where things aren't like they are here. I came back because I had nowhere else to go, but I'm here now because there's nowhere else that I want to be. Give me a chance, and help make things right in this place." He lowered his voice. "Please. Anyone else stands where I'm standing, and they're going to try and push back to business as usual. If your lot had your full way, you'd burn Saekaj to the ground and destroy Sovar in the process. Meet me in the middle here. Let's govern."

Xemlinan did not lose his wariness but looked to either side of him, where he saw reluctant nods, shrugs—and not one blatant refusal. J'anda watched, waiting for it, wondering if there would be one sticky wicket to hold them back, but there was none. "All right," Xemlinan said. "Fair enough. You're right. Any Saekaj blighter standing where you are would pledge to wipe us out or stomp us down, and we were coming to burn you out before." He pushed his lips together. "We'll try it your way and see if peace can be made."

"That's all I ask," Terian said with a faint smile. "Now ... let's get your people fed."

"A wise choice," Kahlee said, and J'anda could feel the relief seep into the room like a cool breeze after a hot day. "On all your parts."

Is this really how it goes? J'anda wondered, watching hands being shaken, heads being nodded, conversations being had. *After all these years, after all the bad blood ... is it really that simple?* He sensed the unease, the lingering tension beneath the surface. *No, perhaps not.*

But it's a start.

94.

Aisling

She packed her things, the very few she had brought with her when she'd begun sleeping in the Grand Palace just a couple months earlier after the battle in the tunnels, putting them all into a bag she could easily carry with her. Things had changed over the last months, both slowly and rapidly, and she could no longer ignore them.

Time to go, she thought, the voice in her head carrying an almost mournful quality.

A knock sounded at the door as she was lifting the pack onto her back. It was enough in the way of supplies to keep her fed for a few days and not much more, sadly. Food was easier to come by now than it had been a few months earlier, but still not exactly in abundant supply. *They can thank the Emerald Fields for that, now that they've had their first harvest of the season and sold the excess to us for quite a pretty pile of gold* ...

"Come in," she said as the knock sounded once more. Her hand fell to the weapon in her scabbard by habit, even though she had not had to draw it in months. She felt uncomfortable on her feet and wanted to sit, but did not wish to project the aura of weakness that it might give.

The door creaked as it opened, bright torchlight falling in from outside in the palace corridor. All the lights were brighter now, oil being the one thing in abundant supply in Saekaj and Sovar. She recognized the armor of the new Sovereign silhouetted in the door's frame and sighed as he stepped in slowly, looking almost exactly like the last wearer of that armor in his careful, pensive motions. "I heard you were packing," Terian said.

"Figured it was time I moved on," Aisling said, drawing the string on her bag closed. "Congratulations, you've done what no one ever thought you could do—united Saekaj and Sovar and made peace between them."

"With your help," Terian said softly, his hands behind his back. The handle of his axe stuck out above his head, far from where he kept his hands. "I couldn't have done it without you, Aisling ... err, Yalina. Whatever you prefer."

"I have no preference anymore," she said heavily. She gave up and sat down on the soft bed, sinking in. She ached all over. "I'm just glad to see it done, though I don't feel as though I've done that much to aid you in this matter."

"You and J'anda have both been invaluable," Terian said. "Your counsel, your advice, your efforts on our behalf. Sovar trusted me not just because of Kahlee's mediations or my part in saving rebel lives, but because you are my advisor, and you have lived and breathed in Sovar for years."

"I haven't been living or breathing in Sovar for a while now," she said, feeling a little out of breath. "And I don't think I can go back, not now."

"Where would you go?" Terian asked, his eyes carefully poised on hers.

"I don't know," Aisling said, looking down. "I'm not really welcome anywhere, I just ..."

"You're welcome here," he said softly, and the abyss threatened to well up within her.

"I have secrets," she whispered. "Secrets to keep. If I stay here much longer ... I'm afraid they're all going to come out."

"You have nothing to fear in this place," Terian said, sounding so much like Alaric she looked up to check for blue skin in the square place above his chin-strap. "This is a ... haven," he said, smiling at his careful choice of words, "for you ... and whoever else."

Aisling looked back down at the grey stone floor. "I let Shrawn push me along for so long with the threat of Norenn hanging over my head. I was so sure that Norenn was it for me, my home—that which I wanted more than anything. Except the place Shrawn sent me ... it was the place that could have been it, and I betrayed everyone there." She blinked her eyes clear. "For years I thought I was trying to save the man I loved from the man who held us both prisoner in different ways. But in the end I freed one and killed the other, and I don't know if I even know which was which. I only know what I feel like I lost in the doing." She took a breath. "I wonder what's left, if there's any part of the original me, if there's anything left of the girl that started this ... because so help me, Terian, I think I enjoyed so much of the journey ... and it doesn't scare me that I was willing to do the things I did."

Terian waited a moment before responding. "Do you have regrets?"

"I have shame," she said, looking at the stone wall to his side, afraid to look him in the eye. "For a few things. A sense of being used against my will that makes me furious in the night, wakes me up sometimes—as if I needed aid in that regard." She shifted uncomfortably on the bed. "But mostly ... I have secrets. I don't want to be seen. I don't want anyone to know me, to know what I did." She blinked and looked at him. "So, yes ... I suppose I do have a few regrets."

"Whatever happens, you are welcome here," Terian said, and she felt a slight sense of warmth. She'd visited her old home a few times, seen her mother and father. They had been ... solicitous, though distant, but growing less so given time and circumstance. Her father, in particular, seemed to be warming to her again, apparently surprised at how his daughter had turned out, and how much sway she had in the new order of things. "Here in the palace, here in Saekaj or Sovar, wherever you choose. This is your home, if you want it to be."

She lowered her head and fixed her gaze on the wall. "I've lied to nearly everyone I've ever met. And these secrets I carry ..."

"Are yours," Terian said, firmly. "And you need not fear your past, nor for your future, not in these caverns. Darkness doesn't rule here anymore, and the only disguise you need place upon yourself is one of your choosing. Hide or do not, but do not fear it either way. You are welcome here, and your secrets are your own, and if I may aid you, all you need do is ask."

She felt some of her worry about the future melt away at his words. She thought about it often—where she could go, what she could do, but never came up with satisfying answers. *I am welcome nowhere else. I am wanted nowhere else, and these worries I carry with me—all I carry with me—would be cause for fear should I be caught.* She looked up at the man in the old knight's armor, and his eyes were warm in a way they'd never been before, in a way she'd perhaps only come to expect from ... well ... the one who wore the helm before him.

"Perhaps I will stay," Aisling said, nodding her head slowly. The bed was soft, after all, and the road ahead was paved with its own sort of trouble if she left. "At least for a while ..."

95.

J'anda

"You're not going to say anything to anyone else before you leave?" Zieran asked. She no longer shared his quarters in the Gathering, the need for that particular illusion gone with the death of the Sovereign those months past, but she remained close by nonetheless and had come to him a few times in the night when he awoke with a hacking cough, the years of his life lost catching up to him more quickly now.

His bag was already packed, cinched tight, and light, with only a few things inside it—a spare robe, some extra sandals, and a little food. "I don't know what I would say." He hefted it on his back. It felt heavy, but when he took up Rasnareke, his staff, it suddenly felt light and easy to manage, like a feather on his shoulder. "I have worked with Aisling, with Terian, with the others for months now to make things stable. Now that they are, I see no reason to spoil the peace with any sort of ... awkward farewell."

"You are the head of the Gathering of Coercers, J'anda," Zieran said with a trace of regret. "You are a man born of Sovar who rose to the tops of Saekaj and helped reform this place—and furthermore, you are the leading exemplar to show others that they need not fear being different in the way that you are. Not anymore."

"I think the point is made," J'anda said with an airy sigh. "Terian has given his word on the matter and emptied the Depths of those accused of my particular crime. Nothing more need be done on my end, and for my part," he looked at the rock walls around him and felt a tightness in his chest, "I don't wish to spend however many days I have left under the ground, no matter how light it is here now."

Zieran nodded her head, her youthful skin folding at her cheeks as she smiled weakly. "It is your life, as you say. I only regret that you do not feel welcome to stay here among us to the end."

"I spent a great many comfortable years feeling uncomfortable about this place," J'anda said, drawing the strap of his sack tighter on his shoulder. "I feel fortunate that events have left me without a trace of those fears—but neither do I wish to spend my last days here, I am afraid. And so I bid my friends goodbye in the only way I know how—by saying nothing at all."

"It's a poor way to go," Zieran said quietly. "To tiptoe out under cover of night like last time."

"Ah," J'anda said, and started toward the door, "but you see, this time I do not need to hide my face, at least." He pulled open the door and blinked in surprise.

His students were lined up in the hall like an honor guard, not quite at attention, but stiff enough that the sign of respect was obvious. It was a salute for a spellcaster, he knew as they raised their hands, and he blinked as he started his walk, pausing to nod in acknowledgment as his feet carried him out of the foyer through the double stone doors, which the students forced open for him—

And revealed a street packed with people on either side, an avenue cleared from the door of the Gathering to a lone, small procession in the middle of the cobblestone road … waiting just for him.

"I could not let you leave in such a way," Zieran said from his shoulder. "Not again."

He kept his face a taut mask, trying to hold back the emotion of the moment as the crowd broke into cheers. He looked out among them on either side and saw the faces of the well-heeled of Saekaj and the slightly more ragged of Sovar, though they looked better now than they had just a few months ago. Gone was the atmosphere of starvation and deprivation, and he could see it and hear it in the way they cheered his name as he made his way to those standing ready to meet him in the middle of the street.

"I heard you were leaving," Terian said, Kahlee upon his elbow, standing even with each other as the equals they were. He looked good in Alaric's armor, J'anda thought once again. *It suits him.* "And I couldn't just let the occasion pass in quiet ignominy."

"So you decided to pass it neither quietly nor ignominiously,"

J'anda said, looking at the streets, which were lined on either side with ... thousands of people. Tens of thousands, perhaps. He blinked in astonishment at the sheer number—

"Last time this man left our home," Terian said, and the crowd quieted in an instant, as if on command, "he was forced to do so in the dark of night, hiding his face, in fear for his life." Terian removed his helm and his black, wavy hair slid out, and his eyes locked on J'anda's. "Never again. J'anda Aimant ... you are always welcome here." He turned and spoke in a booming voice that seemed to echo off the very high ceilings of Saekaj itself. "Make way for a true hero of Saekaj and Sovar!" He laid a hand on J'anda's shoulder, and pressed an envelope into his fingers. "Safe journey, my friend. A wizard waits to take you ..." the white knight smiled, "wherever you want, though I think we both know where that will be. And if you end up there, I'd be much obliged if you could deliver this message to Cyrus."

"I will ... see what I can do," J'anda said, and looked at the crowds lining the street, their colorful attire like a rainbow on a sunny day. "And thank you. For making this place ... welcome."

Terian smiled, and J'anda started his walk, the sound of raucous excitement turned loose around him. Cave cress petals were flung in his path, and the crowds cheered like he was a conquering hero returned to them. J'anda Aimant walked down the streets of his homeland as the sound of celebration paraded him forward, basking in the deafening cheers accorded a hero, and leaving him with no illusions about how the dark elven people of this place felt about him now.

96.

Terian

Terian Lepos sat in the quiet of the throne room, with none but his wife to attend him, and found himself smiling into the light that shone into every corner of the room around him.

"What are you grinning about?" Kahlee asked, sitting in the throne next to him. It wasn't often that they did this, simply sitting here in the silence. There was, after all, always someone to see, someone's problem to smooth over, some matter to attend to. Rare was the quiet moment like this, when Terian could simply sit in his padded chair (it was still somewhat uncomfortable) and stare at the lit corners of a room that until a few months ago had been shrouded in shadow.

"I was just thinking about the way things used to be," Terian said truthfully, glancing over at Kahlee. She wore a wry smile, the sort he still loved about her. "And how they are now."

"And what about that made you smile?" she asked.

He looked down at the armor that wrapped him from chest to boot and felt a tremor of sadness at the thought of its former wearer. *Gone perhaps, but never forgotten.* "The idea that things change. Sometimes for the worse, but ... sometimes for the better."

She gave him a canny look. "Which part of that amused you?"

He smiled again. "Perhaps I simply felt ... a giddy sense of hope."

"You? Giddy?" She placed her hand over her heart and batted her eyes at him in mock surprise. "The greatest white knight in all our land? I can hardly believe it. It hardly seems a fitting disposition for such a man."

"Believe it," he said and rose from the simple throne from which

395

he helped rule the whole of the Sovereignty. She matched his movement and extended her hand, and he took it in his, delicately.

The darkness is gone, hopefully forever.

Thank you, Alaric.

"Where are we going?" she asked, almost playful.

"I can think of a place to while away some time," he said, not without a little playfulness himself.

"Hrmm," she said and let his hand fall from hers as she walked ahead of him. "Well, follow along, then, Sir Knight ..."

And at this he could not but smile and follow his wife along the path she set, never straying from it the whole way out of the throne room.

Epilogue

Aisling

The surging pain brought Aisling's mind back to the center, back to the moment, as it rose to crescendo in the darkness. She sweated against the mattress, bringing wet fingers up to her face and wiping them there, still afraid to cry out, knowing what it would bring. She held it in as long as possible and then let out a scream that echoed down the halls of the Grand Palace, letting her pain flow out of her in one long breath, a surrender that brought little relief.

The door thumped open a moment later and brought with it Kahlee, eyes blinking away sleep. Terian was at her shoulder, just behind, absent his usual armor, though he had his axe in hand. Kahlee gave him an unsubtle look. "Put it away, fool—and get the midwife."

"Right," Terian said, dropping the axe carefully from his shoulder. He stood there only a moment more, stupefied, before he said, "Right," again and ran down the hall.

Kahlee approached the bed carefully, nightgown sweeping about her as Aisling grunted out in pain once more. "How are you feeling, dear?" Kahlee asked.

Normally, Aisling found Kahlee to be one of the most easily tolerable people she had ever come across. "How do you damned well think I'm feeling?" Aisling growled, unable to keep her absolute aggravation at the mere sight of the woman's face from bleeding out.

"I think you're about to give birth," Kahlee said with more sensitivity than sarcasm for once, which annoyed Aisling somehow so much more, but before she had a chance to respond, another terrible, racking pain hit her and she was forced to grab her pillow and throttle the life out of it until the agony passed.

"Found the midwife," Terian said oh-so-helpfully as he came back into view with a woman who was short and squat as a tree stump.

"Get ... out ..." Aisling said to him between breaths.

"Right," Terian said, repeating himself and irritating her all in one. But thankfully, he did leave, which was fortunate for both him and his stupid face, which she found herself quite sick of.

"You're going to need to push when I tell you to," the midwife said, and Aisling found herself looking sidelong at her dagger, which rested on the stand next to the bed. Kahlee caught her looking and neatly slid it out of her reach, prompting Aisling to grunt, then moan as another wave of pain rolled over her.

It felt like hours of torment, of agony, and her assorted curses were many and varied. Kahlee and the midwife took it all in stride, it seemed, like spongy objects that soaked up her bile with aplomb, and that was perhaps the most irritating bit of it all—save for the pain, of course.

When it all passed and was over, she was left with a bundle curled quietly in her arms. She stared at its face—his face, she corrected—in silent amazement. The lines, the cheeks, the closed eyes ... she could not recall ever being in the presence of a baby before, at least not since her own childhood, and it filled her with a sense of awesome wonder and terrible, gut-wrenching fear.

"What are you going to name him?" Kahlee asked. Terian stood at her shoulder now that the fuss was over, peering down at the child she cradled in her arms.

"I could make a suggestion, if you'd like," Terian said with a smirk. His face annoyed her less now, but not much.

"I don't think so," she said, staring at those closed eyes. The baby's lips puckered, skin paler than her own, caught somewhere between pink and blue, a bizarre combination worthy of the mix between the shades of his parents. "I'm sure I'll come up with something, eventually."

Kahlee hesitated, almost held something back, but then spoke. "Should we ... prepare a note for the father?"

Aisling stared at those closed eyes again, her gaze drifting over the sloped forehead and dark patch of hair that crowned the child's head. She'd pondered that very question for a long time, for all the months since she'd found out. She wondered how she'd feel in the moment, and found—most curiously—she felt exactly the same now as she had before, when she'd originally made the decision.

"Cyrus must never know," she said, and she caught the twinge of regret in Terian's expression, but it passed like a cloud on the wind, and she returned to staring at the baby without giving it another thought, focusing instead on that which she held in her arms—that last secret which belonged to her and her alone.

Cyrus Davidon (and Terian) returns in

Warlord

The Sanctuary Series, Volume Six

Coming Late 2015!

Postscript

So here we wrap up my little diversion/excursion into Saekaj and Sovar, following a very unexpected split from the main storyline caused by the inclusion of Terian's father as the dark knight Cyrus and Vara killed on the bridge in Termina way back in Volume Three. That was never originally supposed to happen, unlike much of the series, which had been plotted out in advance. It certainly has led some interesting places, though, but now we find Terian in a most unexpected locale and in an even less expected role. It's all good, though, the story adapts, and I think – if you're a fan of Terian at all – you'll be glad to hear that he's back in WARLORD (As I write this, I am presently about 45% through with the first draft and it's going swimmingly).

If by strange chance you want to know when future books become available, take sixty seconds and sign up for my NEW RELEASE EMAIL ALERTS by visiting my website at www.robertjcrane.com. Don't let the caps lock scare you; I don't sell your information and I only send out emails when I have a new book out. The reason you should sign up for this is because I don't like to set release dates (it's this whole thing, you can find an answer on my website in the FAQ section), and even if you're following me on Facebook (robertJcrane (Author)) or Twitter (@robertJcrane), it's easy to miss my book announcements because…well, because social media is an imprecise thing.

Come join the discussion on my website: http://www.robertjcrane.com !

Cheers,
Robert J. Crane

Acknowledgments

Editorial/Literary Janitorial duties performed by Sarah Barbour and Jeffrey Bryan.

Final proofing was handle by Jo Evans. Any errors you see in the text, however, are the result of me rejecting changes. This story is translated from the original Arkarian, people, make some allowances.

The cover was masterfully designed by Karri Klawiter.

Alexa Medhus and David Leach did the first reads on this one. I also owe many thanks to Alexa for additional customer service help in dealing with bothersome questions that I am simply out of the patience to answer.

As always, thanks to my parents, my kids and my wife, for helping me keep things together.

Other Works by Robert J. Crane

The Sanctuary Series
Epic Fantasy

Defender: The Sanctuary Series, Volume One
Avenger: The Sanctuary Series, Volume Two
Champion: The Sanctuary Series, Volume Three
Crusader: The Sanctuary Series, Volume Four
Sanctuary Tales, Volume One - A Short Story Collection
Thy Father's Shadow: The Sanctuary Series, Volume 4.5
Master: The Sanctuary Series, Volume Five
Fated in Darkness: The Sanctuary Series, Volume 5.5
Warlord: The Sanctuary Series, Volume Six* (Coming in late 2015!)

The Girl in the Box
and
Out of the Box
Contemporary Urban Fantasy

Alone: The Girl in the Box, Book 1
Untouched: The Girl in the Box, Book 2
Soulless: The Girl in the Box, Book 3
Family: The Girl in the Box, Book 4
Omega: The Girl in the Box, Book 5
Broken: The Girl in the Box, Book 6
Enemies: The Girl in the Box, Book 7
Legacy: The Girl in the Box, Book 8
Destiny: The Girl in the Box, Book 9
Power: The Girl in the Box, Book 10

Limitless: Out of the Box, Book 1
In the Wind: Out of the Box, Book 2
Ruthless: Out of the Box, Book 3
Grounded: Out of the Box, Book 4
Tormented: Out of the Box, Book 5
Vengeful: Out of the Box, Book 6* (Coming December 1, 2015!)
Sea Change: Out of the Box, Book 7* (Coming March 2016!)

Southern Watch
Contemporary Urban Fantasy

Called: Southern Watch, Book 1
Depths: Southern Watch, Book 2
Corrupted: Southern Watch, Book 3
Unearthed: Southern Watch, Book 4
Legion: Southern Watch, Book 5* (Coming in 2016!)

*Forthcoming

Made in the USA
Las Vegas, NV
27 September 2023

78220710R00223